RIDE FOR YOUR LIFE

Gavin began firing his Colt, and the rest of the riders joined in. Gonzales shouted his teams into a gallop, and on the very heels of the drag, began firing his Winchester. The herd, already cantankerous and testy from being driven hard and fast, lurched into a run.

Gladstone Pitkin reined up his teams and sat there swearing, watching the galloping longhorns disappear in a cloud of dust. Nell and Naomi, while not understanding the underlying purpose of the stampede, fell into the spirit of it. They rode hell-for-leather after the herd, shouting for all they were worth.

"Glory to God," Woody shouted, when he heard the thunder of hooves and saw the advancing dust cloud.

Woody rode for his life. . . .

St. Martin's Paperbacks Titles
by Ralph Compton

The Trail Drive Series

The Goodnight Trail

The Western Trail

The Chisholm Trail

The Bandera Trail

The California Trail

The Shawnee Trail

The Virginia City Trail

The Dodge City Trail

The Oregon Trail

The Santa Fe Trail

The Old Spanish Trail

The Green River Trail

The Deadwood Trail

The Sundown Riders Series

North to the Bitterroot

Across the Rio Colorado

The Winchester Run

THE SANTA FE TRAIL

Ralph Compton

St. Martin's Paperbacks

This is a work of fiction, based on actual trail drives of the Old West. Many of the characters appearing in the Trail Drive Series were very real, and some of the trail drives actually took place. But the reader should be aware that, in the developing of characters and events, some fictional literary license has been employed. While some of the characters and events herein are purely the creation of the author, every effort has been made to portray them with accuracy. However, the inherent dangers of the trail are real, sufficient unto themselves, and seldom has it been necessary to enhance their reality.

THE SANTA FE TRAIL

Copyright © 1997 by Ralph Compton.

Trail map design by L. A. Hensley.

All rights reserved.

For information address St. Martin's Press, 175 Fifth Avenue, New York, NY 10010.

EAN: 978-0-312-96296-8

Printed in the United States of America

St. Martin's Paperbacks edition / April 1997

10 9 8   7   6

AUTHOR'S FOREWORD

Santa Fe, New Mexico, founded by the Spanish in 1609 on the site of an old Indian ruin, is the oldest capital city in the United States. Isolated trapping parties had reached Santa Fe while it was still under Spanish rule, and they were not welcomed. All trade was forbidden until November 1821, when Mexico won its freedom from Spain.

A trader, William Becknell, brought the news that Mexico was free and that Santa Fe welcomed trade. Becknell himself took the first wagons over the route that was to become the famed Santa Fe Trail. In 1850 a monthly stage line was established between Santa Fe and Independence, Missouri. By 1855, an annual flow of more than five million dollars—in trade goods, horses, mules, oxen, and cattle—moved along the Santa Fe Trail. The coming of the Civil War closed all trails, including the Santa Fe, but following the war, there was an even greater migration, as a nation moved west.

The Civil War slowed or halted progress on most of the nation's railroads, and not until 1880 did the Atchison, Topeka, and Santa Fe reach the capital city. Until the coming of the railroad, the Santa Fe Trail was virtually the only means of bringing settlers to the territory with their horses, mules, cattle, and sheep.

New Mexico entered the Union in 1912 as the forty-seventh state, almost three-quarters of a century after becoming a U.S. territory.

After more than a hundred years, the wagon ruts that mark the old Santa Fe Trail are still visible, for the wagons often traveled four or five abreast. From the air, the old trail is nothing less than awesome, as it seems to wind its way across the plains forever. It is truly a classic in the history of the American West, and I can only describe it as majestic.

Ralph Compton

SANTA

COLORADO | KANSA

Rocky Mts

Arkansas Mts

Sangre de Cristo Mts

River

Spanish Pks.

Trinidad

Raton Pass

CIMARRON CUTOFF

Purgatoire

SAND CR

Taos

Canadian Crossing

Fort Union

Wagon Mound

Santa Fe

La Junta

Glorieta Pass

Las Vegas

San Miguel

Chouteau's Island
Upper Crossing
Fort Aubry
Cimarr

Pa

Jornada o
Lower Spring

Middle Spring

Upper Spring
Cold Spring

TEXAS

CANADIAN RIVER

NEW MEXICO

N

0   40   80   100 Mil

TRAIL

Fort Leavenworth

Fort Osage

Arrow Rock

Old Franklin

KANSAS RIVER

Oregon Trail Junction

Independence

MISSOURI

Council Grove

Shawnee Mission

Boonville

Diamond Spring

Great Bend

OSAGE

RIVER

Dodge

ARKANSAS

NEOSHO

MISSOURI

INDIAN TERRITORY

RIVER

ARKANSAS

CIMARRON RIVER

RIVER

L. A. Hensley

PROLOGUE

Baxter Springs, Missouri. May 15, 1869.

Gavin McCord's range clothes, run-over boots and old hat had seen better days. Only the Colt tied down on his right hip looked new. He was twenty-six, stood about six-four, with hazel eyes and hair as black as a crow's wing. He rode slowly south, dreading to face his four companions, for he bore bad news. In his mind he relived those dark days after they had returned from the war with only the clothes on their backs. Starting with nothing and working like slaves in the hot Texas sun, they had dragged thirty-five hundred wild longhorns from the brakes. Broke, short on grub and horses, they had driven their hard-won herd north, bound for Sedalia or St. Louis. Now there would be no triumphant drive to either railhead, and even if they reached the railroad, a flooded market would render their herd worthless. McCord sighed, for he could hear the restless bawling of the herd. Suppertime was near, and his companions already had a fire going. They waited expectantly until he dismounted.

There were the Pryor brothers, Rusty and Ash. Rusty, with red hair and green eyes, had his Colt thonged down on his left hip, for a cross-hand draw. He was twenty-four, a year younger than his brother Ash, who had the same red hair and green eyes. His Colt was tied down on his right hip. Vic Brodie, twenty-three, had sandy hair, blue eyes, and carried his Colt for a right-hand draw. Woodrow Miles—who had never been called anything but Woody—was twenty-four, with brown hair and deep brown eyes. His Colt rode low on his right hip. All were dressed in typical range clothes. The Pryor brothers were the most temperamental, and Rusty didn't wait for McCord to speak.

"You look downright grim, *amigo*. The trail ahead can't be that bad, can it? Wasn't you able to find any water?"

"There's plenty of water," said McCord, "but there's no graze."

"No graze?" the four shouted in a single voice.

"No graze from Baxter Springs to Sedalia or St. Louis," said McCord. "My God, just the few miles I rode, there must've been twenty thousand cows, with more beyond. I was told there's speculators buyin' herds for two dollars a head."

"Damn it," Vic Brodie shouted, "we can't sell for that. We'll be ruined."

"Oh, we don't have to sell," said McCord, "but our only other choices are as bad or worse. We can drive 'em back to Texas or let 'em starve."

Woodrow Miles, the quiet one, hadn't spoken, and he suddenly found all four of his companions looking at him.

"Don't look at me," Woody said. "I have the same poor choices as the rest of you."

"Yes," said McCord, "but you've been known to dig a mite deeper than the rest of us when we was down to neck meat or nothin'."

"Watch it, McCord," Ash Pryor said. "He made it through the sixth grade, and he's already a mite big-headed."

Woodrow was silent until they thought he wasn't going to speak. Finally he did, and he raised a question.

"When we started this drive, we were hell-bent on Sedalia or St. Louis. Why?"

"Hell," said Rusty Pryor, "the nearest railheads are there. Are you about to suggest we tote these longhorn varmints to Chicago or New York one at a time?''

"I'd do that before I'd sell out for two dollars a head,'' Woodrow said quietly.

They all looked at him for some trace of humor, but he didn't smile. Finally they all laughed, slapping him on the back. When they became serious again, Woodrow spoke.

"Since we face a glutted market and no graze, and we don't aim to drive 'em back to Texas, we'll have to drive 'em somewhere else. Why not Independence?''

"There's no railroad there," Vic Brodie said. "Who's goin' to buy a herd of cows?''

"Back around 'forty-four and 'forty-five," said Woody, "folks was movin' west along the Oregon Trail, and some of 'em bought herds for seed stock, once they got to Oregon or California.''

"I reckon you ain't heard of the Union Pacific Railroad," Vic Brodie said.

"Oh, I wasn't suggestin' our herd might follow the Oregon Trail,'' said Woody. "What I'm thinkin' is that we might sell our herd to some gent travelin' down the Santa Fe Trail into New Mexico. Some hombre wantin' a ranch.''

"That's a long shot, Woody," Ash Pryor said.

"Maybe," said Woody, "but it's the long shots that pay.''

Gavin McCord laughed. "I've seen him bet his roll and draw to an inside straight.''

"Yeah," Vic Brodie said, "but how often does he fill it?''

"Once," said Woody, "but the varmint across the table from me had a royal flush.''

Their laughter died quickly, for the dilemma they faced was all too real.

"It's a gamble," McCord said, "and a big one, but we've been gambling since the day we rode into the brakes and started ropin' these longhorn varmints with the idea of drivin' 'em north to the railroad. Come first light, I say let's head 'em out for Independence. Hell, if we have to sell 'em to butcher shops one at a time, we'll do better than two dollars a head."

"Let's take 'em to Independence," said Rusty Pryor. "I'll go. Who else?"

The verdict was unanimous, and with that settled, they went about preparing a meager supper. Their supplies were dwindling rapidly.

"One thing for sure," Gavin McCord said, "we'll have to do *something* when we reach Independence. Two more days and we'll be out of flour, bacon, beans, and coffee."

"That's the bad news," said Woodrow Miles. "The good news is, we got a nearly unlimited supply of beef."

Independence, Missouri. May 28, 1869.

"My God," Rusty Pryor said, "I'd swap ten cows for one good bite of town grub and a pot of scalding black coffee."

"Then we ain't sendin' you into town to sell the herd," said Vic Brodie.

"There's plenty of graze around here," Woodrow Miles said. "I reckon we ought not be in a big hurry to sell."

"Don't forget," said Ash Pryor, "we been out of grub for near two weeks, and I don't graze worth a damn, even when the grass is high."

"We may be up against a problem we ain't considered," Vic Brodie said. "With all the herds goin' to Sedalia and St. Louis, where do we look for a buyer in Independence?"

"We'll start with the saloons," said Woodrow, "and go from there to the wagon yards and liveries. We'll spread the word that we're lookin' for a buyer to take a herd down the Santa Fe."

"I nominate you to ride into town and scout out a buyer," Vic Brodie said.

"No," said Woodrow. "I'm not takin' all that responsibility by myself."

"Hell," Brodie said, "somebody's got to do it. Pick somebody to go with you."

"If Gavin will side me, I'll do it," said Woodrow.

"I'll go with you on one condition," McCord said, "that bein' that we make no deals on our own. If we find something that looks good, then we all got to pass judgment on it."

"I like that," said Woodrow. "I'll go only if the rest of you agree to what Gavin has suggested."

"I'll buy that," Rusty Pryor said.

"So will I," said Ash.

"Suits me," Vic Brodie said.

"Bein' as how we got no coffee and are on the ragged edge of starvation," said Gavin McCord, "I think we ought to ride in today. It's late, but that's the best time to make the rounds of the saloons. We can check out the wagon yards and liveries tomorrow."

"Then let's saddle up and have at it," Woodrow said. "If we put it off too long, some of those other herds from Baxter Springs may show up here."

Gavin and Woodrow reached town in the early afternoon. Neither had ever been to a town of the magnitude of Independence, and there were so many saloons, they were at a loss as to where to begin.

"Let's try those along the river first," Woodrow suggested. "They look like the kind where a gent's likely to have to step over dead bodies after dark."

"Suits me," said Gavin, "but I can't imagine an hombre with the *dinero* and ambition to ride the Santa Fe Trail hangin' around in slaughterhouses such as these."

Seven saloons later, the pair had gained nothing but hard looks from barkeeps, as they left without buying drinks. The eighth saloon—a place called *Trail's End*—seemed a little more respectable. A poker game was in progress, and in addition to the five men at the table, half a dozen others looked on.

Gavin and Woodrow joined the onlookers. One of the men sat with his back to the wall, a satisfied grin on his swarthy face, and most of the money on the table before him. His hair—black as midnight—curled down to the collar of his boiled shirt. His eyes were of such a dark brown, they at first seemed fully as black as his hair. His hat was a flat-crowned black Stetson, and when he shifted in his chair, the butts of two guns were visible. Briefly his dark eyes met those of Gavin and Woodrow, as he took their measure. But the trouble he obviously expected came from one of his companions at the table.

"Black hat," said the bearded man across the table, "that last card you drawed had better not be a queen."

The black-hatted gambler who had been challenged never had a chance to respond. One of the bystanders slammed a Colt against his head, but the hat partially cushioned the blow, and he came out of the chair fighting. But he didn't have a chance. All the men who had been observing the game piled on the hapless gambler, pounding his head against the floor, clubbing him with drawn revolvers. It was shamefully unfair, prompting Woodrow and Gavin to draw their Colts.

"Back off, all of you," Woodrow said.

One of the attackers, who had been using his Colt for a club, already had it cocked when Woodrow shot him him in the shoulder. The thunder of the Colt got the attention of the others, and they hastily backed away from the fallen man they had been beating. When the barkeep appeared with a sawed-off shotgun, the weapon was pointed at Woodrow and Gavin.

"We don't allow no shootin' in here," the barkeep growled.

"But you don't mind a pack of coyotes gangin' up on a man and beatin' him to death, I reckon," Gavin said.

Gavin and Woodrow stood there with cocked Colts, their cold eyes as unwavering as their weapons. The barkeep swallowed hard, lowered the shotgun, and spoke.

"If you're friends of this cardsharp, gather up the varmint and git out."

"Woodrow," said Gavin, "see can you get that hombre on his feet. I'll keep the rest of these peckerwoods covered, in case they're tempted to backslide."

Woodrow managed to get the half-conscious gambler on

his feet and walk him toward the door. Back-stepping, Gavin followed, covering the men in the saloon until he reached the door. But they refused to stay put. Cursing, several of them followed, swiftly changing their minds when Gavin put two slugs in the door frame. The outside air seemed to revive the injured man. He shook his head and spoke.

"I'm obliged, *amigo*. My horse . . . the bay . . . pack mule . . . mine."

He managed to mount the bay, and McCord took the pack mule's lead rope.

"Unless you have a better place in mind, pardner," Woodrow said, "why don't you go with us to our camp just south of here? You need time to catch your breath."

The stranger nodded, following them as they rode out. Nothing was said until they reached the herd. Sundown was a few minutes away as they dismounted. The Pryors and Brodie said nothing, waiting for some explanation from Woodrow and Gavin. Gavin began and Woodrow finished. Afterward, all eyes turned to the stranger, and he spoke.

"I'm Nip Kelly, from Cape Girardeau, Missouri, and I wasn't cheatin'."

"I'm Woodrow Miles and this is Gavin McCord. Whether you was guilty or not, we reckoned the fight was a mite one-sided. These other gents, from left to right, is Rusty Pryor, his brother, Ash, and Vic Brodie. We're all from Texas, and we just brought a herd of longhorns up the trail."

"I'm pleased to make your acquaintance," said Kelly, "and I regret that we couldn't have met under different circumstances. I am mortally in need of some hot, black coffee."

"We'd be glad to oblige," Woodrow replied, "but we've been out of coffee for most of two weeks. Frankly, all we have is beef, but there's a blessed plenty of that."

"Then allow me to provide the grub for supper," said Kelly. "There's plenty of bacon, beans, flour, coffee, and sugar on the pack mule."

"Mister," Rusty said, "none of us would take a prize for our cookin', but give me a chance, with some decent grub, and you'll know you've been fed."

"Then unpack old Sam and get on with it," said Kelly, "but if you don't mind, fire us up some coffee first."

"Amen to that," Vic Brodie said.

They were camped near a creek, and Kelly removed his shirt and ducked his head in the water. From his saddlebag he took a clean white shirt. Soon there was the pleasant aroma of boiling coffee, and the men got their tin cups. The first cup Rusty filled went to Nip Kelly. There was no conversation until they had finished their first cups of coffee.

"Supper," Rusty announced. "Bacon, more coffee, and plenty of steak."

They all dug in, the Texans enjoying the first decent meal they'd had in two weeks.

"I didn't realize I was so near starved to death," said Ash Pryor, "until I got on the outside of some honest-to-God grub. Too bad we couldn't't've made your acquaintance, Mr. Kelly, without you takin' a beating."

Kelly laughed. "My friends, when I have any, call me Nip."

"Woodrow," said Brodie, "you never got around to tellin' us whether or not you and Gavin drummed up any interest in the herd."

"We didn't," Woody said. "We went through eight saloons, findin' Nip in the last one, but nobody lookin' prosperous enough to afford even one cow."

"There's a newspaper in my saddlebag," Kelly said. "Get it. There's an advertisement that might interest you."

Woody brought the newspaper, published Wednesday and Saturday in Independence. It consisted of eight pages. Kelly folded it to page four and passed it back to Woodrow. Ash Pryor looked over his shoulder.

"My God," said Ash, "it takes up half a page."

"Damn it," Vic Brodie said, "one of you read it to us, if you can."

"Too many big words you wouldn't understand," said

Woody. "I'll just tell you. This gent is an Englishman, name of Gladstone Pitkin, and he's bought a passel of land in New Mexico Territory. He aims to start a ranch there, and he's out to hire a crew."

Vic Brodie laughed. "Gladstone Pitkin? A gent with a handle like that oughta be gut-shot or strung up, just on general principles."

"One problem, as I see it," said Rusty. "We need to sell a herd of cows, not hire on as an outfit."

"If this Pitkin aims to have a ranch," Gavin said, "won't he need cows?"

"My thoughts, exactly," said Kelly. "It won't hurt to track down this hombre and see if he's interested in buying a ready-made herd. I aim to look him up tomorrow, myself. If the money's right, I'll hire on as part of his outfit."

"If he doesn't already have one," Woody said. "This paper's three days old."

"Not yet," said Kelly. "I've been listenin' to talk, learnin' as much as I could before I talk to Pitkin himself. Nobody's takin' him seriously, but I hear he's got a letter of credit from a St. Louis bank, that he could likely afford all of New Mexico Territory if he wants it. Besides that, he's got a pair of daughters you wouldn't believe. They're all settled into the fanciest hotel in town."

"I reckon it won't hurt if we talk to him," Woody said. "Gavin and me can ride in with you, if you don't mind. If he's interested in the herd, he can ride out here and we'll all talk to him. Maybe he'll take the mules and extra horses too."

"Where's your chuck wagon?" Kelly asked.

"We couldn't afford one," said Gavin. "We managed to get four mules, but we lost two of the jug-heads in a stampede, and never did find 'em."

"There's plenty of grub and coffee for breakfast in the mornin'," Kelly said. "That is, if you gents don't mind me stayin' the night."

"Glad to have you," said Woody, "and we're beholden

for the grub and coffee. A gent don't realize how down-and-out he is, till he's out of coffee."

"I'd like to leave old Sam here," Kelly said, as he saddled his horse for the ride into town. "If I hire on with Pitkin, I'm hopin' he'll invest in a chuck wagon and a cook. A man can't eat decent off a pack mule, especially if he's eatin' his own cookin'."

The Texans laughed, appreciating the magnitude of Kelly's statement.

"Leave Sam with our mules," said Rusty. "Maybe they won't be a bad influence."

"Let's ride, then," Woody said. "The rest of you just set tight. If we get beyond the talkin' stage, and Pitkin seems interested in the herd, Gavin and me won't make any deals. We'll invite him out to see the longhorns, and all of you can have your say."

The hotel was everything Kelly had said it was, and more. Kelly inquired at the desk, and was told the Pitkin party had rooms on the first floor. Kelly knocked on the door, and even he wasn't prepared for the sight that greeted them. Pitkin looked to be fifty, and his hair was silver. His robe—which was silver trimmed in blue—swept the floor. But the three men looked past Pitkin to the bountifully set table where the trio had been having breakfast. The two girls had blue eyes and blonde hair, and as for their age, they didn't look more than a year apart.

"Yes?" said Pitkin. "My daughters and I are having breakfast."

"We're here about your notice in the newspaper," Kelly said. "We'll wait in the lobby until you're finished."

"You shall not," said Pitkin. "There's room at the table, and there's plenty of coffee. Or tea, if you prefer."

Woody and Gavin followed Kelly into the room, and the three of them tipped their hats to the women seated at the table.

"I am Gladstone Pitkin," their host said. "My daughters are Nell and Naomi."

"Mr. Pitkin and ladies," said Kelly, "it's our privilege. I am Nip Kelly, and these are my friends, Gavin McCord and Woodrow Miles."

There was room at the table for eight, with a chair at each end, and three more along each side. Without being asked, Nell and Naomi moved to opposite ends of the long table, allowing Kelly, Woodrow, and Gavin to sit facing Pitkin. Nell and Naomi promptly forgot their food and stared in rapt attention at the three visitors. Even Nip Kelly was nervous, but he wasted no time.

"Mr. Pitkin, I am interested in the possibility of hiring on as part of your outfit."

Pitkin nodded. "And you gentlemen?" His eyes were on Woodrow and Gavin.

"We have a herd of thirty-five hundred Texas longhorn cows," said Woody. "If it is your intention to raise cattle in New Mexico, our herd is for sale."

"That is my intention," Pitkin replied, "and I shall be glad to consider your herd. But I must see them, of course, before I make a decision."

"They're ten miles south of here," said Woodrow. "They're ready when you are."

"Allow me a few minutes to get dressed," Pitkin replied. "I'll get a horse from the livery and go with you."

"Get a buckboard, father," said Naomi. "I want to go with you."

"And so do I," Nell said. "I've never seen a herd of Texas longhorns."

"Very well," said Pitkin, "I shall get a buckboard, but I do not intend to wait while the two of you dawdle. We shall be leaving in a quarter of an hour."

Their breakfast forgotten, the girls left the table immediately, going into the next room. They wore only thin dressing gowns, and the trio of visitors watched their departure in admiration.

Pitkin sighed. "Since their mother's death, I have done as well by them as I could, but I fear my best has been less than adequate. As you might expect, they are accustomed to having their own way. Now, gentlemen, if you will excuse me . . ."

He departed by another door, closing it behind him.

"He offered us coffee," said Gavin McCord. "I aim to take him up on that."

There were five extra place settings, and Gavin took a porcelain cup and poured himself some coffee from a large porcelain pot. His companions quickly followed his example.

"With Nell and Naomi taggin' along," Nip Kelly said, "I don't understand why Pitkin don't already have more hands than he needs."

"He looks like a brass-plated dude that don't know one end of a cow from the other," said Gavin.

"A gent with his kind of *dinero* don't have to know cows," Woody said. "He can hire cow nurses for thirty and found, all day long."

"Maybe not," said Kelly. "In this new territory, I hear there's more sheep than cattle, so there may not be as many cowboys as you think. Could be that's why he's hoping to hire riders here."

"Sheep?" Gavin said. "My God, I don't like to think of bein' in the same territory with the wooly varmints."

Kelly laughed. "You'd better get used to it. I hear the government's making some real deals on land in these undeveloped territories, and they're looking for men like Pitkin, who can afford to do what he seems to have in mind."

At that point, Pitkin returned. He wore a derby hat, a white shirt with flowing black string tie, and a gray tweed suit. Instead of boots, he wore gaiters of soft black leather. To his apparent surprise, Nell and Naomi entered the room. Their golden hair had been left loose and they were dressed in simple paisley frocks. Nell's was pale blue, Naomi's buttercup yellow. They waited in the hotel lobby with Gavin McCord, Woodrow Miles, and Nip Kelly, while Pitkin went to the livery across the street for a buckboard. When he returned, and the girls were aboard, Gavin, Woody, and Kelly rode out. Pitkin followed, and when they neared the grazing herd, Gavin and Woody rode on ahead. They sought to warn their three companions of the presence of Nell and Naomi, lest one or more of the three be caught in some embarrassing position. When the Pitkins arrived, Nip Kelly leading, the five cowboys stood with hats in their hands. Woodrow performed the introductions, and without delay, the Pitkins headed for the herd of grazing longhorns.

"Is he buyin'?" Rusty Pryor asked anxiously.

"He's agreed to look at them," said Woody, "but he also aims to have a cattle ranch in New Mexico. I'd say he may be interested."

"Whether he buys or not," Ash Pryor said, "I'd like to get to know them Pitkin girls a mite better."

"He's hirin' hands to go to New Mexico Territory," said Nip Kelly, "and I think I'm his only one, so far. If he hires me, that is."

"If they ain't interested in the herd," Vic Brodie said, "they're takin' a hell of a long time admirin' them ugly critters."

"Here they come," said Woodrow. "I reckon we're about to get the verdict, whatever it is."

"Magnificent beasts," Pitkin said. "How many bulls?"

"A dozen, all not more than two years old," said Woodrow.

"How much are you asking for them?" Pitkin asked.

"We'd settle for twenty-five dollars a head, bulls included," said Woodrow.

"In New York or Chicago," Pitkin said, "the fair market price is thirty-five dollars."

"Yes, sir," said Woodrow, "we realize that, but we were unable to get them to New York or Chicago. We're willing to make allowances."

"So am I," Pitkin replied. "I will take them all, at thirty dollars a head, but there is one condition."

"And that condition?"

"That all of you sign on as my outfit. That you drive the herd down the Santa Fe Trail, to my range in New Mexico Territory, and help me establish my ranch," said Pitkin.

"My God," Vic Brodie said, "that could take years."

"It could," said Pitkin, "but I am prepared to make it worth your while. I will pay each of you fifty and found per month. I will draw up a contract with you for a period of five years. At the end of that period, I will sell you seed stock for ranches of your own, if that's your desire. There are hundreds of acres of government land adjoining my holdings."

"God Almighty," said Rusty Pryor.

The rest of them were struck dumb by the proposal, each doing some rapid mental calculations. The sale of the herd would bring more than a hundred thousand dollars, while unheard-of wages over five years would account for another three thousand dollars per man.

"I'll throw in with you," Woodrow said.

The others agreed, almost in a single voice.

1

"Splendid, gentlemen," Pitkin said. "Mr. Kelly, consider yourself hired."

Nell and Naomi clapped their hands.

"What would you have us do first, Mr. Pitkin?" Woodrow inquired.

"Kindly refrain from referring to me as Mister Pitkin," said the Englishman. You may call me Gladstone or Pitkin."

"With all due respect to England," Woodrow said, "I'd rather just call you Pit, and you can call me Woody."

"So be it," said Pitkin. "How many more men do you feel that I need?"

"Five of us brought the herd from Texas," Gavin McCord said. "The herd's already trail-wise, and with Nip, there's six of us. Unless you know somethin' we don't, the six of us should be enough."

"Provided," said Kelly, "you aim to hire a cook. You'll need a chuck wagon, too."

"Perhaps I'll be more fortunate in the hiring of a cook than I have been in the hiring of a crew," Pitkin said. "Will some of you men inquire as to the availability and the cost of a chuck wagon?"

"A new chuck wagon won't cost more than a hundred dollars," said Woody, "and any wagon yard in town should have at least one. Since you've hired us as an outfit, I'm goin' to suggest something. Why don't you let us find the chuck wagon and scout the town for a cook? Any range cook worth his salt will be able to go to a general store and load the chuck wagon with all the grub and supplies you'll need.''

"Splendid, Woody," Pitkin exclaimed. "What else have I overlooked?"

"Pit," said Vic, "your ladies ought to go to the general store and outfit themselves as cowboys. In men's duds, like us."

"In trousers?" Pitkin said. "In England that would be unheard of."

"You're a long way from England," said Rusty Pryor.

"Father," Naomi said, "they're right, and they're gentlemen enough not to have made a point of the obvious. Nell and me in skirts would make spectacles of ourselves each time we mount or dismount. The men couldn't keep their eyes on the herd for watching us."

Nell and Naomi weren't embarrassed in the slightest, and the men all laughed.

"Very well," said Pitkin. "I wasn't thinking of you riding astride."

"Oh, Father," Nell said in mock horror, "I'd walk from here to Santa Fe before I'd so much as consider a horrid sidesaddle."

Again the men all laughed, and this time Pitkin joined them.

"When I return to town," said Pitkin, "I'll make arrangements to purchase the herd. I will require a bill of sale, of course."

"It's customary to make a count of the herd," Woody said.

"I am trusting you to ride for me, to see to my affairs," said Pitkin. "Therefore, I will trust you for an honest count."

"That's generous of you," Gavin said. "We're Texans, and we'll ride for the brand."

"I should return to town," said Pitkin, "and begin terminating my business here."

"Some of us will go with you," Woody said. "We may be a while findin' a cook."

"Why don't you and Gavin find a chuck wagon and beat the bushes for a cook?" said Ash Pryor.

"Yeah," Rusty said, "and get him and the chuck wagon here in time for supper."

Pitkin and his daughters started for town, with Gavin and Woody riding behind the buckboard.

"Nip," said Vic, "I reckon we owe you one for puttin' us in touch with Pitkin. We was purely out of luck, where the herd was concerned."

"Hell, I was just helpin' myself," Kelly replied. "I ain't sure Pitkin would ever have hired an outfit, the way he was headed. Thanks to you gents, he has a herd, an outfit, and a place for me."

"Thank God on behalf of all of us," said Rusty. "Whatever else happens, we'll all eat regular, and that's almighty important."

When they reached town, Pitkin spoke to Gavin and Woody.

"I am advancing you two hundred dollars. Use part of it to purchase the chuck wagon and the remainder for necessary provisions until you can find and hire a cook."

"We have only three mules, includin' Nip Kelly's," Gavin said.

"Purchase the chuck wagon and find a suitable cook," said Pitkin. "Once you are satisfied with the cook, I will purchase the necessary teams to draw the chuck wagon. I will then arrange credit for all necessary provisions and supplies at a general store."

Pitkin turned away, dismissing them, but they were cheered by smiles from Nell and Naomi.

"He don't waste words, does he?" Gavin said.

"No," said Woody, "and he took us at our word. Now we got to find us a cook that's willing to keep us all fed and drive that chuck wagon from here to Santa Fe."

The eventual cost of the chuck wagon was eighty-five dollars, and they began their search for a cook in the various cafes and restaurants. After making the rounds of better restaurants, their search for a cook having been unsuccessful, they began visiting the hash houses and dives along the river.

"I'm beginnin' to wonder if it was such a good idea, you and me huntin' a cook that's willin' to work a cattle drive," Gavin McCord said. "If we find one down here, he's likely to be so scruffy and rough-around-the-edges, Pitkin won't have him."

"Maybe Pitkin needs to learn somethin' about the frontier," said Woodrow Miles. "The varmint that's all gussied-up like Sunday-go-to-meetin' belongs in town, not on the trail. We got to have an hombre that can boil coffee and make flapjacks in rain or snow, without bellyachin'. A waddy that can use Winchester or Colt, and when there's a stampede, he can grab a horse and ride like hell wouldn't have it."

"Hell, you don't have to convince me," Gavin said. "Let's try that place across the street, the Cattleman's Bar and Grill."

It being mid-morning, most eating places were virtually empty, but when Gavin and Woody reached the door of the Cattleman's Bar and Grill, they could hear angry voices, one of which relied almost entirely on border Spanish.

"Damn it, Gonzales, you call this coffee?"

"*Sí,*" Gonzales bawled. "*Tejano* coffee."

The shouting ceased as Gavin and Woody entered the cafe.

"Sorry, gents," said the man who was obviously the owner, "but I'm without a cook. Gonzales is just leaving."

Gonzales stomped out, his teeth clenched beneath his bushy moustache. Woody and Gavin followed, matching the stride of the irate Mexican.

"What's the trouble, Gonzales?" Woody asked.

Gonzales stopped dead in his tracks. Snatching off his

old hat, he swatted it against his thigh. Turning to face them, he spoke.

"T'ree month I cook for *Tejano* trail drive. *Por Dios*, now I am tell I no can cook, no can make the coffee."

"Gonzales," Woody said, "if you've been a trail cook before, how would you like to be a trail cook again?"

"I like," said Gonzales. *"Tejano coffee, Tejano grub."*

"Our outfit's takin' a herd of Texas cows to Santa Fe," Gavin said. "Mr. Pitkin, our boss, needs a cook for the trail who will become part of the outfit, staying to work for the ranch in New Mexico. Will you go with us to Mr. Pitkin's hotel to talk to him?"

"Sí," said Gonzales. "He like my coffee, my grub, I go."

Not believing their good fortune, Gavin and Woody guided Gonzales to the hotel and knocked on Pitkin's door.

"Pit," Woody said, when the Englishman opened the door, "we've found a man who has been a trail cook. This is Gonzales. Gonzales, this is Mr. Pitkin."

Gonzales grinned, removed his old hat, and bowed.

"His attitude is acceptable," said Pitkin, "but what's the rest of his name?"

"Gonzales is all we know," Woody replied.

"Gonzales *who*?" Pitkin persisted.

"Madre mia," said the Mexican. "You call Gonzales, I come. That not be enough?"

"Yes," Woody said, "I think that will be enough. Don't you, Mr. Pitkin?"

"Yes," said Pitkin wisely. "You will be in charge of the chuck wagon."

"Si," Gonzales replied. *"Caballos, mulos."*

"Gonzales!" Gavin shouted.

He sent his Colt spinning and the Mexican deftly caught it, cocked it, and then eased the hammer down. He expertly border-shifted the weapon, took its muzzle in his left hand, and presented it butt-first to Gavin.

"You'll do, Gonzales," said Gavin.

The Mexican said nothing, and even Pitkin understood

the significance of what he had witnessed. When he spoke, it was to the Mexican.

"Gonzales, I will direct a written message to a general store, authorizing them to load a chuck wagon with all the food and supplies you believe necessary to feed the outfit on the trail and after we establish a ranch in New Mexico. Woody, we *do* have a chuck wagon I presume?"

"We do," said Woody, "but we're lacking teams and harness."

"Then go to the livery—wherever you must purchase teams and harness—get them, and have them charged to me," Pitkin said. "When the chuck wagon has been loaded, take it to your cow camp. My daughters and I will be there sometime tomorrow, prepared to take the trail."

"Pit," Woody said, "if it meets with your approval, Gavin and me will go to the store with Gonzales. There's some things other than grub we're goin' to need on the trail. You'll need bedrolls for your daughters and yourself, and all of you should be armed. If not with Winchesters, at least with Colts."

"Very well," said Pitkin. "You men are much more aware of the needs of an outfit on the trail than I, and I am relying on your judgment."

Woody and Gavin found that Gonzales was a good judge of livestock, for the Mexican quickly chose four young mules of good temperament. They harnessed the mules and led the animals to the wagon yard, where the chuck wagon waited.

"I still have a hundred and fifteen dollars Pitkin advanced us for the chuck wagon and grub," Woody said. "Since we'll be loadin' the chuck wagon today and there'll be plenty of grub, I aim to use some of this money to buy some extra canvas."

"The chuck wagon comes with canvas," said Gavin. "Why do we need more?"

"I aim to buy two twenty-foot squares, with the edges hemmed and brass eyelets at the corners," Woody said. "At least we'll have a shelter where we can squat and eat, without bein' snowed, sleeted, and rained on."

"Might be handy after we reach Santa Fe," said Gavin. "Pitkin's just startin' with open range, and we don't know when there'll be a bunk house."

"*Sí,*" Gonzales said. "Thong one side of shelter to wagon bows, other side to trees, or to poles we bury in ground."

"*Bueno,*" said Woody. "You know what I'm talkin' about."

"*Sí,*" Gonzales said. "If chuck wagon have dry firewood, need possum belly."*

"We can use a cowhide for that," said Gavin. "We saved the last one, brought it on one of the pack mules."

When they reached the general store, Gonzales expertly backed the wagon up to the ramp for the loading of supplies.

"Gonzales, turn in Pitkin's letter," Woody said, "and begin loadin' what you know for sure we'll be needin' on the trail. We'll have to find bedrolls and weapons for Pitkin and his daughters."

While the general store had Winchesters and ammunition, there were no revolvers.

"Let's get three Winchesters and ammunition," said Gavin, "and if they want Colts, then Pitkin can go to a gunsmith's. Maybe I ain't bein' fair to these English folks, but I can't see any of them bein' worth a damn in a fight."

"Frankly," Woody said, "neither can I, but they can change. They'll have to, if they aim to survive on the frontier."

Gavin laughed. "It may shock hell out of Pitkin, but I reckon we'll have to help Nell and Naomi learn cow. Startin' out with thirty-five hundred head, after a couple of years of natural increase, a six-man outfit won't be near enough."

After gathering the extra Winchesters, ammunition, and bedrolls, Gavin and Woody returned to the loading dock.

---

* A cowhide or canvas slung under the wagon box for carrying dry firewood.

Gonzales had three store clerks bringing supplies to the wagon, while the Mexican positioned things so that no available space was wasted. Outside the wagon—on either side of the wagon box—was a water keg, and from each keg to the rear end of the wagon, heavy iron hooks had been bolted to the vehicle's frame.

"What are these for?" Gavin wondered.

"You see," said Gonzales.

The Mexican had secured a dozen yard-long, three-inch-wide leather straps with brass rings at each end. The men loading the wagon brought out four heavy gunnysacks.

"Grain for *mulos*," Gonzales said.

Quickly, Gonzales looped the brass rings on the ends of three of the leather straps over three of the iron hooks on the outside of the wagon box. Two of the men from the store held a heavy sack of grain in position, while Gonzales looped the heavy leather straps over the sack and attached the rings on the loose ends of the straps to three of the hooks along the outside of the wagon box. A second sack of grain was secured in the same manner on the same side of the wagon box, and the remaining two sacks were put into position on the opposite side of the wagon.

"Grub for *mulos* no get in way of grub for outfit," Gonzales explained.

Gavin and Woody looked at one another and grinned. The Mexican was proving himself resourceful when it came to loading the wagon. Now if he could only cook . . .

"Tarnation," said Gavin, "look who's comin' down the boardwalk."

Nell and Naomi Pitkin seemed oblivious to the four men following them. It was Naomi who spoke.

"Father is allowing us to come to the store and choose proper clothing for the drive to Santa Fe."

"Well, he shouldn't have allowed you to come alone," said Woody. "Who are those hombres followin' you?"

"I don't know," Naomi said, looking back. "I never saw them before."

"Well, now," said one of the men, "we ain't introduced ourselves proper."

The four looked as though they had recently departed a saloon, for their faces were flushed. Their hair and beards were unkempt and their clothing looked as in need of washing as their faces, necks, arms, and hands. They became angry when it appeared the two women they were following had come to meet Gavin and Woody. One of the four—big, brawny, weighing maybe three hundred—stepped off the boardwalk into the dusty street, and it was he who spoke.

"I'm Burke Chandler, an' we seen these ladies first. Why don't you an' sonny boy run along, so's we don't hafta hurt you?"

Gavin was nearest. Reacting in a manner that took the big man totally by surprise, he brought his right all the way from his knees. While Chandler didn't fall, he rocked back on his heels and Gavin had to hit him a second time. When he finally went down in a cloud of dust, his three companions charged Gavin. All of them were big men, accustomed to saloon brawling, and when Woody went to Gavin's rescue, the two of them went down under the combined weight of the three men.

"Leave them alone, you brutes," Naomi shouted.

She seized the arm of one of the brawling trio, while Nell went after another. The two of them only succeeded in getting sucked into the fight, and it gradually went from bad to worse. Nell screamed when her dress was ripped from collar-to-waist, and Naomi was faring no better.

"Somebody get the sheriff!" one of the storekeepers shouted.

But the brawl didn't last that long. Gonzales grabbed a Winchester from beneath the wagon seat and slammed the butt of it into the head of one of the four troublesome men. Awaiting an opportunity, he slugged another of the four in the same manner. Naomi and Nell managed to drag themselves out of the fight, while Gavin and Woody each took one of their remaining adversaries. Finally the four intruders were sprawled on the ground, and the victors leaned against the chuck wagon, breathing hard. Gavin and Woody were almost in rags. Naomi and Nell, in their undergarments, sought what was left of their ripped and mutilated dresses. A crowd had begun to gather.

"I reckon you ladies had better go on in the store and get yourselves the duds you had come after," Woody said. "You'll never be in more need of 'em."

"I'm more naked than I want to be, out in public," said Gavin. "I reckon we'd better all go in there and get ourselves covered. Pit will just have to take it from our wages."

"Oh, God," Naomi moaned, "don't tell Father. He'll be furious."

"I don't care," said Nell. "It was a perfectly glorious fight."

"All of you had better get inside," said one of the men from the store. "Here comes the sheriff."

Quickly, Naomi and Nell entered the store, followed by Gavin and Woody. The sheriff arrived in time to witness the awakening of the four men who had been the cause of the brawl. Chandler sat up, blood dripping from his nose and running down his chin. His three companions slowly got to their hands and knees.

"Sheriff Robbins," said one of the men from the store, "these four men had followed two ladies here, and they're in the store, along with the two gents that defended 'em. The *mejicano* here, he cracked some heads with the butt of a rifle. It was all he could do to help his two friends, not to mention the ladies."

"Chandler," the sheriff said, "you and the rest of these varmints git on back to the hole you crawled out of, but don't leave town. If these people—the ladies—want to press charges, I'll jail the lot of you and let the judge decide your punishment."

The four got to their feet and stumbled back the way they had come. Sheriff Robbins went on into the store. Although their hair was a tangled mess, Naomi and Nell were both dressed in men's Levi's and denim shirts.

"Ladies," the lawman said, "I'm Sheriff Robbins. If

you'd care to press charges, I'd be glad to lock up the four varmints that was botherin' you."

"No," Naomi said. "We'll only be in town another day or two. I don't believe they'll bother us again."

Woody and Gavin returned from a dressing room, where they had changed into their new clothes. Each had a black eye, and their faces and hands bled from numerous cuts and scrapes.

"We'll see that they're not alone on the street, Sheriff," said Woody.

The lawman nodded and went on his way.

"Now," Woody said, "if you ladies are ready, Gavin and me will see you back to your hotel."

"I suppose we're ready," said Naomi. "Promise you won't tell Father."

"We won't," Woody said, "but he may learn of it from somebody else."

"He won't have to hear of it from anybody," said Gavin. "All he'll have to do is look at us."

"He won't see us again today," Woody said, "and by the time we see him tomorrow, we'll have had time to patch ourselves up."

Nell laughed. "Then it shall be our secret."

By the time Woody and Gavin returned to the general store, there was very little left to be loaded into the chuck wagon. Gonzales raised the tailgate, closed the canvas pucker, and they were ready to return to the herd. Woody and Gavin mounted their horses and led out, the Mexican following with the chuck wagon. The rest of the outfit saw them coming, and there were shouts of appreciation. When Gonzales reined up the teams, Woody performed the introductions.

"Gonzales," said Vic Brodie, "I know you just got here, but I purely could enjoy some grub cooked by an hombre that knows his stuff."

"*Si*," the Mexican said. "There be firewood?"

"There will be," Brodie said. "Some of you varmints come help me."

With the long trail ahead of them, every man wanted to know just one thing: could the newly hired Mexican actually cook? Gonzales seemed anxious to prove himself, and he seemed to have loaded the chuck wagon in a manner that was most convenient, for he soon had a meal underway. He had bought a supply of Irish potatoes, and while he had a few spare moments, he brought them forth.

"There be biscuits," he said. "Four day, maybe."

"The little *paisano* knows what he's doin'," said Brodie. "Sourdough ain't worth a damn unless it's had time to work."

"Woody," Rusty Pryor said, "I don't know how you and Gavin done it, but you found us a honest-to-God range cook."

"Yeah," said Ash, "and now that we're sure of that, how come you hombres showed up in new duds with black eyes?"

Gavin and Woody told them about the fight, embellishing the story as they went along. When they had finished, there was a moment of silence, and the rest of the outfit began swearing in almost a single voice.

"Just our luck," Rusty said. "Them two Pitkin gals end up in nothin' but their underpants, and it's all wasted on you two unappreciative varmints."

"Whoa up," said Nip Kelly. "They took a pretty good beatin', so I reckon it wasn't all that much fun."

"You're damned right it wasn't," Gavin said. "If Gonzales hadn't grabbed a Winchester and cracked some heads, them four hombres would've made coyote bait of the both of us."

"Just four of them, and you needed help? My God," said Vic, "you're Texans. Gents, I reckon us and the state of Texas is disgraced."

He hung his head, as though in shame, and the others followed his lead. Sorrowfully, they regarded Woody and Gavin, trying mightily not to laugh.

"Damn it," Gavin said, "I'd like to see any two of you

take on them four gorillas and do any better. Where was you when you was needed at the Alamo?"

"Back off, Gavin," said Woody. "They're hoorawing us."

The cowboy humor ended as quickly as it had begun, with a shout from Gonzales.

"Come and get it, or I feed it to the *mulos*."

The Mexican filled their tin plates with fried steak, potatoes, and onions. That was only the start, for Gonzales had fried eggs and bacon on the side, and there were two pots of hot coffee.

"My God," said Vic, when they got to the fried eggs and bacon, "put a sack over the little varmint's head, and I'd marry him."

"You'd have to get in line," Rusty said.

They devoured the food to the last morsel, leaving Gonzales beaming.

True to his word, the following morning Gladstone Pitkin and his daughters arrived as Gonzales was pouring the first coffee. But the Pitkins weren't alone. A bearded rider led three packhorses. Reining up, Pitkin spoke.

"Gentlemen, this is Wilkes Thornton. He has been hired to see to our packhorses."

But Thornton ignored Pitkin. Dismounting, he stood facing the outfit, his right hand near the butt of his holstered Colt. His cold, hard eyes were on Nip Kelly. Kelly seemed totally relaxed, and only Gavin McCord and Woodrow Miles had any idea as to what was about to transpire. Wilkes Thornton was the gambler who had challenged Nip Kelly at the gambling table in Independence!

"Mr. Thornton," Pitkin said, irritated, "may I ask what you have in mind?"

"Pit," said Woody, "stay out of this."

Pitkin, unaccustomed to taking orders, was about to fire off an angry response, but the situation was out of his hands. Thornton went for his gun, and only then did Nip Kelly move. His Colt roared and Thornton stumbled backwards into his horse. The animal shied and the gambler slumped to the ground, his unfired weapon in his hand. Pitkin found his voice and said exactly the wrong thing.

"Mr. Kelly, I will not tolerate such barbaric behavior from any man employed by me."

"Well, then, Mr. Pitkin," said Kelly with exaggerated politeness, "I reckon I won't be employed by you. I'd sell you my time, but not the right to defend myself."

"He's speaking for all of us, Pit," Woody said. "This same hombre tried to kill Nip in town yesterday, and likely would have, if Gavin and me hadn't sided him."

"If Kelly goes, we all go," said Rusty Pryor, his eyes sparking green fire.

Pitkin was speechless until Naomi spoke up.

"Father, Mr. Kelly only defended himself. How can you fault him for that?"

"Daughter," Pitkin said angrily, "how dare you question my integrity in public? Why, I ought to take a strap to you."

"Then you'd as well take a strap to me, Father," Nell said, "because I feel the same as Naomi. "If Mr. Kelly hadn't defended himself, he would be dead, and I don't believe a man should die just to justify your sense of authority."

For a moment, it seemed Pitkin's fury was about to engulf him, but he swallowed his pride and strove mightily to control himself. When he finally spoke, it was to Nip Kelly.

"Perhaps I was hasty in my judgment of you, Mr. Kelly. All of you must be patient with me, for I am unfamiliar with the Western frontier's concept of justice. I hired all of you for your experience, and I shall attempt to rely more fully on that experience in the future. I shall begin by allowing you to do what is legal and proper with the body of the late Mr. Thornton."

"Thornton asked for what he got," said Woody, "and if the law comes nosin' around, Nip's got all the witnesses he'll need. No shootin' was ever more justified, and all we owe Thornton is a decent buryin'."

"Very well," Pitkin said, "I'll accept your judgment,

but who's going to lead the three packhorses with our personal belongings?''

"If you was serious about takın' our advıce," said Rusty, "get rid of the packhorses. What you need is another wagon and some more good mules. You can handle the wagon yourself. All you got to do ıs follow the chuck wagon, and anywhere Gonzales goes, you can go."

It was a sensible suggestion, and it struck both the Pitkin girls as hilariously funny. Pitkin needed a moment to see it as both practical and humorous, and when he spoke again he seemed more like the men he had hıred.

"Woody," Pitkin said, "we're goıng to unload those three packhorses. If I provide the necessary funds, will some of you see to the purchase of four good mules and a suitable wagon wıth canvas?"

"We will," saıd Woody, "and you'll find that second wagon is a good investment."

2

"Mr. Pitkın," Kelly said, "before we put this behind us, there's something you ought to know. I've seen some hard livin', some turbulent times before, durin', and after the war. I've made some enemies, and I can't promise you there won't be more hombres who'd like nothin' better than seein' me laid out in a pine box. But I can and will promise you this: I don't aim to take water, to let them ventilate my carcass, if that's what it takes to stay on the good side of you."

"Very well," said Pitkin. "I have admitted I was wrong in questioning your judgment, and I will go one step farther, if that's what it takes to satisfy you and your companions. I will not object to your defending yourselves in whatever manner you see fit, as long as I can depend on your loyalty to me and my daughters. To my brand, as you might say."

"You got it, Mr. Pitkın," Kelly replied, "and I believe I can speak for everybody else. Am I right, gents?"

"Right," said the others, in almost a single voice.

"One more thing," Kelly said. "You'll need a trail boss, and you should name him before you take the trail with the herd."

"Then why not the same trail boss who brought the herd from Texas?" Pitkin asked.

"That's Woody," said Vic Brodie "He's dependable,

but there's times he's stubborn as hell. Beggin' your pardon, ladies."

"Do it, Woody," Gavin McCord said. "We're all used to your cussedness."

"I'll do it," said Woody, "with the understanding that when I give an unpopular order, I don't have to part somebody's hair with the muzzle of my Colt, gettin' it obeyed."

Everybody laughed, including the Pitkins, but Woody allowed his eyes to linger on each of them just long enough for them to realize he was dead serious. When they again were silent, he spoke.

"There's no point in moving out today, because we've jacked around and lost more than three hours. What we *are* going to do is prepare to leave at first light tomorrow. Pit, if you're willing to buy a second wagon, with mules and harness, I'll have Nip and Gavin ride into town and get it."

"I said I would," Pitkin replied, "and I will. Here's five hundred dollars. Will that be sufficient?"

"Just about," said Gavin. "Good mules are seventy-five to a hundred dollars apiece. I doubt the wagon will be any more costly than the chuck wagon."

"You and Nip get started, then," Woody said. "Pit, do you have further business in Independence?"

"Yes," said Pitkin. "I have yet to close my account with the bank. If I am to purchase your herd, you must decide how you wish to be paid. Do you want gold, or will you be satisfied with a bank draft that can be cashed at the bank in Santa Fe? I intend to have all my funds transferred by the bank."

"Rusty, Gavin, Vic, Ash, will you accept a bank draft?" Woody asked "We'll have no need of gold coin on the trail. It'll just be somethin' else to bother with "

"Bank draft," said Gavin.

Rusty, Vic, and Ash quickly agreed.

"Pit," Woody said, "why don't you return to town with Gavin and Nip? There should be plenty of maps of the Santa Fe. Have you looked at them?"

"Yes," said Pitkin, "and they're somewhat confusing. It

seems there are two different trails. One—the mountain trail—goes through Colorado. The other—the desert trail— is a more direct route, by way of Fort Dodge, and across Indian Territory's panhandle.''

"Then get one of each," Woody said, "and make your arrangements with the bank. While you're doing that, Nip and Gavin can buy the wagon, the teams, and the harness. If there's anything more you'll be needing, the second wagon will provide some extra room."

"Dried apple, more pie," said Gonzales, who had been listening.

That brought a cheer of agreement from the rest of the outfit.

"If it suits you, Pit," Woody said, "when you have the wagon, get a greater supply of dried apples at the general store. Dried apple pie is about the only sweet a man can enjoy on the trail, and the fruit goes a long way, preventin' scurvy."

"An interesting theory," said Pitkin. "I shall do as you suggest. Unless you're opposed to it, I believe we should keep these three extra horses. You don't seem to have that many for the task ahead."

Woody laughed. "You're becoming a mite more observant, Pit. We can use the extra horses."

"Father, while you are gone," Naomi said, "Nell and I can sort out everything from those three pack horses. It will be so much easier, getting to what we need, with a second wagon."

Pitkin nodded and rode out, following Nip and Gavin.

"The rest of you," said Woody, "can unload those packhorses so Naomi and Nell can begin sorting out their things."

The Pitkin girls were amused, for the four cowboys all but fell over one another in their eagerness to reach the packhorses.

Reaching town, Pitkin reined up at the bank.

"We'll bring the wagon here, Pit," Gavin said.

Pitkin nodded, looped the reins of his horse over the hitch rail and went on into the bank. Nip and Gavin watched him go, and Nip spoke.

"He started off a mite rough, but damned if I don't believe he'll be a man to ride the river with."

"He's learned the first important lesson," said Gavin. "Either you bend or you break. There's plenty of give and take on the Western frontier. If you don't give, it takes."

In less than an hour, they had purchased the wagon, the necessary harness, and four mules. With Gavin leading Nip's horse, Kelly drove the wagon to the bank. Pitkin had concluded his business and was waiting. Nip climbed down from the wagon box and passed the reins to Pitkin.

"I'll tie your horse behind the wagon," said Kelly.

Nip and Gavin rode on to the general store, Pitkin following with the wagon.

"We'll wait with the horses and the wagon," Gavin said, "unless you need us."

"I must find some trail maps," said Pitkin. "Why don't you arrange for as much of the dried fruit as you think we'll need?"

When Pitkin returned with the maps, the wagon had been backed up to the loading dock. Two men from the store were loading a large wooden barrel.

"I presume you bought enough," Pitkin said.

"It'll have to do," said Nip. "It's all they had."

"A hundred and fifty dollars' worth," Gavin added.

The storekeeper had his hand out, and Pitkin paid him. Without a word, he mounted the wagon box, following Gavin and Nip when they rode out. By the time they reached the herd, Gonzales had begun supper.

"My God," said Woody, when he saw the enormous barrel in the new wagon, "what's in that?"

"Dried apples," Gavin replied, with a twinkle in his eyes. "We'd've got more, but that was all they had."

"A shame we don't have some sourdough starter," said Rusty, "but Gonzales started it workin' just yesterday. We could use some dried apple pies for supper."

"You hombres didn't dig deep enough in old Sam's pack," Nip said. "There's a quart jar of starter in there, just beggin' to be made into dried apple pies. I'll go fetch it and get Gonzales started."

"Yeeehaaa," Rusty shouted.

Supper was a memorable affair, with plenty of the dried apple pies.

"At first," said Pitkin, "I suspected we were overdoing it with the dried apples. Now, however, I'm not sure we bought enough."

There were still several hours of daylight, and Woody wasted no time in getting down to business.

"It's time we had a look at those trail maps, Pit, and weighed one route against the other."

Pitkin spread the two maps out on the grass, and they had been drawn large enough for the entire outfit to gather around.

"Now," said Pitkin, "you can see what I was trying to tell you. The mountain route—which the map refers to as the Upper Crossing—crosses the Cimarron River perhaps thirty miles west of Fort Dodge. It leads past Bent's Fort through southern Colorado, and finally through Cimarron, New Mexico, to Santa Fe. I would judge it to be at least two or three hundred miles farther than the desert route, which is called the Cimarron Cutoff."

"One thing I don't understand," Woody said. "Why in tarnation is the Cimarron Cutoff referred to as the desert route, when there are so many rivers to cross? There's one stretch—from southwestern Kansas into Indian Territory's panhandle—where the Santa Fe follows the Cimarron River for near a hundred miles."

"Yes," said Pitkin, "but after crossing the Arkansas, what do you see between there and the Cimarron?"

"Cimarron Desert," Woody said. "If this map's drawn to proper scale, that's maybe a five-day drive, at ten miles a day."*

* The *Jornada*—fifty miles of barren plain, without wood or water.

"Yes," said Pitkin, "that's the price one pays for taking the more direct route. While I dare not think of myself as a frontiersman, I know that five days without water is beyond the endurance of man or beast."

"Yeah," Vic Brodie said, "and by the time we get there, it'll be the hottest part of the summer."

"What about it, trail boss?" said Rusty.

"There are two water barrels mounted on each of the wagons," Woody said, "and each of those barrels can be replaced with a larger one. We can utilize some of the extra room in the second wagon, carrying two extra water barrels. All these can be filled before we leave the Arkansas River. There should be enough water for our own use and for watering the horses and mules."

"You are a resourceful young man," said Pitkin, "but what about the herd? They must have water, and there is no possible way we can carry that much."

"We'll have to run 'em dry," Woody replied. "If this Cimarron Desert is all that the name implies, there'll be just dry, flat plain, without drop-offs. We'll have to scout ahead, to be sure, and we'll trail the herd at night. And I mean all night, from dusk to dawn. By the time we allow them to rest, they'll be exhausted, and that's what it'll take. You can't get thirsty cattle to lie down. They'll mill and bawl like lost souls, and if they're goin' to be on the move, it might as well be toward water."

"You seem to have a commendable knowledge of the beasts," said Pitkin, admiringly.

"That's puttin' the best possible face on it," Woody said. "A shift of the wind could turn the herd around and send them stampeding in the wrong direction, but that's all part of the risk. We'll just have to hope their first whiff of water comes from the Cimarron, up ahead."

"Suppose, in spite of all we can do, they run the wrong way, and we lose them," said Pitkin. "What do we do then?"

"We round the varmints up and start all over again," Woody said.

"It sounds like a terrible risk, just to spare ourselves perhaps two hundred miles," said Naomi.

"It ain't as risky as it seems, ma'am," Rusty said. "We lost 'em three times comin' up the trail from Texas. It's just part of trail drivin'. Mostly, a stampede runs all the fat off of 'em, but some good graze puts it back."

"He's right about that," said Woody. "After runnin' 'em dry, once we reach water, we generally take a couple of days' rest before movin' on."

"Someone must return to Independence for the extra water barrels, then," Pitkin said.

"You can take your wagon through there in the morning," said Woody. "We'll drive the herd west and meet you beyond town. I reckon you won't have any trouble finding the Santa Fe Trail. Just follow the wagon ruts."

Naomi and Nell spent the last several hours of daylight packing their belongings in the second wagon. When it came time to turn in for the night, they unrolled their bedrolls beneath the wagon. Rusty, Gavin, and Vic took the first watch. Nip, Woody, and Ash would begin the second watch at midnight. Gonzales again proved his worth as a trail drive cook by filling the two-gallon coffee pot and suspending it over a bed of hot coals so the men on watch would have hot coffee.

Breakfast was eaten in the first gray light of dawn. Nell and Naomi Pitkin surprised Woody with a request.

"We have a lot of cows and not many riders," Naomi said. "Where can we ride that will be helpful to you?"

"Drag," said Woody. "Directly behind the herd. There'll always be a few cows tryin' to quit the bunch and go back the way they came. If you can head them and send them back to the herd, the rest of us can devote all our efforts to keepin' them bunched and movin' ahead."

"We'll really be doing something useful, then," Nell said.

"You most certainly will," said Woody. "Otherwise,

we'd only have one rider at drag, and he'd likely be run ragged.''

"Gavin," Woody said, "today I want you at drag. The Pitkin girls will be riding there too, and it'll be your job to keep an eye on them."

"Damn," said Rusty, "I reckon he won't have any trouble doin' that. Lucky varmint."

"Yeah," Vic said, "why him?"

"All right," said Woody, "none of that. There'll be a new man every day, so each of you will have a turn. Rusty, today I'll want you and Ash ridin' flank. Vic, you and Nip will be the swing riders. I'll be at point, and the wagons will follow the herd."

"What about the extra horses and mules?" Vic asked.

"They'll have to trail with the tag end of the herd, same as they did comin' up the trail from Texas," said Woody. "We can't afford the luxury of a horse wrangler."

"I'm ready," Pitkin said, after he had harnessed the mules to his wagon. "Where am I to find these extra barrels, and how much should I pay for them?"

"You should find them at the wagon yard," said Woody. "If they don't have them, I'd say they can tell you who does. They shouldn't charge you more than two dollars apiece."

"One thing more," Pitkin said. "Naomi and Nell are planning to ride directly behind the herd. Drag, you call it. Will they be safe there?"

"Safer than anywhere else," said Woody "They asked how they could help, and shorthanded as we are, we can use them. Gavin will ride with them today One of the outfit will be with them every day. Both wagons—you and Gonzales—will be following the herd, and we'll be depending on the two of you to always look ahead. First sign of trouble, you can alert the rest of us by firing a shot. I'll be riding point, leading the herd."

Pitkin seemed satisfied, and flicking the reins, sent the mules trotting toward town. The riders already had the herd bunched, and riding west, Woody got around them.

"Move 'em out!" Woody shouted.

Doubled lariats popped bovine flanks, and the herd began slowly moving west. There were stragglers who doubled back, keeping the drag riders busy. Watching Gavin, both the Pitkin girls soon got the idea, and did a fair job heading the bunch quitters.

"Keep 'em bunched," Gavin shouted. "Don't let 'em lag and fall back."

After an hour of difficulty, the trail-wise herd settled down, and by noon, Woody could see water. According to the maps Pitkin had purchased, it was a tributary of the Osage River. They were a few miles west of Independence, and Woody led the herd on until they reached the endless ruts that were the Santa Fe Trail. Woody waved his hat, his signal to the riders to begin milling the herd. Here they would wait for Pitkin. The herd, already thirsty, took advantage of the convenient water. Pitkin soon arrived.

"I had no trouble getting the barrels," Pitkin said, "and I bought another two hundred pounds of grain at the general store. It seemed there might not be enough grain for the mules, with two wagons."

"Good thinking, Pit," said Woody. "There may be times when the graze is skimpy, and there'll barely be enough for the herd. Let's take another look at that map before we move on. I don't recall seeing any water between the Osage and Neosho rivers."

"Where the trail crosses the Osage," Nip Kelly said, "there's four tributaries, spread out like the tines of a hayfork. If this is the first, it's unlikely that we'll travel any farther than the fourth one before sundown."

"This is the first," said Pitkin. "I crossed no river from Independence to here."

"Then we should have water for tonight," Woody said.

"I learned something about the trail while I was in town," said Pitkin. "Council Grove, which is probably a hundred miles west of here, is actually a small village. It is possibly our last contact with civilization until we reach Fort

Union, in northeastern New Mexico. There is a cemetery, a restaurant, and the Last Chance Store.''

"Head 'em up, move 'em out!" Woody shouted.

Pitkin fell in behind the herd, following the chuck wagon, while Woody rode ahead to the point position. The herd settled down and there were fewer bunch quitters. Gavin was watching Naomi and Nell Pitkin covertly, and despite the clouds of dust, they actually seemed to be enjoying their small part in the drive. They had quickly followed Gavin's example, their scarves covering nose and mouth as protection from the dust.

From his wagon, Pitkin had been observing the movement ahead of him, and he marveled at the efficiency of so few men, as they kept the herd bunched and moving. He was fully aware of the effect this extravaganza was likely to have on his impressionable daughters. Following Nip Kelly's gunfight, he thought Naomi and Nell eyed the man with something more than admiration for Kelly's skill with a revolver. It raised possibilities Gladstone Pitkin just wasn't ready to consider, and he forced himself to think of the probable difficulties on the long trail ahead.

The herd had settled down to the extent that horses and riders were able to relax, and to Gavin McCord's surprise, the Pitkin girls had caught up to him. Nell rode to his left, while Naomi rode to his right.

"I am so glad Father bought your cows and hired you and your friends to go with us to New Mexico," said Naomi.

"So am I," Nell said. "Nothing as glorious as this could ever happen in England."

"I've read some about England," said Gavin. "I seem to remember the knights of the Round Table, dragon slaying, and such."

"Horse feathers," Nell replied. "The knights are fat old men who wear powdered wigs and sip tea. The dragons— if there ever were any—are long since dead of boredom."

Gavin McCord laughed until there were tears in his eyes, while Naomi looked reprovingly at her sister.

"Father would take a strap to you," said Naomi, "if he

knew you were spouting such twaddle about jolly old England. An Englishman has his pride, don't you know?''

She spoke with an exaggerated English accent, and the two of them burst into fits of laughter that startled the cows at the tag end of the herd. Gavin's sense of humor got the best of his natural shyness, and he laughed with them. After that, the conversation flowed more easily.

"Tell us about Texas,'' the girls begged.

And Gavin did. They gave him their undivided attention, and when he slacked off, they begged for more.

"Tell us about the Indians,'' Nell pleaded.

"You're likely to meet both Comanches and Kiowa before we reach Santa Fe,'' said Gavin. "If I tell you too much, it might scare you all the way back to England.''

"No,'' they cried in a single voice. "Tell us.''

"I reckon the Comanches are the worst,'' said Gavin. "They've been givin' Texans hell for as far back as I can remember. They'll stampede a herd and then ambush the riders who are tryin' to round 'em up. They stampeded this very herd one night, while I was out in the bushes . . .''

His voice trailed off, and when they sensed his embarrassment, they wouldn't leave him be.

"Why were you out in the bushes during the night?'' Nell wanted to know.

"Yes,'' said Naomi, "I thought you watched the cattle at night.''

"We don't *all* watch the cattle *all* the time,'' Gavin said defensively, "and there will be times at night when you'll want to head for the bushes. But don't do it. There may be a Comanche or Kiowa there waiting for you.''

"Should I have to go to the bushes at night,'' said Nell, "I shall find you and have you go with me.''

Naomi laughed. "So will I.''

They were full of mischief and enjoying themselves at his expense, but Gavin became dead serious, and when he spoke, they listened.

"Anywhere along this trail, we're subject to Indian attack. Neither of you are to move about in the darkness after turning in for the night. It could get you shot.''

They stared at him with frightened eyes, and it was Nell who finally spoke.

"But suppose we have to . . have to . . .''

"Roll out of your blankets and squat right where you are,'' Gavin said.

"You mean that, don't you?'' Naomi said.

"Every word,'' said Gavin. "On the frontier, there's more to lose than your privacy. Such as your hair or your life.''

That sobered them, and the drive went on. Reaching what appeared to be a fourth tributary of the Neosho, Woody waved his hat and the riders began to mill the herd. Gonzales reined up his teams near the water, and Pitkin brought his wagon up directly behind the chuck wagon. The herd wasted no time getting to water. Gonzales and Pitkin began unharnessing their teams, while the riders unsaddled their horses. Nell and Naomi unsaddled their own horses, and the cowboys watched in admiration. The Pitkin women were making it clear they neither expected nor wanted special treatment. Gonzales wasted no time getting supper started. Pitkin approached Woody.

"Woody, I should be standing watch with the rest of you. Starting tonight, I shall be part of the second watch.''

"*Bueno*,'' said Woody. "We'll need you, as we get deeper into Kiowa and Comanche territory.''

"What about Nell and me?'' Naomi asked.

"Maybe the both of you, before the drive's done,'' said Woody.

The sun crept toward its daily rendezvous with the western horizon, and as the blue of the sky changed to purple, the first stars appeared. Prominent in the dusk, far to the west, lightning flickered, vanished, then appeared again for a longer time. Thunder rumbled like a distant roll of drums. The cool, damp fingers of a breeze touched their sweaty faces, as it swept in from the west.

"There's a storm buildin' over yonder to the west,'' Woody said.

"It's a ways off," said Vic. "It may not reach us till sometime tomorrow. Might even rain itself out before it gets here."

"Winds gettin' up," Nip observed. "There'll be rain before dawn, with thunder and lightning a-plenty."

"Just our luck," said Rusty. "Two days out of Independence, and we likely got us a stampede comin'."

"There must be something we can do to prepare ourselves," Pitkin said. "What?"

"When it gets closer—when we know for sure we're in for it—it's every man in the saddle," said Woody. "On stormy nights, there are no designated watches. Nobody sleeps."

"What would you have us do?" Nell asked.

"When it looks like the herd's about to run," said Woody, "I want both of you in the wagon. While I'm obliged for your ambition, a stampede is no place to cut your teeth. If the herd takes a notion to run, we'll have to head 'em, if we can, and that means some hard riding. I saw a rider's horse go down before a stampedin' herd once, and we had to gather up what was left of the hombre with a shovel."

His words had a profound effect on Naomi and Nell Pitkin.

"We'll stay in the wagon," Naomi said. "Perhaps you should join us, Father."

She was serious, and Pitkin seemed torn between anger and laughter. But his sense of humor won out.

"I fear I am as inexperienced as either of you," said Pitkin. "If there's a stampede, with any serious riding to be done, I shall stay out of the way."

Pitkin grinned and the outfit laughed, appreciating his frankness. By midnight, there was ample evidence that Nip Kelly's prediction was about to come to pass. The gentle wind from the west had grown in intensity, sweeping heavy gray thunderheads before it. Lightning shot golden barbs from the cloud mass, and thunder became an ominous, continuous rumble. Woody and the riders were all in the saddle,

circling the restless herd. The cattle were on their feet, milling, bawling their fear and frustration.

"Get ready," Woody shouted. "They're goin' to run."

One blaze of lightning flared into the next, until the sky
was light as day. The rolling thunder reached a peak, sending forth a clap that seemed to shake the earth. It was more
than enough to set the spooked herd in motion, and like a
thundering, bawling avalanche, they lit out toward the east,
running with the wind.

3

*E*ven with the riders anticipating the stampede, they were unable to head the herd, for the running cattle had fanned out almost immediately into a front half a mile wide. Right on the heels of the stampede, the rain came, turning the dusty prairie into instant mud. As the riders rode madly, seeking to head the lead steers, Woody's horse slipped and went down. He hit the ground and rolled, not completely escaping the murderous hooves of the rampaging longhorns. A hoof struck him in the back of the head.

He was brought to his senses by the rain falling in his face. The herd had long since disappeared, and the only sound was the patter of rain and the fading rumble of thunder. Woody got to hands and knees, and then shakily to his feet. The storm clouds were breaking up, and a timid first-quarter moon had appeared. Woody began looking for his horse, hoping the animal hadn't been caught up in the stampede. Suddenly there was the sodden thud of hoofbeats.

"Rein up and identify yourself," Woody said, his hand near the butt of his Colt.

"Nip Kelly," said a voice from the darkness. "I caught a horse runnin' loose, and I was hopin' his rider hadn't been hooked out of the saddle and trampled. Is he yours?"

"I can't see him that well," Woody said, "but he'll do. Have you seen any of the other riders?"

"No," said Kelly. "I was ahead of you, but I think the

others was on the far side of the herd. I've never seen a
herd fan out so fast. The front must have been three hundred
yards across.''

"I hope nobody got caught in front of it," Woody said.
"We'd better see if we can bring them together."

The wagons and the camp had been spared, and slowly
but surely the riders all made their way back. Some of the
horses had been raked by horns, and had to be treated with
sulfur salve. After the wind had died, Gonzales had erected
one of the canvas shelters and there was hot coffee for the
muddy, bedraggled riders.

"I have learned one thing tonight," Pitkin said. "There
is much about the frontier that one can only understand
through experience."

"You'll learn some more tomorrow," said Woody. "All
of us—except for Gonzales—will be roundin' up cows."

"I shall do my share," Pitkin replied. "How far do they
customarily run?"

"Depends on the intensity of the storm," said Woody.
"Right after this bunch lit out, the thunder began to fade.
We shouldn't be more than two days roundin' 'em up."

"You've been hurt," Naomi said, as Woody knelt by the
fire.

"My horse slipped, and before I could get out of the way,
a cow kicked me in the head," said Woody. "A pretty stiff
headache, but I'll live."

"*Medicina* in wagon," Gonzales said.

"Get it for me, please," said Naomi. "We doctor the
horses, and we shall doctor the riders, as well."

She filled the second coffeepot with water and hung it
over the fire. When the water was hot, she cleansed the gash
on Woody's head, bandaged it, and soaked the bandage with
disinfectant.

"Tarnation," Vic said, "if I'd knowed this little lady was
doin' the doctorin', I'd've fell off my horse."

"I didn't fall off my horse," said Woody, with some
resentment. "The horse slipped and fell, makin' it just a
mite difficult for me to stay in the saddle."

There was considerable hilarity, Woody joining in. Gladstone Pitkin marveled at their ability to laugh about an incident that might have cost a man his life.

Gonzales had breakfast ready before first light, and by the time the first golden rays of dawn painted the eastern sky, Woody had all the riders in the saddle searching for the stampeded cattle. They had ridden less than a mile when they sighted the first bunch.

"Might not be as bad as we thought," Rusty said. "There must be two hundred of 'em over yonder."

"Don't get your hopes up too soon," said Ash. "We might have to track down the rest of the varmints in twos and threes."

Since Woody had included Gladstone Pitkin in the roundup, Nell and Naomi had been determined to go. A few head at a time, they began sighting more cattle, and the Pitkins performed surprisingly well. The sun rose in a cloudless blue sky, and by noon, Woody estimated they had recovered a third of the missing longhorns.

"It isn't as difficult as I had imagined," said Pitkin.

"Sometimes you get a break," Gavin said. "A herd that's been spooked by a storm is more likely to run just a mile or two, until the storm lets up. On the other hand, if you're runnin' 'em dry, and they're mad with thirst, the varmints will likely run till they drop, or until they reach the water they're smellin'. Even the smell of rain that's ridin' the wind, from a storm a hundred miles away."

"Then a thirst-crazed stampede in the desert could be far more disastrous than what we have just experienced," said Pitkin.

"It could," Woody said, "because the wind is nearly always from the west or northwest, and if there's rain anywhere between us and the Pacific Ocean, the herd will likely run toward the smell of water."

"And that wind is going to become more intense at night," said Pitkin. "Won't we be increasing the possibility of a stampede, if we drive them at night?"

"Maybe," Woody said. "It's a calculated risk. There's less wind in the daytime, but there's the sun beatin' down, suckin' moisture from man and beast. You'll see, once we're crossin' this desert."

There were fewer cows in the bunches they found during the afternoon, and a quick tally at sundown left them with less than half the herd recovered.

"There's been sun all day," said Ash Pryor. "Another day of it, and there won't be a lot of standin' water from that storm. Them critters ought to come driftin' back to this stretch of river."

"Yeah," Nip said, "unless they run too far. This ain't the only tributary from the Osage. They could've drifted north."

"We'll give it another day," said Woody. "Now we'd better drive our day's gather to camp. As far as the others are concerned, we'll just have to wait until tomorrow."

"I am fortunate to have an outfit that has been through this kind of thing before," Pitkin said.

"We have done that," said Rusty. "We lost the jugheaded varmints three times on the way from Texas."

"It's amazing that you were able to find them all again," Nell said.

"We didn't," said Gavin. "Actually, we started the drive with a few more than the herd we brought to Independence. Be it horses, mules, or cows, you can't drive critters across open country without losin' some."

"I suppose that's the realistic way of looking at it," Pitkin observed.

"Once we reach your holdings in New Mexico, we'll see that you get an accurate head count," said Woody. "You don't pay for cows you don't get."

"While I appreciate your generosity," Pitkin said, "I would be taking advantage of you and your companions. Had I hired someone else to drive the herd, I would have then been obliged to pay you for thirty-five hundred head, and with less experienced men, this same stampede might have been even more costly."

Woody laughed. "Pit, without bein' aware of it, you've adopted the code of the West. Aside from owlhoots and renegade Indians, a Western man will go hungry before he'll take what he believes is unfair advantage."

When they reached camp with the partially recovered herd, Gonzales had supper just about ready.

"Shuck your saddles and let your horses roll," Woody said. "We'll all have time to eat before dark."

The sun had been hot, the day long, and the grateful horses took the time to roll in the grass before going to water.

"By God," said Vic, "I smell dried apple pies."

They had just finished the last of the pies, when the sun dipped below the far western horizon. The first watch saddled up, as early stars twinkled down from a sky that rapidly changed from blue to deep purple. His back to a wagon wheel, Ash Pryor took out a harp and began to play a lonesome melody.

"That's beautiful," Naomi said. "What is it called?"

"I dunno," said Ash. "Daddy used to whistle it."

"He couldn't carry a tune in a jug, when it come to singin'," Rusty said, "but he sure could whistle."

Ash drifted from one lonesome ballad to another, each as nameless as the last. There came suddenly the far away moan of a prairie wolf. The harp became silent in mid-melody, as they listened for a repetition of the chilling sound. It came again, rising, falling, then dying away to silence.

"God," said Vic, "I hope the varmints ain't after our cows."

"If they are," Nell said, "what's to be done about them?"

"Nothing," said Woody, "as long as the herd's scattered. We can't very well protect the cattle still running loose."

"Plains wolves generally ain't a problem," Nip said, "unless there's a really bad winter and game is scarce. But I reckon they could be tempted by good Texas beef."

But the wolves remained silent, and at first light, the riders began their second day of searching for the scattered herd. They quickly found more than a hundred head of cows that apparently had returned to the closest water they remembered.

"We'll have to spread out," Woody said. "Those we don't find today, we may not find at all."

The outfit had been separated for less than an hour, when there was a shot. Quickly the outfit responded to the signal, and they found Ash Pryor near the remains of a cow.

"I reckon this is what quieted them wolves," said Ash. "They didn't leave much, but I sent a pair of coyotes skitterin' into the brush when I rode up."

"It's only one animal," Pitkin observed. "It could be worse."

"Yes," said Woody, "and if we don't round up the rest of our herd, it may well get worse. Two wolves could have killed this cow, but there could be a whole pack of them by tonight. The varmints have that much in common with buzzards. Somehow they get word to others. Let those cows run loose long enough, and every damn wolf within a hundred miles will be after them."

"That's gospel," Gavin said. "We'd best put the rest of today to good use."

"Gavin," said Woody, "you come with me. We'll cross this stretch of river and ride on to the next tributary. The rest of you continue on beyond where we quit the search last night, but not for more than another five miles. It's unlikely they ran any farther east, and the only other possibility is that after the storm, they may have drifted south."

Gavin and Woody rode across the shallow tributary and headed north to the next one.

"I only hope the herd split and some of 'em headed north," said Gavin. "That would explain why they haven't gathered along that tributary where we've been searching."

"For a fact," Woody agreed. "They've got to have water, and these tributaries of the Osage are still the best source."

"There's some of 'em," said Gavin excitedly, when they

were within sight of the line of vegetation that marked the banks of the second stream.

"Not near enough, though," Woody said. "We'll ride upstream a ways and hope for more of them."

Their search was rewarded, for much of the missing herd grazed in large bunches.

"Let's ride amongst 'em and take a quick tally," said Woody. "This may well be the rest of the herd."

Quickly the cowboys took a count, and elated, compared numbers.

"Close to twenty-two hundred," Gavin said.

"I counted nearly a hundred more," said Woody, "so we'll go with your count. Those we rounded up yesterday, added to what's here, brings us within probably three hundred head of our original herd. Ride back and bring the rest of the outfit. I'll go on upstream a ways, and see if there's more."

Gavin galloped away, and the word he brought was met with great enthusiasm by the rest of the outfit.

"It appears we are going to find the rest of them today, then," said Pitkin.

"We'll be close," Gavin said, "but we still can't afford to lose three or four hundred head, only two days out of Independence. There may be other stampedes, some far more damaging than this one."

When they reached the second tributary, there was no sign of Woody.

"Perhaps when we see him, he will have found the rest of the herd," said Naomi.

"They're scattered for another two miles," Woody said, when they met him returning. "Let's bring them up to join the larger herd, and that may finish the gather."

Rounding the cattle up into a single herd, they drove them south, to the tributary on which their camp was located. Within an hour, the much larger herd had been united with the cattle gathered the day before, and it truly looked as though the original trail drive had come together again.

"Tally time," Woody said. "Rusty, Gavin, Vic, Ash, and

Nip, I want all of you to run a tally on the herd."

Quickly the riders ran individual tallies.

"Sing out your totals," said Woody.

"Thirty-four hundred and twenty-five," Rusty said.

"Thirty-four hundred and sixty," said Ash.

"Thirty-four hundred and ninety," Vic said.

"Thirty-four hundred and seventy-five," said Nip.

"Thirty-four hundred and fifty," Gavin said.

"We'll call it thirty-four seventy-five," said Woody. "Tomorrow, before we pull out, we'll ride through here one more time. There may still be a few that'll make their way to water."

"A remarkable feat, recovering so many of the beasts," Pitkin said.

"Not many places for 'em to hole up, on this Kansas plain," said Gavin. "I wouldn't be surprised to find the rest of 'em tomorrow morning."

"I reckon the wolves will let us know if there's any more cows wanderin' loose," Nip said. "If we don't hear wolves tonight, I'd say we've gathered all the cows we're likely to find."

There was no more of the mournful howling, and the night passed uneventfully.

"We have three-quarters of an hour before breakfast," Woody said. "Gavin, I want you and Vic to ride down this tributary and the next one, just on the chance that a few more cows wandered back to water durin' the night."

"I think we're wastin' our time," said Vic, as they saddled their horses.

"Maybe," Gavin replied, "but we need to recover as many as we can. Woody's thinkin' there may be more stampedes, and we purely can't afford to take a big loss on the first one."

They found no more cattle until they reached the second tributary of the Osage. There they gathered fourteen more cows and drove them back to join the rest of the herd.

"This exceeds anything I ever expected," said Pitkin, pleased.

"Let's get breakfast behind us," Woody said, "and get these critters on the trail. We'll have to make up some time. We should reach the fourth tributary of the Osage by the end of the day."

There would be water for the night's camp, and with that assurance, the outfit kept the herd moving at a faster-than-usual gait. Ash Pryor rode drag with the Pitkin girls, and with the herd behaving well, Naomi and Nell kept the young cowboy busy answering their questions.

"What can you tell us about New Mexico?" Naomi asked.

"Not much," said Ash. "I've never been there. We're headin' for the northern part, and from what I've heard, it gets almighty cold in winter. I reckon snow storms blow in from the Sangre de Cristo Mountains, to the west."

"What a strange name," Nell said. "What does it mean?"

"It's Spanish," said Ash. "It means Blood of Christ."

"I don't understand why Father was able to buy so much land," Naomi said. "There is no such open land in England. What the ruling class owns, they keep."

"All of New Mexico Territory was once owned by Mexico, and the Spanish before them," said Ash. "After the war with Mexico, the United States took everything north of the Rio Grande, includin' all of California, New Mexico, and part of Arizona."

"That's terrible, taking so much of another country's land," said Nell. "The United States surely didn't need it, or they wouldn't be selling such enormous parcels of it."

"The spoils of war," Ash replied. "Mexico wouldn't have anything less than war, so we obliged 'em by stompin' their ... whippin' their army. My daddy died in that war, and I don't feel bad about anything we took from Mexico. It wouldn't bother me if we'd kicked the varmints into the Gulf and took their whole damn country."

Nell laughed. "You sound like Father. Some Englishmen

still curse America because the Colonies took their freedom almost a hundred years ago. Father says it was destiny, that it was meant to be, that nothing could have stopped it. We were well off, by English standards, but Father was determined to taste the freedom of the New World, as he put it. So here we are.''

"I'm glad he felt that way," Ash said. "With his ambition and his holdings, someday he'll be a man to be reckoned with. Men are needed on the Western frontier who can see it for what it can be, rather than what it is.''

"You have an unusual perspective, for one so young," said Naomi.

Ash flushed. "I'm not so young. I'm twenty-four.''

"I didn't mean that in a critical way," Naomi said. "Your wisdom, your ideals, are a lot like Father's, yet you're half his age.''

"We can talk about wisdom and ideals some other time," said Nell. "I want to hear more about New Mexico, about the West. Tell me there won't be any of the cold, damp, miserable winters we had in England.''

"I'm from south Texas," Ash said, "so I can't tell you anything first-hand about New Mexico's winters. All I know is that when a blue norther comes rippin' through Texas, it always comes from the west. So I reckon when winter comes roarin' in, it jumps on New Mexico with both feet, before it reaches Texas. I reckon we'll all be wearin' long-handled woollies.''

"What in the world are long-handled woollies?" Naomi asked.

"Woolen underwear that covers your entire body, except for your head, your hands, and your feet," said Ash.

"They sound terribly inconvenient," Nell said. "Why you'd have to remove them every time you . . .''

Her voice trailed off and she dropped her eyes. Naomi laughed.

"You don't remove 'em unless you're takin' a bath," said Ash. "There's a trap door in the seat—a flap with buttons—that works just dandy.''

Nell had turned several shades of red. Ash caught Naomi's eye, and when she laughed, Ash laughed with her. It all proved contagious, and finally Nell joined them.

"Head 'em in," Woody shouted, waving his hat.

They had reached the fourth tributary of the Osage, their source of water for the herd and for their night's camp. The riders started the herd milling, while Gonzales and Pitkin headed their wagons away from the water. The horses and mules would be taken to water at a point along the river where there was no conflict with the thirsty longhorns. The sun was still an hour high when Gonzales got supper under way.

"Pit," Woody said, "let's take a look at that trail map again. As I recall, we ought to reach Council Grove by tomorrow night, where the Neosho River crosses the trail."

Pitkin spread out the map of the trail that led to Santa Fe by way of the Cimarron Cutoff, or desert route.

"Except for the *Jornada*, it looks quite promising," said Pitkin. "After leaving Council Grove, a second fork of the Neosho crosses the trail just west of Diamond Spring. Beyond there, the trail crosses four tributaries of the Arkansas, and just a few miles farther west, we pick up the main body of the Arkansas."

"We'll follow it to a few miles west of Fort Dodge," Woody said, "and it'll be our last sure water until we reach the Cimarron River. Fifty miles, at least."

"Your plan to drive the cattle at night until we're across the desert makes sense to me," said Pitkin. "Is a stampede our only possible problem, or have you been sparing me the others?"

"There's a possibility of Indians," Woody said. "Most likely Comanche. Since we'll be driving at night, we'll have to keep the herd bunched, the riders all close in, and both the wagons right on the heels of the drag. Comanches will stalk and kill at night as readily as in daylight."

"The varmints might stampede the herd," Vic said. "It's happened before."

"It has," said Woody, "and Indians are unpredictable."

"Then there are two possible causes of a stampede as we're crossing the desert," said Pitkin.

"Yes," Woody admitted. "In a way, a thirsty herd stampeding toward the smell of water is worse than a herd spooked by Indians. Most of our wind comes out of the west or northwest, and you can imagine what might happen if there's rain somewhere to the west of us."

"The herd will run toward the smell of water," said Pitkin, "even if it's only rain, and perhaps hundreds of miles away."

"Exactly," Woody replied, "and there's very little we can do about it. A thirsty herd is all but unstoppable. Get ahead of them, and you're risking yourself and your horse."

"All we can do is get them across that waterless desert just as fast as we can," said Gavin. "A cow ain't the smartest critter around, and the varmints have been known to light out down the back trail toward the last water they remember."

"Yeah," Vic agreed, "no matter how far away it is."

"I must say," said Pitkin, "I am receiving an education as to the habits of these Texas longhorn cattle. Do they possess any *good* qualities?"

All the riders laughed, and it was Rusty Pryor who spoke.

"They can survive where anything else would starve. If there's no grass, they'll eat mesquite beans, leaves, even bark. You can run the varmints till they're skin and bones, then lead 'em to some decent graze, and they'll fatten up."

"You forgot somethin'," said Ash. "Even on a good day, they're cantankerous, mean as sin, and if there's nothin' else to hook, they'll hook one another."

"I'm not sure I would consider those good qualities," Pitkin said.

"Come an' get it," Gonzales shouted, "or I feed it to the coyotes."

The following morning, by first light, Woody had the herd moving. Today they were expecting to reach Council Grove, the last civilian outpost until they were near Santa Fe. Nip Kelly rode drag with Naomi and Nell, and while he readily answered their questions, he volunteered nothing. He was friendly enough, yet he seemed distant.

"The other riders are from Texas," Nell said, "but I get the impression you aren't."

"You're right," said Nip. "I am not."

"You were terribly brave, standing up to that gunman from Independence," Nell said. "Did you know him well?"

"No," said Nip.

"Nell," Naomi said, "if you're going to question Mr. Kelly, why don't you do so in a less personal manner? You are behaving like a nosy little wench."

Nell glared at her sister in a manner that would have curdled milk, but she said no more. Curiously enough, it was Kelly who spoke.

"My home—when I had one—was in Missouri, Nell. The man I was forced to shoot tried to kill me during a poker game in a saloon in Independence. I'd never seen him in my life, and it was Woody and Gavin who backed off him and his friends. I don't talk about myself, because I have done little of which I am proud. I am a wanderer, a man with a fast gun and a slow conscience, some have said."

"But you must have a mother, a sister," said Nell.

"No," Kelly said. "My mother died when I was nine, and I've been on my own since then. I never knew who my father was."

Nell looked away, so he wouldn't see the tears in her eyes. Naomi started to speak, but Kelly wasn't finished.

"I knew a girl once, in southern Missouri . . ."

"Then why did you leave her?" Nell asked, in a quavering voice.

"She was dead," said Kelly.

Council Grove, Kansas. June 10, 1869.

One fork of the Neosho River crossed the trail just west of the village, and seeking graze for the herd, the horses, and mules, Woody led the drive well beyond the small settlement. There had been few drives of such a magnitude down the Santa Fe, and the few residents of Council Grove gathered to watch the longhorns pass.

"We'll take 'em downstream a ways," Woody shouted.

When the herd had been bunched near the water, they began sliding down the banks to drink. Gonzales had wisely drawn up the chuck wagon along the trail, a good distance upstream from the thirsty cattle.

"We'll have time to visit the store before sundown," said Woody, as the riders began unsaddling their horses.

"There's a cafe," Vic said.

"You don' like Gonzales's grub?" the Mexican inquired.

"Yeah," said Vic. "Ain't I took seconds as often as I could get 'em? I just said there was a cafe, damn it. I didn't say I was eatin' there."

"*Sí,*" Gonzales said. "There be dried apple pie."

4

"Council Grove bein' the last village between here and Santa Fe," Woody said, "I think we'll stay here through tomorrow. There's good graze and plentiful water. It's a good place to rest our horses and mules, and to maybe fatten the herd some. Then there's the Last Chance Store. There'll be a sutler's at Fort Dodge, but there'll likely be a better choice of goods here."

"Perhaps we can learn something about the trail ahead," said Pitkin.

"Won't hurt to ask," Woody replied. "Anybody wantin' to go to the store today, I'd say there's time before supper. I aim to go there tomorrow."

"I'll wait until then, and go with you," said Gavin.

"Gonzales," Pitkin said, "if there's anything more we're going to need before reaching Santa Fe, see if the store has it."

"*Sí*," said Gonzales. "I go tomorrow, after breakfast."

"Father," Nell said, "Naomi and me need hats. We want the kind the cowboys wear."

"Yes," said Naomi, "and that's not all. I want some Western riding boots."

"So do I," Nell said.

"Both of you have new English riding boots," said Pitkin. "What's wrong with them?"

"As you said, Father, they're English," Nell pointed

out. "Do you want us to look foolish, herding cattle in ridiculous, ugly English boots?"

"Oh, I suppose not," said Pitkin, "but keep those ridiculous, ugly English boots, in case the new ones hurt your feet."

"Let's go to the store now," Naomi said. "If we're getting new boots, we'll have time to get used to them before we take the trail again."

"Very well," said Pitkin. "Woody, do you wish to get your information first-hand, or shall I ask about the trail ahead?"

"Go ahead and learn whatever you can," Woody replied. "We'll inquire again at Fort Dodge, but we're still a long way from there. Might be somethin' we need to know before we reach the fort."

"Yeah," said Ash. "What about Indian trouble?"

"Very well," Pitkin said, "I'll see what I can learn from the proprietor. It will be the least he can do, after my daughters have purchased his supply of hats and boots."

The storekeeper and his wife had obviously been waiting for some business from the trail drive.

"I'm Abel Honicker," the little man said, "and this is my wife, Bessie. What can we do for you?"

"Our pleasure, indeed," Pitkin replied. "These are my daughters, Nell and Naomi. I am Gladstone Pitkin. The girls wish to dress as much like cowboys as possible, while I want to talk to you about the trail ahead."

"Come with me, ladies," said Bessie Honicker.

"Not much to tell about the trail ahead," Honicker replied. "Sometime back—April, it was—Indians attacked a train of a dozen wagons. About halfway between here and Fort Dodge, and seven of their folks was killed. Three of 'em was women."

"That's serious, indeed," said Pitkin. "Have there been other wagons since then?"

"Three," Honicker said. "The day before yesterday. Close-mouthed gent, his two sons and three daughters. Him and his sons each drove a wagon, and I doubt they'd have even stopped here, if one of the wagons hadn't busted a wheel. I wasn't impressed with any of the men, but the women! My God!''

"They weren't aware of the Indian threat?'' Pitkin asked.

"I tried to tell 'em, like I'm tellin' you," said Honicker, "but they didn't seem all that concerned. I asked 'em where they was bound, and was told to mind my own business."

"Most unusual,'' Pitkin observed. "Why would they have been so secretive about their destination?''

"I was inclined to wonder the same thing," said Honicker. "Their wagons was ridin' mighty low, like they was overloaded. When they moved on, I took a look at the trail, and where there was already ruts, their wagons made new ruts.''

"Heavy loads, indeed,'' Pitkin observed. "We are most appreciative for the information about the Indian attack. Now I must restrain my daughters, before they spend me into the poorhouse.''

Returning to camp, Pitkin told Woody and the rest of the outfit what he had learned.

"The Indian attack is bad news," said Woody. "Were they Kiowa or Comanche?''

"Honicker didn't say, and I didn't think to ask," Pitkin replied. "Perhaps you can find out tomorrow.''

"That's interestin', them three wagons ahead of us,'' Gavin said. "If they get through without Indian trouble, we shouldn't have a problem.''

"From what I've heard," said Woody, "the Santa Fe's always been a trade route, and I reckon heavily loaded wagons are always a prime target. While I wouldn't say the Indians will leave us alone, they won't be expectin' a lot of trade goods, us with just two wagons.''

With good graze and plentiful water, the herd posed no problem, and the riders had a day of rest. Gonzales produced some outstanding meals. Pitkin advanced every man a few dollars against his wages, and everybody had a chance to go to the store. Woody took the time to speak to Honicker, but learned no more than what the storekeeper had already told Pitkin.

"You'd best enjoy your time here at Council Grove," Honicker said. "It's one of the most agreeable stoppin' places between here and Santa Fe."*

When Woody and Gavin returned to camp, Rusty, Vic, and Ash left for the store.

"Father," said Naomi, "Nell and I would like to take a walk through the grove."

"Only if one of the men will accompany you," Pitkin said. "I forbid you to go alone."

"Woody and Gavin have just returned from the store," said Nell. "We'll ask them."

Pitkin wasn't surprised when the two cowboys readily agreed. Council Grove consisted of a continuous strip of timber almost a mile wide, extending along the valley of a small, fast-running stream known as Council Grove Creek. It was the principal branch of the Neosho River. Along the creek were fertile bottoms and upland prairies. Among the trees within the grove were ash, oak, elm, maple, and hickory. Many of the trees were clothed in enormous grapevines. The grove consisted of almost a hundred and sixty acres, and its dense shade proved a welcome respite from the glare of the sunburned plains.

"No wonder this is a favored stoppin' place," Gavin said. "I've never seen so many hardwood trees on a single patch of ground."

"With a blacksmith shop behind Honicker's store," said Woody, "there's plenty of all kinds of wood for axles, wagon tongues, and wheels."

"When we're far enough from camp," Naomi said, "I want to take off my boots and wade the creek."

"So do I," said Nell.

"Ah," Gavin said, "missing the old English boots, huh?"

---

* Council Grove took its name from a council held by Osage Indians in 1825, with men sent by the U.S. government to mark a road from Missouri to Santa Fe.

"Of course not," said Naomi. "I just want to enjoy the cool water, while I can. When we take the trail again, we may be under the hot sun all the way to New Mexico."

"Why don't you and Woody remove your boots and join us?" Nell suggested.

"I reckon we'd better not," said Woody. "We'd better just be ready to haul you out, if you get in over your heads."

"We'll find a place where the water's shallow," Naomi said.

They soon found such a place, where they could see the sandy bottom. While Woody and Gavin relaxed in the shade, Naomi and Nell tugged off their boots and rolled their Levi's up to their knees.

"Lord," Gavin said, "I'd forgot how peaceful it can be, with just the chirpin' of birds, the sound of a fast-runnin' stream, without bawlin' cows. Wake me when they're through splashin' around out there."

"I'm likely to doze off," said Woody. "I can't see them gettin' in trouble, when the water's not even to their knees."

But the shallow water extended only so far, until there was a drop-off. There, the water was much deeper, and with a shriek of terror, Naomi and Nell went under.

"My God," Gavin shouted, "where are they?"

As if in answer, two heads bobbed up farther downstream, and again there were two frantic cries for help. Of a single mind, without a word, Woody and Gavin took off their boots and went to the rescue. Neither of the women surfaced again, and when Woody was able to grasp Nell, she was a dead weight. Gavin had just as hard a time of it with Naomi, for all of them were swept downstream where the water seemed deepest. Ahead of them, part of the river-bank had washed out, exposing the gnarled roots of a tree that extended into the water. Keeping Naomi's head above water, Gavin seized one of the roots. Following his example, Woody caught another of the roots.

"Keep their heads above water," Gavin gasped, "until I can climb out."

Gavin struggled out of the water, and seizing Naomi under the arms, lifted her out on the bank. He then hauled out Nell, and Woody scrambled out on his own.

"My God," said Woody, "they look dead."

"Maybe not," Gavin said. "You take Nell, and I'll work on Naomi."

With the women belly-down, Gavin and Woody began forcing the water out of their tortured lungs. Nell came out of it first. She rolled over, and weeping, threw her arms around Woody.

"Hey, now," said Woody, "you're all right."

"I wouldn't have been," Nell sobbed, "but for you."

Naomi took longer to revive, and looking at her so still, Nell wept all the more. As Naomi began breathing normally, Gavin rolled her over and helped her to sit up. Then, to Gavin's total surprise, she kissed him long and hard. When she finally let go of him, he saw something in her eyes that overcame his shyness.

"Miss Pitkin," he said, "I'm tempted to throw you back in and do this all over again."

"Damn," said Woody, "where did I go wrong? I worked as hard as you did."

"And you shall have your reward," the tearful Nell said. He received a longer and more passionate kiss than Naomi had bestowed on Gavin.

"You're right, Gavin," Woody said, when he came up for air. "We'll have to throw them back in and rescue them again."

"If you don't speak of this to Father," said Naomi, "there might be more such rewards for you."

"Yes," Nell said. "Father must not know."

"His daughters practically drown," said Woody, "and he can't be told?"

"He still thinks of us as children," Naomi said. "I fear that if he knew of this, neither of us would ever be allowed out of his sight again."

"We would never be allowed to go anywhere with you

again," said Nell, "and you can be sure that would be the end of your rewards."

"You've convinced me that Pit shouldn't be told," Gavin said.

"I reckon I'm convinced for the same reason he is," said Woody, "but how are we to explain why the four of us are sopping wet?"

"We were caught in a sudden shower?" Nell suggested.

"I don't think so," said Woody. "There's not a cloud in the sky."

"Damn it," Gavin said, "why don't we just tell Pit the truth, and take our chances?"

"Because you won't have any chances," said Naomi. "Neither of us can swim."

"Then why the hell didn't you tell us that, before we allowed you to go in the water?" Woody demanded.

"If we had," said Nell, "you wouldn't have allowed us, would you?"

"You can bet your boots we wouldn't have," Woody replied. "If the two of you had drowned, what would we have told your father?"

"But we didn't drown," said Naomi. "He trusted you, just like we did. Why can't we just stay away from camp until we dry out?"

"Because we'd be here the rest of the day," Gavin said, "and we'd still be damp. Why can't the two of you slip back to your wagon and change into dry clothes without havin' Pit see you up close?"

"Perhaps we can," said Naomi, "but he'll wonder how you and Woody got soaked."

Woody laughed. "Tell him we tried to have our way with you, and you shoved both of us into the river."

"We will not," Nell said hotly. "Even if you had, we wouldn't tell Father."

"We certainly wouldn't," said Naomi. "Just when he's starting to think of us as grown up, he's not going to be told anything that might change his mind."

"Perhaps our clothes would dry more quickly if we removed them," Nell said.

"My God, no!" said Woody. "What do you reckon your daddy would think, if he came lookin' for you and found the two of you settin' here naked?"

"He's right," Naomi said. "Father might think we had done considerably more than fall into the river."

"The chuck wagon's between us and camp," said Gavin, "and your wagon's this side of the chuck wagon. Unless your daddy's in the wagon or under it, the two of you can slip back and change into dry clothes."

"But what about you and Woody?" Naomi said.

"As long as Pit can see us from a distance, and he knows you and Nell have returned, maybe Woody and me can dry out without him suspectin' anything," said Gavin. "Let's go find our boots."

But their boots weren't to be found.

"Damn it," Woody said, "some skunk-striped varmint followed us. Come on out, whoever you are. I aim to stomp your ears down to your boot tops."

Emerging from some willows, their boots in his arms, Nip Kelly laughed.

"By God," said Gavin, "I thought better of you."

"So did I," Naomi said.

"Aw," said Kelly, genuinely contrite, "I just got here, and was havin' some fun with you. I reckoned you was all swimmin'."

"You reckoned wrong," Nell said. "Naomi and I went wading and stepped off into water over our heads. If it wasn't for Gavin and Woody, we'd have drowned."

"Yes," said Naomi, "and now we're in trouble. We don't want Father to know, because neither of us can swim, and we can't slip back without him seeing us soaking wet."

"Sure you can," Nip said. "He got bored in camp and returned to the store. All of you can change into dry duds while he's gone. Nobody's in camp but Gonzales. I reckon I got in his way, and he took to cussin' me in Spanish."

"I swear, Nip," said Woody, "you'd better not be settin' us up for a fall, or I'll fall on you."

"Oh, hell," Kelly said, "I had no idea you was in trouble. Pull on your boots and get back to camp while Pit's at the store."

Only Gonzales was in camp, and if he wondered what had been going on, he contained his curiosity and continued making sourdough biscuits for supper. Naomi and Nell ducked into their wagon, while Woody and Gavin took dry shirts and Levi's from their bedrolls. By the time Naomi and Nell emerged from the wagon in dry clothes, Woody and Gavin had changed.

"We can spread our wet clothes on the grass to dry," Naomi said. "Father will think we washed them while he was gone."

"Thank you, Nip," said Nell.

"Yeah," Gavin said, "we owe you."

"You owe me nothing," said Nip, strangely serious. "I shouldn't have followed."

He turned away, walking along the river, losing himself in the shadow of the trees.

"I can't figure him out," Gavin said.

"I think I can," said Naomi. "He's a sad, lonely man. He's tried to become one of us, and somehow he doesn't fit. He's realizing that, and he's withdrawing from us."

"Damn it," Woody said, "I didn't aim for him to take it so hard. But he really had no business followin' us."

"He seemed to have meant no harm," said Nell. "I hope he won't tell Father."

"He won't," Gavin said. "That's not why he walked away. He's feeling guilty for having followed us."

"But we didn't do anything wrong," said Nell.

"I reckon he knows that," Woody said, "but he's realizing that he might have caught the four of us in . . . well . . . compromising positions."

Nell and Naomi laughed, seeking to hide their embarrassment.

"Sorry," said Woody. "I shouldn't have been so blunt."

"Speak for yourself, Woody," Gavin said. "When Naomi turned to me after comin' out of that river, I saw somethin' more in her than gratitude. What would you say, Naomi Pitkin, if I say I'm more than a little interested in you?"

Naomi reacted in a manner far more eloquent than Gavin expected. Throwing her arms around him, she kissed him long and hard.

"By God," said Woody, "he's the shy one. What am I waiting for? Nell?"

"Nell *what*?" the girl asked.

"Damn it, don't you know I'm as interested in you as Gavin is in Naomi?"

"What does Gavin's interest in Naomi have to do with me?" Nell asked.

Seizing her, Woody kissed her with a force that took her breath away. When he came up for air, she slapped him. Hard.

"I reckon I'm skunk cabbage to you," he said. "You don't care a damn for me."

"Oh, but I do," said Nell. "I just don't like being taken for granted."

"Naomi," Gavin said, "I just developed a powerful hankerin' for some coffee. Will you join me?"

"Yes," said Naomi, striving not to laugh, "I just developed the same hankering."

Nell watched them go, a half-smile on her lips, her eyes twinkling.

"Thanks," Woody said. "You helped me make a fool of myself."

Nell laughed. "You didn't need any help. Now that we're alone, why don't you tell me what you've been trying to say?"

After Woody, Gavin, Naomi, and Nell had gone, Nip Kelly did a strange thing. Taking his Colts from their holsters, he removed the shells. He then began drawing first one Colt and then the other, dry-firing and border-shifting. Growing weary, he reloaded the Colts and returned them to their holsters. He then sat down, his back against an oak, and stared into the swirling water of the river. Again his mind wandered back to that long-ago spring day in southern Missouri when he and Tobe Hankins had fought over Celeste Tilden. Once more, Nip relived those horrifying seconds when the girl, seeking to prevent the fight, had stepped between him and Hankins. Seared into Nip's mind forever was the expression on her face as Kelly's slug—intended for Tobe Hankins—had slammed into her. Hankins had run to the fallen Celeste, and pointing to Nip Kelly, had shouted an accusation loud enough for a dozen witnesses to hear.

"Damn you, Kelly, you've killed Celeste."

A jump ahead of a dozen shouting, cursing men, Nip Kelly had mounted his horse and ridden for his life. Now—remembering—with a groan of anguish, he buried his face in his hands . . .

Westward along the Santa Fe. June 13, 1869.

Outwardly there was no change in Woody and Gavin toward Nell and Naomi Pitkin, for neither of them was ready to explain or defend their fledgling relationships with the Pitkin women. They had no idea how Gladstone Pitkin might react, and cowboys were notorious for feuding among themselves for the affections of a woman. With the worst of the Santa Fe Trail ahead of them, internal strife was the last thing they needed.

"Head 'em up, move 'em out!" Woody shouted.

Rusty Pryor was riding drag with Nell and Naomi Pitkin. Once the herd was moving at an acceptable gait, Woody rode on ahead. After Council Grove, the next stop on Pitkin's map was Diamond Springs. There—from what Woody had learned in Council Grove—was an unfailing supply of clear, cold water. Several miles east of Diamond Springs, there was the evidence of two previous disasters. In a deep gulch was a litter of bones where many oxen had died, probably from having stampeded over the rim. In yet another arroyo, some nameless caravan had come to an end. Whether by fire, Indians, or stampede, Woody had no way of knowing. There was a litter of bones—animal and human—amid the burned-out wreckage of wagons.

"By God, horse," said Woody, "any teamster needin' chains, bolts, or wagon irons of any kind can have 'em for the taking."

Woody rode on to the spring, and after watering his horse, treated himself to a drink of delightfully cold water. Diamond Springs was a large spring gushing from the head of a hollow in the prairie and flowing into Otter Creek. Game trails radiated from the bountiful spring like spokes in a wheel, and Woody wasn't surprised to find tracks of many horses, shod and unshod. Most of the tracks of unshod horses led away to the south, toward the wilds of Indian Territory. It would be unwelcome news to Gladstone Pitkin and the rest of the outfit. Woody drank again from the spring before mounting his horse and riding back to meet the oncoming herd.

"So there's an Indian threat," Pitkin said, when Woody reported what he had found at Diamond Springs.

"Maybe," said Woody. "Maybe just a band passing through, stopping for water, but we can't afford to overlook the possibility of trouble. I think we'll bunch the herd on the high plain east of the spring. They can water at Otter Creek. We'll have to post sentries well away from the spring, so that we don't get trapped in that hollow."

But the drive reached Diamond Springs and the herd was bunched along Otter Creek without difficulty. There was no sign of Indians.

"Don't mean a thing," said Gavin, "them ridin' off to the south. That could have been their way of confusin' them gents with their three wagons."

The truth of Gavin's statement became evident the next morning, as the herd took the trail west. From somewhere ahead came the rattle of gunfire.

"Mill the herd," Woody shouted, waving his hat.

The riders had heard the shooting and had some idea as

to what Woody had in mind. He galloped back to Gladstone Pitkin's wagon.

"Pit, the folks ahead of us are in trouble. It's likely that bunch of Indians. I'm taking the outfit and ridin' ahead. If we don't go after that band of hostiles, they'll come after us. Likely when we're least expectin' it. Keep your eyes open and hold things together here."

Woody galloped away, his five companions following. The firing ahead diminished and then increased in intensity.

"They're likely surrounded," Woody shouted. "Fan out. Maybe we can catch 'em in a cross-fire."

When Woody and his outfit came within sight of the wagons, they counted more than a dozen Indians galloping their horses around the desperate defenders. The attack had taken place out in the open, and the canvas of the three wagons bristled with arrows. The almost continuous roar of rifles was evidence enough that the men with the wagons were armed with Winchesters, but their firing had little effect. The Indians clung to the sides of their ponies, presenting virtually no target. Loosing their arrows, they darted out of range, as other braves galloped in to continue the fight.

"Gun 'em down!" Woody shouted.

The cowboys formed a circle of their own, and the startled Indians clinging to the off-sides of their horses suddenly found themselves prime targets. Six horses galloped away riderless, and as the rest of the attackers broke away and rode for their lives, two more were shot from their horses. The firing from the wagons ceased, and the six defenders came out into the open. None of them spoke until Woody and his companions reined up.

"I'm Levi Stubbs," said the spokesman. "These is my sons Wiley and Whit. My three daughters is Bonita, Jania, and Laketa. We're obliged to you."

"Glad we was close enough to help," Woody replied. "I'm Woodrow Miles. From my left, these other gents are Rusty Pryor, his brother, Ash, Gavin McCord, Vic Brodie, and Nip Kelly. We're the Pitkin outfit, and we have a herd of Texas longhorns up the trail a ways."

"I'm wonderin' if it wouldn't be safer if we all was to throw in together," said Stubbs. "We got trade goods bound fer Santa Fe."

"I'd have to speak to Gladstone Pitkin," Woody replied. "We've seen your tracks, and it appears your wagons are loaded almighty heavy. Breakdowns cause delays, and I reckon Mr. Pitkin will want to consider that."

"Nobody tells me how to load or not load my wagons," said Stubbs resentfully. "We'll pitch camp at the next good water. If this Pitkin's willin' fer us to trail with your outfit, I reckon you can let us know when you git there."

It was an obvious, unfriendly dismissal. Woody and his companions wheeled their horses and rode back the way they had come.

"If it wasn't for the women," Vic said, "I'd favor lettin' the Indians have the whole damn lot. I've never seen three uglier, unfriendlier varmints than Stubbs and them sons of his."

"The girls was as pretty as Stubbs and his sons was ugly," said Rusty. "I'd say they must have took after their mama."

"Yeah," Ash said, "and they should thank God for that, every day."

"Them overloaded wagons is definitely somethin' to be considered," said Nip Kelly. "I reckon the worst part of the trail's ahead of us, and a busted wheel or axle—even if they got spares—could lose a whole day."

"I am considerin' that," Woody replied, "and I aim to mention it to Pit. I reckon we'll have to keep the women in mind, but I don't aim to spend the rest of the summer waitin' for Stubbs to patch up his overloaded wagons."

5

"You are trail boss, Woody," Pitkin said, "and I shall abide by your decision. Even my limited experience tells me it is foolish for so few people to embark upon a journey so dangerous as this. Especially when half of them are female."

"In all fairness," said Woody, "I'd have to say that the three females conducted themselves well. They seemed almighty handy with a Winchester."

"Very well," Pitkin said. "Take that into consideration when you make your decision."

"I am," said Woody. "I'm going to grant them permission to trail with us as far as Fort Dodge, and then only if they can keep up with the herd. If they fall behind, for any reason—and that includes breakdowns—we won't wait for them."

"Suppose they keep up with us as far as Fort Dodge," Pitkin said. "What becomes of them then?"

"If they make it to Fort Dodge without delays, without being a problem to us, then I will consider allowing them to accompany us the rest of the way," said Woody.

"Don't forget the *Jornada*—the fifty miles of desert—beyond Fort Dodge," Gavin said. "We've made provisions for carrying enough water for ourselves and our teams, but I doubt the Stubbs party has. If their overloaded wagons are a problem now, it'll purely be hell on their teams, crossin' that desert.''

"I'm aware of that," said Woody, "and it's one of the things to be considered before we leave Fort Dodge."

Gladstone Pitkin had nothing more to say, and that concluded the conversation. The herd again took the trail, Woody riding point, the wagons trailing. When they were within sight of the three Stubbs wagons, Woody rode ahead. Stubbs' daughters waited, on the boxes of each of the three wagons. Levi Stubbs and his two sons came to meet Woody. He reined up, and without any formalities, told Stubbs essentially what he had told Gladstone Pitkin.

"We generally make camp an hour before sundown," Woody said. "If you fall behind, that'll give you some time to catch up before dark."

Stubbs nodded, saying nothing. Woody waited until the moving herd caught up, and resumed his position at point. Nip Kelly was again riding drag with Nell and Naomi, but the other riders—Vic Brodie, Rusty, and Ash Pryor—had their eyes on the Stubbs girls. When the herd had passed, the three Stubbs wagons fell in behind the chuck wagon driven by Gonzales and the supply wagon Pitkin was driving. Woody looked back occasionally, but was unable to see beyond the dust raised by the herd. West of Diamond Springs some fifteen miles was the far less inviting Lost Springs. It had gained its name by going dry during the hottest part of the summer. Half a mile away, the herd smelled or sensed the water ahead, and broke into a shambling, bawling lope. There was nothing the riders could do, except get out of the way. Woody rode back to meet the wagons, and while the Stubbs outfit was lagging behind, they were doing better than Woody had expected. He rode past his two wagons, wheeled his horse, and rode along between them.

"The spring's down a mite, Gonzales," Woody said, "and you'll have to delay supper for a while. When the herd's had time to drink, we'll have to drive the varmints away, so the water can settle."

"There's the horses and mules," Pitkin said. "Do we water them before supper?"

"Yes," said Woody, "but lead them there and allow them to drink without muddying the water. Then picket them until after supper."

Stubbs and his sons reined up their teams a good distance from the spring. Unharnessing the mules, they waited until the longhorns had been driven away from the water. When the Pitkin outfit's horses and mules had been watered, Stubbs and his sons led their mules to drink. The Stubbs daughters started their cookfire, and without their bonnets, the cowboys noted they all had curly brown hair to their shoulders.

"Them Stubbs men all look like they was weaned on sour pickles," Vic Brodie said, "but that can't be said for the daughters. I aim to get better acquainted with them."

"Don't be such a damn hog," said Rusty. "Choose one of 'em."

"Yeah," Ash agreed. "There's other deservin' hombres in this outfit besides you. Ain't that right, Nip?"

Kelly laughed. "All your choosin' may be for nothin', gents. Old man Stubbs looks as agreeable as a rattler durin' sheddin' season, and them sons of his ain't more'n one jump behind him."

Nell and Naomi Pitkin listened to their banter with interest, covertly eying Woody and Gavin, wondering what their thoughts might be. Neither of the Pitkin girls had spent any time with Woody and Gavin since that day along the river, in Council Grove. While these Stubbs women were distant, it seemed unlikely they would remain so. Nell's eyes met Naomi's in silent understanding. It was time for them to press their advantage with Woody and Gavin, before the Stubbs girls came any closer.

"Pit," Woody said, "it's time we had another look at that trail map. I'd say we're a good hundred miles from the Big Bend of the Arkansas River, and if the water between here and there ain't more plentiful than at this Lost Springs, we're in for it."

"Perhaps you're right," said Pitkin, "but Honicker, at Council Grove, said the maps do not indicate anything less than a major stream. Rivers, most notably. So there may well be numerous streams or springs on which we can rely."

"That means scouting ahead," Woody replied. "It's risky, leavin' one camp, unless you know where the next sure water is."

In the Stubbs camp, Levi was laying down the law to his sons and daughters.

"I don't want none of you messin' around that Pitkin outfit," Stubbs said. "They been complainin' about our wagons already. Give 'em a little encouragement, and some of 'em will have their noses where they don't belong."

"Paw," said Wiley, "we got to pass Fort Dodge. You reckon the army won't have to know what we're haulin'?"

"I don't aim to stop at the fort," Stubbs said. "We'll move on, and Pitkin's drive will catch up to us in a day or two."

"Paw," said Bonita, "if it wasn't for those cowboys, the Indians would have murdered us all. I ain't favorin' us goin' on by ourselves."

"It ain't your decision to make, girl," Stubbs said. "It's mine; and I say we're goin' on past Fort Dodge, even if it means we do it alone."

"Haw, haw," said Whit, "she's got her eye on one of them cow nurses."

"At least they're honest in what they're doing," Bonita snapped. "They ain't haulin' illegal goods that's got to be hid from the government!"

Levi Stubbs struck the girl without warning, and she fell in a patch of briars. Blood dripped from her nose, but she didn't cry out. There was fire in her eyes, and when she fixed them on her father, Stubbs looked away. Bonita got to her knees and her sisters helped her to her feet. Without a word, the three of them walked away, leaving Stubbs and his sons to prepare their supper as best they could.

"Don't do no good to talk to him, Bonita," said Jania,

when she was sure Stubbs was unable to hear.

"Just wait till we get to Santa Fe," Laketa said, "and then we'll leave."

"I'm afraid we'll never get there alive," said Bonita. "I hope the people at Fort Dodge won't allow us to pass without an inspection."

"We could all go to prison," Jania said.

"Better that than lyin' dead on the prairie, full of Indian arrows," said Bonita.

Bonita said no more, but in her mind she began considering some means of forcing the wagons to stop at Fort Dodge. She had been profoundly impressed by the self-assured cowboys who had driven away the attacking Indians. Somehow, without her father knowing, she had to talk to some of the Pitkin riders. Perhaps they would help her . . .

"Pit," said Woody during breakfast, "once the herd's movin', I aim to ride ahead to the next water. I can also look for Indian sign. I'll be back as soon as I can. I want every one of you to keep your eyes open and your Winchesters handy."

Woody rode over level prairie deep in tall, rank grass. There were curious, zig-zag strips where the grass grew thicker and taller than the rest, bringing to mind stories some of the old-timers had told about lightning striking the plains. As a result, they said, the soil was greatly enriched. Woody had ridden not more than five miles when he reached a depression that at first appeared to be a stream, but the vegetation proved deceptive. The stream bed was nothing but mud, and the banks were steep. Someone had rawhided a flat piece of wood to an oak sapling. "Mud Creek" had been painted in crude black letters, and beneath that, some wag had added "The Devil's Hind Quarters."

Woody rode along the muddy streambed until he reached a place where the banks were low enough that the wagons might cross. The Pitkin wagons. He seriously doubted the overloaded wagons belonging to Levi Stubbs would be so fortunate. He urged his horse into a slow gallop, for he must find water and return to the drive in time to warn the wagons of the Mud Creek crossing. Having ridden what he believed was twelve miles, Woody reached a stream which was far from dry. Yet another piece of weathered wood thonged to a cottonwood had a poorly-lettered message: "Cottonwood Creek."

"Damn," said Woody, as he observed the high banks.

Finding a place where the bank wasn't quite as steep, Woody dismounted. He tied one end of his lariat to the saddle horn and secured the other end under his arms. Holding on to the rope, he "walked" down the bank. His boots slipped, and but for the lariat, he would have fallen into the creek. The water, when he reached it, came well above his knees and his feet became mired deep in mud. He tugged on the rope and his horse advanced enough for him to climb out. He rode more than a mile downstream, and while the banks leveled off some, he was still unable to see the bottom. The muddy bed might go on for miles. Still he didn't give up. He rode on, following deep ruts left by previous wagons, until he came to what evidently was the accepted crossing. At best, prospects looked dismal, for there was mute evidence of previous failures. Silt and mud had backed up against what was left of a smashed wagon, and there were the scattered bones of mules and oxen. The more he looked, the more sinister it became, for on the opposite bank was a pair of grassed-over mounds that undoubtedly were graves. If there had been a better cross, somebody would have found it. He rode back the way he had come, taking the unwelcome news to the rest of the outfit. Coming within sight of the herd, he waved his hat. Time was important, but he must tell them what lay ahead. Such information would be doubly important to Stubbs, with his heavily loaded wagons.

"Come on back to the wagons," Woody shouted to the riders. "Trouble ahead."

The Stubbs wagons were half a mile behind, and Woody rode near enough to speak to Stubbs, in the lead wagon.

"Come on up behind our wagons. I've been scouting

ahead, and there's something you should know."

"Then tell us," Stubbs shouted.

"I'm only telling it once," said Woody. "Come on and hear it, or count on some damn unwelcome surprises."

Woody rode on ahead until he reached the two wagons belonging to the Pitkin outfit. Pitkin and his riders waited impatiently for the Stubbs wagons, and Woody could see them advancing. Stubbs and his sons reined up their teams a hundred yards shy, walking the rest of the way. As soon as they were close enough to hear, Woody began speaking. He didn't mince words, and when he spoke of the hazardous crossings, his eyes were on Levi Stubbs.

"We're going to have to make up some time," Woody said, "because we'll want to cross both these creeks today."

"Our teams will be give out, time we git there," Stubbs argued. "Why can't we cross the second creek t'morrow, when the teams is fresh?"

"Because there's a storm buildin' back yonder in the west," said Woody. "There'll be rain sometime tonight, likely fillin' Cottonwood Creek from bank to bank. We could end up settin' there for a week or two, waitin' for the water to go down."

Stubbs didn't like it, but there was nothing he could say, for it was irrefutable logic. Woody rode back to his point position and the herd again took the trail. The three Stubbs wagons followed, lagging behind. Bonita rode the wagon box with her father, and he didn't like the expression on her face.

"What's the matter with you?" he growled.

"You're purposely fallin' behind," said Bonita.

"What if I am?" Stubbs snapped. "If we got trouble crossin' them creeks, we'll handle it ourselves. I don't want no damn cow herders nosin' about."

"There's lots of things I don't know, but I know the truth when I hear it," said the girl. "There is a storm comin', for I can see the clouds. What are we goin' to do if the creeks flood before we can get across?"

"Damnit, girl," Stubbs roared, "that rain may be hundreds of miles away. Might not even git here. Now stop pawin' the ground. You're near as bad as your maw used to be.''

"I wish to God my maw was still alive," said Bonita bitterly. "Maybe she could have pounded some sense into you. We never should've left Missouri."

"We didn't have nothin' in Missouri, an' you know it," Stubbs said. "Nary a pot, nor a window to throw it out. Here, by God, we got us a stake, somethin' we can turn into cash money."

Bonita looked at him pityingly, but said no more. His being so mule-stubborn took her a step further toward seeking help from the Pitkin outfit. Perhaps tonight, if Stubbs didn't allow them to fall too far behind . . .

Before reaching Mud Creek, Woody rode back to speak to Gladstone Pitkin.

"Pit, the banks of this creek are steep, and there's mud aplenty, but I think we got an advantage other outfits haven't had. Hold both wagons back until we've crossed the herd. I believe after a hundred and forty thousand hooves have pounded down that bank and across to the other side, there'll be a pretty decent wagon road. If it still looks a mite too dangerous, we'll have to think of somethin' else. But let's see what the herd can do."

"Bueno," said Gonzales, who had been listening. "I see this done in Texas. Wagons be across *muy pronto*."

Starting with the drag, Woody made sure all the riders knew of his plan to run the herd across Mud Creek. As the cowboys picked up the gait, the longhorns bawled in protest, but they were nearing the creek at a fast lope. The lead steers tried to balk, but the hundreds of lethal horns behind them changed their minds. The leaders plunged into the muddy gulch and fought their way up the opposite bank, and the remainder of the herd quickly became followers. The riders had gotten ahead of the longhorns, and once they had crossed, began to bunch them. Woody rode back to meet Pitkin and Gonzales, with the wagons.

"I go first," Gonzales shouted.

He urged his teams ahead, and without breaking stride, they took the chuck wagon to the opposite side of the dry creek. Pitkin didn't hesitate, and urging his teams forward, crossed to the other bank without difficulty.

"*Bueno,*" Woody shouted.

Already, the riders had the herd moving, and Woody got ahead of them, riding up to the point position. He looked back, but was unable to see the Stubbs wagons.

"Good crossing, eh?" Pitkin shouted to Gonzales.

"*Sí,*" the grinning Mexican shouted back.

Woody allowed the herd to slow to their customary gait, but kept them moving. The Pitkin outfit was already out of sight when the Stubbs wagons approached Mud Creek.

"Why, hell," Levi Stubbs scoffed, "this ain't no problem. Ain't no mud. That creek bed's packed plumb solid from them cows trompin' across it."

Stubbs urged his team ahead, but the stream bed that appeared so solid wasn't ready for the heavily loaded wagons. The rear wheels sank to the hubs and the hapless mules struggled in vain.

"Pull, damn you!" Stubbs bawled.

The mules brayed in fear and pain, as Stubbs flayed them with a whip, but the wagon didn't budge.

"Stop beating the mules!" Bonita cried, seizing her father's arm.

"Get your hands off me!" said Stubbs. "Or I'll use the whip on you."

"Then you'll have to use it on me, Paw," Jania said.

"And on me," said Laketa.

The two of them had left the wagons driven by their brothers, Wiley and Whit, and in the face of such opposition, Stubbs put down the whip. Stepping down from the wagon box, he shouted to his sons who had reined up their teams behind him.

"Unhitch them teams," Stubbs ordered. "We'll use ever' damn mule, if that's what it takes. Then we'll do the same with the other two wagons."

Silently, Wiley and Whit began unharnessing their teams,

wondering what stormy old Levi would do, should the extra mules be unable to move the stuck wagon.

"We'll hitch your teams ahead of mine, Wiley," said Stubbs. "If that don't do it, then we'll hitch Whit's teams ahead of yours."

He glared at them, daring one of them to raise the obvious question. But knowing the futility of it, they kept their silence. Wiley led his teams across to the opposite bank of the creek and backed them into position ahead of Stubbs' stranded mules. When he had all the teams linked together, Stubbs seized the lines and used them to slap the rumps of the first team. Fearing more of the whip, the animals surged ahead, forcing the added teams to move. Time and again, Stubbs forced the straining mules to surge ahead, and while the mired wheels of the wagon moved, they remained stuck.

"Whit," Stubbs said, "unhitch your team an' harness 'em in front of Wiley's."

Whit obeyed, knowing there would be hell to pay if every mule they owned failed to move the stuck wagon. But Levi Stubbs was already considering that possibility. While Whit unhitched his teams, Stubbs worked loose the long hickory pole that served as the wagon's brake handle. He then went on to Wiley's wagon and removed its brake handle. When Whit had the third wagon's teams hitched ahead of Wiley's, Levi Stubbs spoke.

"Wiley, you take one of these poles, an' Whit, you take the other. I want you both behind this wagon, each of you with a pole jammed behind a wagon wheel. When them mules leans into the harness, I want the both of you layin' your backs behind them poles. By God, this wagon better move. Understand?"

Wiley and Whit nodded, taking the poles, dreading the possibility that even this might not be enough to move the bogged-down wagon. Stubbs waited until they were in position. He then took the reins and shouted.

"Heeeeyaaaaa! Heeeeyaaaa! Heeeeyaaaa!"

The mules leaned into their harness, while Wiley and Whit put their shoulders to the hickory poles behind the wagon's rear wheels. Slowly, ever so slowly, the wagon moved. Sensing victory, the combined teams surged ahead, drawing the heavy wagon out of the mud and up the opposite bank. The mules stood trembling from exhaustion. Wiley and Whit stood in mud to their knees, leaning on their hickory poles, sweat streaking the mud on their faces. They were a mess, prompting Bonita, Jania, and Laketa to laugh at them.

"Damn you!" Wiley bawled, charging them with his hickory pole.

"Wiley!" Stubbs shouted.

Wiley froze, knowing better than to disobey the old man.

"Wiley, I want all them mules hitched to your wagon. You an' Whit git busy."

"Hell, Paw," said Wiley, "them mules is got to rest."

"They can rest while they're bein' hitched to your wagon," Stubbs growled. "Git on it, now."

Slowly, Wiley and Whit began unhitching the weary mules from Stubbs' wagon. When all the mules had been harnessed to Wiley's wagon, he climbed to the wagon box.

"Git down," said Stubbs. "You an' Whit's young an' strong. I want the both of you with your backs to them poles, behind the rear wheels of the wagon. I'll take care of the teams."

Silently Wiley got down off the wagon box and took up the muddy hickory pole. Whit seemed about to say something, but one look at grim-faced old Levi changed his mind. He took up his hickory pole without a word. The second wagon met the same fate as the first, and freeing it took an enormous toll on man and beast. The mules stood with heads hanging, their nostrils flared, heaving for air.

"I reckon we'll rest the teams before movin' the third wagon," Stubbs said.

"They're needin' water, Paw, an' there ain't none 'fore Cottonwood Creek," said Whit.

"Then, by God, they'll wait till we git to Cottonwood Creek," Stubbs growled, "if the next water's there. Hell, all we got's the word of Pitkin's trail boss."

"He was telling the truth, Paw," said Bonita. "He had no cause to lie."

"I don't care a damn what you think of Pitkin's trail boss," Stubbs snarled. "Now let's hitch them mules to that other wagon an' git this Mud Creek behind us."

Predictably, the third wagon bogged down, requiring the failing strength of all the mules and the combined efforts of Wiley and Whit, as they put their aching shoulders to the hickory poles behind the wagon's rear wheels. Slowly they freed the third wagon from the mud. Wiley and Whit collapsed on the grass, so covered with mud they were all but unrecognizable.

"Git up an' unhitch them mules," Stubbs ordered. "They'll need a rest 'fore we move on."

"Unhitch 'em yourself," said Wiley. "We been bustin' our backs under them damn poles, while all you done is holler at the mules."

Stubbs said nothing. He had the whip in his hand, and the tip of it bit into Wiley's behind, sending mud flying. Wiley screamed, stumbling to his feet in a rage, but Stubbs still held the vicious whip. Wiley swallowed hard and limped off toward the weary teams, Whit following.

Cottonwood Creek. June 16, 1869.

Nearing Cottonwood Creek, Woody signaled a halt.

"Stay with the herd," he told the riders. "I want to talk to Pitkin. I think maybe we can use the herd to level those creek banks enough for a wagon crossing, but we'll have trouble controlling the varmints until they've watered. Keep 'em bunched until I return."

Pitkin was waiting, his wagon drawn up next to the chuck wagon. Woody wasted no time.

"Pit, those creek banks will have to be leveled some, before we can cross the wagons. Hold fast until I get back to you. Maybe we can use the herd to cut down the banks at a shallow crossing. We'll have to water the herd first, or they'll be hard to handle.''

Pitkin nodded and Woody rode back to the herd, waving his hat to the riders. Again the longhorns took the trail, and when they smelled or sensed the water ahead, they broke into a lunging, bawling frenzy. Letting them go, the riders got out of their way, riding to meet Woody.

"We'll give them time to drink," Woody said, "and while they're doin' that, we'll ride along the creek until we find a shallow place where the wagons won't bog down. I reckon we can drive the herd across a time or two, beatin' down the banks some.''

"Where's the regular crossing?" Nip Kelly asked.

"Downstream a ways," said Woody. "I found it when I was scouting ahead, and we'll have to do better than that. Somebody lost a wagon, and some oxen, some mules, and I found two graves.''

"Then the banks are too high to cross the wagons any-where," Gavin said.

"That's the way I see it," said Woody. "We'll do better, findin' some shallows where there's a solid bottom, and use the herd to level down the banks enough for the wagons. I rode downstream a ways, when I was here before, and all I found was that old crossing that gave somebody a lot of grief. I think we'd better travel upstream and see what we can find, high banks or not.''

They hadn't ridden more than a mile when they found a near perfect crossing, for the water was shallow, passing over solid rock. The problem, when it came to the crossing of the wagons, was the high banks.

"Might be some trouble here," Vic Brodie said. "Bunch them cows too close, and the first ones down that bank is likely to break their necks.''

"All the more reason to let them drink first," said Woody. "Thirsty, nothin' would concern 'em except gettin' to the water. It wouldn't matter if the banks were fifty feet, straight down.''

"This brings to mind the first Goodnight drive to Colorado Territory," Nip Kelly said. "He lost four hundred head, crossin' the Pecos River."*

"God, that must've been some drive," said Rusty. "Was you there?"

"No," Nip said, "but I knew some hombres that was."

"Let's drive a couple hundred head up here," said Woody. "Nip, you and me will be in the creek. Once they come down that bank, it's important that we force them out on the other side. The rest of you force them down that north bank. Don't keep 'em bunched too close. We don't want the second, third, and fourth ranks comin' down on the leaders before they've had time to climb out on the other side."

Woody and Nip found a place where they were able to lead their horses down to the water. They then mounted and rode to the shallows where the longhorns were to come down the steep bank. With a bawling and rattling of horns, several hundred longhorns were bunched and headed toward the creek. The first rank made an ignominious descent, but they slid down, and there were no injuries. Woody and Nip, swinging doubled lariats, forced the bawling, lumbering beasts up the opposite bank. Dirt and rock came down in a small avalanche from both banks. Quickly the fallen dirt became mud, and the churning hooves of the longhorns splattered horses and riders. A horn raked Woody's horse and the animal screamed in pain. When the last of the cows clambered down one bank and up the other, Woody and Nip could see Gavin grinning down at them.

"Ready for another bunch?"

"No," said Nip, "but bring 'em on. There's still too much bank for the wagons."

"I purely admire a trail boss that don't mind gettin' dirty," Gavin said.

"Watch it," said Woody. "The trail boss can swap

* *The Goodnight Trail*. Book One in the Trail Drive Series.

places, if he's of a mind to. You'd better ride back for some more cows.''

Gavin laughed. "Look out below. It's rainin' longhorn cows.''

6

By the time the entire herd had been driven down the steep banks and up the other side of Cottonwood Creek, the slope had been drastically reduced.

"That should be enough of a slope to get our wagons across," Woody said.

"But probably not enough for the Stubbs wagons," said Nip.

"That's not our problem," Woody replied. "He'll have to use extra teams."

Gonzales crossed the chuck wagon first, and Pitkin followed with the second wagon.

"Upstream about half a mile, Gonzales," Woody shouted.

Gonzales waved his sombrero in understanding. Camp must be established well beyond where the crossing of the herd and the wagons had muddied the creek. The importance of getting the crossing behind them became all the more obvious, as the bank of dirty gray clouds shrouded more and more of the western horizon.

Several miles east of Cottonwood Creek, the Stubbs wagons rattled along, with Stubbs swearing at the weary mules. He reined up, and looking back, found that the other two wagons had fallen behind. Stubbs stepped down, bit off a mouthful of plug, and waited for the stragglers to catch up. When they eventually did, old Levi pointed to the cloud mass on the western horizon. He just stood there passing the bullwhip from one hand to the other, and when he spoke, it was in a tone that Wiley and Whit had come to dread.

"We got to cross Cottonwood Creek 'fore that storm gits here. If'n we don't make it, by God, I'm a-goin' to raise hell an' kick a chunk under it, if'n you know what I mean."

Using the whip, he pointed first at Wiley and then at Whit, and they well knew what he meant. Without another word, he mounted the wagon box and slapped the rumps of the mules with the reins. Wiley and Whit pulled their wagons in behind his, and they moved on toward Cottonwood Creek. By the time they reached it, the thunderheads had already swallowed the sun, leaving the sky feathered with crimson.

"There ain't no way we're gonna git these wagons down one bank and up the other'n," Whit said. "The mules will go down headfirst, and the wagon on top of 'em."

"The cows went down these banks to water," Stubbs said, "but you know damn well the wagons didn't cross here. Where Pitkin crossed his wagons, we kin cross ours."

"Yeah," said Whit. "We used their crossin' at Mud Creek. It took us near three hours an' ever' mule we got."

"Hell, we ain't got three hours," Wiley said. "Two, maybe, before dark, an' the mules' rumps is draggin' out their tracks. They're beat."

"We're takin' these wagons across before dark," said Stubbs, "if'n I have to beat ev'ry mule's behind with this whip, ever' jump of the way."

"They're ready to drop in their tracks, Paw," Bonita said. "Beatin' won't change that."

"You better hope it does," said Stubbs, "else I'll have ever' one of you behind these damn wagons, shovin' fer all you're worth."

Stubbs mounted his wagon box, and leading the way, found where the longhorns had been used to level the banks enough for the Pitkin wagons to cross.

"Their wagons crossed here," Stubbs said, "an' so kin ours."

"Not without usin' all the mules," said Wiley. "We might as well unhitch our teams an' hitch 'em up with yours."

"We ain't usin' all the mules hitched to one wagon, unless we got to," Stubbs said, "an' we don't know that we got to. Now git to yer wagons an' foller me."

Stubbs forced his teams down the incline, and while the stone beneath the water kept the wagon from miring down, the weary mules were unable to draw the wagon up the opposite bank. Stubbs applied the whip until his arm tired and the mules were braying in fear and pain, but the wagon remained where it was. Stubbs climbed down from the box and climbed the bank which the wagon had just descended, and when he spoke, his voice shook with fury.

"Unhitch them other teams an' hitch 'em in front of them worthless varmints down yonder. An' be damn quick about it."

Wiley and Whit hastened to obey, for Stubbs still held the whip. Bonita, Jania, and Laketa stood looking at the pathetic mules hitched to Stubbs' wagon. The animals stood with their heads down, trembling, their coats dark with sweat, laced with bloody welts from the vicious whip.

"Paw," said Laketa, "that was a shameful thing to do. You cut the blood out of them, when they was doin' their best."

"A damn mule never does his best, without a taste of the lash," Stubbs snarled, "an' I reckon a woman ain't much better. I want anything outa you, I'll ask fer it."

Wiley and Whit harnessed the extra teams ahead of the Stubbs team. The lead team was halfway up the opposite bank of the creek. Stubbs started to mount the wagon box, and Wiley snatched the whip from his hand.

"You ain't whippin' them mules again," Wiley snarled.

Stubbs eyed his Winchester leaning against the end of the wagon box.

"Reach fer that," said Wiley, "an' you git a taste of what you give them mules."

He took the Winchester, tucking it under his arm. Levi Stubbs climbed to the wagon box and popped the reins, sending the teams surging ahead. With the solid creekbed beneath the wagon's wheels, it lurched ahead, and the combined strength of all the teams was enough to draw the heavy load up the opposite bank. Without a word, Wiley and Whit began unhitching the teams. When they were harnessed to Wiley's wagon, he climbed to the box and drove across to the opposite bank. Again they unhitched the teams, harnessed them to Whit's wagon, and he took it across. Without a word to Levi, Wiley and Whit unhitched the teams belonging to Levi's and Wiley's wagons, but neither of the sons made a move to harness Levi's team to his wagon. Wiley handed him the reins, harnessed his own teams to the wagon, and then mounted the box. He still had Levi's Winchester, and he slid it under the wagon seat. Laketa was already on the box with Whit, and Wiley gave Jania a hand up. Bonita was left with Levi, who was still harnessing his teams to his own wagon. Without looking back, Wiley and Whit drove upstream, seeking a place to make camp for the night. They circled wide of the grazing herd, reining up a hundred yards beyond the two Pitkin wagons. By the time Levi Stubbs arrived with his wagon, Wiley and Whit had unharnessed their teams.

"Damn it," Stubbs growled, "why didn't you wait till I caught up? You done set us in breathin' distance of that Pitkin bunch."

"There's graze here, an' the mules can git to the water," said Wiley, "an' you ain't gittin' no better'n that. Them mules is tuckered out."

Muttering under his breath, Stubbs unharnessed his teams. There was lightning to the west, dancing a jagged pattern above the heavy gray clouds. The wind had picked up, its moist fingers touching sweaty cheeks, promising rain sometime during the coming night.

* * *

"She's gonna blow," Vic Brodie predicted.

"Yeah," said Gavin, "but maybe the thunder and lightnin' won't be as bad."

"We can't count on that," Woody said. "After supper, we'll all take to the saddle and try to calm the herd before the thunder and lightning gets too close."

"Beyond that," said Pitkin, "I suppose there is nothing we can do."

"Right you are," Woody replied. "I'll have Gonzales hurry the supper."

"While he's doin' that," said Nip, "some of us ought to be stretchin' a piece of that canvas between these two wagons. At least we'll have a dry place to hunker and drink our coffee durin' the night."

"Come on," Gavin said. "I'll help you."

The chuck wagon was already positioned with the tongue to the north. Gavin and Nip quickly harnessed a team to the second wagon and moved it parallel to the chuck wagon, at least twenty feet distant. One side of the big canvas was thonged to the bend in the first and last bows of the chuck wagon, while the other side was secured in similar fashion to the upper side of the first and last bows of the second wagon Pitkin had bought. With the bulk of the chuck wagon and its canvas top to bear the brunt of the expected storm, and the tightly stretched canvas between the wagons as protection from the rain, the outfit had the assurance of a fire and a place to dry out, whatever else happened.

"Not be much wood in possum belly," Gonzales suggested.

"There's still time to rustle up some more wood," said Woody, "before supper and before the storm. Some of you get at it."

"Rusty," Vic said, "you an' Ash come on. I ain't wantin' to hunker down at midnight, dyin' for hot coffee, and not a stick of dry wood."

In the Stubbs camp, Bonita, Jania, and Laketa went about preparing supper without much enthusiasm. There was no room in any of the wagons and they had no shelter where they might spread their bedrolls to escape the pouring rain.

"Of all the things I've come to hate," Laketa complained, "the storms are the worst. I am so tired of wet, muddy clothes, trying to start a cookfire in the rain . . ."

"Damn it," Stubbs shouted, "cut out the jabberin' an' git supper done before the storm gits here."

"I swear to God," said Bonita, "if I had anywhere to go, I'd slip away durin' the night and he'd never see me again."

"We've been through this before," Jania said. "We've agreed we'll all leave together, once we reach Santa Fe."

"Yes," said Laketa, "but I'm not sure I can last that long."

The storm came closer and the thunder rumbled, but the lightning never reached the violent proportions that often led to a stampede. The herd bawled their unease, but didn't rise to their feet, for everybody within the Pitkin outfit was in the saddle, except Gonzales. The Mexican had made use of the plentiful dry wood and had started a fire between the two wagons, under the protection of the canvas. There he had both coffeepots on the fire. While the wind rose to gale force and the rain swept down in gray sheets, the presence of the riders calmed the herd. The thunder and lightning moved on, but the rain seemed to have set in for the night. Woody called the outfit together.

"The worst of it's over," Woody said. "Nip, Gavin, and me can take the first watch, with Rusty, Vic, and Ash takin' the second. The rest of you, crowdin' in close under the canvas, can get some sleep."

"That doesn't seem fair," Naomi said. "We trail with the herd during the day, and I think we should take our turn on watch."

"No," said Woody. "We appreciate both of you helping with the drive, but we hired on for that purpose. If there's goin' to be trouble, it's likely to come at night, and I'd not want to risk either of you gettin' hurt."

"Woody's speaking from experience," Pitkin said. "Do as he says."

The camp settled down, and with the herd calm, Woody,

Gavin, and Nip picketed their horses. Eventually the rain ceased, the wind swept away the clouds, and from a deep purple sky, a thin quarter moon smiled down. Stars twinkled like distant splashes of silver.

"I'm ready for some of that coffee," said Nip. "That wind ain't let up much, and in these wet duds, it's enough to chill a gent to the bone."

The three of them got their tin cups, and while they tried to be quiet, they managed to awaken those who had spread their blankets near the fire, under the protection of the canvas.

"Woody," Nell said, "I'm dried out and I'm not sleepy. If I stay close to you, may I walk around some?"

"I reckon so," said Woody.

"I want to come too," Naomi said.

"Then stay close to Gavin or Nip," said Woody. "One of you at a time is about all I can look after."

While Gladstone Pitkin didn't move, Woody thought he heard Pitkin laugh.

"The storm's gone, the herd's calm, and there's goin' to be four of you out there," Nip said. "If nobody objects, I'm goin' to hunker here by the fire, drink my coffee, and see if I can dry out."

Woody and Gavin weren't sure how much Kelly knew and how much he only suspected, but they didn't doubt he was intentionally allowing them some time alone with Nell and Naomi Pitkin. But it was the first time since Council Grove that Woody and Gavin had come even close to such an opportunity, and they said nothing to discourage it. They walked between the herd and Cottonwood Creek, and they could hear the gurgle of rising water.

"Now I see why it was so important that we cross ahead of the storm," Nell said.

"Yes," said Woody. "The creek will overrun its banks by morning."

"But the rain's stopped," Naomi said.

"Somewhere to the west of here, it's still raining," said Woody. "Cottonwood Creek may be on the rise for several more days. Even when the water goes down, there'll be so much mud, crossing would be impossible.''

''There will be other streams ahead of us,'' Nell said. ''Won't we have trouble there?''

''Not necessarily,'' said Woody. ''Every creek or river is different. We're still a long way from the Arkansas. We may have more storms behind us before we get there.''

Woody looked around and found himself alone with Nell Pitkin. Obviously, Gavin and Naomi had sought some privacy of their own. Woody stopped, his hand on Nell's arm. He promised himself he wasn't going to appear as much the fool as he had at Council Grove. Nell was facing him, and even in the pale moonlight, he could see her face. Her lips were parted just a little, and he placed both hands on her shoulders. Only then did he speak.

''If I do what I'm tempted to, are you gonna slug me again?''

''Perhaps,'' she said, ''if you don't do it right. Am I worth the risk?''

''I reckon,'' he replied.

He drew her close to him, kissing her long and hard. Slipping her arms around his neck, she returned the kiss. When they parted for air, Woody sighed. Finally he spoke.

''I reckon I got it right, this time.''

''Yes,'' said Nell. ''You didn't try to justify what you did. You wanted me and you took me. It's what a woman expects of a man.''

''I know that now,'' Woody said. ''I just thought, you bein' English . .''

''That if you got too aggressive with me, I'd burst into tears or fall to pieces in your hands?''

''Somethin' like that, I reckon,'' said Woody sheepishly. ''Do you want me to tell you honestly what was botherin' me . . . before?''

''Yes,'' Nell said softly. ''I think I'd like to know.''

''I had . . . have . . . powerful feelings for you,'' said Woody, ''and I didn't want you to . . to think I was just a clumsy cowboy who had never been with a woman outside some . . . some whorehouse.''

"I never thought that, even when I was angry with you,'' Nell said. "I don't believe you've ever been to such a place. Have you?''

"No,'' said Woody. "Once, when I was just eighteen, there was this girl in Waco . . . she liked me, and well . . . I got her drunk, stripped her . . .''

"And had your way with her?''

"No,'' Woody admitted, "I didn't . . . couldn't . . . do anything. I was afraid. I got her back into her clothes as best I could, and left her there in the barn, to sober up.''

She kissed him on the cheek. "Then what did you do?''

"I joined a trail drive bound for Abilene,'' said Woody, "and I never went back.''

"Woodrow Miles,'' Nell said, "you are an honest cowboy. Would you think me brazen and forward if I told you I want you?''

"I reckon I'd consider myself the luckiest cowboy ever to come out of south Texas,'' Woody said, "and you'd better not be just teasing me. When we get to Santa Fe, I aim to speak to your daddy about you and me goin' before a preacher.''

"I'm not teasing you,'' said Nell, "and when you speak to Father, I think he will be delighted.''

Gavin and Naomi stood beside Cottonwood Creek watching the light from a pale moon and the distant stars dance off the surging water.

"I reckon Woody and Nell are gettin' along some better,'' Gavin said. "So far, I ain't heard a body hit the ground.''

"I can tell you a secret about my sister Nell,'' said Naomi, "but you must promise not to repeat it. Least of all to Woody.''

"I've done my share of hoorawin','' Gavin said, "but I'd never use anything personal against a man. Woodrow Miles is a gent to ride the river with, and I'm hopin' he'll do his best to win Nell, if she'll have him.''

Naomi laughed. "I think I can ease your mind. If Woody wants her, he's got her, but he'll have to conduct himself better than he did at Council Grove. Nell thought he was . . . well . . . afraid of her."

"Hell," Gavin said, "ain't that better than havin' a man try to lay her down and have his way with her?"

"Perhaps up to a point," said Naomi. "I told her to be more patient with him, because he may not have had much experience with women."

"Not many cowboys have," Gavin said, "except in . . . ."

"Where?" she persisted.

"Whorehouses," said Gavin.

"I suppose that's proof enough that Woody's never been to such a place, then," Naomi said.

"Not durin' all the years I've known him," said Gavin. "He was just eighteen when we first met. He'd fought with the Confederacy since he was fifteen, and like the rest of us, I'd say he'd been to hell and back more than once. Woody's next to the youngest man in the outfit, but he's trail boss. He may be a shorthorn when it comes to women, but as a man, he's nine feet tall and a yard wide."

Naomi said nothing. Slipping her arms around Gavin's neck, she kissed him.

"I ain't complainin'," Gavin said, "but what was that for?"

"For justifying my faith in Woody, and what I told Nell," said Naomi, "and for telling me something about Gavin McCord that I'd never have dared ask."

"What have I told you about me?"

"You said that in the years you've known Woody, he's never gone to a whorehouse. That tells me you haven't gone there, either," Naomi said.

"I'm two years older than Woody," said Gavin. "How do you know I didn't make the rounds before we met?"

"If you did," Naomi said, "you've kept away from them for a long time. But I don't believe you've ever been there."

"You're right," said Gavin, "but I can't truthfully say

I've had no experience with women. I'm a long ways from perfect.''

"Then don't tell me about . . . the others," Naomi said.

"You'll have me like I am, then?"

"Yes," said Naomi. "A woman has no right to condemn a man for his past, unless it's still part of his life. You're not a drunkard or a gambler, are you?"

Gavin laughed. "No, ma'am. Even if I was so inclined, I couldn't afford either one, on a cowboy's pay."

"When are you going to speak to Father, to tell him . . . about us?"

"When we reach Santa Fe," said Gavin, "unless you want me to do it sooner."

"I want you to do it much sooner," Naomi said. "I'm fond of the other riders, but I'd feel better if they know about us. Then I won't feel guilty about spending so much of my time with you. Does that make sense, or am I just a nervous female?"

"It makes sense to me," said Gavin. "I don't want them thinkin' you're neglectin' them and being partial to me without a good reason. I'll talk to Pit in the morning."

Rusty, Vic, and Ash were two hours into the second watch, when they heard a footstep. Instantly the three had Colts in their hands.

"You're covered," Vic said. "Identify yourself."

"Bonita. Bonita Stubbs."

"What is it?" Vic asked. "Is something wrong?"

"No more than usual," said Bonita. "I'm wet, cold, and lonely. I . . . I just wanted to do something . . . to walk . . . and my brother Whit's on watch near the wagons. I thought I'd best stay near the creek, so I didn't get lost in the dark."

"Good thinkin'," Vic said. "I'm Vic Brodie, and the gents with me is Rusty and Ash Pryor. Would you like to have some hot coffee?"

"Lord, yes," said Bonita. "We have no shelter from the rain."

"I'll get you some coffee," Ash said.

"Life on the trail is hard on a woman," said Rusty. "I'd've thought your daddy would've left some room in the wagons for you and your sisters."

Bonita's laugh was bitter. "He don't think as much of us as he does the mules, and he hates them."

Ash returned with a tin cup of hot coffee, and Bonita sipped it gratefully. She held the cup in both hands, seeming to relish its warmth.

"Ma'am," said Rusty, "if I ain't bein' too bold, do you folks aim to settle somewhere around Santa Fe?"

"I . . . I don't know," Bonita said. "Thank you so much for the coffee. I must go, before I'm missed."

As suddenly as she had appeared, she was gone.

"Damn it, Rusty," said Vic, "you scared her away."

"I didn't mean nothin'," Rusty said. "They're three mighty handsome gals, and if they aim to be around Santa Fe, I might just go callin' on 'em."

"Don't let me discourage you," said Vic, "but old man Stubbs strikes me as the kind that'd greet you with a loaded shotgun."

"I wonder what the old varmint's got loaded on them wagons," Ash said. "It wouldn't take much for me to sneak over there and have a look."

"Like hell," said Rusty. "You'd be asking for a dose of lead poisoning. You heard her say one of her brothers is on watch."

Bonita returned cautiously to her own camp, only to find that her absence had been discovered.

"You sneaked off somewhere," Jania hissed. "Where did you go?"

"For a walk," said Bonita, "if it's any of your business."

"You went to the Pitkin camp, didn't you?" Laketa said.

"Yes, if you must know," said Bonita. "I wanted coffee, and they gave me some. Tell Paw, either of you, and I'll claw your eyes out."

"We're not telling Paw anything," Jania said. "Tell us what you did, what you said."

"I told them I was cold, wet, and lonely," said Bonita, "and nothing more. They had hot coffee and offered me some. I took it."

"Who did you talk to?" Laketa demanded.

"The three men watching the herd," said Bonita. "Vic Brodie, Ash and Rusty Pryor. They're no older than we are, and they were very nice to me."

"But they must have asked about us," Jania said. "What did they ask?"

"Rusty asked if we would be settling near Santa Fe," said Bonita. "I told them I didn't know. Then I left."

"I'm surprised they didn't ask why we're going to Santa Fe, and what we're hauling in the wagons," Laketa said.

"You sound like Paw," said Bonita in disgust. "They were interested in me . . . us."

Jania sighed. "It would be so nice to have something to look forward to in Santa Fe. Something better than cooking and washing for Paw, Wiley, and Whit."

"Paw would take the whip to you, if he heard you talking like that," Laketa said.

"That's all Paw knows how to do, takin' the whip to anything or anybody that crosses him," said Bonita.

"We all made plans to leave, when we get to Santa Fe," Jania said. "I still want to."

"So do I," said Laketa.

"I may not wait until then," Bonita said.

"You're going back to see those cowboys again, aren't you?" said Jania.

"I am," Bonita said.

"When you do," said Jania, "please take me with you."

"Only if I can go," Laketa said. "My God, I'm twenty-six years old, and I've never so much as had a man look at me twice."

"These three cowboys are somewhere within a year or two of us," said Bonita. "Next time we're close enough to them, maybe all of us can slip into their camp."

"Paw may never let us get this close again," Jania said.

"He wouldn't have, this time, if Wiley and Whit hadn't already unharnessed their teams."

"Paw may surprise you," said Laketa. "I was watching him after the Pitkin riders came to our rescue during that Indian attack, and he was scared. For all his cussing and yelling, he was afraid. He put his hands in his pockets so we wouldn't see them tremble. I believe we'll be staying close to the Pitkin outfit because of the Indians."

"You may be right," Bonita said. "He was determined to get our wagons across the creek before the storm brought high water. I suppose we'll know, after we make camp for tomorrow night."

"Pit," Gavin said, while they waited for breakfast, "there's something I need to ask of you."

"Then ask," said Pitkin. "I am listening."

"I have asked Naomi for her hand," Gavin said, "and she has accepted. Now, I reckon the proper thing for me to do is ask for your blessing."

"Yes," said Pitkin, "that would be proper, but it strikes me this is hardly the time or place. Couldn't this have waited until we reach Santa Fe?"

"Yes, sir," Gavin said. "It could, but Miss Naomi wants your permission now."

"Very well," said Pitkin, "you have it. However—and I am addressing this as much to Naomi as I am to you—I am not granting approval for anything less than proper conduct until this relationship has been legalized in Santa Fe."

"Father," Naomi wailed, "what a perfectly horrid thing to say!"

Until then, only Pitkin, Gavin, and Naomi had been involved, but her outburst quickly alerted the rest of the outfit.

"What did Father say?" Nell demanded.

"He says I'm not to sleep with Gavin until we reach Santa Fe and find a preacher," said Naomi.

"Then I suppose he's going to tell me the same thing, where Woody's concerned," Nell said.

"I say," Pitkin bawled, "what is going on here?"

"Yeeechaaaa!" shouted Rusty, Vic, Ash, and Nip.

"Oh, damn," Woody groaned.

Santa Fe, New Mexico Territory. June 16, 1869.

Tobe Hankins was the last to enter the room in the rear of the saloon he owned. The six men who waited for him sprawled in chairs, their glasses full, savoring the whiskey Hankins had provided. There was Deuce Rowden, York Eagan, Watt Grimes, Grady Beard, Haynes Wooten, and Jude Epps. They were a disreputable lot, several with prices on their heads, and they would kill for money. Taking the chair behind his desk, Hankins grunted in satisfaction, poured himself a drink, and then he spoke.

"There's seven men I want dead. One of them is Gladstone Pitkin. The rest are gun-throwing cowboys that's bringin' a herd of Texas cattle from Independence."

"When will they be gettin' here?" Deuce Rowden asked.

"They won't be getting here," said Hankins. "I want them dead somewhere along the Santa Fe, so if there's ever any questions, it can be blamed on Indians or renegades."

"It'll cost you," Rowden said. "We want sixty-five hundred dollars. Five hundred for expenses, and a thousand for each of us."

"Too much," said Hankins.

"Not enough," York Eagan countered. "Not when we got to ride two or three hunnert miles up the Santa Fe."

"Yeah," said Watt Grimes. "It'll be hotter than hades, and we're likely to end up with the damn Indians after us."

"Fifteen hundred for each of us," Haynes Wooten said.

"A thousand for each of you," said Hankins, "and you keep the cattle."

"What'n hell are we goin' to do with a herd of cows?" Grady Beard asked.

"Yeah," said Jude Epps. "I ain't hirin' on as no cow nurse."

"Take it or leave it," Hankins said, "and don't waste any more of my time makin' up your minds."

The six men looked at one another. They had done Hankins' dirty work before, and they understood him only too well. They had pushed him to the limit, and he was about to dismiss them, penniless.

"We'll take it," Rowden said. "Half in advance?"

"Five hundred for each of you, in advance," said Hankins. "The rest when I'm sure the job's been done."

"What about our expenses?" Eagan asked.

"You're gettin' a herd of cows for free," said Hankins. "Pay your own damn expenses. Now take your advance and get the hell out of here."

Casting him dirty looks, they took the money and left, the last one out closing the door. Tobe Hankins leaned back in his chair, put his feet on the desk, and lighted a cigar. From his desk drawer he took a report that included the proposed right-of-way for the railroad to be built into Santa Fe. Silently he cursed the fate and blind luck that had made it possible for Gladstone Pitkin to buy literally thousands of acres of land for a few cents an acre. Land that would be worth millions, once the railroad came. Hankins dared not contest Pitkin's ownership, for the Englishman had money. So much, in fact, that Hankins was intimidated. He had but one chance, and that was to see that Pitkin and his riders did not reach Santa Fe alive.

Eastern Kansas. June 17, 1869.

After Naomi revealed her relationship with Gavin, and Nell had further shocked everybody with news about herself and Woody, breakfast was a silent affair. The rest of the riders covertly eyed Gavin and Woody, tempted to hooraw them, but aware that Gladstone Pitkin had become decidedly cool to them all. After breakfast, when it was time to move out, Nell and Naomi approached Pitkin.

"Father," Naomi said, "we have something to say to you."

"I believe the two of you have said quite enough for one day," said Pitkin.

"No we haven't," Naomi insisted. "Perhaps you have a right to be furious with us, but it's unconscionable of you to be so cold to everyone else. None of the men have said or done anything to you. Not even Gavin and Woody. They have been perfect gentlemen, and it was Nell and me who pushed them to speak to you."

"I can believe that," said Pitkin, "and I am not faulting Woody and Gavin for having been captivated by you. When we reach Santa Fe, if they still want you, they shall have you, with my blessing. Or perhaps with my apology. While we're on the trail—however difficult it may be— you will conduct yourselves in a manner so as not to embarrass me further. Otherwise, I shall take a strap to one or both of you, as the occasion demands. Have I made myself clear?"

"Yes, Father," they said meekly.

Woody and Gavin had crept close enough to hear Pitkin's ultimatum, and they grinned at one another.

"Head 'em up," Woody shouted. "Move 'em out!"

In the Stubbs camp, the teams had been harnessed and the wagons readied for the trail well before the Pitkin outfit was ready to depart. Bonita, Jania, and Laketa exchanged hopeful looks, for it seemed Levi Stubbs intended to remain close to the Pitkin outfit. The Pitkin wagons fell in behind the drag, and the three Stubbs wagons followed.

After they left Cottonwood Creek, the vegetation changed. There were cottonwood, elm, box-elder, and willow trees. There was some wild plum, and goldenrod abounded. While there was plenty of buffalo grass, there was seldom any tallgrass, except in the bottoms. Occasionally they saw crumbling buffalo bones, and wallows long since grown up in weeds and grass. But to everybody's surprise, the trees began to thin out, and there were none that had been struck by lightning or windblown. Gavin McCord rode with Nell and Naomi at drag.

"There are fewer and fewer trees," Naomi observed. "If they disappear entirely, what will we use for firewood?"

7

"We filled the possum bellies on both wagons last night, before the rain," Gavin said. "We'll be all right for a day or two. After that, we may all be gathering buffalo chips."

"Buffalo chips? What are those?" Nell asked.

"Dried buffalo droppings," said Gavin.

Nell wrinkled her nose, and Naomi looked as though she doubted the truth of it.

"You'd put your hands on *that*?" Nell asked.

"I would," said Gavin, "and so will you, if there's nothin' else to burn."

"More important," Naomi said, "will Gonzales wash his hands after adding to the fire, before he prepares our food?"

"I doubt it," said Gavin, with a straight face. "Most range cooks have learned to save water, when they can. When a frontier woman settles down, roundin' up buffalo chips is one of her duties."

"Gavin McCord," Naomi said, "you'd just better hope there's plenty of wood where we are going. I won't gather buffalo chips for *any* man. Or for myself, for that matter."

Once the herd was moving, Woody rode ahead, seeking water. Long stretches on the map Pitkin had bought showed little or no water. Twenty-five miles west of Cottonwood Creek, Woody reached another creek whose name he didn't know. There was good water and abundant graze, but not a stick of wood!*

"There'd better be some buffalo chips," said Woody aloud, "for there's nothin' else."

Suddenly there was a sharp pain at the back of his neck, and Woody swatted at what proved to be an enormous mosquito. Woody rode along the creek a ways, finding there were three forks. The banks were bright with scarlet flowers he didn't recognize, and in the clear water of one of the forks, he could see fish. But there was danger too. There was the ominous whirring of a rattlesnake, and Woody's horse backstepped. He wheeled the animal and rode back the way he had come. It was time to return to the herd and tell the outfit they were an impossible distance from the next decent water. He rode back in a slightly different direction and began seeing more and more of the bleaching bones of long-dead buffalo. There were numerous buffalo wallows, grassed over and knee-high in weeds, that could prove troublesome for wagons. When Woody met the herd, he rode on around. He would first report to Pitkin, and then inform the riders they were facing a dry camp for the night. Despite the fact there had been plentiful water, Pitkin had wisely taken the precaution of filling the extra barrels he had bought to help them across the desert. While the herd would be dry, the barrels would hold enough water for drinking and cooking, as well as a small ration for the horses and mules. The wagons were traveling side-by-side, and Woody, after passing them, turned his horse and rode back between them.

"Dry camp tonight, *amigos*," Woody said. "It's a good twenty-five miles to the next creek."

"*Malo*," said Gonzales.

"We have enough water in the barrels to see us through tonight," Pitkin said.

"That was a smart move, filling those barrels," said Woody. "Since that map has long stretches with no water

* Turkey Creek.

showing, we can't count on there being any. When we reach this next water, we'll want to refill those barrels."

"I shall see to it," Pitkin said, obviously pleased that his foresight was appreciated.

Woody, starting with the drag riders, told the others of the impending dry camp. He caught Gavin's eye, and winking at him, Gavin followed it with a question.

"How about firewood? Is there plenty ahead of us?"

"Funny you should mention that," said Woody. "There's not a stick of wood between here and that creek. But there's plenty of buffalo bones. We can gather buffalo chips, if we have to."

Nell and Naomi turned up their noses, and Gavin laughed. Woody quickly caught on and played along.

"Should be plenty of buffalo chips. Since we're in dry camp tonight, we can stop well before sundown. That'll give Nell and Naomi enough time to gather a pretty good load of that prairie firewood."

"Woodrow Miles," Nell said, "if you're expecting us to put our hands on those horrid things, then you're as . . . as full of it as the buffalos were."

Woody and Gavin slapped their thighs with their hats and laughed until they cried. It was Gavin who recovered first, and when he spoke, he seemed dead serious.

"I reckon we'll have to tell Pit we've changed our minds about these ladies. When a woman won't do the little things, how can you depend on her for important stuff?"

"I dunno," said Woody with a straight face. "It gets cold as all get-out in northern New Mexico. When a blizzard blows in across the Sangre de Cristos, we'll likely freeze to death for want of a fire."

"I think we'll just call your bluff," Naomi said, getting wise. "Father's barely speaking to us, as it is. He has virtually no sense of humor. Irritate him further, and he may just forbid us to have anything more to do with either of you."

"I reckon they got us, Woody," said Gavin. "We'll have to gather our own buffalo chips. Pit's a hundred years away from understandin' cowboy humor. If he ever does.''

"I'd better talk to the rest of the riders," Woody said. "They'll wonder what's goin' on back here."

Woody passed the word to the rest of the riders and then took his place ahead of the herd, at point. As he rode along, the Stubbs outfit came to mind. How were they going to survive a night in a dry camp? He grudgingly concluded he would probably share some of their water with Stubbs, but only if the old varmint kept a civil tongue.

Once the herd had traveled what Woody believed was half the distance to the next water, he chose a level plain with good graze and waved his hat. The riders began heading the leaders, starting them milling. As the herd settled down, Pitkin and Gonzales reined up their teams and began unharnessing. Within a few minutes, Levi Stubbs reined up his sweating mules. His other two wagons were close behind.

"Where is the water?" Stubbs demanded.

"Twelve miles ahead," said Woody calmly.

"We can't spend the night here," Stubbs all but shouted. "We got no water, not even for cookin'."

"Mister Stubbs," said Woody as calmly as he could, "on the frontier, there is never any assurance there'll be water within a day's drive. You generally carry a water barrel on the outside of each wagon box. That will see you through a dry camp, with enough water for drinking and cooking. Your teams will have to go without, and you'll have to rest them more often on the next day's drive. Where are your water barrels?"

Stubbs looked uncomfortable, and when he didn't say anything, Wiley answered for him.

"Paw left the barrels behind. He said haulin' water was foolish, that it would just be extry weight, cuttin' down on our payload."

There was a prolonged silence, and every eye was on Levi Stubbs. The man had fallen victim to his own ignorance and greed, and nobody had any sympathy for him. However, there were others to consider, and the worry in the eyes of the three Stubbs daughters got to the Pitkin outfit. Even Pitkin looked to Woody for an answer to the dilemma.

"Stubbs," said Woody, "there's no gettin' around the fact that you're a damn fool for havin' left your water barrels behind. If it was just you, I'd let you do without, but your sons and daughters shouldn't have to suffer for your ignorance. We'll share our water with you, allowin' you enough for cookin' your meals and drinkin'.''

"Why, damn you," Stubbs bellowed, "I wouldn't . . ."

"But we would," Wiley interrupted, "and we'd be obliged."

"You are most kind," said Bonita, "and we're all thanking you."

"Well, by God, I ain't," Stubbs said. "Our mules is thirsty too."

"Sorry," said Woody, "we don't have enough for your mules. You'll take what we can spare, or leave it alone."

"You didn't act like you cared all that much for them mules, Paw," Whit said. "Way you was whippin' 'em while we was crossin' them creeks, I thought you was beatin' them to death. There's sores from the whippin'.''

It was a telling argument. On the frontier, even outlaws and killers didn't abuse their animals, and it prompted the cowboys to take a closer look at Stubbs' teams. There was no mistaking the marks of the lash, and the men looked at Levi Stubbs in a manner that sent chills up his spine.

"Stubbs," said Woody through clenched teeth, "if you don't doctor those wounds and keep the blowflies away, those mules are goin' to die."

"Hell," Stubbs said, "it ain't that bad."

"Bad enough," said Nip Kelly, "and it may get worse. If we find you've been beating those animals again, it's you that'll die. I believe I speak for every cowboy here."

There were shouts of agreement from everybody, including all the Pitkins, and even Gonzales, the cook.

"I don't have to take that kind of talk," Stubbs bawled.

He stalked back to his wagon, climbed to the box, and slapped the rumps of his mules with the reins. He finally reined up a hundred yards beyond the Pitkin camp. Wiley and Whit didn't follow him. Instead, Whit approached Woody.

"Do you have any medicine we could buy that will heal them lashes on the mules?"

"Nothing you can buy," said Woody, "but we'll share our sulfur salve with you, if we can count on you making use of it."

"You can," Whit replied. "Me an' Wiley will see to it."

"Gonzales," said Woody, "get them one of those tins of salve from the medicine chest in the chuck wagon."

While the Mexican was fetching the salve, the three Stubbs daughters came closer. It was Bonita who spoke.

"Please let us have a little water for drinking and cooking. Whatever we can do to pay you, we'll gladly do."

"There's no pay wanted or expected for the sharin' of water," Woody said. "At least, not for them that's deservin' of it. Rusty, you and Vic take one of those small barrels of water from Pit's wagon, and carry it where these ladies tell you."

Rusty and Vic hastened to obey, and when they were well away from the Pitkin camp, Bonita spoke.

"You all have been so kind to us, after Paw treated you so shamefully."

"Yes," Jania said, "I'm so sick, I could just die."

"Don't be feelin' like that," said Vic. "None of us has got much choice, when it comes to our kin. We're stuck with 'em."

"Oh, God," Laketa said, "why did we have to get stuck with him?"

"After midnight," said Rusty, "Ash, Vic, and me will be on watch, and there'll be hot coffee. Why don't the three of you slip away and join us for a while?"

"Yeah," Vic said. "All we'll do is just talk," he added hastily.

"We will if we can," said Bonita.

"If Wiley or Whit's on watch, we can," Jania said. "It's him we got to worry about."

Rusty and Vic left the keg of water a few yards behind Stubbs' wagon. He ignored them and continued unharnessing his team. As the cowboys returned to their own camp, they met Wiley and Whit with the other two wagons.

"They're a decent enough bunch," said Vic, "except for old Stubbs. That old bastard oughta be gut-shot and fed to the coyotes."

"The girls must have taken after their mama," Rusty said. "I'd near about tolerate the scruffy old varmint from here to Santa Fe, just to get to know the girls better. I believe the three of 'em would leave old Stubbs and go with us, was they asked proper."

"Yeah," said Vic, "but I reckon that would be stretchin' Pitkin's patience to the limit. He's stuck with two females in the outfit, because they're kin. What in tarnation would it be like with three more?"

"I reckon we won't ever know," Rusty said, "but I do hope the three of 'em are able to join us on the second watch. Pitkin don't have to know about that."

There was considerable conversation during supper, as Pitkin's outfit discussed all they had seen and heard. The longhorns, without water at the end of the day's drive, were in full voice, bawling their frustration. The horses and mules had been given only a little of the available water, but that was better than nothing, and with another small ration before taking the trail the next morning, they would survive.

"Supper's ready," Bonita announced.

Levi Stubbs sat on a wagon tongue and said nothing. Wiley and Whit wasted no time getting to the supper fire. After the boys took their portions, Bonita, Jania, and Laketa served their own plates. Not until they had all left the fire and settled down to eat did Stubbs take a tin plate and cup and serve himself.

"Damn him," said Wiley quietly, "we shouldn't've loft him nothin'."

"I'm glad we did," Bonita said. "After the shameful way he acted, he'll have trouble not chokin' on every bite."

Stubbs was hungry and thirsty, and that overcame his

fury. He realized he had played the fool and regretted having done so, but his iron-bound pride forbade his saying or doing anything to make amends. While the girls had prepared supper, Stubbs had watched Wiley and Whit applying the sulfur salve to the rumps of his mules where he had lashed them with the whip. It galled him that Woody Miles had spoken the truth about blow flies worsening the wounds he had inflicted, and he hated them all for having ridiculed him for beating mules that belonged to him. He had accepted their water and their medicine because he'd had no choice, but if the opportunity ever presented itself, he would see that Woody Miles paid. When he had finished eating, he dropped his eating tools, plate, and cup on the ground. It wasn't quite dark, but Stubbs took his blankets and crawled under his wagon. He hadn't forgotten how his two sons had sucked up to the Pitkin bunch. If there was a watch, he decided, it would be up to Wiley and Whit.

"Lookit the old varmint," said Whit. "Pilin' up under his wagon to sleep, and it ain't even dark. That means the watch is up to us."

"No," Bonita said. "We can't make him do what he ought, but we can keep everything from falling on you and Wiley. The two of you stand watch until midnight, and we'll take over until dawn."

"That's decent of you," said Wiley, "but it ain't your responsibility. It's for a man to do, but we're shy one."

"That's why we're offering to help," Laketa said. "We're close enough to the Pitkin camp that they would help us, if there was a need for it. Sometime after midnight, we'll get word to them Paw's still got a burr under his tail, and that we're standing watch for the rest of the night."

"That's smart," said Wiley. "Do that, so's me an' Whit can git some sleep. Just holler long an' loud if somethin' goes wrong."

Bonita and Jania said nothing, but they smiled their approval at their older sister. Old Levi, in his selfish, evil way, had played into their hands.

* * *

"We'll have to keep a close eye on the herd tonight," Woody said, after supper. "It's likely they'll keep to their feet and mill around all night, them bein' thirsty."

"They might stampede again, even without thunder and lightning?" Pitkin asked.

"Yes," said Woody. "They're naturally ornery. Add thirst and frustration to that, and anything can happen."

"One thing we can do," Vic said, "is keep any two of them bulls from gettin' close to one another."

"Yeah," said Gavin. "All it takes is for one of the varmints to hook another, and them that's closest may stampede at the smell of blood."

"I never realized they are such temperamental beasts," Pitkin said.

"Little of that comes into play," said Gavin, "when there's good water and graze. But on a trail drive, you don't always have that."

"We never had much trouble, drivin' from Texas north to the railroad," Rusty said. "After a drive or two, you know where the water is. None of us has ever been down the Santa Fe before."

"I can understand that," said Pitkin, "and I regret that the available maps are of little help. They seemed reliable enough, until after we left Cottonwood Creek."

"That's generally the trouble with early maps of the frontier," Nip Kelly said. "They're good about showin' major rivers, but tell you little or nothin' about the hard miles from one river to the next."

"All the more reason to see that all our water barrels are full, before we leave the next good water," said Pitkin. "Just do your best with the herd tonight. I expect nothing more."

"There'll be some dewfall later tonight," Woody said. "If they'll graze, that'll help to slake their thirst."

By the time Rusty, Vic, and Ash took over the second watch, the herd had begun to settle down. Woody, Gavin, and Nip had managed to separate the troublesome bulls during the first watch. There was some braying from the mules in the Stubbs camp.

"Longhorns ain't the only ones that gets ornery when they're thirsty," Vic observed.

"Between their mules and our ornery cows, I hope there's no trouble," said Rusty. "I want some time to talk to the Stubbs gals."

"Which one you reckon is the oldest?" Ash asked.

"Laketa," said Vic. "There's crow's feet around her eyes."

"Hell, that don't make her old," Rusty said. "There's crow's feet around my eyes, and I'm just twenty-four. Laketa's the quietest, and I like her best. Lord, a man could get lost in them big brown eyes."

"They all have brown eyes," said Ash, "but I like Jania."

"Then I reckon it's just as well I like Bonita," Vic said. "She's all that's left."

"I wonder what they'd think," said Rusty, "if they knowed we was pickin' and choosin' 'em like heifers at a beef sale."

"I reckon they wouldn't mind too much," Ash said, "when you consider what a hard-headed, scruffy old varmint their daddy is. I say we talk to 'em like we aim to go courtin', when we all get to Santa Fe."

"Maybe you're right," said Vic. "They could do worse. Accordin' to my figgerin', that check we got from Pitkin is for a hundred and five thousand dollars. That's twenty-one thousand for every man of us."

"Why don't we just keep our mouths shut about that?" Rusty suggested. "Me, I want a woman that's wantin' me, even though she believes I'm a dirt-poor trail herder. Get too free with your money, and you'll never be sure that ain't what she's after."

"That kind of makes sense to me," said Ash. "Vic, can we count on you to bridle your tongue?"

"I reckon," Vic replied. "We may be countin' our chickens before they're hatched, anyhow. Them gals may not want any of us.''

When the Stubbs women arrived, they quietly identified themselves.

"We're glad you all could get away," said Rusty.

"It wasn't all that difficult," Laketa said. "Paw was mad enough to bite himself and die from the poison. Wiley and Whit would have had to stand watch all night. They agreed for us to take the second watch, if we asked you all to look out for us. Will you?"

"Consider yourselves looked out for," said Vic. "It ain't likely anything will happen in your camp, it bein' so close to ours. We need to stay near the herd, them bein' restless, and they're right behind your wagons."

"We're ever so grateful to you for the water," Bonita said. "How can we ever repay your kindness?"

"When you get to Santa Fe," said Vic, "wherever you settle, we'd like to come callin' in a courtin' way."

The three of them giggled, chattering like excited geese, and Vic wasn't completely sure they weren't laughing at him. He said no more, while Rusty and Ash seemed nervous beyond speech. Suddenly the women became serious, and Bonita spoke.

"We don't know ... what ... will happen, after we get to Santa Fe, except we know we'll have to get away from Paw. But wherever we are, we'd like for you to come calling. You'll be welcome."

"You certainly will," Laketa said, "but who will be calling on who?"

"I hope this ain't gonna be embarrassin'," said Rusty, "but we kind of already made up our minds. I like you, because I reckon you're about my age. Well ... there's some other reasons, too, but I ain't gettin' into them, with these other two big-eared varmints standin' here listenin'."

Laketa laughed. "I'm twenty-six, and I'll look forward to you getting into those other reasons."

"Bonita," said Vic, "I'm twenty-three, an' if I ain't too

old and ugly, I'd admire to see you as often as we can manage it."

"I'm twenty-four," Bonita said, "so if you're old, so am I. Let's take a walk."

"Ash," said Jania, "it's down to you and me. I hope you're satisfied, because I am."

8

The dewfall had done little to slake the thirst of the herd, and the riders had trouble heading them west. They bawled like a demented chorus, and it was difficult keeping them bunched so they couldn't break ranks. Many a flank was raked by the horns of an unruly, irritated companion. Ash was riding drag with Nell and Naomi Pitkin, and it was to them that Woody spoke first.

"You'll have to push 'em hard all the way. Keep 'em bunched so's all they can see is the next cow's behind, while a pair of horns is rakin' their own."

Despite all their efforts, there were bunch quitters, keeping the flank and swing riders busy. While Nell and Naomi had become more adept at heading the animals, they lacked the skill of trail-wise cowboys, and Ash Pryor had his work cut out for him. By the time the sun was noon-high, the riders and their horses were coated from head-to-toe with dust.

"By God, they've run us ragged," said Gavin, "but their tails is draggin' too. It won't be as bad from here on."

Gavin was right. The lack of water and their own cantankerous nature had sapped the strength of the longhorns, and they became easier to manage. Their tongues lolled out, and their bawling ceased, for they no longer seemed to care. Mile after weary mile they kept the herd moving. Two hours before sundown, the longhorns smelled or sensed the water ahead, and there was no holding them. The riders could only get out of the way and let the herd run. They waited for Gonzales and Pitkin to catch up with the wagons, and then they moved on toward the three forks of the creek ahead.

"There's fish in at least one of the forks of that creek ahead," said Woody.

"They'd be mighty tasty for supper," Vic said, "but how do we catch 'em, scoop 'em up with our hats?"

"I'll bet you ten dollars Gonzales has lines and hooks," said Woody.

"You're on," Vic replied, "and if he has, I'll sweeten the pot by cleaning all the fish you can catch."

They all fell into the spirit of the thing, and riding close to the chuck wagon, Woody shouted at Gonzales.

"Gonzales, there's fish in the creek ahead. How many lines and hooks you got?"

"*Muchos,*" the Mexican shouted back. "*Diez, per'ap.*"

Woody laughed. "Listen up, all of you. There's fish in the creek ahead, Gonzales has hooks and lines, and Vic's just volunteered to clean all we can catch."

"Whoa, damn it," said Vic. "I said I'd clean all *you* can catch."

"That ain't what I heard," Rusty said.

"Me neither," said Ash. "I ain't been fishin' in a coon's age, 'cause I hate cleanin' the critters. With old Vic takin' care of that, I'll catch a good string."

"All of you had best be careful around these three forks," Woody said. "When I was here before, my horse almost stepped on a rattler."

Reaching the three forks, they found the cattle had taken over all three, and the water was muddied.

"Let's run the varmints out of there," Gavin said. "They've had time to drink, and it won't clear up with them sloshin' around in it."

But Gonzales had thought of that. He veered away with the chuck wagon, choosing a place to set up camp upstream, well beyond the herd. Pitkin followed with the other wagon. The riders unsaddled their horses, while Gonzales and Pitkin unhitched the teams.

"We'll hold the horses and mules a few minutes," Woody said. "They ought to cool some before they drink, after bein' dry for so long."

The Stubbs wagons circled wide, going well beyond the Pitkin camp. When Woody judged it was safe for the horses and mules to drink, they were turned loose. Thirsty as the animals were, they took the time to roll before going to the creek. Rusty and Ash had wasted no time getting hooks and lines from Gonzales. The Mexican had also given them bacon strips for bait.

"Anybody wantin' to fish, come on," Rusty shouted. "Gonzales is greasin' the skillet, and he ain't gonna wait forever."

Except for Gladstone Pitkin and Gonzales, everybody got into the spirit of it, walking upstream past the Stubbs wagons. Stubbs sat on a wagon tongue, while Wiley and Whit leaned against the front wheels of their wagons.

"Wiley, Whit," said Woody, "there's fish in this creek. We have extra lines, hooks, and bait. You're welcome to join us."

"We ain't takin' nothin' from you," Stubbs snarled.

"I wasn't offering you anything," said Woody coldly. "I spoke to Wiley and Whit."

"We're obliged, and we'll go with you," Wiley said. "A mess of fresh fish would sure be welcome."

There were sun perch and catfish, and within an hour, more than enough fish had been caught. Wiley and Whit returned to their camp triumphant, each with a decent string of fish. "I reckon we'll have to pitch in and help old Vic clean these fish," Woody observed. "It's hard work, cleanin' catfish."

"Why are catfish more difficult to clean?" Naomi asked.

"They have to be skinned," said Gavin, "and it's a two-man job."

Despite the bet between Woody and Vic, everybody pitched in and helped clean the catch. Gonzales had two fires going and two frying pans ready. He dunked the fish in cold water, rolled them in corn meal, and then fried them a golden brown.

"I got to admit I ain't never been fed this well on a trail drive," Rusty said.

It was a sentiment with which everybody else agreed, and even Gladstone Pitkin seemed to have overcome his aggravation with the outfit. Gonzales beamed, continuing to fry fish until nobody could eat any more.

"Thank God we ain't got to listen to them bellerin' cows all night tonight," said Vic.

"The Santa Fe is unfamiliar to us," Woody replied. "We could be facing a dry camp at any time. We were lucky last night. When a herd's mad for water, anything can stampede 'em. Even somebody sneezing."

The three Stubbs girls again visited Rusty, Vic, and Ash on the second watch, and they were jubilant.

"Thank you so much for inviting Wiley and Whit to go fishing," Laketa said. "The fish were a welcome treat."

"More than that," said Bonita, "it gave Wiley and Whit a chance to stand up to Paw. They've always taken his orders, however selfish and foolish they were. Now I feel they're finally becoming men."

"That's what it takes," Vic said. "If a gent wants to be treated like a man, he's got to stand up on his hind legs and act like one."

After breakfast the following morning, Woody again asked Pitkin to spread the map so they might get some idea where they would find the next water.

"The Little Arkansas," Pitkin said, "but how far is it?"

"We can't tell from this map," said Woody, "but I'll know after riding to it. If there's any possibility of reaching it today—even if we arrive after dark—then I think we ought to make the sacrifice. An occasional dry camp is bearable, but it's a mite soon for another. There was some lightning last night, and there may be more tonight. Worse, if there's rain somewhere to the west, just a hint of it on the wind can start a thirsty herd running.''

"We're traveling west," Pitkin pointed out.

"More to the southwest," said Woody, "and even if they stampede in that direction, you can count on 'em fanning out. We'll still lose a couple of days rounding 'em up.''

"Best not to gamble with a thirsty herd and a building storm," Nip Kelly said. "We'll be far better off to drive to the next water, even if it's twenty miles.''

"Soon as the herd's movin'," Woody said, "I'll ride ahead and see just how far we are from the Little Arkansas.''

"I smell smoke," said Gavin.

"It's from the Stubbs' breakfast fire," Vic said.

"I don't think so," said Gavin. "Look.''

Somewhere to the west, a plume of gray smoke dirtied the blue of the sky. The wind was from the west, and there was no fire in the Stubbs camp, for Stubbs and his sons were harnessing their teams.

"Perhaps it is Indians," Pitkin said.

"If that's all it was, we'd be in luck," said Woody. "Too much smoke on too wide a front. We're seeing the results of that lightning last night. That's a prairie fire, and it's on its way to overtaking us.''

"What are we going to do?" Nell asked.

"We're going to try to reach the Little Arkansas ahead of it," said Woody.

"Suppose we just stay here until it passes?" Pitkin asked.

"Because it's comin' with the wind," said Woody. "By the time it reaches us, the front may be ten miles wide. We must reach the Little Arkansas and cross it. With the wind behind the flames, they'll jump this creek like it wasn't here. Get the herd moving, while I go and warn the Stubbs outfit.''

The riders wasted no time getting the herd moving. Gonzales and Pitkin pulled both wagons in behind the drag. Woody reined up before the Stubbs wagons. Levi Stubbs said nothing, and there was no welcome in his hard eyes.

"There's a prairie fire comin' this way," Woody said, pointing to the distant smoke. "We must reach the next water—the Little Arkansas—and cross ahead of the fire."

"We don't *know* that's a prairie fire," said Stubbs, "an' we don't *know* it'll be of any trouble to us. All we got is your word, cow stink, an' that ain't enough fer me."

"It's enough fer me an' Whit," Wiley said. "Paw, these men has got experience that we ain't got. You kin piddle around an' take your chances with that fire, if'n you want to, but we're makin' a run fer that river. Ain't we, Whit?"

"Damn right," said Whit. "Even if the fire ain't a danger, we still got to make it to that river, so what we got to lose?"

He climbed to his wagon box and gave Jania a hand up. Wiley mounted the box and Laketa followed.

"Make room for me," Bonita cried. "I won't ride with him."

Laketa gave her a hand up, and when Whit's wagon moved out, Wiley's was right behind him. Without a backward glance, Woody rode away. He could hear Stubbs cursing, but he could also hear the rattle of the wagon.

"I'm ridin' ahead to the Little Arkansas," said Woody, as he rode alongside Pitkin's wagon. "Then I'll try and get some idea as to how close that fire is, and how wide a front the flames are coverin'."

Pitkin waved his understanding, and Woody rode on. The rest of the riders knew the danger and the necessity of knowing how far they were from the Little Arkansas. Each of them lifted a hand as Woody rode past. He kicked his horse into a slow gallop, and soon was lost to the riders driving the herd.

"Have you ever been through a prairie fire, Gonzales?" Pitkin asked, as his wagon rattled along beside the chuck wagon.

"*Si,*" said Gonzales. "Lose chuck wagon, grub, and much cows."

Pitkin bit his lip and pushed his teams all the harder. He

was rapidly learning that his resourceful outfit did not exaggerate.

Woody rode on, ever aware of the billowing smoke on the horizon. While there was a slim possibility the blazing front might burn itself out without extending all the way to the Little Arkansas, he couldn't be sure of that. If the fire's front stretched all the way to the river, the herd would have to reach and cross the Little Arkansas ahead of the flames. Only one thing could Woody see in their favor, and that was the total lack of any timber. A truly terrifying fire could race up resinous trees, turning them into towering torches. With a treacherous wind at its heels, such a fire could leap from one tree to another, often crossing creeks and rivers as though they didn't exist.

Sparing his horse, Woody rode at a slow gallop. Reaching the Little Arkansas, he estimated that it was an alarming fifteen miles from where he had left the herd. Now he was better able to judge the progress and potential danger of the prairie fire. Studying the smoke, it appeared the flames might already have reached the river. While that might halt the advance of the fire, it still would be necessary for the Pitkin outfit to cross the Little Arkansas before the flaming front reached them.

"Before we start back, we might as well get us a drink, horse," said Woody.

Woody found a shallow place and watered his horse. He was about to belly-down and satisfy his own thirst, when a movement on the opposite bank caught his eye. An Indian arrow whipped so close to his cheek, he felt the passing of it.

"My God," Woody said, under his breath.

The Comanche who had loosed the arrow shouted, and a dozen mounted comrades rode whooping toward the river. In an instant, Woody was in the saddle, kicking his horse into a fast gallop. But there was absolutely no cover, and Woody knew they would soon flank him, leaving him but two choices, one as unappealing as the other. He could force them to shoot him out of the saddle in a deadly crossfire, or he could take refuge in the tallgrass, killing as many of them as he could, before their arrows found him. Woody rode his tiring horse as fast as he dared, aware that every yard took him a little closer to the oncoming herd. Were they near enough to hear his desperate plea for help? Having nothing to lose, Woody drew his Colt and fired three times, spacing the shots so there would be no mistaking their purpose. Over the bawling of the herd, the riders were able to hear the distant shots.

''Woody's in trouble,'' Gavin shouted.

It was a situation the outfit had been up against more than once, and experience told them it was Indians or outlaws. They were unable to desert the herd because of the advancing prairie fire, so their decision was quick and unanimous. They would take the herd with them, a thundering hooved avalanche, to counter whatever danger threatened Woody. But their decision went beyond Woody's plight, for there was no other way of getting the herd to the Little Arkansas ahead of the prairie fire. Gavin began firing his Colt, and the rest of the riders joined in. Gonzales shouted his teams into a gallop, and on the very heels of the drag, began firing his Winchester. The herd, already cantankerous and testy from being driven hard and fast, lurched into a run.

Gladstone Pitkin reined up his teams and sat there swearing, watching the galloping longhorns disappear in a cloud of dust. Nell and Naomi, while not understanding the underlying purpose of the stampede, fell into the spirit of it. They rode hell-for-leather after the herd, shouting for all they were worth.

''Glory to God,'' Woody shouted, when he heard the thunder of hooves and saw the advancing dust cloud.

The herd galloped on, fanned out in a line half a mile wide. Dust obscured the farthest ranks, presenting a formidable sight to the Comanches pursuing Woody. Wheeling their horses, they fled before the fast-moving stampede. Woody rode for his life, and when he was out of the path of the running longhorns, he slid out of the saddle. He flung his arm around the neck of his horse, for the gallant animal was lathered and heaving for air.

"Nice of you to bring us company," Gavin said, as the riders reined up. "Comanches, I reckon?"

"Yeah," said Woody, "and I'm obliged for the welcomin' committee. I had that prairie fire on my mind, and got a mite careless. They jumped me at the river. A dozen of them."

"I ain't playin' down the Comanches," Vic said, "but how serious is the fire? How wide is the front?"

"Looked like it might extend all the way to the Little Arkansas," said Woody. "While I don't relish the idea of explainin' it to Pitkin, that stampede serves two good purposes. It got rid of the Comanches—at least for now—and maybe it'll get the herd across the Little Arkansas ahead of the fire."

"Hell," Nip Kelly said, "tell it to Pitkin straight. Even if there was no Comanches and no prairie fire, without a stampede, that bunch of longhorned catamounts wouldn't get to the Little Arkansas until sometime tomorrow."

"Maybe not even then," said Rusty. "We've pushed 'em hard all day, and a dry camp would've been hell with the lid off. A breath of air with the smell of water could've sent 'em skalley-hootin' in exactly the wrong direction. At least they're fifteen miles farther on the trail they got to travel."

"Howsomever," Gavin said, "we'll have to do some fast talkin'. Yonder comes old Gladstone, and all the smoke ain't from the prairie fire. He's spoutin' of it."

Pitkin reined up his teams, and after glaring at them all, fixed his gaze on Woody. He spoke, making no effort to conceal his anger.

"All the way from Independence, I have been warned of the many dire consequences of stampedes. I have seen you gentlemen go to great lengths to avoid them, and now, before my very eyes, you create one. Perhaps you'd like to justify what I have witnessed?"

"I reckon I can do that," said Woody, "but this is not the time or the place. If you don't get your wagon and teams across the river, the prairie fire's goin' to cut you off."

Pitkin could now see the advancing flames, as they fed on the tallgrass. He also could see the chuck wagon far ahead, as Gonzales raced for the safety of the river. Shouting at his teams, Pitkin urged them on. The riders fell in behind, and crossed the Little Arkansas at the same shallows Gonzales had used just moments before.

"Here comes the Stubbs wagons," Rusty shouted.

Despite the heavy loads, the wagons rattled along at a frantic pace, for the wind was blowing great billows of smoke, and the Stubbs mules were terrified. Wiley and Whit got to the river and crossed ahead of Stubbs, for he had remained behind until the very last minute. His teams were ready to drop, and once across the river, he had the good sense to rein up. Wiley and Whit regarded him with some amusement, while everybody else just ignored him. Woody wasted no time settling his score with Gladstone Pitkin.

"Pit, under normal conditions, a stampede is bad news. Other times, it can serve some useful purposes. This is one of those times. If we hadn't got those brutes to water, they'd have run during the night, and not necessarily toward the Little Arkansas. There was no way to get them across the river before dark, even if there had been no prairie fire. When I reached the Little Arkansas, a pack of Comanches jumped me. The outfit heard my warning shots and stampeded the herd. The cows discouraged the Comanches, saved my hide, and got themselves across the river ahead of the fire. You got a problem understandin' the stampede?"

"Father," said Nell, "it was a perfectly marvelous thing. How could you not see it?"

"I didn't know about the Indian attack," Pitkin said. "I can see the need for saving ourselves and the herd from that."

"That, as well as the fire," said Naomi. "It's burning its way right up to the water."

"The fire might have been a lot worse," Rusty said. "If there were trees, with help from the wind, it could jump from tree to tree."

"The fire wasn't the danger it might have been," said Woody, "but that won't be the case with the Comanches. They'll be back."

"I ain't seen no Comanches," Levi Stubbs growled. "I think cow stink, here, just come up with that as an excuse fer them longhorn varmints gittin' spooked an' runnin' off."

"Stubbs," said Woody grimly, "by the time *you* see the Comanches, you'll have your hair lifted, your throat slit, and arrows in your belly. When you sleep—if you do—you'd better have a gun in your hand."

Levi Stubbs said nothing, but Wiley and Whit swallowed hard. The duo had seen the truth. Too often had the Texas trail boss been right, proving their stubborn old father dead wrong.

"While Gonzales is gettin' supper," said Woody, "there'll be just about enough time to bunch the herd. We'll need to talk before first watch."

What Pitkin only vaguely suspected, Woody's Texas companions knew very well. The Comanches had been taken by surprise and put on the defensive, but it wouldn't last. Just as soon as supper was ready, Gonzales doused the supper fire.

"Obviously the Indians know we're here," Pitkin observed. "What's the purpose in extinguishing the fire so quickly?"

"I want them to know we realize they're not finished with us," said Woody. "They'll be less likely to ambush us. There's no good time for a visit from the Comanches, but it's always better if we see them first."

After supper, before the first watch took its position, Woody spoke.

"The usual watch, but when it's your turn to sleep, don't remove anything but your hat, and keep your Winchesters handy. We'll keep the remuda bunched with the herd for the next few nights."

The Stubbs wagons were much nearer the Pitkin camp than usual, and it appeared that Wiley and Whit had been responsible for that. Following Woody's instructions to his outfit, Wiley and Whit approached.

"When Paw was havin' his doubts about the Indians," said Whit, "he wasn't talkin' fer us. We'd like to help, if there's anything we kin do."

"Yeah," Wiley said. "They just ain't enough of us, and we're scairt they'll run off our mules."

"If they aim to stampede your mules," said Woody, "a hundred men can't stop them. But if it'll make you feel any better, you can bunch your teams near the herd and take your turns standin' watch with us."

"That'll make us feel some better," Wiley said. "You know the ways of these Indians, an' we don't. They could slip up on us in the dark, an' we'd be dead 'fore we knowed they was there."

"Woody," said Vic, "we ought to invite the Stubbs women into our camp."

"I have no objection to that," Woody replied. "It's up to them."

The Stubbs wagons were near enough for Stubbs and his daughters to have heard, and the most immediate response came from Stubbs himself.

"They ain't a-goin' nowhere. They got rifles, an' they kin shoot."

"We can't see in the dark, Paw," said Bonita.

"No," Laketa said, "and we're goin' with them."

The three did exactly that, ignoring Stubbs. Taking his Winchester, he seated himself defiantly on the box of his wagon.

"Stubborn old pelican," said Nip Kelly. "He'll be a prime target."

Woody, Gavin, and Nip took the first watch. Wiley and Whit Stubbs insisted on joining them.

"Just one of you," Woody said. "Whit, get some sleep and join the second watch."

Wiley took his place with the first watch, but Nell and Naomi Pitkin weren't quick to welcome the Stubbs girls.

"Where should we spread our blankets?" Bonita asked.

"Anywhere you like," said Nell shortly. "It's a big country."

Naomi said nothing, and the Stubbs girls said no more. The spot they chose happened to be near to where Rusty, Vic, and Ash would sleep until they assumed the second watch.

"Don't let it bother you, Bonita," said Vic, for he had heard Nell's snobbish response to the girl's question.

"Yeah," Rusty said. "They're English, and there's times when they still suffer from touches of it."

Both cowboys had spoken loudly enough for Nell and Naomi to hear, had they been listening, and they had been.

"Listen to them," Nell hissed. "They're making up to those . . . those range riff-raff."

Naomi said nothing. Vic had called Bonita by her name, with a familiarity that said he had more than a neighborly interest in her. That left Jania and Laketa for Ash and Rusty. Suppose these three females, bound for Santa Fe, were spoken for by the three cowboys from the Pitkin outfit? Whatever Nell and Naomi thought of the Stubbs girls, any hostility toward them might cause a rift within the outfit, reason enough to further antagonize their father, Gladstone Pitkin. Perhaps it was time for Nell and Naomi to bridle their tongues, for Pitkin had become increasingly irritable, less inclined to forgive foolish blunders.

"They ain't no moon," said Wiley Stubbs. "How we goin' to know if they're sneakin' up on us?"

"We may not know," Nip Kelly said. "That's about all we got in our favor. The same dark that keeps us from seein' them pretty well keeps them from seein' us. When they come skulkin' around in the dark, it's generally with the idea of runnin' off the stock. Then while we're scattered all over hell roundin' 'em up, the Comanches will try to pick us off, one or two at a time."

"Then all we kin do is wait fer 'em to make their move," said Wiley.

"That's pretty much the way it is," Woody replied. "I've seen them shoot flaming arrows into a herd, shielding the flame with a blanket until the arrow's ready to be fired."

"One thing in our favor," said Gavin. "The herd, the mules, and the horse remuda's all lined out along the river. It's unlikely they'll come after us from that direction. All we got to worry about is the other three."

There was grim laughter from his companions, as they settled down to wait for whatever tactic the resourceful Comanches might employ. It came just a few minutes before midnight, when the second watch was about to take over. From downriver came a patter of hooves and the nervous nickering of a horse.

"What the hell?" Nip muttered. "One rider?"

But when the horse appeared, galloping along the river in the dim starlight, there was no rider. In a second, Woody was in the saddle, galloping after the riderless horse, but the damage had been done. The horses and mules lit out first, and the panicky longhorns followed, all of them running southwest. Woody caught the frightened horse, as the animal fought the rope secured to a bloody wolf carcass.

"I have seen or heard no Indians, and no sound of a fight," said Gladstone Pitkin. "I have, however, heard and seen every animal we have—or had—galloping wildly away to the southwest. Will one of you enlighten me as to what has happened?"

"The Comanches roped a bloody wolf carcass to a horse and ran it through camp," Woody said. "The wolf smell and the smell of blood did the rest."

"I suppose there was nothing you could do to stop it?" Pitkin said.

"Nothing," said Woody. "It's a trick as old as time, and it almost never fails. There's nothing that will stampede horses, mules, or cows quicker than wolf or cougar smell."

It was a poor time for Levi Stubbs to show up, complaining, but he did.

"My mules is gone, by God, an' all because they was bunched in with your fool cows. What do you aim to do about 'em?"

Any man in the outfit might have responded in similar fashion, but Woody was first. His fist thudded into Stubbs' chin and sent him tumbling down the bank and into the river.

9

Stubbs crawled out of the river on hands and knees, cursing.

"I'll kill you fer that," he bawled.

"You'll do nothing of the sort," said Gladstone Pitkin. "Under the circumstances, I am sure your mules would have stampeded for the same reason our stock did."

"Mr. Pitkin is dead right," Woody said. "Come daylight, you can join us when we begin our search for the stampeded stock. Until then, there's not one damn thing any of us can do. Now just kindly shut up."

Stubbs said no more, wandering off in the darkness toward his wagons.

"What are we goin' to do the rest of the night?" Whit asked.

"Stand watch as planned," said Woody. "I doubt the Comanches will bother us again tonight, but we won't risk it. Tomorrow we'll start our gather."

"Woody," Pitkin said, "I wish to speak to you. Tonight."

Woody followed Pitkin to his wagon. When they were alone, the Englishman spoke.

"I do not wish to appear ungracious, but I do not believe it is in my best interest to further accommodate Mr. Stubbs, beyond possible protection from Indian attacks. He may trail with us, but his teams are his own responsibility."

"I've reached the same conclusion," said Woody. "The man's unreasonable, and I only allowed their teams to mix with ours because Wiley and Whit requested it. I reckon they can see why you've had enough of their mule-headed old daddy."

"I am aware that Stubbs' daughters are spending the night in our camp," Pitkin said, "and for their safety, I am not opposed to that. I will leave that to your discretion, and your ability to keep Stubbs in line. I am also aware that three of our riders have shown more than a passing interest in the young ladies, and I am trusting you to see that Stubbs is in no way allowed to twist that to his personal advantage."

Woody laughed. "You are an observing man, Mr. Pitkin. I understand you perfectly. I believe the three ladies in question are of age, and I doubt they'll allow themselves to be used in ways harmful to you. As you may have noticed, I've had a bellyful of Levi Stubbs, and there'll be no more foolishness from him. Now you'd best get what sleep you can. We have a long, hard day ahead of us tomorrow."

There was no sign of the Comanches during the night, and by first light, Woody had the outfit ready to begin the gather. Accompanying them were Whit and Wiley Stubbs. Levi had ignored them all. Woody approached Nell and Naomi as they were about to saddle their horses.

"I want both of you here in camp during this gather," Woody said. "There may be Indian trouble. Keep your Winchesters ready, because they could attack the camp, planning to burn the wagons and take scalps. We'll be depending on the two of you, your father, and Gonzales."

Woody had expected an argument from them, but they had meekly accepted his order to remain in camp. The three Stubbs girls had heard, and responded as Woody had hoped they might.

"We have rifles and we can shoot," Bonita said. "We've already had a fight with the Comanches, and we're not afraid. If they come after us, we'll make some of them sorry."

"I reckon you will," said Woody. "I've seen you shoot."

He turned away before Nell and Naomi could see his grin, aware of their displeasure. The two could stand some experience in humility, and the more down-to-earth Stubbs girls might well be able to administer it. He mounted and led the outfit in the direction the stampede had taken. After several miles, they began seeing bunches of grazing longhorns, but there were no horses or mules in sight.

"I was afraid of that," said Woody. "They've cut out the mules and the remuda horses and lit out."

"South, toward Indian Territory," Nip Kelly said. "If the trail don't lead that way, I'll eat my boots and spurs."

It was a safe bet, and when the tracks began to come together, the trail led south.

"Fresh trail," Vic said. "They couldn't gather stock in the dark any better than we could, so they ain't that far ahead of us."

Gavin laughed. "That's the good news and the bad news. They know they can't outride us, so that means we can expect an ambush."

"It won't be easy, even for Comanches," said Rusty, "unless they can get to Indian Territory ahead of us. There's no cover on these Kansas plains."

"They'll never make it, drivin' horses and mules," Nip predicted, "but that ain't likely to bother 'em. I never seen a Comanche yet that couldn't make you think he was just part of the earth, until you was close enough for him to shoot your gut full of arrows."

"Oh, Lord," said Whit, "Paw will skin us alive, if we don't find them mules. He's got him a feelin' it's mine an' Wiley's fault they was run off."

"It was nobody's fault," Woody said. "The blood and wolf scent would have sent them running hell-for-election, even from your own camp."

"We got to get ahead of them and find that ambush," said Gavin. "Who'll ride south with me?"

"I will," Vic said. "Suit you, Woody?"

"Yes," said Woody, "but don't do anything foolish. Ride wide enough of them so that neither of you stumble into that ambush on your own. When you have some idea as to where they are, come on back. Then we'll decide how best to overrun them."

Gavin and Vic rode out, Gavin to the southeast, Vic to the southwest. There was no defined method for flushing out the hidden Comanches. Each man had to depend on his own skills and powers of observation. The Comanches would be expecting advance riders, and their deadly arrows killed silently, without warning the rest of the pursuers. While the Indians might rely on one ambush, a second one wasn't out of the question, so Gavin and Vic rode with that in mind. Their task was made all the more difficult by the total lack of timber of any kind on the Kansas plain. While the two riders were half a mile apart, they could still see one another, and that was a small advantage.

A hundred yards ahead of Gavin, a flock of birds swooped down, and without touching the ground, flew away. Vic reined up, and waved his hat. Gavin waved back. They now knew where the bushwhackers waited, but they didn't know how many were there, or if there were others ahead, concealed in a different location.

Following Woody's orders, one of them was to stay put while the other rode back for the rest of the outfit, but that option was quickly lost. The wind was out of the west, and with Gavin to the east of the hidden Comanches, his horse sensed or smelled them. The animal nickered nervously, and four Comanches seemed to rise out of the earth itself.

Gavin kicked his horse into a gallop, riding toward them. Two of the quartet began loosing arrows at him, while the other two were concentrating on Vic, who galloped his horse in their direction. Gavin and Vic drew their Colts and began firing. The Comanches had made their play too soon, and the arrows fell short. The four went down under deadly fire, as Gavin and Vic rode on, meeting and reining up.

"Woody ain't goin' to like this," Vic said.

"I don't like it for the same reason," said Gavin. "We

nailed their bushwhackers, but the rest of 'em are down-wind from here. They've heard the shots, and they know we're still on their trail. If there's enough of the varmints, they can set up another ambush.''

"With that possibility in mind," Vic said, "do we ride on, or do we report back to Woody?"

"We'll report to Woody," said Gavin. "We didn't obey his orders, but we done what we had to. He's been followin' that trail long enough to have some idea how many Indians we're dealin' with. He needs to know there's four less.''

No sooner had they wheeled their horses than the wind brought the distant rattle of gunfire.

"My God," Vic said, "there's more of 'em, and they're attackin' Woody and the rest of the outfit."

"I don't think so," said Gavin. "The shooting is too faint and far away. I reckon the varmints have attacked the wagons. With only Pitkin, Gonzales, and old man Stubbs there for defense, there may be hell to pay."

"Don't forget those three Stubbs women," Vic said. "In a fight, I'd as soon be sided by any one of them, as Pitkin or Stubbs. Gonzales will do his part."

They galloped their horses back the way they had come, knowing there was little any of them could do. Gladstone Pitkin was on his own, with the Mexican cook, an unpredictable Levi Stubbs, and three women . . .

"Madre de Dios," Gonzales shouted, *"Indios."*

It was all the warning they would get, and all they needed. A dozen Comanches were less than half a mile distant, fanned out in a skirmish line. They were still out of range, but they came on, knowing there were few defenders.

"Get into the wagon," Pitkin ordered his daughters.

Nell and Naomi did, but only long enough to get their Winchesters. They were only too well aware that the Stubbs women already had their weapons in hand, waiting. Stubbs, for all his ignorance and mule-headedness, stood with his Winchester at the ready, and a grim look of determination on his craggy face. Whooping, the Comanches began circling the defenders. Each brave clung to the off-side of his horse, presenting no target. As they came within range, they began firing arrows under the necks of their horses. One of the deadly missiles buried itself in Nell Pitkin's left thigh, and she screamed. Pitkin killed the horse of the Indian who had fired the arrow, and when the Comanche fell free, Pitkin shot him. It set the tone for the fight, and the rest of the defenders began firing at the Indian horses. The Stubbs girls were firing as rapidly as they could pull the triggers, and none of the Comanches whose horses were shot escaped. Seven horses and seven men were down when the Indians gave up the attack. Bonita Stubbs leaned against a wagon wheel, the right side of her shirt bloody. Blood was rapidly soaking the leg of her Levi's. Her father stood there gripping his Winchester, staring at her. He swallowed hard, and despite her wound, Bonita laughed at him. It was Gladstone Pitkin who began giving orders.

"Gonzales, get a fire going and put on some water to boil. We must treat the wounds as best we can."

When Gavin and Vic caught up to Woody and the rest of the outfit, they were headed for camp at a fast gallop. Hearing Gavin and Vic coming, they slowed their horses until their comrades caught up. Quickly Gavin explained what had happened.

"No help for it," Woody said. "You did what you had to. The varmints didn't put all their eggs in one basket. They're attacking the camp, figurin' to buy themselves some time, in case their ambush failed."

"They figured right," said Nip Kelly. "They're likely to get clean away with the mules and horses, while we're ridin' back to camp."

"Maybe," Woody said, "but we can't ignore the possibility that some of our bunch has been wounded. Nobody there—except possibly Gonzales—is likely to know how to treat arrow wounds. We can't gamble somebody's life on mules and horses."

They rode into camp, all too aware of the dead horses

and Comanches. Nell Pitkin sat with her back to a wagon wheel, the shaft of the grisly arrow protruding from her hip. At the other end of the wagon sat Bonita Stubbs, bloody from waist to knees. Gonzales had a fire going and water heating. Gladstone Pitkin still held his Winchester in the crook of his arm, and it was obvious that he didn't know what to do next. He seemed about to speak, but one look at Woody changed his mind. Woody swung out of the saddle, his eyes on the white, pinched face of Nell Pitkin. He knelt beside her and she clung to him.

"That arrow will have to come out, *querido*," he said.

Vic had wasted no time in getting to Bonita. She tried to reassure him with a smile, but pain stole it from her pale lips, and she groaned. With trembling hands, Vic pulled the tail of her shirt free of her Levi's, exposing the wound. While the arrow hadn't remained, it had torn a ghastly wound in her side, and she was rapidly losing blood. Jania and Laketa hovered close, and old Levi Stubbs showed more concern than Vic had ever thought possible.

"What can we do for her?" Jania asked anxiously.

"Spread some blankets under one of your wagons," said Vic, "and take her there. We must stop the bleeding."

Meanwhile, Gladstone Pitkin had confronted Woody.

"Obviously, they have created this diversion so that they might escape with our mules and horses," Pitkin said.

"Obviously," said Woody, "but the wounded come first. That arrow must be removed from Nell's thigh, and Bonita's bleeding to death."

"I trust you have the knowledge and skill to treat such wounds," Pitkin said.

"I can remove the arrow from Nell's thigh and treat the wound," said Woody, "and I believe Vic intends to treat Bonita's wound. I'm going to ask Gavin to take the rest of the outfit and pursue those Comanches who have taken our horses and mules. Vic and me will follow, after we've seen to these wounds."

"Four men," Pitkin said. "That's scarcely enough."

"Six," said Wiley Stubbs. "Whit an' me are goin'."

"I'd go," Levi Stubbs said, "but I got no mount."

"Then stay here and guard the camp," said Woody. "Once we've taken care of these wounds, Vic and me will be needin' our horses."

Woody went to the chuck wagon, and without being asked, Gonzales passed him a quart bottle of whiskey. Woody returned to the Stubbs wagon where Nell waited. Helping her to her feet, he led her to the Pitkin wagon. Naomi was waiting.

"I've spread some blankets in the wagon," Naomi said.

"Help me get her in there," said Woody.

He let down the wagon's tailgate, untied the pucker, and with Naomi's help, moved the wounded Nell inside. Woody pulled the cork with his teeth and passed the open quart of whiskey to Nell.

"You'll have to drink about half that," Woody said. "It's whiskey. Likely not very good whiskey, but it'll knock you out long enough for me to rid you of that arrow."

"Why can't you just pull it out?" Naomi asked.

"There's a barb on the end of it," said Woody. "I'll have to drive it on through."

"Oh, God," Nell groaned, "I don't know if I can stand that."

"You'll have to," said Woody. "It's the only way. Now drink the whiskey."

She tried, but it gagged her. Again and again she tried, downing a little of it each time, until half the fiery brew had been consumed.

"Do you want me to remove her Levi's?" Naomi asked.

"Not until I've driven the arrow on through," said Woody. "Then we'll have to take them down to treat the wound."

Nell tried to laugh, but it dwindled off into a groan.

"Don't worry," Naomi said. "I'll see that he keeps his mind on removing the arrow."

When the whiskey took effect, Nell began snoring.

"This won't be easy to watch," said Woody.

"I'm sure it won't be," Naomi said, "but perhaps it's

something I need to know. I'll try to see it through."

Woody punched the shells out of his Colt. He then broke off the feathered end of the shaft and began the gruesome task of driving it the rest of the way through Nell's thigh. In short, rapid strokes he struck the broken shaft of the arrow with the butt of his Colt, and progress seemed agonizingly slow. Even with Nell unconscious, she grunted with pain each time the cruel barb advanced.

"My God," Naomi cried, "is there no other way?"

"None that I know of," said Woody.

He stopped to sleeve the sweat from his face and to dry his sweaty hands on the legs of his Levi's. Naomi's face was white, and her hands were clenched into fists, but when her eyes briefly met Woody's, she was shocked at what she saw. His hands were steady and sure, but there was pain and fear in his eyes. Kneeling beside him, she placed a hand on his shoulder, and he continued pounding the shaft of the arrow. Finally the cruel barb was driven through, and he was able to extract the arrow intact from the exit wound. He fell back, spent. It was a moment before he could speak.

"Now we'll have to remove her Levi's to get at the wound."

Realizing that Woody felt self-conscious, Naomi removed the Levi's. She then removed Nell's shirt.

"You didn't need to remove the shirt," said Woody.

"Why not?" Naomi replied. "She's in the wagon, and she's sweating terribly. I'll go for some hot water, so you can cleanse the wound. Do you need anything else?"

"No," said Woody. "I have the medicine chest, with disinfectant and bandages."

While she was gone, Woody took Nell's hand, and was surprised when she squeezed his own. Her eyelids fluttered and when she spoke, her voice was slow and slurred.

"Am I . . . drunk?"

"I'm afraid so," Woody said. "The hangover may be the worst of this whole ordeal."

"My . . . clothes," said Nell. "I . . . I'm naked."

"Naomi took them off," Woody said, "but you're in the

wagon. There's nobody but me. Naomi's gone for some hot water to cleanse your wound."

"The arrow's gone, then?"

"Yes," said Woody, "but you'll be almighty sore for a few days, and there may be infection tonight. If there is, you'll have to drink more whiskey and sweat it out."

"Please," she shuddered, "no more whiskey."

"Here's the hot water," said Naomi, passing him the wooden bucket. "Do you want me to stay out of there, out of the way?"

"Yes," Nell said. "You stripped me naked and left me alone with him. The least you can do is close the wagon flap and wait outside."

"Nell," said Gladstone Pitkin, "I will not tolerate such disgraceful carrying on."

"Father," Naomi said, "the arrow has been removed, but she's delirious. Please leave her alone until she's feeling better."

Woody squeezed Nell's hand and climbed out of the wagon. Pitkin had followed Naomi and stood behind her, looking concerned.

"She'll be all right, Pit," said Woody. "When Vic's taken care of Bonita to his satisfaction, we'll catch up to Gavin and the others."

Woody found Vic buttoning Bonita's shirt over a massive bandage that he had wound about her middle.

"I got the bleedin' stopped," Vic said. "I want her to stay here in our camp until she feels like bein' up and about."

"Fine with me," said Woody. "Have Jania and Laketa stay with her. You and me have to catch up to Gavin and the rest of the outfit."

Vic found Jania and Laketa. He expected an argument from their father, when he asked the girls to stay with Bonita, but Stubbs said nothing. Woody already had their horses saddled, and soon they were galloping away to the south.

Miles ahead, Gavin and his five companions reached the place where the Comanches had staged the ambush. Not surprisingly, the bodies of the dead had been taken away.

"Well, that cost 'em a little time," Nip Kelly said.

"But not nearly enough," said Gavin. "When we pick up their trail again, maybe we'll have some better idea as to how many of 'em we're up against."

"I'd say there's a substantial war party," Rusty observed. "We've accounted for four who aimed to ambush us, and seven more was gunned down when they attacked the camp. If they've gathered all the mules belongin' to Pitkin and Stubbs, as well as the extra horses in our remuda, that's more than thirty animals. They ain't used to Indians, and if I'm any judge, they'll be ornery as hell."

"All the better for us if they are," said Gavin.

"Maybe if they have enough trouble drivin' the horses an' mules, they won't bother layin' another ambush," Whit Stubbs said hopefully.

Ash Pryor laughed. "Don't we wish? A Comanche never gets too busy for that."

"We oughta be seein' Vic and Woody pretty soon," said Nip.

"Don't count on it," Gavin said. "Woody's got something up his sleeve. We'll just ride careful with our guns ready."

Woody and Vic had ridden southeast, following the Arkansas. Woody eventually reined up. Vic looked at him questioningly.

"When we left their trail this mornin', those Comanches was pretty well followin' the Arkansas," said Woody. "Can you think of any reason for 'em to change direction?"

"No," Vic replied. "The Arkansas runs clean through Indian Territory and it's a ready source of water. If they're bound for the Territory, why shouldn't they follow the river?"

"My thinkin', exactly," said Woody, "and don't you reckon they'll know Gavin and the rest of our outfit are trailin' 'em?"

"Damn right they'll know," Vic said. "Hell, they not only took the mules that's needed for the wagons, they got every horse we owned, except the eight that was saddled. What are you leadin' up to, *amigo*?''

"Suppose we ride due south, stayin' well to the west of the Arkansas?'' said Woody. "While those Comanches are worryin' with Gavin and his riders on their back-trail, we'll get ahead of them and do a little bushwhacking of our own.''

Vic laughed. "Pard, you're one to ride the river with. But won't Gavin be sendin' two advance riders—or maybe goin' himself—to look for an ambush?''

"No," said Woody, "because I told him not to. He'll ride careful, his riders with their guns ready.''

"Then let's ride like hell,'' Vic said. "We got to head this bunch off before dark.''

In the Pitkin camp, Gladstone Pitkin stood on the bank of the river, looking anxiously toward the southeast. While his faith in his outfit hadn't wavered, he feared the time they had lost returning to camp might have given the Comanches enough of an edge to escape with the horses and mules to Indian Territory.

"How do you feel, Bonita?'' Jania asked.

"Sore,'' said Bonita. "Where's Vic?''

"Him and Woody rode after the Comanches that took our mules,'' Jania said. "Did you think he was going to stay here with you, while his friends fought Indians?''

"I thought he might,'' said Bonita, "since the two of you stripped me naked. Why, for God's sake? The wound is in my side.''

Laketa laughed. "You were bloody to your knees. How could we know you hadn't been wounded somewhere down there? You never said anything.''

Bonita blushed furiously.

"Tell me what Woody did while I was unconscious,'' Nell begged. "How did he remove the arrow from my leg?''

"He drove it on through with the butt of his pistol,'' said Naomi. "I suppose it's a terrible thing to say, but I envied you.''

"My God,'' Nell said. "Why?''

"There was pain and fear in his eyes," said Naomi. "Each time he struck the shaft of that arrow, he was hurting for you. Dear God, I wish I could be sure that Gavin feels all that strongly about me."

Nell laughed. "He was overwhelmed, seeing me stark naked."

"You little fool," Naomi said scornfully. She climbed over the wagon's tailgate and walked away.

"We've come a good twenty miles," said Vic, when they reined up to rest the horses.

"Still not far enough," Woody said. "They got more than six hours on us."

"Another ten miles, then," said Vic.

"At least that," Woody agreed. "Let's ride."

Half a dozen miles to the northwest, on the bank of the Arkansas, Gavin and his five riders were resting their mounts.

"If we don't end this chase 'fore sundown," said Nip, "we'll lose 'em. This country's so flat, they can ride all night, ambushin' us anytime they take a notion."

"Likely that's what they have in mind," Gavin said. "If they can hold out until after dark, they can wait until we're right on top of 'em, without bein' seen."

"From their tracks," said Wiley, "they ain't more'n a dozen. Why don't we git as near as we kin, and rush the varmints?"

"No," Gavin said. "There's a better, safer way. We'll get within sight of them, if we can, and we'll attack when the time comes. You'll know when."

They rode on, and when the sun wasn't more than two hours high, they could see the horses and mules topping a distant rise.

"Thirteen riders pushin' 'em," said Nip. "An unlucky number."

"Unlucky for them," Gavin said. "They're just tryin' to stay ahead of us until dark. We'll keep them in sight for a while."

Woody and Vic rode eastward until they reached the Arkansas.

"No tracks," said Woody. "We're ahead of them."

"You aim for us to ride into 'em, headlong?" Vic asked.

"No," said Woody. "We can't be that far ahead. There's no real cover, so we'll picket our horses on this side of that ridge over yonder. When the horses and mules cross that ridge, we'll cut loose, stampedin' 'em right back into those Comanches. By now, Gavin and the rest of the outfit should be close enough to attack."

"Most of 'em will cut and run," Vic said, "but they can't take the horses and mules with 'em."

"Don't sell Gavin and the outfit short," said Woody. "There'll be some confusion, and it should buy them enough time to get within range before the Comanches can run for it. They've already lost eleven men. If we can account for half of what's left, they won't come after us again."

"It'll be just a hell of a lot more dangerous for us," Vic said, "but we'd better picket our horses another mile downriver and hoof it back to here. A nickerin' horse—be it one of ours, or one of the bunch the Comanches are drivin'—could warn the varmints. Then they could stampede the horses and mules in our direction, catchin' us afoot and with six of 'em to one of us."

"I never pass up good advice," said Woody, "and I reckon you're a mite ahead of my thinkin'. You're right. We'll picket our horses downriver far enough so they don't give us away. Come on."

Picketing the horses, Vic and Woody hadn't been in their former positions more than a few minutes when the first of the horses and mules topped the ridge. Both men ran forward, firing their Winchesters. Horses nickered, mules brayed, and the entire lot of them stampeded back the way they had come. With the high banks of the Arkansas to their right, the only logical path of escape was to the south, and the Comanches broke for it. But with the first rattle of gunfire, Gavin and his riders kicked their mounts into a fast gallop, bringing them within range of the fleeing Comanches.

"Cut them down," Gavin shouted.

10

Nine of the surprised Comanches escaped to the south. Gavin and his riders had all the horses and mules gathered by the time Woody and Vic got to their picketed horses and rode back to meet their comrades.

"Woody," said Gavin, "you and Vic done that just right. It was as slick a piece of work as I ever seen. I reckon them nine that escaped will be thinkin' of us as bad medicine from now on."

"It all depended on you gents bein' right behind 'em," Woody said, "and we're obliged to you for bein' there. Are all the horses and mules accounted for?"

"Every last one," said Gavin.

"If we move fast, we can get them back to camp before dark," Woody said. "We'll go after the herd tomorrow."

"They ain't scattered all that much," said Nip. "There's pretty good graze and plenty of water. You got to drive a longhorn away from that."

They drove the horses and mules hard, reaching camp just minutes before dark. Gladstone Pitkin shouted and waved his hat, and even Levi Stubbs seemed pleased.

"Supper be ready," Gonzales said.

"We'll unsaddle our horses and eat," said Woody. "First and second watches as usual. There shouldn't be any more Indian trouble, but all of you keep your guns handy and don't let your guard down for a second."

"You want Whit an' me to stand watch with you?" Wiley Stubbs asked.

"You're welcome to," said Woody. "One of you on each watch. Leave your mules with our mules and horse remuda. Might as well join us for supper too."

Woody caught Gladstone Pitkin's eye, but the Englishman still seemed elated over the return of the horses and mules. While everybody else got in line for supper, Woody and Vic had more important things in mind. Woody headed for the Pitkin wagon, while Vic made a similar move toward the Stubbs wagon. Bonita still lay under the wagon, but had been covered with blankets. Obviously she slept, but Jania and Laketa were there.

"How is she?" Vic asked.

"Feverish," said Jania. "Gonzales brought us a bottle of whiskey, and we've been forcing her to swallow it."

"Good," Vic said. "I'm on the second watch, and I'll be lookin' in on her, if you and Laketa need to get some sleep."

"We've dozed some during the day," said Laketa. "We'll sit up with her. But please do come around when you can. When she's awake, she's asking for you."

"I'll be around as often as I can," Vic said, pleased.

Woody found Naomi sitting on the wagon's lowered tailgate. Anticipating his question, she answered it before he could say a word.

"She has a temperature. I've been giving her whiskey, and she's been giving me hell. She's throwing off the blankets faster than I can cover her."

"I'm on watch until midnight," Woody said. "I'll watch her the rest of the night, while you sleep."

"I know how you feel," said Naomi, "but you've had a long day. I'll sit up with her, and you can look in on her as often as you like."

"I'm obliged," Woody said.

It was still light enough for him to see her eyes, and she beheld him with a softness he had never noticed before. He could hear Nell's ragged breathing, and he looked into the wagon. She had flung the blankets aside, and he could see where her wound had bled into the white bandage. He swallowed hard and was about to turn away, when Naomi put her hand on his arm.

"Woody . . ." her voice broke and trailed off.

"Yes?" said Woody.

"Sometimes . . . we have hard words, but she's my sister, and I . . . I care. I watched your eyes while you were . . . working . . . over her. Thank you, Woody, for . . . caring . . ."

A lump rose in Woody's throat and he found himself at a loss for words. He then did what seemed the most natural thing in the world. He kissed Naomi on the cheek and went to supper . . .

Two hours into the first watch, Woody took the time to ask about Bonita Stubbs.

"She's feverish," Laketa said. "Gonzales brought us a bottle of whiskey, and we've had a terrible time getting it down her."

"I know it's vile stuff," said Woody, "but we have nothing else to break that fever."

"Vic," said a sleepy voice from beneath the wagon, "Vic."

"She's out of her head," Laketa said, embarrassed.

"Maybe not as much as you think," said Woody, touched by the urgency in Bonita's voice. "Vic's on the second watch, startin' at midnight, so you'll be seein' him. Maybe her fever will be broken by then. Keep givin' her the whiskey, and keep the blankets on her."

"We will," Laketa said, "and thank you."

Woody returned to his position on the first watch, more impressed than ever by the three Stubbs girls. He even sympathized with Whit and Wiley. They weren't a bad lot, if one overlooked Levi Stubbs for the cantankerous old varmint he was.

"Almighty quiet tonight," said Gavin.

"Yeah," Nip said. "Makes you wonder why."

"Cut it out," said Woody. "We spent the whole damn day hunting, chasing, and shooting Comanches. Tomorrow, we have to round up the herd. We don't have the time for anything else."

"I'm almighty glad of that," Gavin said. "After a day like we just had, wrasslin' cows is a Sunday-school picnic. How is Nell?"

"Feverish," said Woody. "Naomi's with her, giving her whiskey."

"I reckon we can handle this watch, if you'd like to set with her a while," Nip said.

"I'm obliged, Nip," said Woody, "but Naomi's agreed to stay with her tonight. I'll go look in on her again at the end of the watch, and I aim to spread my bedroll close by, so Naomi can wake me, if she needs to."

A few minutes before the end of the first watch, Woody wasn't surprised to see Vic making his way to the Stubbs wagon.

"She's still feverish, Vic," Jania said, "but she's awake."

"I'll talk to her, then," said Vic.

Bonita had thrown off the blankets to her waist, and removing his hat, Vic was able to hunker down beside her, beneath the wagon.

"*Querida*," Vic said, "you're sweatin' out a fever. You ought to stay under all them blankets. This night air won't help."

"But I am so hot," said Bonita. "Feel my face."

Vic did, and his heart leaped, for there was a dampness.

"You're beginnin' to sweat, babe," Vic said. "Your fever's broke."

"No more whiskey?"

Vic laughed. "No more whiskey, unless you need some for the hangover."

Forgetting Jania and Laketa, he kissed her and she returned it.

"Tomorrow I can get up," said Bonita.

"Not so fast," Vic said. "Tomorrow we have to round

up the herd, and you're going to lay right here and rest. Get up too soon, and that wound can bust loose and start to bleed some more. You want to do this all over again, whiskey and all?''

"My God, no," said Bonita.

"Rest, then," Vic said. "I'm on watch until dawn. Jania and Laketa will be with you, and I'll be lookin' in on you as often as I can."

At the end of his watch, Woody made his way to the Pitkin wagon. Naomi sat with her back to a wagon wheel, head bowed, asleep. Woody looked into the wagon, and Nell still lay there without the blankets. Trying not to disturb Naomi, Woody climbed into the wagon and knelt beside Nell. She seemed to be breathing more normally, and her face felt cool to his touch. Silently she took his hand in both of hers.

"Your fever's gone," he said softly.

"I know," she replied. "I've been waiting for you. Where's Naomi?"

"Asleep," said Woody. "She must be exhausted. Do you want me to fetch you a pot, a bucket, or . . ."

She laughed, sensing his embarrassment.

"It's too late for that. Fortunately, the bottom of this wagon box has cracks in it, but it also has splinters, some of which are in my behind. When I raise up some, see if you can get one of those blankets under me."

Woody managed to get one of the blankets between her and the wooden floor of the wagon box. He tried to cover her with another of the blankets, but she wouldn't have it.

"I've sweated so much and feel so dirty, I'd like to jump in the river," she said.

"Don't you dare," said Woody. "Remember, you can't swim."

"Whatever gave you that idea?" she asked. "I swim like a fish, and so can Naomi."

"But you . . ." Woody's voice trailed off.

"Oh, that," said Nell. "I'd forgotten about the river at Council Grove."

"Damn it," Woody said, "you scared hell out of Gavin and me for nothing."

"*Was* it for nothing?" she whispered, still holding his hand in both of hers.

Finally it all dawned on him, and he laughed.

"I heard that," said Naomi, from outside the wagon. "Nell, you promised."

"I suppose I did," Nell replied. "But Woody won't tell Gavin, will you, Woody?"

"Hell, yes," said Woody. "If he's asleep, I'll wake him. We both got snookered."

Naomi sighed. "I suppose there's no help for it. It was a dishonest thing to do."

"Aw, hell," Woody said, "if you want Gavin to know, tell him yourself. It's generally the last draw that counts, and I reckon old Gavin come out as much a winner as I did. I'd say he's waitin' for me to say good night. Then he'll be around to see how Nell's feeling."

Nell laughed. "He'll be around to see how Naomi's feeling. When will I see you again, Woody?"

"Tomorrow," said Naomi. "He's had a long day. He'll be around before breakfast to pull the splinters out of your behind. Won't you, Woody?"

"Sorry," Woody said. "As much as I'd like to, I'll have to pass. There's cows to be gathered. Take care of those splinters for me, Naomi, and try not to leave any scars."

With that, he was gone. Naomi waited a moment longer before she spoke.

"You don't *really* have splinters in your bottom, do you?"

"Of course not," said Nell. "Whatever gave you that idea?"

Breakfast was ready well before first light. Woody spent a few minutes with Nell, and Vic enjoyed a similar time with Bonita. By the time the first rays of the morning sun crept over the eastern horizon, Woody and the outfit had begun rounding up the scattered longhorns. Nip Kelly's prediction

proved accurate, and none of the cattle had strayed any farther from the river than was necessary to find good graze.

"After the day we had yesterday," Rusty said, "we deserve a break, and it looks like we're about to get it. We'll
have this herd together before sundown."

"It's lookin' good," Woody agreed. "We'll ride downstream for as far as we can see any cows, and then haze
'em back this way. Then we'll run a tally, learn how many
we're short, and the real gather begins."

The obvious place for most of the cattle was the south
bank, and they concentrated all their efforts in that direction.
When they had ridden five miles, and saw no more cattle,
they began pushing the grazing remnants of the herd westward, along the Arkansas. Once they were within several
miles of their camp, they bunched the newly gathered herd.

"We'll run some tallies," Woody said. "Rusty, Gavin,
and Vic."

Though they had no interest in the herd, Wiley and Whit
Stubbs had ridden along on the gather. They watched with
interest as the cowboys ran their tallies.

"Twenty-seven hundred," Rusty said.

"Twenty-six fifty," said Gavin.

"Twenty-seven seventy-five," Vic announced.

"We'll call it twenty-seven hundred," said Woody.
"That means there's eight hundred of the varmints somewhere along this river."

"At least, we hope that's where they are," Nip said.

"We'll search the north bank," said Woody. "There's
plenty of shallows where they could have crossed."

"With graze over here," Whit said, "why would they
cross?"

"Texas longhorns are strange critters," said Ash. "They
like to drink from the water they're standin' in. When they
decide to climb out, they ain't smart enough to go back the
way they waded in. That brings 'em out on the opposite
bank."

"I hope that holds true in this case," Gavin said.
"There's no cover, no place for them to hide. If we don't

find 'em on the other side, then we got our work cut out for us.''

"There's some ridges," said Woody, "and there's generally good graze at the foot of them. We'll find some of 'em there, where we can't see 'em from the river. Let's ride.''

They crossed the Arkansas, riding north, and somewhere ahead, a cow bawled. Reaching the crest of a low ridge, they reined up. There they found the missing cattle had been gathered, and eight mounted men waited.

"Trouble," said Gavin.

"Maybe," Woody said. "All of you keep your Colts handy and follow my lead."

They rode down the ridge, reining up twenty yards shy of the mounted men.

"Howdy," said Woody. "I see you've gathered the rest of our herd."

The eight riders were all armed, and the one who trotted his horse to the forefront carried twin Colts in a *buscadera* rig. He laughed, and then he spoke.

"Pilgrim, we rounded up these cows grazin' free, and that makes 'em ours. Unless you got some proof, otherwise.''

"We have the rest of the herd," said Woody. "They were stampeded by Comanches. All these animals you've gathered are branded Circle Five. That's our brand, registered in Texas.''

The two-gun man laughed. "You ain't in Texas, an' we're contestin' your claim. Now, if these critters was in Texas, they'd be worth maybe ten dollars apiece, on the hoof. Just to prove we're reasonable hombres, we're willin' to take ten dollars a head. There's a few more than eight hunnert, and we'll throw in the extry ones for free.''

"As far as you're concerned," said Woody, "we're taking them all for free. They're not yours to sell.''

It was an ultimatum no Western man could ignore or fail to understand. The two-gun man drew, but he wasn't quick enough. Woody Miles drew and shot him out of the saddle.

Just as suddenly, the rest of Woody's outfit had flaming Colts in their hands. It began and ended in half a second. Two of the outlaws escaped, riding for their lives. The rest lay dead or dying.

"Great God Almighty," said Wiley Stubbs.

The Stubbs brothers stared at the dead men in dismay, cutting their eyes back to their companions who were calmly reloading their revolvers.

"We can use those extra horses," Woody said. "Let's round them up and move these cows across the river."

Quickly they caught up the horses belonging to the dead outlaws. They then drove the newly acquired horses and the eight hundred cows across the Arkansas. With the longhorn herd again intact, they drove them upriver, beyond their camp, to the nearest graze. The sun was two hours high when Woody reported to Gladstone Pitkin.

"Commendable, Woody," Pitkin said. "Commendable. I thought I heard shooting."

"You did," said Woody. "Some outlaws had gathered part of the herd. We persuaded them to return them to us. We'll be ready to move out tomorrow at first light."

Woody found Nell hobbling around, despite the wound in her thigh, refusing to spend another minute in the wagon. Vic found Bonita just as determined. While she was weak, her wound had been tended and bound, and she was on her feet. Gonzales prepared supper an hour early, and there was jubilation within the camp.

"Pit," said Woody, "before dark, let's have another look at the trail map."

Pitkin spread the map on the wagon's tailgate, and they studied the trail ahead.

"Looks like we'll reach the main fork of the Arkansas just before we reach Pawnee Rock," Woody said. "If the map's accurate, we should be following the Arkansas beyond Fort Dodge, to the point where we enter the desert. The *Jornada*."

Far to the west, there was lightning. The wind had died away to nothing, and the heat seemed oppressive. It was then and there that man and beast became acquainted with the buffalo gnat.*

"Dear God," said Naomi Pitkin, "I'm familiar with mosquitos, but I've never seen any insect as vicious as these small black ones. What are they?"

"Buffalo gnats," Nip Kelly replied, swatting at a swarm of them attacking his face. "I have never experienced them until now, but I've heard it said they can drive horses, mules, and cows mad. They've been known to cause stampedes."

"I've heard that too," said Woody.

"Hell, we'll all be up with the herd tonight," Vic said. "There won't be no sleepin', with these little varmints chawin' on us."

"They ain't satisfied just eatin' on your hands and face," said Rusty. "They've sneaked up my shirt sleeves and britches legs, and they're just hangin' on. I wonder would it help if I dunked myself in the river?"

Nip Kelly laughed. "For a few minutes maybe, but soon as you got out, they'd all be after you again. You can't spend the night in the river."

"This will be our third night here," said Gladstone Pitkin. "Where have they been until now?"

"I have no idea," Woody said.

"I think it's got something to do with the weather," said Nip. "There's not a breath of air stirring tonight."

Darkness was only minutes away, and the two or three cows that had begun bawling had been joined by many others. They stood there shaking their heads and switching their tails, as swarms of buffalo gnats attacked them. Mules brayed and horses nickered in pain and frustration, as they suffered attacks by armies of vicious insects against which they had no defense.

"Come on, first watch," Woody said. "We're in for a night of it."

---

* The buffalo gnat was a small black insect that drove humans and animals half mad with pain and aggravation. Their bites caused intense irritation and swelling.

After supper Vic had spent some time with Bonita, and eventually, Jania and Laketa joined them. Sleep being out of the question, Rusty and Ash wandered over, as well.

"I've never been so miserable in my life," said Bonita. "These gnats are hurting me as bad or worse than my wound ever did."

"They're up the legs of my Levi's," Laketa said, "all the way to my . . ."

Her voice trailed off in embarrassment, and she laughed nervously. "They're chewing on mine, too," Jania said.

"I'll get some piggin' string," said Rusty. "Maybe if we tied it around our legs, above our boot tops . . ."

"Too late," Vic said. "The varmints is already up to my belt, and another herd of 'em is headed up my shirt sleeves. I had me a case of cooties one time, and they wasn't near as bad as these damn gnats."

"You'll have to excuse his language, ladies," said Ash. "He gets a mite carried away, sometimes."

"He'll have to come up with stronger words than that, before the night's over," Bonita said. "I'm ready to learn them myself."

Jania laughed. "You already know them all. I've heard you get a mad on."

"What are cooties?" Laketa wondered.

"Body lice," said Ash helpfully. "They bite somethin' awful, and they get together any place you got hair."

They all looked at Vic, and when he became embarrassed, they laughed.

"Damn it," Vic snorted, "it ain't funny when a man's itchin' in places where it purely ain't polite to scratch."

The longhorns continued to bawl their misery, refusing to lie down. Woody, Gavin, Nip Kelly, and Wiley Stubbs circled the herd, as well as the mules and the horse remuda. Finally, as it grew late, there was a light breeze from the west, and it lessened the massive hordes of buffalo gnats. The longhorns bedded down for the night, while the horses and mules seemed more resigned to their lot. The men on watch dismounted, unsaddled their weary horses, and allowed the animals to roll. When the first watch ended, Woody took the time to say goodnight to Nell, and found her with Naomi and Gavin.

"I reckon I'll just set here the rest of the night," said Gavin. "There ain't a place on me I ain't been bit a hundred times by them damn buffalo gnats."

Woody laughed. "The sound of your scratchin' is likely to keep Naomi awake."

"No chance of that," said Naomi. "I'll be scratching too."

"Nell's got a sore leg," Woody said. "Why don't the two of you take a walk?"

"Nell," said Gavin, "are you sure you're ready to be alone with this cow-nursin' Texas varmint?"

"I think so," Nell said. "I've already been alone with him, stark naked. Naomi can't say the same for you."

"Oh?" said Naomi. "How would you know? You were drunk all night and part of a day."

"Come on, Naomi," Gavin said, embarrassed.

Naomi laughed and followed him into the darkness, toward the river.

Thanks to the buffalo gnats, Vic had slept little, and before it was time for him to begin the second watch, he sought out Bonita. He found her awake, alone, and expecting him.

"The buffalo gnats finally let up on us," she said, "so Jania and Laketa are sleeping."

"And you should be," said Vic.

She laughed. "Not yet. I haven't seen you since supper, and I knew you'd be here."

"I reckon I'm a predictable varmint."

"Come sit beside me. Thanks to those gnats, I'm itching in places I can't reach."

"I know the feeling," Vic said. "How about your wound?"

"Sore as all get out, but with all these gnats biting me, I forgot everything else."

Unlike the rest of the outfit, Vic tended to be shy, even

with Bonita, and the silence became embarrassingly long. Suddenly she leaned over and kissed him.

"Why did you do that?" he asked.

"Two reasons," said Bonita. "Because I wanted to, and because you seem to be afraid of me. When I was hurt, you undressed me, tended my wound, and it didn't bother you. I'm the same as I was then, except more interested in you. Why are you afraid of me? Is it because the others—the men—have been making jokes?"

"No," Vic said, "they'd never do that. They're my pards. It's . . . somethin' else . . ."

"Tell me."

"No," said Vic. "You'd just laugh."

"I promise I won't."

"There was this girl . . . I wasn't more than a kid . . . and I liked her a lot. But there was others that she run around with, and they didn't like me. Well, they put her up to flirtin' with me, and damn fool that I was, I took her serious. When I made a big play for her, they all laughed in my face, includin' her."

"How terribly cruel," said Bonita. "How could she live with herself? I'm flattered by your interest in me."

"You are?"

"Yes," Bonita said. "Please don't be afraid of me. I realize it isn't easy for us to be together, on the trail like this. You have part of the responsibility for the herd, and I . . . well, there's Paw. The burr under his tail gets bigger every day, and I just can't get over the feeling that . . . something . . . will happen before we reach Santa Fe. I'd just . . . like to be happy . . . for a little while. Then if I . . . I lose it, at least I'll have the memory . . . of what it was like . . ."

Her voice trailed off into a sob, and she wept as though her heart were broken. She needed very little encourage ment, and when Vic put his arms around her, she leaned on him until no tears remained. Her hopelessness, the wistfulness in her voice, overcame Vic Brodie's shyness, and he began talking to her.

"Whatever happens between here and Santa Fe, I'll side you," he said. "Even if I have to quit the drive to do it."

"Oh, no," she cried, "I wouldn't want you to do that. These men are your friends, and you have an obligation to Mr. Pitkin."

"Because these hombres are my friends, they'd understand," said Vic, "and while I've hired on to help Pitkin build a ranch, he don't own me. I'd fold my hand and throw it all down for you, if you'll have me."

She wept again, and it was a while before she could speak. When she finally did, he had to lean close to hear.

"I want you, Vic, but we have no privacy here, and this isn't the time or the place for me to prove it. I can only be as honest with you as you've been with me. I fear that we won't be allowed to travel beyond Fort Dodge."

"Why?" Vic demanded. "What's in these wagons?"

"Whiskey," said Bonita. "Barrels and barrels of trade whiskey."

Vic laughed. "There's no law against that, Bonita, unless he aims to sell it to Indians, and the military at Fort Dodge won't have any proof of that."

"It's not just that," Bonita said. "Paw once rode with Quantrill, and after Quantrill was killed, the remnants of his outfit stole two army payrolls. Those payrolls were never recovered, and the government's been watching Paw. That's why we're bound for Santa Fe."

"So they think your paw knows where those stolen payrolls are," said Vic. "Why him?"

"He's the only one of that particular bunch that's still alive," Bonita said, "and they're convinced he knows where that gold is."

"And you think so too," said Vic.

"Yes," Bonita replied. "I think the barreled whiskey's just an excuse to quit Missouri. I also think—although I have no proof—that in one or more of those barrels, there's near fifty thousand dollars in gold."

11

Whit Stubbs was on the second watch with Rusty, Vic, and Ash. Not until Whit took the time to go to the bushes did Vic get a chance to relate what Bonita had told him about Levi Stubbs and the expected difficulty at Fort Dodge.

"So she thinks the whole family's likely to be placed under military arrest," Vic said.

"That don't seem right," said Rusty. "Did she say anything about Wiley and Whit bein' involved?"

"No," Vic replied. "She didn't say anything about Jania and Laketa either, and I was so shook, I didn't think to ask."

"My guess is, old Levi's guilty as hell," said Ash, "but I don't believe the others are. Whatever happens to Levi, Wiley, and Whit, we got to save the girls."

"I already promised to stand by Bonita," Vic said, "even if it means quittin' the drive and quittin' Pitkin."

"I'm makin' Jania the same promise," said Ash.

"Then I can't do any less for Laketa," Rusty said.

"Whoa," said Vic. "You can't say nothin' to Jania or Laketa until I talk to Bonita. She may be wise to somethin' the others don't know."

"When Whit gets back," Rusty said, "you take a trip to the bushes. Talk to Bonita again, even if you got to wake her. If everything does go to hell when we reach the fort, I think Jania and Laketa ought to be as sure of Ash and me as Bonita is of you.''

"I reckon you're right," said Vic. "I'll talk to her again.''

As quietly as he could, Vic crept to the wagon under which Bonita slept. Jania and Laketa slept under the next wagon, a few feet away. To Vic's surprise, Bonita was awake, and sat up.

"Vic?''

"Quiet," Vic hissed. "I need to talk to you some more.''

"Then lie down beside me," said Bonita, "and speak softly.''

Quickly, quietly, Vic explained his need to talk, of the stand Rusty and Ash had taken for Jania and Laketa.

"They just want Jania and Laketa to know they won't be alone, if there's a showdown at Fort Dodge. They aim to stand up for Jania and Laketa just like I'll stand up for you, but we didn't know if they're as savvy as you about . . . your paw . . . and the stolen payrolls.''

"They share my suspicions," Bonita said. "They just haven't had the chance to talk as much as I have, thanks to that Comanche arrow. I think perhaps they're a little afraid that none of you would have us, if you knew who Paw is, and what he's done.''

"Wrong," said Vic. "We're all the more anxious to help you. Now will you tell Jania and Laketa we all know about the possible trouble at Fort Dodge, and that we'll stand by the three of you?''

"Yes," said Bonita, "I'll tell them. I'll tell them tonight.''

"Do it," Vic said. "Rusty and Ash will likely be here sometime before dawn, and they want to be sure the girls know where they stand, before they say anything.''

"What are you two whispering about?" Laketa asked.

"Oh, God," said Bonita, "they've been listening to every word we said.''

"We heard you whispering," Jania complained, "but we

couldn't understand the words. The least you could have done was whisper a little louder."

"Come on over here, both of you," said Bonita. "Vic's brought messages for you from Rusty and Ash. And be quiet."

"I got to get back to the herd," Vic said.

It was a while before he was able to convey the message to Rusty and Ash, and after he had, they resolved to talk to Jania and Laketa at the end of their watch.

"Head 'em up, move 'em out," Woody shouted.

The herd moved on, trailed by the horse remuda and the two wagons. Behind them rattled the three Stubbs wagons. Woody rode far ahead, not to search for water, but to look for Indian sign. Cow Creek, according to Pitkin's map, was twenty miles distant, and just beyond that, they would reach the Grand Arkansas. The land became more verdant, and buffalo wallows—some thirty feet across—stood full of water. Woody rode on, finding level plain except for occasional drop-offs into the unused buffalo wallows. Obviously, some of the lightning they had witnessed had been accompanied by rain a few miles ahead of them. When Woody reached Cow Creek, he found it running bank-full. He rode downstream a mile and upstream two miles, without finding a place the wagons might cross without considerable work. He found no tracks except those of animals. Almost under the hooves of his horse, a covey of quail whirred into the air. According to what Woody had learned at Council Grove, once they reached the valley of the Arkansas, they would be two hundred and sixty-five miles from Independence. The Santa Fe Trail would then follow the Grand Arkansas one hundred and twenty-two miles, to the Cimarron Crossing. There they must leave the river, where the treacherous Desert Route would lead them in a more southwesterly direction. Woody watered his horse and rode back to meet the oncoming herd. He had nothing unusual to report, but he trotted his horse aside until the drag had passed. He then fell in alongside Pitkin's wagon. Nell smiled at him from the wagon box, for she had taken his advice and stayed out of the saddle. Her horse trotted behind the wagon on a lead rope. Naomi and Gavin rode drag.

"The trail ahead looks good," Woody reported, "but there's lots of buffalo wallows, some of 'em deep enough to topple a wagon. We'll have to cross Cow Creek, and it's got mostly high banks. There's been recent rain ahead of us, and the creek's running bank-full. We may have to use shovels and dig down the banks for a crossing for the stock as well as the wagons."

"If that's what we must do, then so be it," said Pitkin. "Are we moving at a gait that is rapid enough for us to reach Cow Creek today?"

"I think so," Woody replied, "but if we can't, we can make do. Most buffalo wallows are standing full of water, and we can use what's in our barrels for drinking and cooking."

Woody rode on ahead of the herd and took up the point position. There was almost no dust, the herd was behaving well, and riding drag was pleasant enough for Gavin and Naomi. They rode their horses close enough that they might talk, and Gavin found Naomi much different. It seemed Nell's being wounded had been a sobering experience for both girls, and Gavin asked Naomi about it.

"I won't say it was a good thing, Nell being wounded," said Naomi, "but I think both of us learned from the experience. In England, women tend to lead passive lives, while the men go to sea, fight wars, duels, and the like. While Nell and I were firing at all those circling, shouting Indians, I felt what might have been my soul rise to new heights, and I wanted to shout. I have never felt more vibrant, more alive. Does that make sense?"

"It does to me," Gavin said. "You don't really appreciate life until you're living it on the very edge, until there's a very real chance it may be taken from you."

"Yes," said Naomi excitedly, "that's exactly how I felt. From what Nell's told me, she had the same feeling, even after she'd been hurt."

"Without danger, without risk," Gavin said, "we sometimes lose sight of our own mortality. Gettin' shot generally
brings the reality of it all back to us, pronto."

"I believe it was all coming home to me while I watched
Woody removing the arrow from Nell's leg," said Naomi.
"I have never seen so much compassion in a man's eyes,
but there was fear too. But he knew he could remove the
arrow. What was he afraid of?"

"Infection," Gavin said. "I've never known anybody to
die from it when there was plenty of whiskey, but there's
some that can't keep the whiskey down. When you're hurt
on the Western frontier, far from a doctor, death is always
near. Whether or not he goes away empty-handed often depends on the circumstances, maybe even luck. If that had
been you with an arrow in you, and I had been in Woody's
place, I'd have been afraid, just as he was. Nobody ever
takes a hand against death without considering that, on the
final, fatal draw, he may lose."

"Dear God, Gavin McCord, you're a philosopher. You
have looked into my very soul and described my feelings."

Gavin laughed. "I'm just a Texas cowboy that's done a
lot of livin' and seen my share of dying. I hope I never have
to remove an arrow or piece of lead from you."

"Not even if you were allowed to strip me naked?"

Gavin didn't respond, and for a long moment, he didn't
look at her. When he did, what she saw in his eyes shocked
her. She was immediately ashamed of herself, and tried to
make amends.

"Gavin, I'm sorry. That was a foolish, insensitive thing
for me to have said."

"It was," said Gavin. "If you were lying wounded,
maybe dying, that . . . what you just said . . . would be the
last thing to ever cross my mind."

"I know that," she said, her voice trembling. "Oh, God,
I'm so sorry. Can you ever forgive me?"

Tears ran down her cheeks. Finally he tilted his hat back
on his head and looked at her, and her heart leaped.

"Consider yourself forgiven, ma'am. In Texas, it ain't

the way of a man to strip his woman until he's got his brand on her. Diggin' out lead and Comanche arrows is the only exception.''

She laughed, he laughed with her, and the unpleasant moment ended.

''I'm almost afraid to open my mouth, after that,'' said Naomi. ''Tell me about gathering the herd, after the stampede. I heard Woody tell Father there was some trouble.''

''We were still missing eight hundred,'' Gavin said, ''and when we found them, there were eight men claiming them. They wanted to sell them to us at ten dollars a head, and we had to change their minds.''

''How did you manage that?''

''You don't want to know,'' Gavin said.

''Of course I do,'' said Naomi. ''If we're going to New Mexico Territory and I'm going to live on a cattle ranch, shouldn't I know as much about it as I can?''

''There are some things unfit for a woman's ears,'' Gavin replied.

''Not this woman's ears,'' said Naomi. ''In England maybe, but this isn't England, thank God.''

''Woody demanded that they give up the cows,'' Gavin said, ''and they refused. When the leader of the pack went for his gun, Woody shot him. Rusty, Vic, Ash, Nip, and me had to shoot five more, when they drew on us. Two of them ran for their lives, and we let them go. Now are you satisfied?''

''Yes,'' she said, in a small voice. ''You tried to spare me, and I wouldn't let you. Am I rebelling too much against an old English custom that so often has a woman seen, but seldom heard?''

Gavin shrugged. ''It all depends on how much you can take. I'll make a deal with you. Any time you resent not being exposed to the cold, hard facts—to the naked truth— just tell me. I'll lay it on you, no matter how raw it gets. *Comprender?*''

''I . . . I . . . yes,'' she replied.

Gavin said no more, and when Naomi looked at him, his

eyes seemed fixed on something only he could see. The drive moved on.

"We ain't gonna make it at this pace," said Nip Kelly, his eyes on the westering sun.

"I'll have to agree with you," Woody said. "I'll get the word to the rest of the outfit, and we'll push 'em harder."

Woody spoke to the flank and swing riders, and finally the drag riders. He then rode alongside Pitkin's wagon.

"We're steppin' up the pace, Pit," said Woody. "It's our only chance of makin' it to Cow Creek before dark."

Pitkin nodded, and Woody rode back to his point position. He could hear the bawling of the herd, as some of them protested the faster gait. The Stubbs wagons began falling behind.

"Damn 'em," Levi Stubbs shouted, "they're tryin' to kill our mules."

"They're tryin' to git to water before dark," Wiley said.

Wiley and Whit already had their teams neck-and-neck with Levi's, passing him when he refused to try and keep up with the Pitkin outfit. Only when he fell seriously behind did Stubbs call on his teams for more effort.

"Keep 'em moving," Woody shouted.

Their determination was rewarded when they reached the creek just as the sun had begun to paint the western sky with towering strokes of crimson. It was near dark when the three Stubbs wagons arrived. Supper was a jovial affair, for they had avoided another dry camp. Pitkin had studied the map while it was still light enough to see, and had found a definite camp they could logically reach the following day.

"Pawnee Rock," Pitkin said. "Where Walnut Creek flows into the Grand Arkansas. I am unable to understand the logic of the parties who drew this map. Cow Creek is a vital stop between the Little Arkansas and the Grand Arkansas, yet it does not appear on this map. However, Walnut Creek, which isn't all that necessary, is included."

"That's exactly why I believe in scouting ahead," said Woody, "even when the map says there's water. The only thing that looks fairly certain is the trail following the Arkansas, after we reach Pawnee Rock. Any idea how far it is from there to Fort Dodge?''

"There's no mileage figures on the map,'' Pitkin said, ''but I got some estimates from the storekeeper at Council Grove. Once we pick up the Grand Arkansas at Pawnee Rock, we'll be about a hundred miles from Fort Dodge. We'll reach Cimarron Crossing twenty-two miles beyond Fort Dodge. That's where we'll leave the Grand Arkansas and begin crossing the desert.''

"We'll be maybe two weeks following the Arkansas, then,'' Gavin said. ''That is, if we don't have any more Indian or outlaw trouble, and no more stampedes. Do you aim to lay over a day or two at Fort Dodge, Pit?''

"I haven't decided,'' said Pitkin. ''Woody, what do you think?''

"I think we should lay over an extra day, and meet with the post commander,'' said Woody. ''They'll have the telegraph, and maybe we can get some word as to conditions on the trail between Fort Dodge and Santa Fe.''

"So be it,'' Pitkin replied.

He didn't notice the looks of consternation on the faces of Rusty, Vic, and Ash. The three of them shared a single premonition. They recalled the disturbing things Bonita had told Vic about old Levi's past. An hour before the trio would begin the second watch, the three of them quietly approached the Stubbs wagon beneath which the three girls slept.

"Bonita?'' Vic said quietly.

"Here,'' said Bonita. ''We're still awake.''

The trio crept out from beneath the wagon so that the cowboys might kneel beside them. Rusty and Ash said nothing, allowing Vic to tell them of the proposed delay at Fort Dodge.

"If nothin' goes wrong,'' Vic concluded, ''we'll be there in maybe two more weeks. Has anything changed, after what you told me?''

"No," said Bonita. "We still don't have any proof of . . . what . . . we're most afraid of, and we still suspect that it may be true."

"We're fearful that if the army searches these wagons and finds . . . anything, they'll be angry enough to arrest all of us, along with Paw," Jania said.

"That don't make any sense to me," said Ash. "How can they hold a man's whole family responsible for somethin' he's done?"

"We don't know that such a thing is possible," Laketa said, "but we fear the worst. A few of the men who rode with Quantrill were captured. When they couldn't or wouldn't reveal any information about the stolen payrolls, their families suffered."

"Whatever your paw's done," said Rusty, "we won't stand by and see any of you mistreated. And I'm includin' Wiley and Whit."

"It's wonderful, knowing the three of you care enough to stand up for us," Bonita said. "That's one thing that's hurting us, the possibility that we may all be kept at Fort Dodge until the military chooses to let us go. Then we wouldn't be able to go on to Santa Fe with you. Now do you understand our feelings?"

"Yeah," said Vic, "and like I told you before, I'll quit Pitkin before I'll leave you at Fort Dodge."

"I'll be right behind you," Rusty said.

"So will I," said Ash. "We'll camp right there at Fort Dodge until they let all of you go, and we'll be raisin' hell all the while."

Despite their anxiety, the three women laughed at the deadly serious cowboys, and for the next few minutes, each man paired off with the girl of his choice for a short interval of privacy before the start of the second watch.

Pitkin had thoughtfully brought half a dozen long-handled spades. To avoid a possible lengthy search for low banks where the wagons might cross Cow Creek, the cowboys set out to lower the banks and create a crossing.

"Find a shallows with a solid bottom," Woody said. "Then we'll lower the banks."

Cow Creek wasn't wide, and there were places where it flowed shallow over stones. It was in just such a place that the men took turns manning the shovels, creating a decent slope down one bank and up the next. Wiley and Whit were there, taking their turns with the shovels.

"When we're done," Woody said, "we'll cross the herd and the horse remuda first, so they can pack down those banks hard enough that the wagons won't bog down."

It proved to be excellent strategy, and even the heavily loaded Stubbs wagons crossed without double-teaming. As had become his custom, Woody rode ahead, uncertain as to the distance to Pawnee Rock and the next water.

Pawnee Rock. June 25, 1869.

While at Council Grove, Woody had heard talk about Pawnee Rock. It had become the most famous landmark along the Santa Fe. Literally hundreds of travelers had carved their names into it. But he rode past Pawnee Rock almost without looking at it, for something more he had heard at Council Grove bothered him. The entire outfit had relished the idea that, once they passed Pawnee Rock and reached the Grand Arkansas, they would then be able to follow the river for some one hundred and twenty-two miles. There would be unlimited water all the way to the Cimarron Cutoff. But the old storekeeper at Council Grove had said something that had bothered Woody. He had said that the hundred and twenty-two–mile route along the Grand Arkansas to the Cimarron Cutoff didn't actually follow the river. Instead, while it paralleled the Arkansas, it was sometimes as far as ten miles from the river, following less hazardous terrain.

When Woody reached the point where Walnut Creek flowed into the Arkansas, he rode on along the river until he came to what obviously was a fork in the trail. Wagon tracks veered away from the river, while others followed it. Woody rode along the river, looking for some reason why the trail had split. Why had some wagons chosen to travel parallel to the Grand Arkansas, while too far away to avail themselves of the ready water? Following the Arkansas half a dozen miles, Woody saw no difficulty that might have convinced teamsters to leave the river for a distant trail where water was in short supply.

Wheeling his horse, he rode back to meet the oncoming herd. They would reach Pawnee Rock, where Walnut Creek joined the Arkansas, before dark, and it would be a good time to study Gladstone Pitkin's map. He had an uneasy feeling there was much the map wasn't telling them.

When he eventually met the herd, he took over the point position. There was no need to convey his doubts about the accuracy of the map to Pitkin until they were able to study it. Once the herd had been bedded down and Pitkin had unharnessed his teams, he wasted no time in seeking out Woody.

"I have become accustomed to you reporting back to me, after scouting ahead. Today, however, you did not. May I ask why?"

"I wanted to wait until we stopped for the night, so that I can study that map again. I learned something that the storekeeper at Council Grove only hinted at. After reaching Pawnee Rock, and the point where Walnut Creek flows into the Grand Arkansas, it appears there are two trails. One follows the river, while the other leads away from it. Probably far from it. I think this hundred and twenty-two miles we're looking at is the distance to Cimarron Crossing if we follow this second trail. I also think, while it's probably shorter, there may be a problem of little or no water."

"Why, confound it," Pitkin shouted, "the map shows the trail following the Arkansas from its confluence with Walnut Creek all the way to the Cimarron Cutoff, well beyond Fort Dodge. I will not leave the river and its readily available water for some unknown and uncharted trail that isn't even recorded on the map.''

Pitkin's outburst had drawn the attention of the rest of the outfit, including Gonzales, and there seemed a good possibility the Stubbs outfit had heard him, as well. Woody did his best to silence Pitkin until they had studied the map further.

''I have no objection to following the river,'' said Woody, ''even if it's a longer route. I have told you what I discovered. There's no need for an immediate decision, and I believe we should have another look at the map.''

''Perhaps you're right,'' Pitkin said. ''There's time before supper. I'll get the map.''

Pitkin spread out the map, and it told them nothing regarding the alternate route that Woody had discovered.

''So we know nothing about this second route,'' said Pitkin, ''except that it exists. Do you have any suggestions or opinions?''

''Yes,'' Woody replied. ''Since the map tells us nothing, we'll have to rely on some good old horse sense. We know we're lookin' at a hundred and twenty-two miles, if we follow the Grand Arkansas, as the map suggests. We also know we're goin' to have water all the way. I think this alternate route may be shorter, but without sure water, and maybe some dry camps. This follows the same principle as the desert route that we aim to take, when we reach Cimarron Crossing. While we could take the longer route through southeastern Colorado, avoiding the *Jornada*, the distance would be greater.''

''So we have two choices,'' said Pitkin. ''We can stay with the Grand Arkansas for the distance from Pawnee Rock to Cimarron Crossing, or we can risk this alternate route which may be shorter, but perhaps without water.''

''That's what it amounts to,'' Woody said, ''and given a choice, I'd follow the Arkansas to Cimarron Crossing. We know there's fifty miles of desert, once we reach the crossing. Suppose we take this alternate route and find it dry? We'll be leaving one dry trail for one as bad or worse, when we reach Cimarron Crossing."

"So you favor the hundred and twenty-two miles, along the Grand Arkansas," said Pitkin.

"I do," Woody replied. "I'm not one to risk the unknown, where water—or the lack of it—is concerned. We've never driven this trail before, nor have you."

The rest of the outfit had gathered around, and Pitkin studied their faces. When he had nothing to say, Gavin spoke.

"I reckon we'd better stay with the river. If you're lookin' for a reason, I'll give you one. If we're parallel to that river, on a dry trail, all it'll take is a snifter of wind and the smell of water. Every horse, mule, and cow will stampede toward that river, no matter if it's ten miles away."

"He has a point," said Woody. "On that alternate trail, we'd be down wind from the Grand Arkansas. Thirst will create a stampede quicker than thunder, lightning, Indians, and outlaws combined."

There was a chorus of approval from the rest of the outfit.

"Very well," Pitkin said. "We know there'll be water all the way, as long as we follow the Grand Arkansas. I believe we are justified in taking the trail where there's an assurance of water."

Supper was a jubilant affair, for there would be abundant water for at least two more weeks. The fifty miles of desert beyond Cimarron Crossing was strong on their minds, and whatever assurances the trail afforded were welcome.

At first light, they soon left Pawnee Rock behind. While there was abundant water, Woody still rode ahead, for he knew not what dangers might await them. Woody reached the cutoff that veered away from the river, and he couldn't help wondering why some of the teamsters that traveled the Santa Fe had taken such a route. He rode on, following the river, and he covered twelve miles without seeing anything to arouse his suspicion. There were no recent tracks, and between those ruts that marked the trail, he found no tracks of unshod horses. He rode back to meet the oncoming herd, thankful for the proximity of the river and its abundant water.

"No problems, then," Pitkin said, when Woody reported to him.

"None that I could see," said Woody.

He rode back to the point position. Gavin again rode drag with Nell and Naomi Pitkin.

"I'm so tired of the trail," Nell said. "When we reach Fort Dodge, I'd like to take a wild turn, create some excitement, do something daring."

Gavin was amused. "What do you have in mind?"

"Won't there be a preacher—perhaps a chaplain—at the fort?"

"I reckon," said Gavin. "Why?"

"I'm thinking perhaps Woody and me will get married."

"Tarnation," Gavin said, "that's contrary to what your daddy's been told. Is this your idea, or Woody's?"

"It's hers," said Naomi, "and she's planning on you breaking the news to Woody."

"Oh, no," Gavin said. "Pit will raise hell, and I wouldn't blame him."

"Not if you and Naomi will stand up with us," said Nell. "Please?"

Gavin looked suspiciously at Naomi. "Are you in on this?"

"No," Naomi said, "but I could be persuaded. How do you feel about it?"

"I favor doing exactly what we promised Pit we'd do," said Gavin, "and I can tell you that Woody's goin' to feel the same way. This is the kind of thing that can wait until we're in Santa Fe."

"But I don't want to wait," Nell said. "I have these . . . feelings . . . that I . . ."

Naomi laughed. "So do I, but I have no intention of explaining them to Father."

"I reckon Woody and me has them feelings, too," said

Gavin, "but the Santa Fe Trail ain't the place to give in to 'em."

"You don't want us, then," Nell pouted.

"We don't want to wrassle you around under a wagon, with the rest of the outfit all gettin' their enjoys out of it," said Gavin. "Speakin' for myself, I want my marryin' day to be special, and knowin' Woody, he'll feel the same way. After dark, I reckon the both of you ought to find a shallow place in the river and set there a while."

Naomi laughed, while Nell described her feelings in a very unladylike manner.

12

᭜᭜᭜

Santa Fe, New Mexico Territory. June 26, 1869.

*D*euce Rowden and his five companions were reluctant to take the Santa Fe Trail with the intention of ambushing Gladstone Pitkin and his outfit, because they didn't want to be away any longer than necessary. There were virtually no accommodations for men who relished town living. After considerable discussion, the six killers came up with what they considered a legitimate reason for calling on Tobe Hankins.

"Hell," said Haynes Wooten, "it's three hunnert an' fifty miles from here to the cutoff, an' we don't know if this Pitkin will take the dry trail or the mountain trail. I purely don't aim to ride all the way from here to the Cimarron Cutoff an' wait. Besides, it ain't all that far to Fort Dodge, an' we could have the military after us."

"Damn it," Deuce Rowden said, "why didn't you think of that when we was in Tobe's saloon, an' he was talkin' down to us? We go back in there, raisin' hell, he'll want all his money back. How many of you has got that five hundred on you?"

The five of them looked at him in silence, and that answered his question.

"There's one thing he could do for us that ain't unreasonable," said York Eagan. "He's got to find out for us which way this Pitkin outfit aims to go. If we know which trail they aim to take, we can ride out maybe a hunnert miles an' earn our money.''

"Damn right," Watt Grimes said. "Not only is it three hunnert an' fifty mile from here to Cimarron Crossing, fifty of them miles is across desert.''

"They got the telegraph at Fort Dodge," said Grady Beard. "Why can't Hankins telegraph the fort an' find out which trail Pitkin's outfit aims to take?''

"I dunno," Deuce Rowden admitted. "Maybe he can. But we already took his money, and we ain't done a damn thing to earn it.''

"Then git over there an' tell him we got to know which trail Pitkin's takin'. There's got to be a way he can find out, usin' the telegraph," said Beard.

"If I stand up to him, by God, then you hombres got to side me," Rowden growled.

"Then come on," York Eagan said. "We'll all go with you to face the varmint."

"No," said Rowden, "I'll go. Just remember, the rest of you are neck-deep in this.''

Woody continued riding ahead each day, but there was no Indian sign. That bothered him, and while he said nothing to Pitkin, he spoke to others whose judgment he trusted. On watch with Gavin McCord and Nip Kelly, he sought their opinions.

"I'm as puzzled as you," said Gavin. "We're a good hundred miles from Fort Dodge, and I don't doubt for a minute the Comanches know we're here.''

"They didn't fare so well, the last time they tangled with us," Nip Kelly said. "Could be they're aimin' to strike while we're crossin' the *Jornada*. If they know anything about Texas longhorns, they'll know the varmints get ornery as hell when they're thirsty. What better time and place to hit us than when we're in the middle of a desert?''

"You could have something there," said Woody. "I'm considerin' drivin' the herd at night, when it's cooler, but it'll also be more risky. Whatever superstitions the Comanches have, attackin' at night ain't one of 'em.''

"That," Gavin said, "and if there's any wind, it'll likely be out of the west, bringin' the smell of water."

"If that's goin' to be a problem," said Nip, "it won't matter if the herd's bedded down or on the move. They'll still run."

"Not if they're exhausted," Woody replied. "Suppose, before movin' into that desert, we let the herd have all the water they can drink, and then drive the varmints all day and all night?"

"We'd likely be halfway across," said Nip.

"Exactly," Woody said. "Suppose we rest the herd until sundown, and then drive 'em all night?"

"They'll be dyin' on their feet," said Gavin, "and so will we."

"Maybe," Woody admitted, "but by dawn of the second day, we'll be within a dozen miles of the Cimarron River. We can stampede them that far, if we have to."

"Like hell," said Gavin. "They won't have the strength to run. They'll be staggering."

"Damn it," Woody said, "maybe we ought to forget the dry trail and take the longer one through Colorado."

Nip laughed. "You're the trail boss. It's your decision."

"Yeah," said Gavin, "and it ain't us you got to convince. Pit's been reasonable up to now, but he's never crossed a desert with a bunch of thirsty, cantankerous, hell-raising longhorn cows."

Wiley Stubbs had been listening with interest, and it was he who finally spoke.

"When we git to Fort Dodge, I aim to ask Paw to buy some water barrels to go on the outside of our wagons. Without water, our teams won't never make it across that desert."

Woody said nothing more about the trail across the desert. Embarrassed, Gavin and Nip kept their silence, not wishing to make Woody's position more difficult than it already was. Neither man envied Woody the necessity of preparing Gladstone Pitkin for the trials that might confront them during the crossing of the *Jornada*.

In Santa Fe, in his saloon office, Tobe Hankins stood behind his desk, while Deuce Rowden leaned across it. With gritted teeth, the two regarded one another like two hostile hounds just before the fur begins to fly.

"I paid you and your bunch half the money we agreed on," Hankins snarled, "and the whole sorry lot of you are still lyin' here in town."

"I done told you why we're still here," said Rowden, with equal hostility. "We got to know which leg of the Santa Fe this Pitkin outfit aims to take. Damn it, we ain't of a mind to ride three hunnert an' fifty mile, to Cimarron Crossin', and then set there on our duffs waitin' to see which trail this bunch will be ridin'. All you said was, you don't want 'em bushwhacked in Santa Fe. Well, we'll ride a hunnert miles and do your dirty work, but we got to know which damn trail they'll be takin'. There's telegraph to Fort Dodge, and all you got to do is have a reason for the military to wire you when Pitkin's bunch shows up. When they leave Fort Dodge, we'll ride out, but not without knowin' which trail they'll be takin'. Ain't I said that clear enough for you?"

"I reckon you have," Hankins replied in a slightly more civil tone. "I got a contact at Fort Dodge. I likely can learn when Pitkin's drive pulls out, and the trail they'll be takin'. Where will I find you and your bunch?"

"One of us will call on you every day, until you get the word," said Rowden.

"Like hell you will," Hankins snorted. "When you leave here, I don't want to see any of you in here again. Not even for a drink. Do you understand *that*?"

Rowden laughed. "Yeah. We're good enough to do your killing, but not good enough to be seen with you. We're at the Pecos Hotel."

Rowden got up to leave, but only got as far as the door.

"Rowden!"

His thumb hooked in his gunbelt over the butt of his Colt, Rowden turned.

"If anything goes wrong, Rowden," said Hankins, "and by God, I mean *anything*, you and your bunch had better ride and keep ridin'."

Deuce Rowden swallowed hard and stepped out the door, closing it behind him. There had been rumors of other gunmen Tobe Hankins had paid to kill, and to a man, they had all mysteriously disappeared.

Fort Dodge, Kansas. July 7, 1869.

The day finally came when Woody, scouting ahead, caught up to a patrol from Fort Dodge. They saw Woody coming, and reining up, waited for him. There was a lieutenant, a sergeant, and four privates. Woody introduced himself and told them of the Pitkin outfit.

"I am First Lieutenant Fields," the officer said, "and this is Sergeant Oliver."

He didn't bother introducing the privates, and Woody nodded to them. He then spoke to Lieutenant Fields.

"How far from here to the fort, Lieutenant?"

"Maybe ten miles," Fields replied. "How far back is your outfit?"

"A good fifteen miles," said Woody. "We won't reach the fort until tomorrow."

"You can ride on to the fort with us," Fields said, "and meet our post commander, Lieutenant-Colonel Hatton."

"I'm obliged," said Woody. "I'll do that."

Hatton proved to be a gracious host, and Woody spent a pleasant hour with him.

"There's something you should know about the *Jornada*," Hatton said, "if you have intentions of taking the Cimarron Cutoff."

"Unless I change my mind," said Woody, "that's the trail we'll be taking. What else can you tell us about the *Jornada*?"

"There won't be a drop of water for at least fifty miles," Hatton said. "Not until you reach the Cimarron. But I suppose you already know that. What you may not know is that the lack of water may not be your only problem. The Comanches—some of them, I hear—are holed up in northwestern Indian Territory. They'll wait until you're a day or two into the *Jornada* and then come calling, usually on a moonless night. How many wagons do you have?"

"Only two, includin' the chuck wagon," said Woody, "but the Stubbs family is trailing with us. They have three wagons."

"That name, Stubbs, is somehow familiar," Hatton said. "Are they traders who may have traveled the Santa Fe before?"

"I doubt it," said Woody. "Their wagons are loaded too heavy, and they left both the water barrels behind that usually ride each side of the wagon box."

Hatton laughed. "They are green, aren't they? Do you know where they're from?"

"Somewhere in Missouri, I think," Woody said. "There's old Levi, his two sons, and three daughters."

"I'll talk to them when they reach the fort," said Hatton. "I like to be familiar with all folks who come down the Santa Fe. So many of them have died along the way— usually at the hands of hostile Indians—it helps, knowing who they are and where they're from, so we can notify their next-of-kin."

"We'll be here sometime tomorrow," Woody said. "We'll see you then."

When Woody had ridden away, Lieutenant-Colonel Hatton did a strange thing.

"Corporal," he said to the young man in the orderly room, "I need you to go to the telegraph shack. Tell Hastings I want that sheaf of reports from Fort Leavenworth, dealing with stolen payrolls."

"Thank God," Gladstone Pitkin said, when Woody told him of the nearness of Fort Dodge. "We are at least halfway to Santa Fe."

But there were some who didn't feel like celebrating their arrival at the fort. Rusty, Vic, and Ash recalled only too well what the Stubbs girls had told them about old Levi's outlaw past. If Stubbs had any portion of a stolen military payroll in his possession, the post commander might place the entire family under military arrest. It was a fear shared by the three Stubbs girls, and during the second watch, they slipped away to join Rusty, Vic, and Ash.

"Now that we're almost there," Bonita said, "I have this bad feeling—a premonition—that we'll all be in trouble."

"Well, you know where we stand," said Vic, "and we ain't changed our minds. If your paw's done anything wrong, then he's the one to pay. If they try to hold the rest of you, the three of us will raise hell and kick a chunk under it. I'm bettin' Woody will side us, and maybe even Pitkin."

"I think so too," Rusty said.

"Whether they do or don't," said Ash, "you can depend on us."

"Bless all of you," Laketa said. "Thanks to Paw's reputation, we went through hell back in Missouri. We hoped all that would be left behind."

"You don't know that it won't be," said Rusty.

"No," Jania agreed, "but we've never had a minute's peace or happiness. It just seems like we never will."

Rusty, Vic, and Ash did their best individually to cheer up the girls, but they seemed to expect the worst.

"Damn it," said Vic, when he again was alone with Rusty and Ash, "they've got me to thinkin' everything's about to go to hell."

"Yeah," Rusty agreed. "Instead of us buildin' them up, they dragged us down."

Two hours before sundown, Woody had the herd bunched across the Arkansas from Fort Dodge.

"We'll be here tonight and tomorrow night," said Woody. "I'm goin' to report to the post commander, Lieutenant-Colonel Hatton. I'll get permission for us to go to the sutler's store tomorrow. There's enough daylight left for anybody needin' to wash clothes or bedrolls. Just because the fort's across the river, don't get careless and wander too far away.''

Woody noted that Levi Stubbs had seen to it that Wiley and Whit had followed him with their wagons, and that all three were almost a mile upriver from the fort. His action wasn't lost on Rusty, Vic, and Ash.

"The old varmint's actin' almighty guilty," Rusty observed.

"Yeah," said Vic. "Looks like the girls knowed what they was talkin' about."

"We may all be sweatin' for nothing," Ash said. "Until we see somebody from the fort ridin' over yonder to the Stubbs wagons, we got nothin' to worry about."

Woody was shown into the post commander's office, and Lieutenant-Colonel Hatton greeted him cordially.

"We aim to lay over through tomorrow night," said Woody, "and I'd like permission for my outfit to visit the sutler's store."

"Permission granted," Hatton said. "Are the Stubbs wagons still trailing with you?"

"In a manner of speaking," said Woody. "They went on around us, and are quite a ways beyond the fort. The sons and daughters are neighborly enough, but Stubbs is a mite stand-offish."

"I'll be leading a patrol down there within the hour," Hatton said. "I would advise you and your outfit to remain within your camp until I have questioned Stubbs."

"I'll see that my outfit is told," said Woody.

He was surprised at the thinly veiled warning from Hatton. He was hopeful the officer might reveal to him the military's interest in Levi Stubbs, but Hatton said no more. Without further conversation, Woody excused himself, left the fort, and rode across the river. He found everybody waiting expectantly. First, he told them they had permission to visit the sutler's the next day. He then told them of Hatton's strange request regarding old Levi Stubbs and his wagons.

"That is indeed a strange request," Gladstone Pitkin observed.

"Maybe not," said Nip Kelly. "Stubbs has been treated kindly by you, by Woody, and as far as I know, by everybody in this outfit, but he's been hostile as hell. I've known too many men who were running from something or somebody, and he fits the pattern."

"He does, for a fact," Gavin agreed.

"Wiley, Whit, and the girls ain't done nothin'," said Vic. "Somebody oughta stand up for them."

"I don't believe that's our responsibility," Gladstone Pitkin said.

"If it comes down to that," said Vic, "it's my responsibility to speak up for Bonita."

"I'll be standin' up for Laketa," Rusty said.

"And me for Jania," said Ash.

"It's no more than I expected," Pitkin said. "Need I remind you that it is my prerogative to dismiss the three of you, if your conduct warrants it?"

"No," said Rusty, "and I reckon you don't need remindin' that it's our prerogative to quit, if your conduct warrants it."

"All right, damn it," Woody said, "before anybody gets his tail up over what may or may not happen to the Stubbs outfit, maybe we oughta see what interest the military has in Stubbs."

"I will subscribe to that," said Pitkin stiffly.

Rusty, Vic, and Ash had nothing to say. Their eyes were on the fort across the river, and even as they watched, Lieutenant-Colonel Hatton led a patrol of nine men toward the Stubbs wagons.

"Oh, God," Whit groaned, "here it comes."

"Git your Winchesters ready," said Levi. "Them Federals ain't snoopin' through my wagons an' my goods."

"Paw, no," Wiley begged. "You can't fight the army."

"He can't afford not to," said Bonita. "There's something he can't let them discover."

"Barreled whiskey," Whit said. "Ain't no law agin that."

Laketa laughed bitterly. "There's more than whiskey. Tell him, Paw."

"Shut your mouth, woman!" Levi bawled.

Stubbs jacked a shell into the chamber of his Winchester. Wiley and Whit clutched their weapons, fearful and uncertain. Lieutenant-Colonel Hatton raised his hand, and the patrol reined up fifty yards away. Hatton spoke.

"Mr. Stubbs—if that's your name—I am Lieutenant-Colonel Hatton. I am an officer in the army of the United States of America. It is my right and my duty to inspect those wagons and examine their contents. Lay down your arms."

"These wagons an' their cargo is private property," Stubbs snarled. "Now you ride back the way you come. Trot that horse a step closer, an' I'll kill you."

"Paw, no," Whit cried.

Wiley dropped his Winchester and raised his hands. Whit quickly did the same.

"Sergeant Hardesty," said Lieutenant-Colonel Hatton, "prepare to fire."

Levi Stubbs fired, but his shot went over Hatton's head, for when he made his move, Sergeant Hardesty had obeyed orders. Stubbs stumbled backwards, blood pumping from a hole in his chest. He dropped the Winchester and collapsed in the dust. While the remaining soldiers held their rifles at the ready, Sergeant Hardesty dismounted, walked to the inert Stubbs, and knelt beside him. He then got to his feet and spoke to Hatton.

"He's dead, sir."

Wiley, Whit, Bonita, Jania, and Laketa stared at the body of their father in horrified silence. It was to them that Hatton spoke.

"It is regrettable that he chose to follow such a course. Will the rest of you stand aside while my men search these wagons?"

"Yes, sir," Wiley said.

"Sergeant Hardesty," said Hatton, "take charge of the search."

All of Pitkin's outfit had witnessed the shooting, and stricken by the suddenness of it, nobody said anything for a moment. Nip Kelly recovered first.

"My God, I've never seen a man make such a fool move. He didn't have a chance."

"He must have been hidin' something that purely couldn't stand the light of day," said Gavin. "They're searchin' the wagons."

"He wasn't a very sociable man," said Naomi Pitkin, "but I feel sorry for his family."

"So do I," Woody said. "Under certain circumstances, the military can confiscate some or all of a man's property. Old Levi's sons and daughters could be stranded here. Or worse, if they share his guilt, they could be arrested and sent to prison."

"Damned if I'll stand by for that," said Vic.

"I thought," Pitkin said, "we had agreed not to make any hasty decisions regarding the Stubbs family until we know the outcome of all this."

"I thought so too," said Woody. "After they've completed their search of the wagons, I'll call on Lieutenant-Colonel Hatton. While he can always tell us to mind our own business, I'm counting on him being fair enough to explain this Stubbs affair."

Hatton's men searched Wiley's wagon first, opening the whiskey barrels.

"Nothing in that one, sir," Sergeant Hardesty said, "except barreled whiskey."

"Certainly not worth a man's life," said Hatton. "Search the other wagons."

A search of Whit's wagon revealed only barreled whiskey. Hatton said nothing, his face turning grim, as the soldiers moved on to the third wagon. Their search had barely gotten underway when there was an excited shout from Sergeant Hardesty.

"We found it, sir!"

Two of the men rolled a barrel out on the wagon's tailgate and then lifted it to the ground.

"Open the rest of the barrels," Hatton ordered. "This may not be all of it."

But upon opening the remaining barrels, the soldiers found only whiskey. None of the Stubbs survivors were allowed near the open barrel, and Whit asked a timid question.

"Sir, ain't we allowed to know what's in that barrel that's worth our Paw gittin' kilt?"

"You'll know tomorrow," said Hatton. "I will conduct a hearing in the morning in an attempt to learn to what extent the rest of you are implicated in this. Until then, all of you are under military arrest. You will hitch your teams to these wagons, and they will be taken to the fort. Sergeant Hardesty, have that barrel returned to the wagon, and assign a man to take the reins and follow us to the fort. You Stubbs men will bring the other two wagons."

"If you got to arrest somebody," Whit said, "then take me an' Wiley, my brother. Let our sisters stay the night in the Pitkin camp."

"All of you will go to the fort, as ordered," said Hatton firmly. "There will be suitable quarters for the ladies."

Wiley and Whit harnessed the teams to their wagons, while a pair of the soldiers soon had the mules harnessed to the third wagon. Almost as an afterthought, Hatton seemed to remember Levi's dead body. He spoke to Wiley.

"Do you want me to send a burial detail to take care of your father?"

"With all of us under arrest an' bein' took to the fort," said Wiley, "what choice have we got?"

"Yeah," Whit said bitterly, "you kilt him. Now you kin bury him."

Hatton looked at Bonita, Jania, and Laketa, and while they were pale and shaken, they glared back at him defiantly.

"Very well," said Hatton. "Sergeant Hardesty, have the

body loaded in one of these wagons. Then assign a burial detail when we reach the fort."

Whit helped Bonita and Jania up to his wagon box, and Laketa mounted the box with Wiley. The Stubbs brothers guided their teams in behind the wagon driven by one of the soldiers, who led them to a place in the river shallow enough for the wagons to cross. The mounted soldiers, led by Hatton, followed.

"By God," said Gavin, "they're all bein' taken to the fort, along with the wagons."

"Yeah," Nip said. "The blue bellies must have found what they was lookin' for. Can't help wonderin' what was so all-fired valuable in that wagon."

"Woody," said Rusty, "Vic, Ash, and me has got to know what's goin' to happen to Bonita, Jania, and Laketa. Will you try and find out, or you want us three to go knockin' on that blue belly officer's door?"

Gladstone Pitkin looked as though he might erupt, but Woody silenced him without speaking a word. He then answered Rusty's question.

"You wouldn't get anywhere with a breach of military etiquette except in trouble. I'll ride to the fort, express your interest in the Stubbs women, and see what I can learn. I'll be back before supper, and I'm depending on all of you to keep the lid on, until we get some answers."

When Woody reached the fort, there was no sign of Wiley, Whit, or the three Stubbs women. The wagons had been lined up next to the orderly room. Two soldiers—obviously sentries—paced back and forth. Woody nodded to them and stepped into the orderly room where a corporal sat behind a battered desk.

"I need to talk to Lieutenant-Colonel Hatton," Woody said.

"And you are?"

"Woody Miles," said Woody impatiently. "I was here not two hours ago."

There was no friendliness in the soldier's manner, as he knocked on Hatton's door.

"Yes," Hatton said. "What is it?"

"Woody Miles is here to see you, sir," the corporal said.

"Send him in," Hatton replied.

Woody entered the office, closed the door, and wasted no time explaining the purpose of his visit. Hatton looked at him long and hard before he spoke.

"This entire affair is most regrettable, and while I can appreciate your concern for the Stubbs family, I am unable to divulge any information concerning their arrest at this time. I am awaiting a response to several telegrams I have sent to Fort Leavenworth. Tomorrow there will be a hearing in the post chapel. Perhaps at that time I'll be at liberty to answer your questions. You are welcome to attend this hearing, accompanied by the three young men who are concerned about the ladies in question. Good day."

It was a curt dismissal that invited no response. Woody stepped out the door, closing it behind him. He nodded to the corporal, left the orderly room, mounted his horse, and rode back across the river. When he dismounted, his words were for Rusty, Vic, and Ash.

"There's a hearing in the morning, at the post chapel. The three of you are invited to be there with me. Hatton's waiting for telegrams from Fort Leavenworth, likely to help him decide if the rest of the family's involved in whatever old Levi Stubbs had going."

"I am not to accompany you, then," Gladstone Pitkin said.

"No," said Woody. "You're welcome to go in my place, if you want."

Pitkin's eyes met those of Rusty, Vic, and Ash, and a chill crept up his spine. If the scheduled hearing didn't go to suit these three hellions from Texas, the Englishman had not the slightest doubt there would be hell to pay. In spades.

"I think not," Pitkin said. "I trust you to act on my behalf, doing what must be done."

13

Fort Dodge, Kansas. July 9, 1869.

*W*oody, Rusty, Vic, and Ash reached the fort a few
minutes before the hearing was to begin. The soldiers
who had searched the Stubbs wagons were already seated
near the front of the chapel. There was no sign of any of
the Stubbs family, and when they appeared, it was under
the watchful eyes of armed guards. Briefly, Vic's eyes met
Bonita's, and in them was a frightened, desperate appeal.
Lieutenant-Colonel Hatton was the last to enter, and he took
his place behind the podium.

"We have concluded an investigation into a matter of
utmost importance to the military," Hatton said. "Just this
morning, I received clearance from Fort Leavenworth, and
the details surrounding this bizarre circumstance are no
longer classified. The purpose of this hearing is to settle,
once and for all, the guilt or innocence of the surviving
family of the late Levi Stubbs. The family and friends of
the family seem unclear as to the military's interest in
Stubbs. Let it be known that the shooting yesterday afternoon became necessary as a result of Mr. Stubbs' hostility,
and the military is under no obligation to justify it. As a
courtesy to the family and friends, I am about to relate to
you the activities of one Levi Stubbs that led to his death
yesterday."

Hatton cleared his throat, opened a file, and began to read.

"Levi Stubbs rode with Quantrill. Finally, when Quantrill fled Kansas, Stubbs joined a band of former Quantrill riders, and their many nefarious activities included the theft of two army payrolls in gold, exceeding fifty thousand dollars. Through the Secret Service and Pinkerton operatives, the military kept tabs on all former Quantrill men. Levi Stubbs was the only known survivor, and the Pinkertons lost him in Kansas City. His description was telegraphed to every frontier outpost west of the Mississippi. Yesterday, in one of the Stubbs wagons, we found most of the two missing payrolls. Now is there anyone present who would refute all or any part of what I have related?"

Nobody had anything to say, and all eyes were on Hatton when he spoke again.

"Will the family members accompanying Levi Stubbs please stand?"

Wiley, Whit, Bonita, Jania, and Laketa stood.

"I have questioned all of you individually," Hatton said, "and have been told basically the same story. I believe that if any one of you were lying, there would be some conflicting answers, and there were none. I have therefore concluded that Levi Stubbs acted alone, without the knowledge of any of you. At the conclusion of this hearing, you are free to go. Good luck."

Bonita, Jania, and Laketa wept, while Wiley and Whit didn't seem far from it. Rusty, Vic, and Ash made haste to get to the Stubbs girls, while Woody sought out Lieutenant-Colonel Hatton.

"I trust the hearing was conducted to your satisfaction," Hatton said drily.

"It was, sir," said Woody. "Stubbs was a hard man, and while none of us thought highly of him, we had no idea . . ."

"The Quantrill saga was a sorry episode in American history," Hatton said. "Let us hope this final act will close the curtain on it for all time."

Woody found Rusty, Vic, and Ash, each with one of the Stubbs girls.

"I reckon all of you are satisfied," said Woody.

Vic laughed. "I reckon we are. Hatton looks like a hard-nosed old coyote, all spit and polish, but beneath all that brass, he's got a heart."

"He strikes me that way," Woody said. "Where's Wiley and Whit?"

"They're gone to the sutler's store," said Rusty. "There's just the two of them now, and with one wagon too many they're lookin' to sell one of 'em. Wagon, teams, whiskey, and all."

"That's a hell of a lot of whiskey," Woody said. "I doubt the sutler can take all of it, and he certainly won't have need of a wagon and team."

"Let's mosey over that way and see," said Vic.

They encountered Wiley and Whit as they were leaving the sutler's.

"More whiskey than he needs," Wiley said, "an' he's got no use for the wagon and the mules."

"But they's a town in the makin' about eight miles west of here," said Whit. "There's already a general store an' two saloons. We're goin' there an' try our luck."*

"You'd better get started, then," Woody said. "We'll be leaving here tomorrow at first light."

"Maybe some of us oughta ride along with 'em, leadin' some extra horses," said Vic. "If they sell the whiskey, the wagon, and the team, it'll be a long walk back."

"What about us?" Bonita asked.

"You can return to our camp," said Woody. "Wiley, you and Whit can take the other two wagons there, if you like. Vic, bring the third one."

With Bonita on the wagon box with Vic, Jania with Whit, and Laketa with Wiley, they left the fort and crossed the river. Woody, Rusty, and Ash rode along behind, and when they reined up in camp, the rest of the outfit was waiting.

* The beginning of Dodge City. The railroad would reach Dodge in 1872.

Woody quickly explained what had taken place, and Gladstone Pitkin was obviously relieved. In fact, he extended a most gracious welcome to the Stubbs girls, fully aware that he was making a most favorable impression on Rusty, Vic, and Ash. Woody took it a step further when he spoke to Pitkin.

"Pit, there's the makings of a town west of the fort, along the river. Wiley and Whit aim to take one of the three wagons there and try to sell it, along with the teams and the whiskey. Rusty, Vic, and Ash aim to ride along."

"I have no objection," said Pitkin. "In fact, if there's a store there, it might be to our advantage to know what they sell. I'm going to the sutler's, at the fort."

"We'll check out this general store for you," Vic said. "We'll need a couple of extra horses, in case Wiley and Whit sell the wagon."

Pitkin nodded. Wiley and Whit climbed to the wagon box, while Rusty and Ash began saddling a pair of extra horses. When Pitkin—accompanied by Nell and Naomi—set out for the fort, the wagon, trailed by Rusty, Vic, and Ash, was headed west along the river.

"This place has got a ways to go," Vic said, as they neared the cluster of tents along the Arkansas.

"I reckon," said Rusty, "but somebody's got big ideas. Look."

A crudely painted sign before a newly erected tent read: *Real Estate. Town lots for sale.*

"Tarnation," Ash said, "look at the size of that general store. I was at a circus once, in St. Louis, and the big top wasn't as long or as wide as this one."

The tent was massive, with more than a dozen uprights down the center supporting the high-peaked top. Surprisingly, there was a nearby corral with half a dozen mules. The saloon tents were smaller, but more gaudy. From one came the out-of-tune jangle of a piano.

"Jiminy," said Whit, climbing down from the wagon

box, "if we don't have no luck at the saloons, we kin try the general store."

"Yeah," Vic said. "Pit knew what he was doin', when he wanted us to have a look at that store."

"Go with us to the saloons, first," said Wiley. "We kin all go to the store together."

Rusty caught Vic's eye, and Vic nodded. They suspected Wiley and Whit, probably on their own for the first time, were nervous and uncertain. The five of them headed for the first saloon. It was still early, and a lone man sat at a table shuffling and dealing cards. He stood up, and Wiley spoke.

"We're lookin' for the owner."

"Jeff Sartain at your service. I am the owner."

"We got a wagonload of barreled whiskey for sale," Whit blurted. "We're sellin' the whole shebang. Whiskey, wagon, an' mules."

Sartain laughed. "Do I look like I need a wagonload of whiskey? This place won't be a town till the railroad gets here."

"When it does," said Vic, "you'll be ready. Who owns the other saloon?"

"An old fool name of Darby Calhoun, and he's about as flush as I am. Why don't you see Jonas McClendon, at the store? He's been tryin' to buy out me and Calhoun. That old coyote still has the first dollar he ever got his hands on."

"God," Whit said, "we're runnin' out of chances mighty fast."

"Sounds like this McClendon might be the man you're lookin' for," said Rusty. "Why don't we go see him?"

They entered the enormous tent and stood there in awe. Never had they seen such an array of merchandise on the frontier. The man who came to greet them was in his fifties, in a boiled shirt with tie. There was a white knee-length apron over his dark trousers.

"I'm Jonas McClendon. What can I do for you?"

Wiley and Whit seemed suddenly at a loss for words. Wiley finally spoke.

"I'm Wiley Stubbs an' this is my brother, Whit. We're bound for Santa Fe, with three wagonloads of barreled whiskey. We had some trouble an' lost a teamster, so we're lookin' to sell one wagon, the whiskey in it, an' the teams. Would you be interested?"

"Maybe," said McClendon cautiously. "What's your askin' price?"

"We ain't familiar with prices on the frontier," Whit said. "Why don't you tell us the most you're willin' to pay, an' we'll consider it? The wagon an' the team is outside."

"How much whiskey?" McClendon asked.

"Ten barrels," said Wiley.

"A hundred dollars a barrel for the whiskey," McClendon said, "and five hundred for the four mules, the harness, and the wagon."

Wiley and Whit looked at one another, uncertain. They had no idea how much Levi Stubbs had paid for the wagon, the teams, or the whiskey. Wiley caught Vic's eye, and Vic nodded.

"We'll take it," Wiley said.

"I'll want a bill of sale for it all," said McClendon.

"Git us pencil an' paper," Wiley said, "an' we'll write one."

While Wiley and Whit—with help from Vic—wrote the bill of sale, McClendon went for the money.

"Count it," said McClendon, handing Wiley a canvas bag.

Wiley upended the bag, pouring double eagles out on the counter. He carefully placed them in stacks of five, until there were fifteen stacks.

"We're obliged," Wiley said, returning the gold coins to the sack.

McClendon studied the bill of sale which both Wiley and Whit had signed. He nodded his head, and the sale became final. It was time for Vic to speak.

"I'm Vic Brodie, and these hombres is Rusty and Ash

Pryor. We're riders for the Pitkin outfit. Wiley and Whit are trailin' with us. The three of us and our three pards are trailin' a herd of Texas longhorns to Santa Fe for Gladstone Pitkin. I reckon you got more goods than the sutler at Fort Dodge. We'll likely stop and do some business with you, as we take the trail to Santa Fe."

"You'll be welcome," said McClendon. "Dodge will be a railroad town, and I aim to be ready. Until then, there's the soldiers from the fort. It's almost up to strength, and yes, I have a far better stock of goods than the sutler. I have to, if I'm going to get the soldier trade."

"We'll likely be seein' you tomorrow, then," Vic said.

The five of them were about to leave the store, when they noticed a glass case with a variety of jewelry. Being of a single mind, Rusty, Vic, and Ash stopped to look.

"Marryin' rings," Vic said. "What would the girls say, if we stopped here and bought each of 'em one?"

"Why don't we do it, and find out?" said Rusty.

"I'm game," Ash said.

McClendon had noted their interest and was standing hopefully by.

"How much is these marryin' rings?" Vic asked.

"Ideally," said McClendon, "they come in sets. There's a diamond engagement ring the lady wears immediately, to show she's spoken for. Then, on the day she marries, she adds the gold band. You can get a respectable set—with a small diamond—for less than fifty dollars. The very finest ones, with large diamonds, are three hundred dollars."

"I hope you got three sets of them three-hundred-dollar ones," Rusty said. "Ash, Vic, and me is each goin' to need one, I reckon. Believe it or not, these Stubbs hombres, ugly varmints that they are, has got three beautiful, brown-eyed sisters. We aim to each get our brand on one of 'em before they get to Santa Fe."

"Excellent," said McClendon. "Bring the young ladies in, and I will guarantee a perfect fit."

"God," Wiley said, when they had left the store, "you fellers aim to spend that kind of money on Stubbs women?"

"Yeah," said Vic, "and I'm proud of the opportunity."

"We aim for it to be a surprise," Rusty added. "If either of you breathes a word of it to 'em, we'll beat your ears down around your boot tops."

Whit laughed. "We won't say nothin'. I got to see the looks on their faces when they git a look at such finery."

"Yeah," said Wiley. "Paw never bought any of us anything we could do without, and he never told us nothin' unless he had to. We might of took a beatin' on the whiskey, the mules, an' the wagon, because we got no idea what he paid for any of it."

"Maybe," Vic said, "but I don't think so. The whiskey might go for a hundred and fifty dollars a barrel in Santa Fe, but this ain't Santa Fe. Pitkin paid less than a hundred for each of his wagons, and no more than a hundred apiece for the mules."

"Yeah," said Ash, "you won't be goin' into Santa Fe broke. You'll have money that'll see you through a year, if need be, until you've had a chance to sell the rest of that whiskey for the best price you can get."

"One thing we aim to do," Wiley said, "is buy a pair of water barrels we can mount on the outside of our wagon boxes."

"Vic," said Rusty, "there's somethin' we need to discuss with Woody, so's he can talk to Pit about it. With Wiley, Whit, and the girls trailin' with us, they should be taking all their meals with us. Don't you reckon?"

"Yeah," Vic said. "If I'm investin' three hundred *pesos* in a gal, I want her where I'm sure nothin' will happen to her."

"We still have considerable grub we can add to the chuck wagon," said Wiley, "and now we got money to buy more. If Mr. Pitkin allows us to eat with you, be sure you tell him we'll pay for our share of the grub."

"Yeah," Whit said. "Gonzales can cook better'n any of us, includin' the girls."

"Damn it," said Vic, "don't go tellin' me I'm sparkin' a gal that can't cook better'n a *Mejicano*."

Rusty laughed. "If you think more of your belly than you do of Bonita, maybe you'd better marry Gonzales. I bet he'd go for a set of them rings."

"By God," Vic said, "I'm goin' to pretend you ain't ignorant enough to have said a disgraceful thing like that, and if you was fool enough to've said it, then I'll pretend that I didn't hear it."

They all laughed, slapping their dusty thighs with their dusty hats, until Vic replaced his offended look with a grin, and laughed with them.

Pitkin listened with interest as Rusty, Vic, and Ash spoke of the enormity of the tent-housed general store in the fledgling village that would become Dodge City.

"The sutler's store is somewhat limited in its selection of goods," Pitkin said. "We'll take the time to visit McClendon's store tomorrow."

The three Stubbs girls had watched enviously as Nell and Naomi had accompanied their father to the fort. Never had they been allowed to visit a store, not even to look. Great was their surprise when Wiley and Whit sought them out.

"We got fifteen hunnert dollars for the wagon, the team, and the whiskey," Wiley said. "Split five ways, that's three hunnert dollars apiece."

"You'd divide the money with us?" Bonita asked wonderingly.

"We aim to," said Whit. "You're our kin, an' you're all entitled."

In a burst of affection he had never experienced, Bonita threw her arms around him.

"Damn it, woman," Whit mumbled, "stop slobberin' on me."

On the tailgate of one of the remaining wagons, Wiley counted out the money. There were five stacks of double eagles, fifteen to a stack. For a while, none of them touched the money. It was Laketa who finally spoke.

"We never had anything, because Paw never *wanted* us to have anything. It would be a mortal sin to say I'm glad he's gone, but now there's hope for us being something more than white trash.''

"You're all goin' to be considerable more than that," Wiley said. "Don't waste any of that money at the sutler's store. Save it for the big general store where we sold the mules, the wagon, an' the whiskey."

After reporting to Pitkin, Rusty, Vic, and Ash went looking for Woody. Quickly they explained their idea of allowing the Stubbs family to take their meals with Pitkin's outfit.

"They already have considerable grub they'll put in the pot," Vic explained, "and they got money to help pay for anything else Gonzales may need."

"You got it all figured out," Woody said. "All I have to do is sell Pitkin on the idea. While I'm neck-deep in that, is there anything else I can do for any of you?"

"Matter of fact, there is," said Rusty. "We each got twenty-one thousand comin' from the sale of the herd. We each want five hundred dollars for that visit to the general store tomorrow."

"You aim to do some big spending, I reckon," Woody said.

Ash laughed. "You won't believe what we have in mind."

"Yeah," said Rusty. "I hope it ain't too rough on you and Gavin."

They said no more, leaving Woody to wonder what they had in mind. He decided to go ahead and speak to Pitkin about the Stubbs family, and while he was about it, he would ask for the money Rusty, Vic, and Ash had requested. Fortunately, Pitkin seemed in a jovial mood.

"I have no objection to such an arrangement," Pitkin said, "as long as they're willing to contribute some foodstuffs. In all fairness, I must say the Stubbs ladies accounted for themselves favorably during the Comanche attack."

"I'm glad you feel that way," said Woody, "because I thought so too. There's just one more thing. Rusty, Vic, and Ash each want five hundred dollars when we reach the general store tomorrow."

"None for Gavin and yourself?" Pitkin asked.

"I have no idea why we'd need that much," said Woody, "but I haven't been to that general store. I reckon you might as well advance Gavin and me equal amounts."

Woody told Wiley and Whit the good news. He then told Rusty, Vic, and Ash. They would waste no time in telling the Stubbs girls. Not until suppertime did Pitkin tell Woody of an incident at the sutler's store.

"This gentleman's name was Damon Urbano," Pitkin said. "He had an unusually strong interest in the herd and the trail we planned to take to Santa Fe."

"That's bad news," Woody said. "I hope you didn't tell him anything."

"I told him we will be taking the Cimarron Cutoff," Pitkin said. "I saw no harm in that."

"There may not be," said Woody. "On the other hand, he could be a front man for a pack of renegades. It's not uncommon for a gang to keep a man at the outposts, watching for wagon trains and outfits like ours. When a likely bunch comes along, word is passed to the outlaws, who then decide when and where to attack."

"Dash it all," Pitkin exclaimed, "I had no idea . . ."

"No real harm done, I reckon," said Woody. "You didn't tell him anything he couldn't have learned on his own, just by trailin' us to Cimarron Crossing."

After the stranger had talked to Pitkin, he had gone immediately to the on-post building that housed the telegraph. Taking a blank, he addressed it to Tobe Hankins, Santa Fe. The message consisted of one word: *Jornada*.

"That's all?" the telegrapher asked.

"Yeah," Urbano said. "How much?"

"Seventy-five cents."

Urbano paid, watched the telegrapher send the brief message, and departed.

"From now on," Woody said, after supper, "Wiley will join Gavin, Nip, and me on the first watch. The second watch will include Whit, Rusty, Vic, and Ash. We'll move out tomorrow at first light, but it'll be short day. We'll make camp eight miles upriver, near the general store. Far as I know, it'll be our last chance before reaching Santa Fe.''

After supper, when the first watch had taken over, Rusty, Vic, and Ash spent almost an hour with the Stubbs girls. For the first time, they were all part of the same outfit, and spirits were high.

"We couldn't believe it," Bonita said. "Wiley and Whit gave each of us a share of the money they got for the wagon, the teams, and the whiskey."

"I'm going to that store tomorrow," said Laketa, "and buy me some honest-to-goodness female clothes. Something I've never had."

"So am I," Jania said.

"None of you owns any dresses?" Ash asked. "We reckoned you was wearin' britches and shirts 'cause you was dressed for the trail."

Jania laughed. "Paw didn't believe in female finery. All we have is men's clothes, and they're mostly hand-me-downs."

"God, yes," Bonita said. "I want socks and underwear."

"Tarnation," said Vic, "you mean none of you. . . . under them shirts and britches . . ."

His face went red, and all the women laughed at his embarrassment. Jania spoke.

"Under these men's clothes there's only bare hide. What did you think was causing all the commotion in the fronts of these shirts?"

Rusty laughed. "I have noticed considerable activity in them shirt fronts, but I been careful not to give it too much attention. I wouldn't want to be thought of as less than a gentleman."

"Me neither," said Vic and Ash, in a single voice.

"Gentlemen have eyes too," Bonita said. "Each of you has stood up for us, and each of you has spoken for one of us. We don't know how it is among high-falutin' town girls, but we want you to be men first, and gentlemen second."

"Or perhaps third," said Jania.

"Or even fourth," Laketa added.

The three of them laughed uproariously, and the three cowboys—taking them at their word—joined in. Nell and Naomi Pitkin heard the laughter, and from a distance, looked on in envy.

"Head 'em up, move 'em out," Woody shouted.

The herd took the trail, the four wagons following. Nell and Naomi continued to ride drag, and they had been joined by Ash Pryor. The longhorns, trailwise, well-watered, and grazed, caused no trouble. Nell and Naomi wasted no time engaging Ash in conversation. While they knew Rusty, Vic, and Ash were more than a little interested in the three Stubbs women, they craved a more intimate knowledge of the relationships. But Ash volunteered nothing, and they found it exceedingly difficult to engage him in conversation about any of the three women.

"I think it's kind of you, Rusty, and Vic to spend some time with the Stubbs girls," Nell said. "They must be terribly upset over what happened to their father."

"They're bearin' up tolerably well," said Ash.

He said nothing more, and seemed not to notice the pained expression on Nell's face. Naomi tried a more direct approach.

"What do they intend to do when they reach New Mexico Territory?"

"They ain't talked to us about it," Ash said. "Why don't you ask them?"

Naomi blushed. "I fear they would think it's none of my business."

"That's what I think too," said Ash, looking her in the eye.

That silenced them. Neither spoke another word to Ash. The sun was noon-high when they reached the town site and the general store, eight miles distant. Once the longhorns had been bedded down, Ash rode away without a backward look. He, Rusty, and Vic hadn't said anything to the Stubbs girls about escorting them to the store across the river, and he quickly joined Rusty and Vic.

"We'd better talk to 'em pronto," Ash said. "That money's likely burnin' holes in their pockets, and they might leave without us."

"That ain't likely," said Vic, "unless they swim the river. We'll have to tell Woody we aim to go, and see if he'll let us saddle some horses for the girls."

"You're in an almighty hurry to get to that store," Woody said. "In my saddlebag, I have the five hundred dollars each of you wanted. Am I right in thinkin' this money, the three Stubbs girls, and that store are all part of some scheme you three Texas coyotes have strung together?"

The trio laughed delightedly, fueling the flames of his suspicions.

"Could be," said Vic. "I reckon you'll just have to wait and see."

"Yeah," Rusty added, "and it might be a good idea if you and Gavin had Pit advance you some money. At least three hundred dollars apiece."

Enjoying the puzzled expression on Woody's face, the trio laughed until they cried. It was typical cowboy humor, and Woody had recognized it as such. He turned away, and Vic spoke.

"Woody . . . ?"

"Yes," said Woody over his shoulder, "you're welcome to saddle horses for the girls."

Rusty, Vic, and Ash didn't have to go looking for the Stubbs girls. Instead, the trio came looking for them, and it was Bonita who spoke.

"Wiley and Whit won't take us to the store. They say they're too tired. Will you—all of you—go with us?"

Rusty, Vic, and Ash silently blessed Wiley and Whit, and with as straight a face as he could manage, Vic spoke.

"I reckon we can escort you over there. Come on, and we'll saddle some horses."

Suddenly Rusty patted his empty pockets, a motion that

wasn't lost on his two companions. They had forgotten to get their money from Woody!

"I got to see Woody before we go," Vic said. "Rusty, you and Ash be saddlin' our horses."

Woody spoke before Vic could say a word.

"All the money's in your saddlebags. Don't start anything you can't finish."

14

❦

Reaching the store, Rusty, Vic, and Ash carefully avoided the glass showcase with the jewelry. They would save their surprise until the excited trio had satisfied their lust for new clothing. Vic caught McClendon's eye and winked, lest the storekeeper say something to give away their plot. Bonita, Jania, and Laketa wasted no time, but went directly to the women's section. They eyed the three cowboys for signs of embarrassment as they began selecting lady's underwear, but their escorts seemed perfectly at ease. In fact, they appeared to be fascinated by the female unmentionables they had seen only a few times in their entire lives. Bonita held up a pair of frilly, white ankle-length bloomers.

"What do you think of these, Vic?"

"I reckon they'll do," Vic said, "but I thought you was gettin' away from britches."

"Vic," said Rusty solemnly, "I think them fancy pants goes under a dress."

There was much laughter at Vic's expense, and the search went on. After more than three hours, there were three enormous piles of underwear, gowns, stockings, and shoes on the counter.

"Is that it?" an exhausted Vic asked hopefully.

"Perhaps," Bonita said. "We'll have to see how much money we have, after we've paid for this."

"Oh, Lord," said Jania, "suppose we don't have enough?"

"I suppose we all went a little crazy," Laketa said.

"Like cows that's been grazin' on locoweed," said Rusty.

He was saved from the consequences of that remark by the arrival of McClendon, as he began separating the items and making note of prices. Eventually, he placed a bill with the total beside each girl's purchases.

"Oh, I'm afraid to look," Bonita said.

Vic laughed. "It's twelve hundred dollars."

With a frightened squawk, Bonita snatched the bill.

"Why, it's a hundred and twenty dollars," she cried.

"Sorry," said Vic cheerfully. "I never was good with numbers."

It prompted Jania and Laketa to seize their own bills before Rusty or Ash could tease them in a similar manner.

"Mine's a hundred and twenty-eight dollars," Jania said.

"I owe a hundred and thirty-five," said Laketa. "We can go through the store again."

"My God, no," Rusty groaned.

"You can't wear none of that finery on the trail," said Vic desperately. "Can't the rest of it wait till we get to Santa Fe?"

"If you're goin' through all that again," Ash said, "you'll be doin' it without me. I'm plumb dead from the knees down."

"Why, you poor boys," said Bonita, a twinkle in her eyes. "I suppose we can get by with these few things until we reach Santa Fe."

The three of them paid for their purchases and waited while McClendon wrapped them in brown paper and tied them securely with string.

"I suppose we're ready to go," Laketa said.

"None of us has had a chance to buy anything," said Rusty.

"Nobody's stopping you," Laketa said. "We'll wait."

"No," said Rusty, "I'm not so good at this kind of thing. You'll have to help me."

"Bonita," Vic said, "I aim to buy just one thing, and I can't do it without you."

"Whoa," said Ash. "I'm gettin' left out. Jania, I want you to go with me."

The three women looked at one another and then at the three cowboys, but there wasn't a telltale grin among them. Each was solemn as a judge.

"Mr. McClendon," Vic said, "bring out them goods we was lookin' at yesterday."

McClendon brought out three little boxes, giving one to each of the cowboys. Quickly, each man took the left hand of his intended, removed a diamond ring from the box, and placed it on her ring finger.

"You don't get the gold band until the preacher reads from the Book," Vic said.

For a long moment, the three women stood there as though in shock. But they came out of it quickly, and with shrieks of joy, began bestowing kisses on the three delighted cowboys. They broke away long enough to pay McClendon for the rings, and with the three excited women taking the lead, rode back across the river. Knowing what was about to take place, Wiley and Whit were waiting, grinning.

"Wiley, Whit," Bonita shouted, "look!"

She seemed to forget her many parcels, dropping them as she all but fell off the horse. Jania and Laketa followed her lead, and the three of them stood there, their left hands in the air. The rest of the outfit wasn't as surprised and pleased as Wiley and Whit. Gavin and Woody looked at one another, the implication of what they were seeing bringing frowns to their faces. Only Nip Kelly laughed.

"Congratulations, ladies and gents," Nip said. "I've never seen so many diamonds all in one place. They're enough to blind a man."

But after the initial shock, Gladstone Pitkin had shifted his attention to his daughters, Nell and Naomi. The two seemed struck dumb, but they cast stormy looks at Woody and Gavin that said their silence was only temporary. Of a single mind, they stomped off down to the river and stood there as though contemplating drowning themselves.

"Tarnation," said Vic, "they're clouded up enough to rain all over Kansas, Texas, and New Mexico Territory."

"I reckon we know who's responsible for that," Gavin said. "Thanks a lot."

"Yeah," said Woody. "You're pards to ride the river with."

To the total surprise of everybody, Gladstone Pitkin laughed. Slapping his thighs like a cowboy, he roared. None of them had ever seen Pitkin laugh before, and Nip Kelly regarded him as though he had taken leave of his senses.

"Come on, Gavin," Woody said. "We got some talkin' to do."

Like condemned men, they made their way toward the river where Nell and Naomi had their backs turned. Woody didn't beat around the bush. He walked around in front of Nell but before he could say a word, she pushed him in the river. Gavin was careful not to offer Naomi a similar opportunity. Remaining behind her, he spoke.

"Naomi, we didn't know they aimed to do this. Damn it, Woody and me didn't know a frontier general store even had such finery."

Woody climbed out of the river, shaking his head to clear his eyes and ears of water. Nell regarded him with a half-smile, and it was more than he could take. Seizing her, he dropped her into the river. That prompted Gladstone Pitkin to break into yet another fit of laughter. It proved contagious, and soon he was joined by Nip Kelly, Rusty, Vic, and Ash. Bonita, Jania, and Laketa resisted the urge to laugh, for they understood what had piqued the two Pitkin girls. Nell crawled out of the river, voicing her opinion of Woodrow Miles in spectacular terms that left the listening cowboys envious. Gavin stood behind Naomi, and in a fury, she turned to face him.

"You wouldn't dare!" she snapped.

"Oh, but I would," said Gavin.

He gave her a gentle shove and sent her head-first into the river. It was deep enough that when she struggled to her feet, the water came to her armpits. She stood there and called Gavin some choice names that would have done credit to a bull-whacker. Gladstone Pitkin had apparently exhausted his new-found sense of humor. When Nell climbed the river bank on hands and knees, Pitkin was there to greet her.

"That will be quite enough out of you, young lady," Pitkin said. "I tend to think you got what you deserve."

"Father!" said Naomi, "how can you . . ."

"That goes for you, as well," Pitkin snapped. "If I ever again witness so unladylike a tantrum, I'll take a strap to both of you. Now you're going to apologize to everybody for your childish attitudes."

"Never!" Nell shouted.

"I suppose you are of the same mind," said Pitkin, his eyes on Naomi.

"Damn right I am," Naomi said.

"Very well," said Pitkin. "The two of you will go to the wagon, where you will remain until you see fit to apologize for your crude behavior."

Unrepentant, the two started for the wagon. When they were out of hearing, Woody spoke to Pitkin.

"Pit, maybe Gavin and me should talk to them."

"No," Pitkin said. "You handled them exactly right. Don't spoil it."

"If they apologize," Gavin said, "maybe we ought to take them to the store and buy them rings."

"No," said Pitkin. "They're of age, and if you and Woody still want them when we've reached Santa Fe, then take them with my blessing. But until then, they're going to behave as ladies, if it kills them."

Nell and Naomi spent the rest of the day sulking in the wagon, and when suppertime came, Pitkin forbade the taking of any food to them.

"They got to be half-starved," Gavin said sympatheti-
cally.

"I reckon they are," said Woody, "but Pitkin's laid
down the law."

The camp was asleep except for the men on the first
watch and the unrepentant Pitkin women. They crept out of
the wagon seeking Woody and Gavin.

"How can you let him treat us like ... children?" Nell
cried.

"He believes that's the way you were acting," said
Woody, "and I agree."

"Same here," Gavin said.

"All men are heartless brutes," said Nell bitterly.

"Maybe," Woody replied, "but we're all you've got.
What have you accomplished by sulking, hunkered here in
the wagon, without your supper?"

"Nothing, I suppose," she replied in a small voice.

"He's right," said Naomi resignedly. "We were jealous
of the Stubbs girls, and father knew it. We took it out on
Gavin and Woody. We behaved like a pair of harpies."

"That you did," Gavin said cheerfully, not completely
sure what a harpie was.

"Very well," said Nell. "In the morning we'll apologize.
Then do we get rings like the Stubbs girls have?"

"No," Woody said. "Your daddy forbids it. If you
hadn't let your jealousy override your common sense, Gavin
and me would likely have bought the two of you a set of
rings. Now your daddy says you'll wait till we reach Santa
Fe."

"Damn him," said Nell venomously, "I can't wait to be
out from under his thumb. Him and his proper English
ways."

Gavin laughed. "His English ways ain't all that different
from Texas ways. You was plumb lucky, gettin' pushed into
the river. When I get my brand on you, and nobody else is
around, I'll strip you and take a piggin' string to your bare
behind."

"I couldn't have said that better, myself," said Woody.

"Then maybe you won't be getting your brands on us," Nell said spitefully.

"Maybe we won't," said Woody. "Your daddy's already said we're free to change our minds when we reach Santa Fe."

"Yeah," Gavin added. "Pitch another fit like you did today, and your daddy will be stuck with you from now on."

"I can't believe he'd treat us this way," said Naomi. "Those Stubbs trollops . . ."

"They're not trollops," Woody said, "and nobody knows that better than the two of you. I don't blame Rusty, Vic, and Ash for buying them the rings. They've never said an unkind word to either of you, while you've cut them down at every turn in the trail. Here on the frontier, we don't abide by snooty, stuck-up behavior. Damn it, you're going to be civil to them, if it kills you."

Neither of the furious women said a word, which left Woody and Gavin with all the excuse they needed to terminate the stormy conversation. They returned to the first watch.

Santa Fe, New Mexico Territory. July 11, 1869.

The note from Tobe Hankins was brief. Deuce Rowden read it aloud.

Crossing the Jornada. Ride.

"We still don't know *when*," York Eagan said.

"This is all we're about to get," said Rowden. "We know they've reached the fort, and it's maybe twenty miles from there to the crossin'. They'll be comin' out of the desert six days from now. We got two hundred miles to ride, and that's a good four days."

"I don't like the last word in that message," Jude Epps said. "It sounds like a threat."

Rowden's laugh was ugly. "Threat, hell, that's a promise. If we don't carry out Tobe's orders, we're finished in Santa

Fe, among other places. We got to get us some grub and be on our way.''

"Look yonder," Wiley said proudly, pointing to his and Whit's wagons.

Each of the wagons had a brand new water barrel mounted on each side of the wagon box.

"It's the sensible thing to do," said Woody approvingly.

Breakfast was ready, but Pitkin restrained them.

"My daughters have something to say to all of you," Pitkin said. "Especially, I think, to Woody and Gavin."

The apology didn't come easy. Nell and Naomi stood with their heads down, and it was Nell who spoke first.

"I am sorry for my display of temper yesterday. Woody, I'm sorry I pushed you in the river."

She paused as though she half expected Woody to apologize for his similar treatment of her, but Woody said nothing.

"I am sorry I lost my temper yesterday," said Naomi. "Gavin, I'm especially sorry for what I did to you."

Her eyes couldn't meet Gavin's, and like Woody, he said not a word.

"Now that we have the necessary unpleasantries out of the way," Pitkin said, "let us all have breakfast and be on our way."

Once the herd was moving, Woody rode on ahead. He wanted to be sure just how far they had to travel before reaching the Cimarron Cutoff. He rode twenty miles, and still the wagon ruts continued following the Arkansas. Ten miles later, he found what he was seeking, for there the trail forked. One set of ruts continued almost due west, following the Arkansas, while the other veered away to the southwest. He reined up, looking into the formidable *Jornada*. As far as the eye could see there was only sand, seeming to stretch on into infinity. There wasn't a tree or clump of grass. Miles away, in the painful blue of the sky, buzzards circled. It seemed like they always took a hand in the game, and when a man had played his last cards, the macabre scavengers were there to collect all bets. Wheeling his horse, Woody rode back to meet the outfit.

"Another inaccuracy in the map," said Woody, as he rode beside Pitkin's wagon. "I'd say it's more like thirty miles from Fort Dodge to the Cimarron Cutoff."

"I can't see that it matters," Pitkin replied. "Even if we reach the crossing at midday, shouldn't we wait until the following morning to begin the trek across the desert?"

"Not necessarily," said Woody. "Half the distance across that desert will be in the daytime, at the mercy of the sun. Suppose we watered the stock, and at sundown, drove them all night? At first light we keep them moving and drive them all day."

"It is my belief that you would have an unruly herd, completely out of control," said Pitkin.

"The second night," Woody said, "we would rest them until midnight and then drive them on as far as they would go. With any luck, we can get them three-quarters of the distance across the desert and then stampede them the rest of the way."

"I don't like to question your experience on the trail," said Pitkin, "but I must remind you that the Arkansas will be to the northwest of us. As you have so often pointed out, the mere hint of water on the night wind can drive a thirsty herd crazy."

"I'm considering that," Woody said. "It's a calculated risk."

"Going by way of Bent's old fort and across Raton Pass is almost five hundred miles," said Pitkin, "but we would avoid the desert. Suppose we considered the mountain trail through southern Colorado?"

"I would consider the mountain trail if we had pack mules," Woody said, "But there are the wagons. A stampede, with cattle taking to mountain draws, and we'd be there until snow flies. Even with a desert to cross, it's the shortest way."

Woody stuck to his guns, and Pitkin said no more, something he would later regret.

"Tomorrow," said Woody, after they had bedded down the herd for the night, "we'll reach Cimarron Crossing. I want every container—every barrel—filled with water. We'll see that the herd gets all the water they can drink. Then we'll drive them all night and all the next day. That should take us halfway across the *Jornada*."

"Then we'll have a thirsty herd in a dry camp," Nip Kelly said, "with two more dry days and nights ahead of them. You're asking for it, *amigo*."

"Maybe," said Woody grimly, "but it's my decision. If it's a bad one, then I'll take the blame."

Cimarron Crossing. July 13, 1869.

They drove the herd into the Arkansas, within sight of the formidable desert.

"Drive 'em in," Woody shouted. "Make them drink."

Pitkin's wagon followed the chuck wagon, as Gonzales drove upriver away from the herd.

"After supper," said Gonzales, "we fill the water barrels."

Supper was a hurried affair, for they knew they must take full advantage of the night hours. Time was their enemy, bringing with the dawn a vicious sun that would suck the moisture out of man and beast. After supper, Woody, Gavin, Rusty, and Nip began filling the barrels in Pitkin's wagon. Wiley and Whit filled their newly acquired barrels, and then helped Gonzales fill the barrels on either side of the chuck wagon.

"Head 'em up, move 'em out," Woody shouted.

It was time to rest, to graze, and the longhorns resisted all efforts to drive them into the desert. It required the efforts of every rider, and almost an hour to get the herd moving. Even as they took the trail, the longhorns bawled their displeasure, and the drag riders had their hands full heading the animals that broke ranks and headed down the backtrail. The herd was tired, and they made their displeasure evident by raking their companions with their razor-sharp long horns.

"Keep 'em bunched," Woody shouted. "Let every cow see nothing but another cow's behind."

They fought the herd every step of the way. When they finally settled down, it was at a gait of their own choosing. The riders used their lariats to pop the behinds of the longhorns, but all to no avail. After three hours, the riders had to change their mounts, lest the animals become exhausted. Come the dawn, they milled the herd, while Gonzales got breakfast. The cattle bawled mournfully. The cowboys had to eat two at a time, while their companions strove mightily to keep the herd bunched. Time after time, steers broke ranks and lit out down the backtrail.

"Head 'em up, move 'em out," Woody shouted.

It was all they could do, keeping the herd headed in the same direction. The sun rose with a vengeance, and soon every rider's shirt was dark with sweat.

"My God," said Nell, at drag, "we'll never get them across this desert."

"We got no choice," Rusty said. "You and Naomi watch that left flank, and I'll try to cover the rest."

But they simply didn't have enough drag riders. Bonita waved her hat, getting Vic's attention. He dropped back beside Whit's wagon.

"You need more drag riders," said Bonita. "If Woody will allow you to saddle horses for Jania, Laketa, and me, we'll help out at drag."

"Bless you all," Vic said. "I'll talk to Woody."

It wasn't easy, for Woody was everywhere. When Vic was finally able to talk to Woody, he found the trail boss willing to try anything.

"Saddle them some mounts," said Woody.

Vic made haste to catch up three of the horses they had taken from the outlaw gang who had tried to claim part of the herd. There were extra saddles in Pitkin's wagon.

"What are you attempting to do?" Pitkin asked.

"We just picked up three more drag riders," said Vic.

"The Stubbs girls are goin' to fill in at drag."

Pitkin said nothing, but Vic thought he saw approval in the Englishman's eyes. As it turned out, the Stubbs girls rode well, and began to make a difference. Ahead, beyond the sand hills, was a barren plain without wood or water. There wasn't a single landmark, and Pitkin constantly consulted his compass. The first few miles through the sand hills was heavy pulling, and the wagons fell behind. By the time the mules reached the level plain beyond, they were already hot, tired, and thirsty. By noon of the first day there was distant thunder, accompanied by lightning.

"Could it be about to rain?" Pitkin wondered.

They soon had their answer, and it was the last thing any of them expected. Egg-sized hailstones began pelting them, raising painful lumps. This assault from the sky was too much for the weary, thirsty, cantankerous longhorns, and they stampeded. Horses reared and mules balked as the merciless barrage continued. Riders hung onto their hats, trying to protect their heads, while arms, shoulders, and thighs took a beating. It lasted not more than a few minutes, but seemed much longer. By some miracle, the horse remuda had not run with the herd.

"Gavin," Woody shouted, "you and Rusty stay with the remuda. The rest of you riders come with me. We have to catch up to the herd."

Because the hail stones had struck them from behind, the longhorns had run virtually in the same direction they were being driven. Woody was gratified to find his five female riders had followed. He would need all the help he could get. They had ridden more than five miles before they began seeing small clusters of longhorns. Having no graze and no water, they stood there bawling their misery, like a chorus of lost souls.

"We'll drive this bunch until we can combine it with the next one," Woody said.

"The only damn thing in our favor," said Nip Kelly, "is that they managed to run the way we wanted 'em to go."

Looking back, Woody could see the horse remuda and

the wagons following. After ten miles, half the herd was still missing.

"What I was afraid of," Vic said. "The varmints didn't all run straight. Some of 'em fanned out. We'll have to circle."

"We'll wait for the wagons," said Woody. "We're likely to be a while, and for safety's sake, we may have to make camp right here."

Pitkin reined up his teams and Woody explained the situation.

"Very well," Pitkin said, through thinly-veiled exasperation, "I suppose there is no help for it."

The riders fanned out in a half-circle, but with only a small measure of success. They would have to ride back to near the start of the stampede and swing farther out. Leading the way, Woody bypassed Pitkin's wagon. He didn't feel like explaining their need for riding back the way they had come. But there were others who didn't understand.

"Vic," Bonita said, "why are we riding back the way we've just come?"

"Because all the herd didn't run straight," said Vic. "Some of them broke ranks, slewing off to one side or the other. Riding a straight line, we've missed them."

It proved to be the case, and slowly they brought the herd together. Sundown was an hour away when a final tally satisfied Woody. He called the outfit together, and they all listened glumly as he told them what they didn't want to hear.

"We move out after supper. A small ration of water for the horses and mules."

"At the risk of seeming to question your judgment," said Pitkin, "do you really think these cattle are physically able to stand another night on the trail?"

"We're about to find out," Woody said. "They mustered up enough strength to scatter themselves over twenty miles of desert."

The first stars were flowering silver in a purple sky when they again took the trail. The mournful lowing of the cattle had become a dirge, and the riders were grimly silent. If they had doubts about Woody, they remained silent, for he was trail boss. The showdown came at dawn, when Gavin rode forward from drag.

"Woody, some cows are down and can't get up."

"We'll rest the herd for a couple of hours, while we have breakfast," Woody said. "If there's some that can't get up when we're ready to move out, shoot them."

Nell Pitkin had followed Gavin, and she listened unbelievingly to Woody's order.

"Woodrow Miles," she said, "you are a heartless, unfeeling brute."

"I reckon," said Woody, "but I'm also the trail boss."

But all Woody's plans changed in an instant. The outfit was having breakfast when the Kiowa struck. There were two dozen of them, and they seemed literally to rise out of the desert sand.

The attack was a total surprise, and they galloped their horses near enough to loose a barrage of arrows before a shot could be fired. Gladstone Pitkin was the first to get off a shot, and the first to take an Indian arrow. Wiley and Whit had left their Winchesters under their wagon boxes, and before reaching their weapons, each took an arrow in the thigh. An arrow struck Woody in the back, high up, slamming him face-down in the sand.

An Indian was about to drive a lance through Woody, when Bonita Stubbs shot the brave off his horse. There was a scream as Naomi Pitkin fell with an arrow in her side. But the defenders fought back, and the deadly Winchesters took their toll. More than half the attackers had been shot off their horses when the survivors gave up the fight and rode away.

"My God," Gavin said, kneeling beside the wounded Naomi.

An arrow had struck Gladstone Pitkin below the collarbone, but he ignored it, instead concerning himself with those who were more seriously wounded. He looked questioningly at Gavin.

"A flesh wound," Gavin said, "but she's losing blood."

"Woody's wound appears to be much more serious," said Pitkin. "Perhaps you'd better see to him."

Rusty and Vic had raised Woody to a sitting position, and Nell was kneeling beside him, weeping.

"He took a bad one," Vic said. "Drivin' it on through could puncture a lung."

To their surprise, Woody grunted. He lifted his head, and they could see the pain and uncertainty in his eyes. Fixing them on Gavin, he spoke.

"Gavin . . . you're . . . trail boss. Good luck . . . *amigo*."

15

❦

The next several hours were a nightmare. Quickly, Gavin saw to Naomi's wound. His first priority was to stop the bleeding. He appealed to Rusty, Vic, and Nip Kelly.

"Some of you will have to help me drive these arrows on through. If any one of you believe you're more qualified than I am, then you're welcome to remove that arrow from Woody."

"My God, no," said Rusty. "You and Woody's been pards too long. He'd want you to drive that arrow out of him."

"Unless Pit has some objection," Nip said, "I'll take that barb out of him."

"Then I reckon Rusty and me can drive them arrows out of Wiley and Whit," said Vic. "Rusty, are you game?"

"I reckon," Rusty replied, swallowing hard. "Gavin's got the hardest task of all, so the least we can do is help where we can."

"I bring all the whiskey," said Gonzales. "There is no more."

He produced four quart bottles.

"Wiley and Whit's got two wagonloads of the stuff," Gavin said. "We'll tap a keg of that, if we need to. Nip, Rusty, and Vic, take a bottle of this. See that Pitkin, Wiley, and Whit drink at least half of this, and give it time to knock them out."

With Nell standing fearfully by, Gavin examined Woody, studying the angle of the arrow. It hadn't yet pierced a lung, or there would be bloody froth on Woody's lips. The trick would be to drive it on through, missing any vital organs.

"Is he . . . can you . . . save him?" Nell asked.

"I don't know," said Gavin. "All I can do is try. The arrow must be driven through, and there's always the danger of piercing a lung. It's one of those devilish situations where his life can be saved only by risking it. While I support him, I'll need you to get at least half this bottle of whiskey down him."

Woody being unconscious, it was difficult getting him to drink the whiskey, but Nell was determined.

"He'll need maybe half an hour for it to put him under," Gavin said. "While we're waiting for that, I'll cleanse and disinfect Naomi's wound. Gonzales should have water boiling by now."

Nell brought the hot water and a quantity of clean white muslin that Gonzales had thoughtfully purchased. Cows bawled mournfully, but lives hung in the balance, and there was no time to consider anything else. Nobody noticed the clouds gathering ahead of them until the distant lightning began dancing across the heavens. Thunder boomed.

"Rain!" Nell shouted.

"Somewhere ahead of us," Gavin said, "but not close enough to save the herd."

But the turmoil in the heavens and the several hours' rest did wonders for the cattle. Somewhere ahead there was the smell of water, and the longhorns responded. It started with a few cows in a shambling run, escalating into a full-blown stampede. The thundering herd was soon lost in the distance, the clouds of dust the only sign of their passing.

"Well, by God," Nip Kelly said, "I never seen the like. Don't look like there's ever been any rain on this cussed desert, and that means it's somewhere beyond. Twenty-five miles, at least."

"They'll run all the way to the Cimarron," said Vic. "At least, when we're able to go on, we'll stand a chance of roundin' 'em up. I ain't puttin' Woody down, but them cattle purely wouldn't have made it without that storm."

Pitkin was under the influence of the whiskey and wouldn't learn of the stampede for a while, and that suited Gavin. Woody's life was in his hands, and the burden lay heavy on his mind. Finally he had put it off as long as he could, and it was time to drive the arrow on through. Nell had spread a blanket and Woody lay on it, facedown.

"This won't be pleasant," Gavin said. "It'll be hell on me, but you don't have to watch it."

"I know," said Nell, "but I want to stay. I can't forget the last words I said to him. I called him a heartless brute."

The recollection reduced her to tears, and Gavin said nothing. He broke off the end of the shaft, getting rid of the feathers. He would need most of the arrow's length to drive it through. He removed the shells from his Colt, and taking it by the muzzle, began pounding the shaft of the arrow. Despite the whiskey, Woody grunted with every blow, but there was now cause for hope. As long as there was life, it was unlikely the deadly arrow had penetrated a lung. Gavin's shirt was soon soaked with sweat, and it dripped off the end of his nose. The muzzle of the Colt slipped in his sweaty hands, for the pressure was almost more than he could stand. He could tell when the barb of the arrow exited, and he drew a long breath of relief. Nell was pale as death, silent tears dripping off her chin.

"Help me turn him over," Gavin said. "The arrow's out."

Gavin said a silent prayer that when they turned Woody over, there wouldn't be that telltale red froth on his lips. There wasn't, and Gavin wiped his sweating brow on the sleeve of his shirt.

"Gavin," said Nell. Overcome with emotion, she seemed about to put her arms about him.

"While I lift him up," Gavin said, "yozu remove his shirt."

Surprisingly, the wound hadn't bled much. Gavin poured disinfectant into the wound, and preparing two large pads from the muslin, placed one over the wound, front and back. He then used strips of muslin to bind the pads in place, soaking them with disinfectant.

"I'll need you to watch him," said Gavin. "If he gets restless, he'll lose both those pads. I've soaked both these pads in disinfectant, and they'll need soaking again, as quickly as they dry out. Will you do that?"

"Yes," Nell said. "I'll do it."

Lightning still blazed across the heavens, and the tantalizing smell of the distant rain made it seem imminent. But with the wind, thunder, and lightning, there was no rain as far as the eye could see. With Woody resting, Gavin made his way to the blanket on which Gladstone Pitkin had been stretched out. Nip Kelly raised the arrow triumphantly.

"He'll make it," said Nip. "He's such a tough old rooster, I had trouble drivin' the arrow on through. Hardest part was gettin' the whiskey down him. He ain't much of a drinkin' man, or he's used to better whiskey."

Nip disinfected the wound, padded it front and back, and then soaked the pads with the disinfectant. Gavin moved on to see what progress Vic and Rusty had made with Wiley and Whit.

"I reckon we must've done somethin' right," Vic said. "The arrows are out, and these two is still breathin'."

"Disinfect their wounds, bandage them, and let them sleep," said Gavin. "I reckon we have enough barreled water to keep ourselves, the mules, and the horses alive. Without the herd, we can survive. This is a poor excuse for a camp, but with so many wounded, we'll have to make do."

"We can't be sure that bunch of Indians won't come lookin' for revenge," Vic said.

"No," said Gavin, "but we won't have to worry about them comin' after us after dark. They were Kiowa."

"I've never seen weather like this, since the Llano Estacado," Rusty said. "All we'll get out of all that wind, thunder, and lightning is a little relief from the sun."

"Don't knock it," said Vic. "As long as that's goin' on, and there's a smell of water, them longhorns will be runnin' hell-bent-for-election toward it. Sure as hell, it's saved the herd for us.''

In the late afternoon the distant storm began to subside. The thunder and lightning became less frequent, and the anxious riders could only hope that its duration had been sufficient for the thirst-crazed herd to free itself from the desert and reach water.

"Pitkin's conscious and wantin' to talk to you," Nip Kelly said.

"He has no business awake and talking," said Gavin. "Why didn't you give him enough whiskey to knock him out again?"

"He wouldn't have it," Nip said. "Not until he talks to you."

Pitkin lay under a blanket, his head on a saddle. Gavin hunkered down beside him.

"Kelly wouldn't tell me anything," said Pitkin, "except that the arrow has been taken out, and that I should be dead drunk. Where is the herd? I can no longer hear them."

"There was a storm—with wind, thunder, and lightning—maybe twenty-five miles ahead of us," Gavin said. "All it took was a hint of water, and they were off and running."

"I suppose it was for the best," said Pitkin, "with so many of us wounded. What are our chances of rounding up at least some of the herd, when we're able to catch up to them?"

"Better than you'd expect, I think," Gavin replied. "Accordin' to your map, maybe ten miles this side of the Cimarron, is Sand Creek. Back in Council Grove, Woody and me was told Sand Creek is dry most of the time, flowin' only after a cloudburst. I'd say what we just witnessed was the grandpappy of all cloudbursts. If there's water in Sand Creek, we'll find every last cow alive and well. But we can't travel. We'll just have to wait and see.''

"Thank you," said Pitkin. "How are Woody, Naomi, Wiley, and Whit?"

"They'll all need time to heal," Gavin said, "but they're not facing anything worse than massive hangovers."

"Excellent," said Pitkin. "Now you may have Kelly fetch that venomous whiskey."

"There ain't enough in this bottle to see him through a bout of fever," Kelly said. "We'll be needin' more whiskey by sometime tonight."

"When the bottle's empty, bring it to me," said Gavin. "I'll refill it from one of the barrels in one of the Stubbs wagons."

Gavin found Bonita, Jania, and Laketa watching over Wiley and Whit.

"We feel terribly useless, just doing nothing," Bonita said.

"There's not much any of us can do, with so many wounded," said Gavin. "All of you held your own during the Indian attack, and that's when it counted. You can all watch over Wiley and Whit during the night, giving them more whiskey when it's needed. We're just about out of the stuff, and we may have to tap a keg in one of your wagons."

"Take it," Bonita said. "I'm just thankful it's here, when there's a need for it."

After supper, Gavin spoke to the outfit.

"It's unlikely there'll be any Indian trouble at night, unless there's some Comanches around, but we'll still need a watch. That'll depend on Nip, Rusty, Vic, Ash, and me. Let's go with two of us on the first watch and three on the second. I'll be one of the three on the second."

"I want to help in some way," said Nell.

"You're goin' to," Gavin said. "I'm putting you in charge of dosing Woody and your daddy with whiskey until their fever breaks."

"What about Naomi?" Nell asked.

"I'll be checking on her," said Gavin.

"We'll be looking after Wiley and Whit," Laketa said, "but isn't there something more we can do?"

"Yes," said Gavin. "Keep your Winchesters handy, and if there's more trouble, meet it like you did that Indian attack."

Before the first watch took over, Gavin saw to it that the horses and mules each had a small ration of water. It wasn't enough, but it would keep them alive. Before the start of the second watch, Gavin enlisted Vic's help in drawing enough whiskey from one of the barrels to fill the four whiskey bottles. There was no moon, and the desolation of the desert made the silence seem all the more intense.

"Sometime during the night," said Gavin, "those Indians will reclaim their dead. We'll allow them to, as long as thcy don't make any hostile moves."

"Good thinkin'," Vic said. "They had one hell of a bad day in battle, and sometimes it hits 'em as a bad omen, and they'll give it up."

"I'd settle for that," said Rusty.

The three saw and heard nothing. Gavin went twice to look in on Naomi, and finding her with a fierce fever, forced her to drink more whiskey. At first light, there was not a sign of the Indians who had fallen on the sandy plain. While Gonzales prepared breakfast, Gavin made the rounds of the wounded.

"Father and Woody began sweating a short while ago," Nell announced.

"They're back among the living, then," said Gavin. "No more whiskey."

When Gavin touched Naomi's face, he found it moist. She opened her eyes.

"How do you feel?" Gavin asked.

"Like I've had nothing to drink in months, and my head's about to explode."

"I'll bring you some water," said Gavin, "and then you'll have to take another slug of that whiskey. You, dear girl, have a man-sized hangover."

Gavin found Wiley and Whit conscious, begging for water.

Gavin laughed. "Don't complain, gents. You've been drinkin' your own whiskey."

"God," Whit said, "we should've sold all of it while we

was in Dodge. We'll likely git run out of Santa Fe for ped-
dlin' this stuff.''

The sun rose hot and merciless, and the sandy plain was
devoid of any movement except an occasional dust devil.
By noon, all the wounded were able to take nourishment,
and for the first time, Woody learned of the stampede.

"I reckon it saved my bacon," said Woody. "God
knows, I'd played my last card, and needin' an ace, drew a
deuce. How's Pit takin' it?"

"Better than you'd expect," Gavin replied. "You remember, back at Council Grove, we was told somethin'
about Sand Creek, eight or ten miles this side of the Cimarron?"

"Yeah," said Woody. "Except after a cloudburst, Sand
Creek's nearly always dry."

"Well, the cloudburst that stampeded the herd may have
left Sand Creek runnin' bank-full," Gavin said. "That bein'
the case, it means the herd was maybe fifteen miles away
from water. Like I told Pitkin, there's a good chance we
can round up the herd when we catch up to them."

"I reckon you didn't mention the possibility that Sand
Creek may have dried up again, before we can get there,"
said Woody.

"Damn it," Gavin said, "you'd pile a heavy burden on
a man, wouldn't you?"

Gavin found Pitkin cheerful enough, despite the fact he
likely had a massive hangover, and was restless because of
the delay.

"How much longer must we remain here?"

"I figure two more days," said Gavin. "By then, our
barreled water will be low, and we'll be forced to move on.
Do you think you'll be up to it?"

"I shall be ready to go tomorrow," Pitkin said stiffly,
"but I suppose I must consider the others. I suppose you
have seen to Naomi?"

"Yes," said Gavin. "She's in no danger."

"I suppose you are posting an adequate guard, should the
Indians return."

"I am," Gavin said, becoming irritated by Pitkin's apparent doubt of his capabilities.

But that very night, the Indians returned. Not to fight, but to take captives. Not until Gavin, Vic, and Rusty were about to begin the second watch did they learn something had definitely gone wrong.

"Where's Bonita?" Vic asked.

"She had some business away from camp," Laketa said.

"Which way?" Vic asked, becoming alarmed.

"Over there beyond the wagons," said Laketa.

"Rusty," Gavin said, "get the lantern from the chuck wagon."

Rusty brought the lantern on the run, and by its dim light, they found exactly what Gavin had feared. There were three sets of moccasin tracks.

"It wouldn't take three Indians to subdue Bonita," Gavin said. "I'm afraid they might have taken Nell or Naomi, or perhaps both. Wait for me."

Gavin found Naomi asleep, and a few feet away, Gladstone Pitkin also slept. Gently as he could, Gavin awakened Naomi.

"Naomi, do you know where Nell is?"

"No," said Naomi. "Why?"

"Indians have taken Bonita Stubbs," Gavin said. "There were three of them, and I had to be sure they hadn't taken you or Nell."

"But now you believe they have," said Naomi.

"Yes," Gavin replied, "and we can't trail them until first light. Don't wake Pit, and by all means, keep it from Woody. I'm asking you to trust me. Will you?"

"Yes," she said quietly. "I've been nasty and mean to you when you didn't deserve it, but I'd trust you with my life, as well as Nell's. Please do what you can, before they . . ."

She didn't finish the dreaded sentence, nor did she need to. Gavin quickly rejoined Vic and Rusty.

"Looks like they took Nell too," said Gavin. "We'll make the rounds of the camp with the lantern."

They quickly found Nell's tracks leading away from the Pitkin wagon, and finally the place where one of the Indians had taken her. There were only moccasin tracks leading away.

"There ain't a damn thing we can do in the dark," Vic said, "but let's track the three varmints to their horses and find out which way they went."

They quickly found the place where the three sets of moccasin tracks came together, and followed them to where the Indians had left their horses.

"As if we needed proof," Rusty said, "look at them moccasin tracks. Two sets of 'em are deeper than the others. Them varmints was carryin' Bonita and Nell."

"That means two horses are carryin' double too," said Vic.

"Yes," Gavin said, "and it may be our only hope of finding the girls. There's been no rain here in months. Maybe years. Do you know what a decent wind could do to all those tracks?"

"My God, yes," said Vic. "Them horse tracks is headin' south, but we don't know they won't change direction to throw us off the trail."

"Why in tarnation are they ridin' south?" Rusty wondered. "What's down there?"

"Pit's map don't go that far," said Gavin, "but if I'm any judge, they'll eventually get to the Cimarron River. Or beyond that, the North Canadian. Indians must have water, and I doubt there's a drop anywhere in this desert."

"What are we goin' to do until it's light enough to trail 'em?" Vic asked.

"There's nothing we can do," said Gavin, "and I know how you feel. Remember, they have Nell, too."

"Lord, yes," Rusty said, "and before we do anything else, you'll have to tell Pitkin."

"I know," said Gavin, with a sigh. "He asked me if I was postin' proper sentries, and I felt like cussin' him for insultin' my intelligence."

"It's the kind of thing fifty sentries couldn't have prevented," Rusty said. "The girls had no business goin' off in the dark."

"They're on their way, but they're not yet Western women," said Gavin. "I'm to blame for not specifically telling them to remain in camp at night."

"I reckon maybe all of us are some to blame," Vic said. "Remember, we was thankin' our lucky stars that bunch that attacked us wasn't Comanches, that they wouldn't come after us at night?"

"I remember only too well," said Gavin. "While it may be true the Kiowa don't attack at night, we know now they aren't afraid of taking hostages."

"I don't even like to think about it," Vic said, "but suppose these varmints *ain't* Kiowa? They could be Comanches."

"My God," said Gavin, "you're right. That bunch of Comanches that came after us had to know there were women in the outfit. There's nothing Comanches like better than captive white women. Remember Cynthia Ann Parker?"*

They all knew the sad saga and its tragic ending. There was little they could do except keep watch until dawn. Then Gavin remembered he hadn't told Jania and Laketa Stubbs the Indians had taken Bonita, nor had he cautioned them against going in search of her.

"I'll be back," Gavin said. "There's something I must attend to."

They might have hoorawed him for slipping away to visit with Naomi, but it wasn't the time or place for cowboy humor, nor was Naomi likely to be in a romantic mood. The Stubbs girls were awake, worried, but had remained near the wagon where Wiley and Whit slept.

"I didn't forget you," Gavin said softly. "We had to do some looking around. Indians took Bonita. They also got

---

* Cynthia Ann Parker, captured by Comanches in 1836, became the wife of a Comanche chief and the mother of Quanah Parker, the last great chief of the Comanches.

Nell Pitkin. We found their trail by lantern light, but there's no way we can go after them until first light.''

These were practical women who had seen more than their share of hardship, and they accepted the bad news without breaking down. Bonita was the youngest of the three, and the most outgoing, and her sisters were afraid for her.

"What will the Indians do . . . to Bonita and Nell?" Laketa asked.

"They likely won't be physically harmed," said Gavin. "These may not have been the band of Kiowa we fought, but the bunch of Comanches you were fighting when we rode to help you. Comanches generally force captured white women to become the wives of their tribal chiefs."

"Dear God," Jania said, "that could be worse than death."

"No," said Gavin. "It'll buy us some time."

"Is there anything we can do?" Laketa asked.

"Just one thing," said Gavin. "Keep quiet about this until morning. I'll have to break the news to Pitkin, and I might as well tell everybody else at the same time."

"We'll be quiet," Jania said. "We know you'll do your best, and you'll probably have a time of it, leaving Woody behind."

"I expect I will," said Gavin. "I'll face that when I have to."

It seemed to Gavin he had been waiting forever when, like a heaven-high rosy headdress, dawn feathered the eastern horizon. Pitkin, Naomi, Woody, Wiley, and Whit lay on blankets near enough that Gavin could speak to all of them at the same time.

"Sometime during the night," Gavin said, "Indians took Bonita Stubbs and Nell Pitkin. By lantern light we found their trail and are preparing to go after them."

"Who was on watch when this took place?" Pitkin demanded.

"That would have made no difference," said Gavin.

"The girls left the camp for some reasons of their own. They avoided the sentries."

"I still wish to know who was on sentry duty at the time," Pitkin said.

"Ash and me was on the first watch," said Nip Kelly. "You want me to quit, or would you rather fire me?"

"Nobody quits and nobody gets fired," Woody shouted. "Hell, half of us are wounded and of no help. Pit, this is no time to exercise your temper."

"Woody," said Gavin, "shut up. This happened while I was trail boss, and damn it, I'll do what must be done to rescue Bonita and Nell."

"Then do it," Pitkin snapped. "You are precisely correct. I've nothing but admiration for a man with the courage to take responsibility."

Woody shrugged his shoulders, and the rest of the outfit would have laughed if the circumstances had been different. The fiery confrontation Gavin had expected had been avoided, and Pitkin's response had a sobering effect on Woody. He didn't insist on being included in the rescue party.

"It'll be Vic, Rusty, and me," Gavin said. "Nip and Ash, I'm leanin' heavy on the both of you. You'll be the only two defenders without wounds, and if we don't make it back by tonight, you'll have to do a full night of sentry duty. Jania and Laketa, your Winchesters will be needed if there's trouble. Wiley and Whit, your leg wounds won't prevent you from shooting, and I'm counting on you to do it, if there's a need."

"We'll be ready," said Wiley.

"Yeah," Whit added. "Just find the girls and bring 'em back."

"Jania and me can stand watch tonight, if need be," said Laketa. "We can still have two watches."

None of the others who had been wounded—Pitkin, Woody, and Naomi—had a word to say. They didn't need reminding that their wounds were recent, and any exertion, such as the recoil of a Winchester, could undo the healing that had begun. Gonzales had heard enough of Gavin's shocking revelation to know there was a need for haste, and by the time Gavin had reached an understanding with the rest of the outfit, the Mexican had breakfast almost ready.

"Vic, Rusty, get your plates, cups, and eatin' tools and go first for grub. I'll be right behind you. After we eat, load your saddlebags with enough jerked beef for three days, and plenty of ammunition for Colt and Winchester."

Breakfast was a hurried affair. Gonzales took food and coffee to those who had been wounded. Nip and Ash finished their meal along with Gavin, Vic, and Rusty, following the trio when they went to saddle their horses.

"I reckon this is a bad time to bring it up," said Nip, "but we'll be so near out of water by tomorrow night, there won't be enough for the horses and mules."

"It's somethin' that's got to be dealt with," Gavin said. "I aim to talk to Woody once more before we leave. You and Ash come with me, and I'll do it now."

Woody looked up questioningly as they approached.

"Woody," said Gavin, "I'm leavin' some orders that I'll expect you to carry out, if they become necessary. By tomorrow night, the barreled water will be dangerously low, with none for the horses and mules. If we're not back by then, I want you to push on to Sand Creek, the Cimmaron, or the nearest water. Nip and Ash can harness the teams. It'll be hard on Pitkin, likely, but he'll have to ride his own wagon box. Wiley and Whit won't have that much trouble, with leg wounds. You'll ride the chuck wagon with Gonzales, and Naomi will ride with Pitkin."

"Not bad, *amigo*," Woody said. "I reckon you have plans for the horse remuda."

"I have," said Gavin. "We're takin' two extra horses for Bonita and Nell. That leaves a dozen. Using lead ropes, Nip and Ash will tie four of them behind each wagon. There's no herd, so Nip and Ash can act as outriders for the wagons. You'll be in no more danger and no worse off than settin' here without water. *Comprender*?"

"*Sí,*" Woody replied.

Nip and Ash nodded their understanding. It was time for the rescuers to mount up and ride. Laketa followed Rusty to his horse, while Gavin answered a cry from Naomi. Vic waited impatiently, his mind on Bonita, while his companions said their goodbyes. Finally Gavin and Rusty took their leave and mounted their horses. As the three rode away to the south, their companions watched them go.

"*Vaya con Dios, amigos,*" said Nip Kelly softly.

Only Ash Pryor heard him, and he understood. The trio would be facing they knew not how many hostile Indians—perhaps Comanches—and they might never return. Gavin had made allowances for that. A true Texan would save his comrades if he could . . .

16

*B*eing "horse Indians," the Comanches stalked their prey for as many days or miles as was needed. The trio had been particularly attracted to the "yellow-haired squaws," and in the aftermath of the attack by the Kiowa, had awaited their opportunity to take captives. The Comanche method was simple. With one hand over the captive's mouth to prevent her from crying out, he fisted his other hand and knocked her senseless. Thus Bonita Stubbs and Nell Pitkin were taken without a sound, and when they became conscious, each was bellydown over the withers of an Indian horse.

"Where are you taking me?" Bonita shouted.

There were only guttural sounds from the rider. To Bonita it sounded like laughter. In the starlight she could see the legs of another horse, and when she lifted her head, her eyes met those of a very frightened Nell Pitkin.

"So they got you too," Nell said. "What are they going to do with us?"

"I don't think they're taking us home to meet mama," said Bonita. "From what I hear, if we're lucky, they'll only share us with the rest of the tribe."

"Well, I don't intend to go any farther," Nell said.

She sank her teeth into the Indian's bare leg, letting go when he again knocked her senseless. Bonita began beating the horse's belly with her fists, spooking the animal. Buckjumping, it threw her and the Comanche. The third Indian, mounted, caught the horse, while its thrown rider went after Bonita.

"*Diablo* squaw," he muttered, seizing her by the belt. Again he flung her down over the horse's withers and climbed up behind her. No sooner had he done so, than he felt a wetness flowing beneath him and down his legs.

"*Agua!*" he shouted. "*Agua!*"

He slid to the ground, seized Bonita by the shirt collar, and dragged her off the horse. Water began pooling in the sand around her bare feet, and the two mounted Comanches thought that hilariously funny. Aware the rest of the tribe would hear of this disgraceful incident, her captor clubbed Bonita with his fist, knocking her down. But she was game. Getting to her hands and knees, and finally to her feet, she began shouting at the top of her voice.

"What did you expect, you heathen varmint? You dragged me away before I had a chance to go."

While the Comanches didn't understand her words, there was no mistaking her intent, no denying her spirit, and this time, all the Indians laughed. Bonita chose that moment to retaliate. Lightning-quick, she kicked the nearest of the three in the groin. His companions were amused at first, but their fun ended swiftly when Nell slid off the horse and ran. One of the mounted Indians quickly rode her down, only to have her bite his hand while he had it over her mouth. He flung her back onto the horse, but no sooner had he mounted behind her, than she began raking his bare leg with her nails.

"*Garras,*" the Comanche snarled.

He flung Nell to the ground and slid off the horse. She was about to get up, when he shoved her back. She was rolled over, bellydown, and her hands were bound behind her back with rawhide thongs. Her feet were similarly tied together. Another of the Comanches had bound Bonita in the same fashion. Again they were thrown across the withers of Indian horses, and the journey continued.

* * *

"Lord," said Rusty, as they rested the horses, "I wish we'd had some way of bringing along some water."

"We could easily have bought canteens at Fort Dodge," Gavin said, "but how were we to know we'd end up trackin' Indians across a desert?"

"Couldn't have brought enough in canteens for our horses," said Vic. "We'll have to find water for them by tonight, and that'll mean water for us. Indians got to have water, too, and it can't be that far off."

"Then we'd better be ridin' on. Our best—and probably only—chance to rescue Nell and Bonita will be after dark," Gavin said.

"They must not be ridin' too far," said Rusty. "They're pushing their horses, and they ain't stopped for a rest."

But within the hour, they reined up where Nell and Bonita had rebelled. There were numerous tracks in the sand, including the bare ones left by the girls.

"There was a puddle here," Vic said. "One of the girls. Sun's dried it up long ago, but you can see where it was."

"I doubt they stopped for that," said Gavin. "Comanches aren't known for their consideration or compassion."

"Bonita and Nell was givin' 'em some grief," Rusty said. "One of 'em was put bellydown. There's an outline of part of a belt buckle in the sand."

"Here's another," said Vic. "Likely this is where they was tied hand and foot."

"That's a pretty good picture of it," Gavin said, "and it makes me feel better. If the girls can keep their nerve, we'll pull them out of this yet."

"Yeah," said Vic. "If Nell can unload on them Comanches like she's unloaded on poor old Woody, them Comanches will be offerin' us boot to take her back."

Rusty had to laugh, and despite the gravity of the situation, Gavin joined in. Quickly they mounted their horses and rode on.

Back in camp, time lagged. Gladstone Pitkin, Woody, and Naomi sat in the shade of the wagon, and when the burning sun reached its zenith and began its descent, they moved to the other side of the wagon. Wiley and Whit languished in the shade of one of their wagons, with Jania and Laketa. Nip and Ash hunkered beside the chuck wagon exchanging idle conversation with Gonzales. Occasionally, the three of them walked around, relieving their own boredom and that of the others, expressing a few words of confidence.

"It humbles a man some, gettin' cut down by an Indian arrow," Ash said.

"If you're referrin' to Pitkin, I'd have to agree," said Nip. "It kind of reduces it all to the least common denominator. I'd bet my horse and saddle this is the first time in Pit's life that he's had to depend on others, maybe the first time he's ever taken enough booze to get snockered. It has an equalizin' effect, makin' him realize he's a mortal, like everybody else."

"The first time I see the Señor Pitkin," Gonzales said, "I think per'ap in this place call England, the Señor Pitkin make the rain come."

"He did tend to come on a mite strong," said Nip. "Like he was just a cut or two below God. Leave him here amongst us lesser mortals a while longer, and there's a chance he may adapt."

Nip walked over to spend a few minutes with Naomi, Woody, and Pitkin, while Ash broke the monotony for Wiley, Whit, Jania, and Laketa. All their minds were on the two captives taken by Indians and the three friends who sought to rescue them, so all their conversation leaned in that direction.

"I got all the confidence in the world in them three gents," said Whit, "but I never seen 'em go agin a bunch of wild Indians that's took captives. Is there really a chance they kin git the girls loose an' all of 'em come back alive?"

"If it can be done, they can do it," Ash replied, "and I ain't sayin' it 'cause Rusty's my kin. They're Texans, born and bred, and that's the first thing a Texan learns. How to outsmart and outfight Indians. Especially Comanches."

"Do you think these Indians were Comanches?" Jania asked.

"I won't be surprised," said Ash. "I've always heard it said the only thing a Comanche likes better than takin' scalps is takin' female captives. The varmints have always had some kind of hankerin' for fair-haired white women."

"Bonita has dark hair," Laketa reminded him.

"Indians—especially Comanches—don't limit themselves to the fair-haired," Ash said. "Bonita's young and pretty. That's enough."

Nip Kelly was cautious in what he said, because of Woody's precarious situation. His intended had been taken by Indians while Woody lay wounded. This morning, he had been forced to watch acting trail boss Gavin McCord ride to the rescue. There were times when all a man had was his pride and his shadow on the ground behind him. Woody Miles had swallowed a lot of pride, passing the duties of trail boss to Gavin, and much more when Gavin had taken over with as much or more determination than Woody himself. Nip had said little to Woody directly, and Woody had left most of the conversation to Naomi and Pitkin. This time, Woody only nodded, while Pitkin and Naomi spoke.

"Four more hours of sun, and then darkness," said Nip. "The only relief from the heat."

"I'd welcome the night, for that reason," Naomi said, "except that Gavin, Rusty, and Vic can no longer track those Indians."

"Perhaps they will have caught up to the savages before then," said Pitkin. "Wouldn't you say that's a possibility, Woody?"

"Yes," Woody replied. "I'd have gone, had I been able, but there is nothing I could do that Gavin McCord won't try. With Vic and Rusty siding him, they'll find a way to take Bonita and Nell from those Indians. I'd put my life in the hands of any one of them, and the three combined may be the strongest fighting force to ever come out of south Texas."

"Woody Miles," said Naomi, "you are a noble, generous man. Were you in England, you would be knighted by the Queen."

"I dare say she's right," Pitkin said, cutting in before Woody could reply. "I must say that events of the last several days have been an humbling experience for me. Frankly, I did not expect you to appoint Gavin acting trail boss, nor did I expect you to take orders from him. It takes a strong man—a confident man—to measure up as you did this day."

"Thanks," said Woody, a bit overwhelmed by the unaccustomed praise.

Nip laughed. "Sir Woody, I haven't known you that long, but I'd have to agree. From what I've seen of Gavin and the rest of your *amigos*, I'm ready to believe they can walk on water, if you say they can. I'm a Missourian, but I've never known a Texan who would not challenge hell with a bucket of water, if the need arose. I just hope, if I ever have my back against the wall, about to play my last hand, one of you will remember me."

Kelly spoke with an eloquence that touched them all. None of them had ever heard him speak in such a manner. There were tears in Naomi's eyes, while Woody and Pitkin had some difficulty responding. The time would soon come when Kelly would play that last card, and all of them would remember . . .

Indian Territory, along the Cimarron. July 16, 1869.

The three Indians bearing their captives crossed the Cimarron into Indian Territory's panhandle two hours after sunrise. Bonita and Nell were shoved unceremoniously off the horses. Stiff and sore after the long ride belly-down, with hands and feet tied, they fell, striking the backs of their heads against the hard ground. The horses danced nervously away, when a dozen barking dogs approached. Bonita and

Nell were dismayed to discover they were in an Indian village of many teepees. Women stood in silence, while naked and near-naked children peered from behind their long skirts. Several dozen braves approached, while others watched from a distance. One of the Indians knelt beside Nell and ran his fingers through her yellow hair. That angered the Indian who had brought her in, and an argument followed. After much shouting, it appeared that some kind of decision had been made. The girls were released from their bonds, lifted to their feet, and led to one of the teepees. One of the braves shouted, and half a dozen Indian women came forth. In their eyes was a venomous look that suggested they were about to enjoy what was to follow. One of them pulled aside the teepee's flap, while the rest shoved Bonita and Nell inside. A dozen hands snatched at them, ripping the buttons from their shirts. They fought back as best they could, but their hands and arms were still stiff and numb from having been tied for many hours. Their shirts were stripped away. While each of them was held helpless by two of the squaws, a third began slashing with a knife. Their belts were cut and remnants of their Levi's ripped away, leaving them naked. The squaws left the teepee, closing the flap behind them. Nell looked at Bonita.

"What do you suppose they're going to do with us?"

"Whatever it is, we won't be needing clothes," Bonita said. "Does that give you any ideas?"

"Yes," said Nell, shuddering. "We must escape."

"Naked, without weapons or horses? We wouldn't stand a chance," Bonita said.

"We haven't a chance, anyway," said Nell fearfully. "With Woody and so many of the others wounded, who would come for us?"

"Gavin," Bonita said. "Gavin will come, if he has to come alone. But he won't be by himself. Vic will be with him."

"Woody won't let him," said Nell. "Woody will try to come himself."

"Woody's no fool," Bonita replied.

"I suppose you know him better than I," said Nell angrily.

"Yes," Bonita replied. "In some ways, I do. They are proud men, these Texans. They are a kind of family, Vic says, and nobody can hurt one of them without fighting all the others."

"So Gavin and your knight in shining armor will be coming for you," Nell said, with all the sarcasm she could muster.

"Yes," said Bonita, matching the sarcasm with confidence. "They'll be here sometime tonight, and when they arrive, I'm going to help them turn this Indian camp inside out."

"My God," Nell said, "you actually believe that, don't you?"

"Of course I do," said Bonita, in a more kindly voice. "Woody's hurt, and can't ride, but he won't forsake us. How can you care for him, yet have no confidence in him?"

To her surprise, Nell Pitkin dropped to her knees and burst into tears. Bonita knelt beside her, offering what comfort she could.

"I'm a coward, and I'm frightened out of my wits," Nell wept.

"I'm afraid, too," said Bonita, "but I believe in Woody and Gavin, just as I believe in Vic. If neither Woody or Gavin could come, Vic would. They'd have to kill him."

"Oh, God," Nell cried, "if I only had your faith."

"Just promise me you won't do anything foolish," said Bonita. "They're holding us for somebody—maybe a chief—and if we can hold out until dark, we have a chance."

"I won't . . . do anything," said Nell. "I don't know what I could do."

"There's really nothing either of us can do, except perhaps get ourselves shot full of arrows," Bonita said. "After dark, when some of our outfit gets here, they'll know what to do. It'll be up to us to listen for them, so we can somehow help them to find us. I don't know about you, but I didn't sleep much, belly-down across that horse. Why don't we see if we can sleep?"

"I've never slept with my bare behind on the ground," said Nell, "but I'm exhausted, and I'm willing to try."

So they stretched out on their backs, removing as many of the troublesome stones as they could before they further injured their already sore bodies. But sleep was elusive, and after a while, Nell spoke.

"Bonita, are you asleep?"

"No," said Bonita. "There are too many rocks."

"Bonita, I'm sorry for . . . for so many things."

"You don't have to say that," Bonita replied. "We come from different worlds, and we each saw this Western frontier in a different light. I suppose it seemed like a step down for you and Naomi, but the Stubbs family was Missouri white trash. Unlike yours, our daddy was an ex-renegade, on the run from the law. Until Wiley and Whit sold that wagonload of whiskey and shared the money with us, Jania, Laketa, and me never had a pair of socks or underwear among us. We had nothing, we were nothing, and that's why I suppose we just went crazy when we were given those rings by Vic, Gavin, and Rusty. We should have been ashamed of ourselves for . . . for crowing over them. I'm truly sorry. Can you forgive us?"

Nell Pitkin was so choked up she couldn't speak for a while. She only wept. When she was finally able, she moved over close to Bonita.

"Bonita Stubbs, you've *always* been somebody. It's the Pitkins I'm unsure of. All of us had to fall off the throne. I just hope Naomi and my father hit as hard as I did. If we live through this, I'll be a friend to you and your family. Humility is a new and strange feeling, but I think I'm going to like it. Will you help me?"

"Every step of the way," Bonita assured her. "Now let's try to sleep. We may be up and awake again tonight."

The sun was noon-high when Gavin, Rusty, and Vic reined up to rest their horses.

"I've never been so dry, and the sun never seemed so hot," Rusty said. "For our sake and our horses' we got to reach water by sundown."

"The Indians would have the same problem," said Vic, "so I reckon we'll be reachin' the Cimarron before long."

"The Indians had an edge," Gavin said. "Most of their ride was in the dark, without the sun suckin' 'em dry. We got to be almighty careful, once we reach the river. I expect the Comanches to have a village, and there may be dogs. Besides that, one of their horses or one of ours could nicker and give us away."

"There's got to be some greenery along the Cimarron," said Vic. "Long before we're close enough for horses nickerin' or barkin' dogs to give us away, we'd best get off this trail we're follerin'. We can go upstream or downstream to water our horses and ourselves. If we stay dead on this trail, we're likely to come out across the river from the Comanche camp."

"I expect you're right," Gavin said. "We'll have to find the Indian camp, figure out where they're holding Nell and Bonita, and discover how many Comanches we're facing. That's the easy part. It gets a mite complicated when we have to devise a plan to get us all out of there alive."

"If we had a dead wolf or cougar," said Rusty, "we could pull the same trick on them that they pulled on us. We could stampede their horses all over hell and half of Texas."

"If we had some ham," Gavin said, "we could have ham and eggs, if we just had some eggs."

Despite the seriousness of their mission, they laughed at that. Then it was time to mount up and ride on, for they and their horses desperately needed water.

Suddenly the teepee flap was drawn aside. A squaw left a large pot and a bowl, and the flap was closed.

"If there's water in just one of those," Nell said, "I don't care about the other."

The clay pot—an olla—contained water, and they shared

it gratefully. Bonita poked a finger into the murky contents of the bowl and tasted it.

"What is it?" Nell asked.

"It tastes like corn mush," said Bonita. "With no salt, no sweetener, it's just a little better than nothing."

"It's been a long time since supper last night," Nell said. "Are we supposed to eat it with our hands?"

"I suppose," said Bonita.

"We could wash our hands in what's left of the water," Nell suggested.

"No," said Bonita. "We may have to drink that water. We don't know when they'll bring us more, or if they will. Tilt the bowl and swallow some of the mush. It's not all that thick."

Nell did, wiping her lips on the back of her hand. "I left you half."

"You can have it all," Bonita said. "I grew up on the stuff."

Time lagged, and with a July sun overhead, the teepee grew unbearably hot. Bonita and Nell were unable to sit or lie down, lest their sweaty bodies bathe them in mud.

"Perhaps that's why they stripped us, because of the heat," said Nell.

"I don't think so," Bonita replied. "It's getting noisy out there, like they're preparing for a celebration. I have this cold feeling down in my belly that tells me we may be part of it."

"I'm going to open that flap and see what they're doing," said Nell.

"That's not as important to us as the time of day," Bonita said. "If I can, let me poke my head out and see where the sun is."

Bonita was able to get her head out the open flap for only a few seconds before one of the squaws caught her. She was beaten over the head repeatedly with a heavy stick until she withdrew and closed the flap.

"What are they doing?" Nell asked.

"I don't know," said Bonita. "One of the female varmints was bashing me on the head with a stick, and I didn't have much time. By the sun, it must be some time in the afternoon. There's maybe four or five more hours of daylight."

"Oh, God," Nell moaned, "I'm afraid we can't hold out that long. They're preparing to do something with us, if all the shouting and laughter means anything. Why do you think these Indian women hate us?"

"They don't like the way their men are attracted to us," said Bonita. "They're jealous of us."

"If only we could talk to them and tell them we have men of our own," Nell said. "It might be enough for them to set us free."

"That's the last thing they have in mind for us," said Bonita. "We must buy ourselves some time. Whatever they do—or try to do—to you, don't take it without a fight. Some of the men will try to take us, if we're here long enough. Use your hands, your feet, your teeth. Remember, a foot in the right place can make any man think of other things."

"Like killing us," Nell said gloomily.

Bonita and Nell had been spared the unwelcome attention of the Indian men because of discontent among some of the squaws. Buffalo Nose, who had taken Bonita, already had a pair of wives. Wolf Tail—son of a chief—had claimed Nell, although he had three wives. The discontented wives, united in their fury, had succeeded only in getting themselves disciplined by the old ones within the tribe. By right of having stolen these white squaws, Buffalo Nose and Wolf Tail would be allowed to take them as wives. Triumphant, they made their way to the teepee where the captives were held. The vigilant squaw with her stick stepped aside, allowing Buffalo Nose to draw the flap to one side. He stepped into the dim interior of the teepee, followed by Wolf Tail.

"*Esposa,*"* said Buffalo Nose, pointing to Bonita.

"*Esposa,*" Wolf Tail repeated, pointing to Nell.

* Wife.

Bonita and Nell had retreated as far as they could their bare backs against the skin of the teepee Bonita tried to kick Buffalo Nose in the groin but he was cat quick Seizing her foot he twisted it until she cried out in pain Nell swung her small fists as hard as she could aiming for Wolf Tail s face Laughing the Comanche caught both her wrists in his powerful hands When she tried to knee him in the groin he released one of her wrists and slammed a fist into the side of her head He then slung the unconscious Nell over his shoulder headdown and stepped out of the teepee Buffalo Nose had shouldered Bonita in similar fashion ignoring her as she pounded his broad back with her fists The two stalked through the Comanche village to the laughter of the braves and the stony silence of the squaws Two teepees had been prepared for the occasion: one for Buffalo Nose and Bonita the other for Wolf Tail and Nell Each man bearing his new wife drew aside the flap and after stepping into the teepee closed it behind him

That s got to be the Cimarron up yonder   Vic said

I m sure it is   said Gavin   It's the first hint of green since before we entered the *Jornada* It s time we rode a couple of miles west and then south to the river

'The sun s still three hours high   Rusty said   We ll have to hole up somewhere until dark

Not until we ve had a shot at finding that Indian camp said Gavin   According to Pit s map, we ll likely be in Indian Territory s panhandle after we cross the river If there s any cover at all I want to at least find the camp If we can get close enough to see it in daylight we ll be better able to plan our moves after dark

Nearing the water the horses wanted to run and it was necessary to restrain them When they reached the Cimarron roughly two miles west of where the trio of Indians had likely crossed they found it flowing shallow over a sandy bottom When the horses had rested, they led the animals to water and allowed them to drink Only then did they slake their own thirst

"My God," Vic said, "if the Cimarron's this shallow, that blasted desert may swallow it before our outfit can get there."

"I don't think so," said Gavin. "The fact that there's water here at all is proof enough that it's flowing from a source that's kept it from drying up. I'd say that distant storm that stampeded the herd has helped. Let's find a place to hide the horses, and then make our way upstream as far as the cover will allow."

They secreted the horses in a thicket through which the river flowed. The banks were low enough for the animals to reach the water, and there was even a little graze. The trio took their Winchesters, and following the south bank of the river, headed downstream. To their surprise, the brush along the river—combined with the undergrowth—afforded more cover than they had expected. A portion of the river bed was dry, allowing them to walk upright, peering through the brush. Suddenly a dog barked, a host of others joining in, and the three Texans paused.

"Let's get a little closer, if we can," Gavin said. "It's not much help, knowing where the camp is, if we can't see it."

They crept closer, and suddenly where the Cimarron took a sudden southward turn, they could see many Indian teepees in the bend of the river.

"God," Vic groaned, "with that many teepees, there must be a hundred warriors."

Before Gavin or Rusty could respond to that, Buffalo Nose and Wolf Tail exited the teepee with their naked captives. They could see Bonita's small fists pounding the broad back of the Indian who had her slung over his shoulder. When the shock wore off, Vic leaped to his feet.

"Them sons a bitches," he snarled.

He was just seconds shy of leaping out of the brush with his Winchester, when Gavin caught the back of his pistol belt and dragged him to his knees.

"Damn it," Gavin hissed, "you want to get all of us killed?"

"But they got Bonita," said Vic, with a moan, "and you know what they aim to do to her . . ."

"The three of us being shot full of arrows won't change that," Gavin said. "They've got Nell too. You think I want to have to tell Woody . . ."

"Tarnation," said Rusty, "all hell's busted loose in them two teepees. Look!"

17

*T*he moment Buffalo Nose set Bonita on her feet, she threw herself against the inside of the teepee. Her weight was enough to crack one of the lodge poles, and when Buffalo Nose lunged for her, she seized his arm. Off balance, he fell against her, and they both smashed into the side of the already weakened teepee. Their combined weight was too much. Several more lodge poles snapped and the entire teepee began to sag. Buffalo Nose began shouting words Bonita didn't understand, but the Indians observing the spectacle seemed to. There was much laughter, as the teepee collapsed. Bonita managed to sink her teeth into the Indian's thigh. Buffalo Nose bellowed like a bull and intensified his efforts to get his hands on her.

In the other teepee, Nell Pitkin had tried a different approach. On her feet, she had lunged for Wolf Tail. While she hadn't caught him entirely off guard, her weight caused him to stumble, and the two of them went down in a tangle. She managed to knee him in the groin, and momentarily free, she scrambled for the teepee's open flap. She almost made it, but Wolf Tail caught her by an ankle. She seized one of the lodge poles, it broke, and using a length of it for a club, she began beating Wolf Tail over the head. Little by little, she inched her way out of the teepee, the stubborn Indian clinging to her ankle. All this, added to the spectacle of Bonita and Buffalo Nose struggling under the collapsed teepee was entertainment that staggered the imagination of the Comanche gathering. Dogs barked, men shouted, and women laughed.

Suddenly Bonita emerged from the collapsed teepee and made a run for it. Not one of the laughing squaws attempted to stop her, and one of the braves had to run her down. Eventually, Buffalo Nose crawled out from under the ruins of the teepee on hands and knees. He had a nasty cut above one eye, and blood dripped from his nose. The brave who had captured Bonita brought her, kicking and clawing, back to Buffalo Nose. He just looked at her without enthusiasm.

"*Perro,*" Buffalo Nose growled. "*Diablo squaw. Malo medicina.*"

But his companions would have none of it. The Indian who had seized Bonita held her at arm's length to escape her kicking and clawing, clearly waiting for Buffalo Nose to claim his new wife. Buffalo Nose got up, and despite Bonita's struggles, grabbed her and again flung her head-down over his shoulder. He then stalked back to the teepee from which he had taken her, drew aside the flap, and flung Bonita inside. It was an admission of failure, an invitation to the tribe to do with the captive what they would, and the squaws howled their delight. They now turned their attention to the other teepee, from which Nell Pitkin had emerged, Wolf Tail clinging to her ankle. Having witnessed Bonita's victory, Nell took to beating Wolf Tail with new enthusiasm, swinging the broken lodge pole like a club. Wolf Tail wasn't about to accept disgrace without a fight. Springing to his feet, he seized Nell's weapon and flung it away. He then caught the girl's flailing arms and began forcing her back into the teepee, but Nell went limp and slipped out of his grasp. Before he could get hold of her again, she grabbed a large stone and smashed it against his knee. She then drove her head into his groin. He stumbled into the side of the teepee, and it collapsed with him. The same Indian who had stopped Bonita from running away now caught Nell, and stood there grinning. Wolf Tail crawled out of the ruins of the teepee, limping because of his injured knee. The Indian holding Nell shoved her toward Wolf Tail, and he had to take her. She clawed his face, and while he fought to control her flailing arms, she drove a knee into his already aching groin. Wolf Tail fell on top of her, and lying there, tried to catch his wind. When he was able, he rolled over and slammed his fist into Nell's jaw. He got to his feet, and ignoring the laughter of the squaws and the ridicule of the men, threw the unconscious Nell over his shoulder, facedown. Returning to the teepee from which he had taken her, he flung Nell inside, with Bonita. Yellow hair or not, the tribe could do with her what it wished. To a Comanche, ridicule was a fate worse than death.

"I never would've believed it, if I hadn't seen it with my own eyes," Rusty said.

"Bonita and Nell done it just right," said Vic, "but them Comanches ain't done with 'em yet. Unless some of the other braves wants a chance at 'em, they'll likely be turned over to the squaws."

"Yes," Gavin agreed, "and they won't be long about it. Indians being superstitious, I'd say they've already decided their white squaws are bad medicine."

"That means we can't wait for dark," said Rusty.

"No," Gavin said. "We'll have to see what kind of sport the Comanches have in mind, and go from there. Count on the squaws to come up with somethin' that will inflict the most pain and sufferin'."

"The gauntlet," said Vic. "That'll be hell."

"It won't be easy, savin' 'em from that," Rusty said.

"We can try," said Gavin. "If it's the gauntlet, there's a play Woody and me pulled off once, in Texas."

They watched the Indians, and it soon became evident the gauntlet was indeed what they had in mind for Bonita and Nell. Beyond the village was a path along the south bank of the river, and the squaws began clamoring for position. Many had knives, some stones, some clubs. It would be a formidable run, for there were many squaws who would be lined up along each side of the path, each striving to hurt or kill the desperate captives as they ran for their very lives.

"The supper fires are goin'," Vic said. "Is the runnin' of the gauntlet to come before supper or after?"

"Generally after," said Gavin. "Comanches like to prolong the agony of it as much as they can. If either or both the captives get through alive, they're taken back to the start of it and forced to run again."

"If I got anything to say about it, they won't be runnin' it even once," Vic said.

"We sure won't be takin' Nell back to Woody in very good shape," said Rusty.

"Vic," Gavin said, "I want you to ease on back to the horses. Take yours and the two we brought for Nell and Bonita. I want you to take a round-about way downriver, so you are as close as possible to where that gauntlet's goin' to end. Rusty and me will be takin' the minds of those Comanches off the gauntlet. It'll be up to you to get the girls on their horses and out of there. With any luck, the Comanches won't have any horses to go after you."

"From this end," said Rusty, "it sounds like a sure thing. I can't wait to hear what you and me are goin' to contribute to make it possible."

"Then I won't keep you in suspense any longer," Gavin replied. "You and me will bring our horses up here. Once the Comanches have gathered to witness the runnin' of the gauntlet, you and me are goin' to get busy with our Winchesters. We're within range from here. I'm gamblin' that Indian wearin' the buffalo horns is a medicine man. I aim to cut him down first, and we'll plug as many more as we can without reloading. Mounting our horses, we're goin' through that Comanche camp like retribution with the fuse lit. I aim to scatter those Indian horses from hell to breakfast."

"I can follow it from there," said Rusty. "If we're still alive, we ride north, catchin' up to Vic, Nell, and Bonita."

"That's how it should turn out," Gavin replied, "but like

every plan where Comanches are involved, we can't be sure they'll do what we're expectin' of 'em.''

"That ain't the only problem," said Vic. "When that gauntlet falls apart, we don't have any way of knowin' Nell and Bonita won't run like hell in the other direction."

"No," Gavin agreed, "but those squaws won't be armed with bows and arrows. Once Rusty and me start gunnin' down the braves, they'll be devotin' all their attention to us. If Nell and Bonita run upstream, go poundin' after them. Rusty and me, when we stop shootin', will have those Indian horses on the run. Comanches are horse Indians, and I'm gamblin' that when they're about to lose their horses, they'll forget everything else."

"Yeah," Rusty said. "Everything except killin' you and me graveyard dead."

"I'm countin' on total surprise," said Gavin. "Remember, our shootin' will have to be rapid and dead-center. We must gun down enough of them to draw their attention to us, and then stampede their horses before they can get to them. If too many of them are able to reach their horses, they'll ride us down."

"Then don't try to gun down too many," Vic cautioned. "You're right about scatterin' the squaws from the gauntlet. It'll be strung out along the river, and with three horses, I'll ride some of them squaws right into the water. You're lettin' me out of this too easy. 'Stead of me gettin' the girls mounted and ridin' downstream, I oughta be doin' just the opposite. Let me come bustin' through the bunch of squaws, and they'll scatter like quail."

"That kind of makes sense," said Rusty. "With Vic roarin' through from the far end, Bonita and Nell can see him comin', and all they'll have to do is wait."

"Let's think beyond me gettin' the girls mounted," Vic said. "I got a Winchester too, and I reckon you both know I'm fair-to-middlin' good with it. Once the girls are mounted and in the clear, I'll rein up and help cover the two of you. It's damned important to keep them Comanches from catchin' up even one horse. While you and Rusty are scatterin' them horses, I can cut down any Comanches that might be tempted to fill you full of arrows.''

"Maybe you have something there," said Gavin. "I just want to be sure you have Nell and Bonita in the clear. Use your own judgment, but don't get your tail in a crack tryin' to side Rusty and me. We'll be shootin' like hell wouldn't have it, and then we'll be doing some almighty fast ridin'.''

"I'm goin' after the horses," Vic said. "Another hour before sundown, and that bunch is eatin' supper now."

Vic moved swiftly, using the available cover, and was soon out of their sight.

"There won't be much daylight left, after we bust loose," said Rusty. "All we got to do is get out of there alive, after Vic gets to Nell and Bonita."

"You handled him just right," Bonita said, when Nell regained her senses.

"I couldn't have done it without you showing me how," said Nell. "Now what do you suppose they'll do with us?"

"I don't know," Bonita said. "I think we disgraced the pair that tried to take us, and it may discourage the others. At least we've gained some time. Before much longer, it'll be dark."

But there was no more time. Four squaws came for them, forcing them to their feet, prodding them along with sharp sticks. A hundred yards beyond the camp, Nell and Bonita could see the two lines of squaws alongside the river. Indian braves, while not wishing to get too close to an event involving squaws, had gathered outside the teepees where they could see what was about to take place. The medicine man—wearing buffalo horns—sat on his horse so that he had a better view.

"I don't like the looks of this," Bonita said, as they neared the squaws lined up along the river. "They're going to beat us."

"Let's run for it," said Nell. "What do we have to lose?"

"Not yet," Bonita said. "Something has to happen."

Something did. There was the sharp crack of a Winchester, and the horned medicine man pitched off his horse. In the stunned silence that followed, the roar of one Winchester became the echo of another, as braves scrambled for their weapons. Then came thundering hoofbeats, as yelling, pistol-wielding horsemen swept down on the camp.

"*Caballos!*" a brave shouted. "*Caballos!*"

But they were too late. The shooting and shouting had spooked the horses and they broke into a run. The squaws lined up for the gauntlet found themselves confronted by a galloping horseman and three horses. They dropped clubs and knives, scampering out of harm's way, but some of them were tumbled into the river.

"Vic!" Bonita shouted. "Vic!"

"Mount up!" Vic shouted.

Bonita leaped into the saddle, but Nell wasn't quite as adept. Vic seized her hand and set her astride the horse, letting her find the stirrups as best she could. It had all taken no more than a few seconds. Some of the squaws swung their clubs, but their targets were moving. The sticks swatted the flanks of the horses, and they leaped ahead.

Three hundred yards upriver, Vic reined up, passing the reins of the horses to Nell and Bonita. From its saddle boot he drew his Winchester, but there was no need for it. The stampeding of the horses had been successful, and there was no sign of Gavin or Rusty. Few if any of the Comanches had loosed any arrows, and those who hadn't taken cover from the deadly fire apparently had pursued their horses. Crossing the Cimarron, Vic rode west, followed by Bonita and Nell. When they were far enough from the Indian camp, Vic reined up. Bonita edged her horse as near his as she could get, and for the first time since her capture, she wept.

"I knew you would come!" she cried. "I told Nell you would."

"I didn't come alone," said Vic. "Gavin and Rusty are back yonder somewhere. All this was Gavin's idea, and it was him and Rusty that done the shootin' and stampeded the Comanche horses."

"Bless all of you," Nell said. "If Naomi ever speaks another unkind word to Gavin, I will personally tear her hair out by the roots."

"We tried to get here before they . . . done anythin' to either of you," Vic said.

"They tried," said Bonita, "but we changed their minds. I think you saved us from a terrible beating."

"They was goin' to make you run the gauntlet," Vic said. "If you'd got through it and was still on your feet, they'd have made you do it again."

"I don't suppose you have a blanket with you?" Nell asked hopefully.

"No," said Vic, "and I doubt Gavin or Rusty will. We was ridin' light, not expecting to need our bedrolls or saddlebags. But it'll soon be dark."

Nell and Bonita laughed at his obvious embarrassment.

"I'm not complaining," Nell said. "I'm just thankful to be alive."

"We'll be all right," said Bonita. "Without protection, the sun would have ruined us, but we'll be back in camp before morning, won't we?"

"Yeah," Vic said. "I'm wonderin' what's happened to Gavin and Rusty."

"While we're waiting for them," said Nell, "why can't we get into the river and wash ourselves? I'm sweaty and I've been pawed by Indians, and I feel dirty."

"So do I," Bonita said.

"Have at it," said Vic, "but don't get out of my sight, and be ready to run for it if you have to. I'll keep watch."

Nell and Bonita had barely gotten into the water when Gavin and Rusty arrived.

"Where in tarnation have you been?" Vic asked. "I was startin' to wonder if some of 'em had got to their bows and arrows and had pincushioned the both of you."

"We got through without a scratch," said Gavin. "We got their horses on the run, and wanted to be sure they didn't catch any of them in time to come after us. You should have ridden on."

"Looked like we was rollin' nothin' but sevens," Vic said. "I wanted to see if Bonita and Nell was all right, and they wanted to wash, while they had water. There won't be any to spare, once we're back in camp."

"You're right about that," said Gavin. "I reckon we should have remembered to bring some blankets with us."

"Nell and Bonita ain't complainin'," Vic said, "and the sun won't be a problem."

"We'd better take the time to water all the horses," said Rusty.

"Good idea," Gavin replied.

They all dismounted and led the animals to water a few yards below where Nell and Bonita were washing. By the time the horses had drunk their fill, Bonita and Nell were out of the water. Without a word, her hair dripping, Nell put her arms around Gavin. Before he recovered from the kiss, she thanked Rusty in a similar manner.

"Hey," Vic said, "what about me?"

"Sorry," said Nell. "I wasn't sure that Bonita would approve."

"Under the circumstances, Bonita doesn't care," the girl said.

Nell then presented Vic with a similar reward.

"I don't want to seem ungrateful," said Bonita. "Vic?"

"Go ahead," Vic replied.

Bonita went to Gavin and Rusty first, saving her most generous reward for Vic.

"That was more than I ever expected," said Gavin.

"Same here," Rusty said, "and I promise not to tell."

Vic laughed. "When we ride in with the two of 'em jaybird-naked, I reckon we won't have anything to tell. I'm just glad Bonita's alive, and I reckon the rest of her folks will be of the same mind."

"Then let's mount up and ride," said Gavin. "If our wounded are able, we ought to be on the trail at first light tomorrow. We still have the herd to gather, if we can find them."

*   *   *

Jania and Laketa had volunteered to stand watch so that Nip and Rusty wouldn't have to take the entire night. Nip and Laketa had taken the first watch, and at midnight, Ash and Jania had taken over. They were talking quietly when Ash drew and cocked his Colt.

"What is it?" Jania whispered.

"Someone's out there," said Ash. "Stay where you are."

Moonset was only minutes away, and Ash knelt in the shadow of one of the wagons. Anyone but an Indian would have a difficult time finding him in the dark. He spoke softly.

"Identify yourself."

"Three hell-for-leather Texans, and two naked females we took from the Comanches," Rusty answered.

"Send in the naked females, and the rest of you varmints vamoose," said Ash, in as gruff a tone as he could manage.

They all exploded in laughter that awoke the rest of the camp. Weeping, Jania threw her arms around Bonita. Everybody—including Gonzales—was there within seconds. Even Gladstone Pitkin lost his reserve and caught up Nell in an affectionate manner that she had not experienced in years.

"Excuse me," Nell said, "but will someone bring me a blanket? I've been naked since yesterday morning, and I'm freezing."

"I'd like one too," said Bonita, "for the same reason."

"Gonzales," Gavin said, "I reckon it's a mite early for breakfast, but all any of us has had since leavin' here is a handful of jerked beef. What about it?"

"*Sí,*" said Gonzales. "Hot coffee *muy pronto,* then grub."

Woody had waited until the excitement had died down, and even then he didn't go immediately to Nell. Without a word, he offered his hand to Rusty, then to Vic. When he eventually took Gavin's hand, he spoke just one word.

"*Bueno.*"

It was enough. Woody then welcomed Nell, who had donned a blanket. Within minutes Gonzales had hot coffee ready, and Gavin had taken the opportunity to report to Pitkin.

"We were considerably outnumbered," Gavin said, "so we had to use some tricks to free the girls from the Comanches. I'm pleased to report that they conducted themselves well under dangerous circumstances."

"I am pleased with the overall manner in which you and your riders resolved what had all the earmarks of a disaster," said Pitkin. "You exceeded my expectations."

"I'm obliged," Gavin said. "I must say I didn't like takin' Vic and Rusty away, leavin' so many of you wounded, but I had no choice."

"I have learned much in the last several days," said Pitkin. "Most important, I think, is that the responsibilities of a trail boss are diverse and difficult. Further, I believe I can say without reservation that we have truly come together as an outfit."

Gavin laughed and went looking for Naomi. He found her sipping coffee, watching Nell and Woody. Naomi had been expecting him, and produced a second cup of coffee.

"Had Nell *really* been naked since yesterday morning?" Naomi asked.

"I expect she had," Gavin said, "and so had Bonita. Indians generally treat female captives that way. Nell and Bonita were about to run the gauntlet when we took them away."

"Father and Woody are proud of you," said Naomi, "and you know I am."

"That's behind us," Gavin replied. "More important, are those of you who have been wounded able to travel?"

"I am," said Naomi. "You treated my wound superbly, and it's healing well. I believe I can ride without difficulty. I'm sure Father won't have any trouble with the wagon. Wiley and Whit still limp, but I heard them say they're ready to move on. You'll have to make up your own mind about Woody."

"I aim to," Gavin said. "I hope he's able to ride, so he

can take over as trail boss. I'll talk to him as soon as I'm able to pry him loose from Nell.''

"When you do," said Naomi, "send her over here to talk to me. I want to hear every detail of her adventure.''

"Especially the part about her ridin' naked across the desert with three men," Gavin said.

Naomi laughed. "Yes, especially that part.''

"Grub," Gonzales shouted. "Eat, or I feed it to the *mulos*.''

The recent captives and their rescuers were half-starved, and everything else had to wait while they had breakfast. First light was still an hour away when Gavin had a chance to talk to Woody.

"Woody," Gavin said, "we need to move out at first light. Are you able?''

"Yes," said Woody. "I'm still sore, but by the time we give the horses and mules a little water, our barrels will be dry. Without the herd, I won't be under that much strain. Have you talked to the others who were wounded?''

"Mostly just to Naomi," Gavin said. "I reckon I'd better ask the others. Are you in a mood to become trail boss again?''

Woody laughed. "I'm in no hurry. Pitkin's so pleased with you, why don't you just keep the title? All I could get out of Nell is how wonderful you are.''

Gavin didn't respond to that, but called the outfit together. They listened as he spoke to them.

"I realize some of you who were wounded haven't had time to fully heal, but we're in no position to remain here any longer. There's about enough water in our barrels for a small ration to our horses and mules. We must move on. Perhaps to Sand Creek, perhaps to the Cimarron River, the nearest source of water. I've been to the Cimarron, and I know there's water. Somewhere ahead of us, we should find the herd. The gather will take some time, and those of you who were wounded will have a chance to heal and become stronger. Are there any questions?''

There were none.

"Let's water the horses and mules," Gavin said, "and then we'll move out."

They took the trail, the riders driving the horse remuda ahead, followed by the three wagons. Nell and Naomi were mounted, as were the three Stubbs girls. Riding ahead, Gavin was accompanied by Woody, and they were gratified to find the tracks of the stampeded herd led on.

"We needed a miracle," Woody said, "and the stampede could have been it. Now, if we can only find the herd."

"No reason why we shouldn't," Gavin said. "Cows ain't too bright, but they're smart enough not to stray from water. There's nobody to drive 'em away, unless Indians have got mighty ambitious."

"Longhorns might wander along a creek or river," said Woody. "They'll have to go with the graze, but we can live with that."

Gavin said nothing. It was he who had suggested to Pitkin the herd might be gathered along Sand Creek or the Cimarron, and the Englishman's hopes were now riding on that. Now it seemed that Woody had taken hold of that same slender straw of salvation. While the missing herd should be scattered along creek or river, suppose they were not?

"What's ahead of us?" Naomi asked, trotting her horse beside Gavin's.

"Sand and cow tracks," said Gavin.

"Then we will find the herd, won't we?"

"I hope so," Gavin replied. "Even if they reached water, they still may have drifted up- or downstream, lookin' for graze. We may be a while roundin' 'em up."

"I don't care how long it takes," said Naomi, "as long as we're off this hot, miserable desert. I want to see trees and green grass."

Woody and Nell rode together, while Vic accompanied all three of the Stubbs girls.

"Vic," Jania said, "Bonita won't tell us about her time with the Indians. Will you tell Laketa and me?"

"Ain't much to tell," said Vic cautiously, aware that Bonita was watching him. "Rusty, Gavin and me got there just in time to save Bonita and Nell from bein' beat to death by a bunch of squaws.''

''I always thought Indians stole white women for . . . another purpose,'' Laketa said, with a twinkle in her eyes.

''I reckon they do,'' said Vic, aware he was on thin ice, ''but that don't . . . always work out. A woman can discourage a man—even a Comanche—if she tries hard enough.''

''I suppose Bonita could discourage a man, if she set her mind to it,'' Jania said, ''but what does a woman do when she's stark naked, and that man's a Comanche?''

''That's somethin' only Nell or Bonita can tell you,'' said Vic.

''That's an idea,'' Laketa said. ''Nell was nice to us during breakfast. We'll talk to her tonight.''

Bonita glared at Vic, and he shrugged his shoulders.

Sand Creek. July 18, 1869.

Again Gavin rode ahead, and again Woody accompanied him. Eventually they could see a faint line of green on the horizon.

''That's got to be Sand Creek,'' Gavin said.

''I reckon,'' said Woody. ''Do we ride on ahead and make sure, or go back and hurry the others?''

''Let's go back and hurry the others,'' Gavin said.

They rode back, waving their hats. The riders pushed the horse herd to a faster gait, while Pitkin, Wiley, and Whit urged their teams on. Gavin and Woody waited for all to catch up and then swung in ahead of them.

''Sand Creek?'' Nip Kelly shouted.

''Yeah,'' Gavin shouted back. ''It has to be.''

There were cattle tracks everywhere, and the bed of the creek was still muddy, but there was no water . . .

18

"*T*here's mud," Woody said. "That means there was water after the cloudburst. Break out the shovels."

Nip and Rusty brought the shovels, and the men took turns digging. Soon they had three holes several feet deep, all of them slowly filling with muddy water.

"We'll dig a few more holes," said Gavin. "This will have to do until we can go on to the Cimarron."

"Perhaps that's where we'll find the herd," Pitkin observed.

"Maybe," said Gavin. "When the creek began dryin' up, there may have been some low places where there was still water for a while. We may have to ride the length of this creek, as well as the Cimarron, before we find them all."

Pitkin looked at Woody, and Woody nodded.

"The water in the first holes is startin' to clear up," Rusty said.

"Dip out as much as you can, and put it in the barrels," said Gavin.

Wiley and Whit had been manning two of the shovels, beginning new holes as earlier ones began to fill. Ash and Vic took over the shovels, allowing Wiley and Whit to fill their own barrels.

"After supper," said Nip Kelly, "there'll be time before dark for a couple of us to ride along this creek a ways. Maybe we can find out if any of our herd's still here."

"It might be worth the ride," Gavin said. "Take it up-stream half a dozen miles, and then downstream an equal distance. If there are no cows, it's on to the Cimarron."

Supper over, there was still more than an hour before sundown.

"Ash and me are ridin' downstream," said Nip. "Who's gonna ride the other way?"

"I will," Vic said. "Bonita, why don't you ride with me?"

Bonita nodded, and Vic went to saddle their horses. Pitkin had brought out the map and was studying it. Gavin and Woody joined him.

"Another four hundred miles to Santa Fe," said Pitkin, "but if this map is accurate in the slightest, our water problems should be over."

"Sorry," Woody said, "but I don't trust that map. It's been wrong too often. I think we'll continue scouting ahead."

"That's about the way I feel too," said Gavin.

"Very well," Pitkin said.

Nip and Ash rode what they believed was seven miles down Sand Creek without seeing a single cow.

"No tracks," said Nip. "This bein' a dry stream most of the time, there's not enough graze to keep a goat alive. I reckon there was plenty of water here, after that cloudburst, but that herd was needin' graze as much as water."

"No use ridin' any farther, then," Ash said. "I'll gamble there won't be any cows the other direction, either."

Vic and Bonita found no cows upstream, nor had Vic expected to. He had wanted to spend some time with Bonita, and after half a dozen miles, he reined up.

"There are no cow tracks," said Bonita. "Why are we looking for cows?"

Vic laughed. "It seemed like a fair excuse for gettin' you away from the rest of the outfit. I reckon you're some give out, after ridin' bellydown on a Comanche's horse all of last night, and then ridin' most of the day, gettin' back to the outfit."

"My bottom's a little raw," Bonita said, "but after what you did this morning, you've got the right to ask anything of me that you want."

"Anythin'?"

"Anything," said Bonita.

"That bein' the case," Vic said, "let's dismount and set a spell under that tree."

They sat down with their backs to an oak. Vic reached for her, she came to him, and for a prolonged time they shared the embrace.

"What did you think," she asked, "when you found the Indians had taken me?"

"I thought if they hurt you, I'd have killed every damn Indian on the frontier."

She laughed. "Suppose they had .. violated me? Would you have left me to them?"

"My God, no," Vic said. "I was just prayin' that you'd be alive. You think I'd blame you, if some highhanded Indian forced you to give in to him?"

For a long moment she looked into his fierce blue eyes. Then she spoke.

"It would be your right to forsake me, if another man used me. That was all I could think about, when that Indian was trying to . . . force me."

"I'm glad you brought him up short," Vic said, "but even if he had taken you, then I'd still want you. For whatever it's worth."

"It's worth everything to me," said Bonita. "Do you suppose Woody would .. feel this strongly toward Nell, if an Indian had taken her?"

"I almost know he would," Vic replied. "He never asked any of us—Rusty, Gavin, or me—what happened in that Indian camp."

"Perhaps Nell told him."

"Not for him havin' asked her," said Vic.

"The more I see of Texas men, the better I like them," Bonita said.

"I hope so," said Vic, "because I can't be nothin' else.

I reckon it's time we started back. We both need some sleep. If you wake up later tonight, you can track me down on the second watch."

"Don't be surprised if I do that," Bonita said. "Jania and Laketa will be spending some time with Ash and Rusty, and I wouldn't want you feeling neglected."

All the holes they had dug in the bed of Sand Creek had clear water the following morning, so the horses and mules had more than enough to quench their thirst before the outfit moved on to the Cimarron.

"I'm ridin' ahead for a look at the Cimarron," Gavin told Woody. "Care to ride along with me?"

"Yes," Woody said. "I'm anxious to see if the herd— or any part of it—is there."

While there were some cow tracks leading toward the distant river, it was obvious the stampede had lost its momentum at Sand Creek. Neither rider said aloud what both were thinking. The herd, if it had drifted on to the Cimarron, had done so not in a mass, but was likely strung out for miles. Strangely enough, well before they reached the river, the cow tracks began to come together, as though the scattered herd had smelled the water.

"They picked it up along here, and started to lope," Woody observed.

"They shouldn't have been that thirsty," said Gavin, "unless they hung around at Sand Creek until it dried up. But that wouldn't have made any sense, with no graze."

Woody laughed. "Me boy, don't ever underestimate the stupidity of a cow."

Their first look at the Cimarron was encouraging, for there was some green along the banks that proved to be young willows. While there was no abundance of grass, there was some, with a promise of more. The river was by no means bank-full, and in places, there were wide sand bars where the stream narrowed to the extent that a man could step over it without muddying his boots. But the sand bars revealed many more cow tracks.

"Water—or the lack of it—is a mite disappointin'," Gavin said. "East of here, where we found the Comanche camp, the water was deeper and wider."

"That's important information," said Woody. "Proof enough that as long as we follow the Cimarron, there'll be water."

Three miles after reaching the Cimarron, they came up on nine longhorn cows. Picking at the graze along the river, the animals lifted their heads, watching the riders.

"Look at 'em," Gavin said. "They know who we are, and the cantankerous varmints know they run off and left us in the desert."

Woody laughed. "You're givin' 'em credit for more smarts than I would, *amigo*. All I'd be willin' to admit is they know when they're dyin' of thirst, and that nothin' matters except the next water hole."

There were more and more cattle, as they continued along the Cimarron, and when they eventually reined up, they were feeling better about the herd.

"More than a thousand head, so far," Woody said.

"At least that many," said Gavin, "and every reason to believe we'll find the rest of them somewhere along this river. But I reckon it's time we rode back and told the others. I was reachin' for straws when I told Pit we'd likely find 'em scattered along the Cimarron. Now he'll believe anything an old Texas trail driver tells him."

"Well, let's ride back and find out," Woody said. "We've probably ridden farther than the outfit will travel today, but we needed to know if we could actually gather the herd, or if we've just been givin' Pit false hopes. Now we can promise him somethin' he can sink his teeth into."

"Splendid," said Pitkin, when he was told about the many cows Woody and Gavin had discovered along the Cimarron. "We can gather them as we progress."

"It should work out that way," Gavin said. "We'll run a tally every day until we have them all."

* * *

The second day of travel along the Cimarron brought them to Willow Bar, a ridge of sand covered by a heavy growth of willows. Many cattle had taken refuge there from the sun, and riders flushed them out from beneath the trees. Several miles beyond the willows, everybody—even Pitkin—reined up to stare at the massive piles of bones.

"Tarnation," Rusty said, "what happened here? An Indian massacre?"

"Ain't likely," said Vic. "I don't see nothin' but mule bones. See them skulls?"*

They traveled on, not wishing to spend the night near the mounds of bleaching bones.

"Beginning right now," Gavin said, after supper, "I'm steppin' aside as trail boss. I'm passing the honor back to our *amigo*, Woodrow Miles."

"He *never* calls me Woodrow unless I'm about to draw another deuce," said Woody. "What is it? Indians? Rustlers? Another prairie fire?"

They all laughed at the two Texans hoorawing one another, all of them knowing and appreciating what Gavin had accomplished while Woody had been wounded.

"Señor trail boss, suh," Vic said, with a cockeyed, left-handed salute, "requestin' permission to run a tally on the herd, suh."

"Go on," said Woody, "but take somebody with you for a second count. You never get within two hundred cows, on your own."

Rusty went with him, and the count they brought back was encouraging.

"At least twenty-five hundred," Rusty said. "That's Vic's count. I say there's more."

"Then we'll go with the low count," said Woody. "That means we have to come up with another thousand of the varmints, to reach the number we started with."

Their third, fourth, and fifth days following the Cimarron,

---

* An area along the trail known as the Hundred Mule Heads. The mules perished there in a blizzard during the winter of 1844–45.

the number of longhorns grew to thirty-four hundred.

"It's been nothing short of a miracle, finding as many as we have," Woody said. "The rest may have been taken by Indians, or wandered so far, we'd never find them."

"We shall take what we have, and consider the gather finished, then," said Pitkin.

At their last camp before leaving the Cimarron, Pitkin again took out the map. He had noted distances between points according to what he had been told at Council Grove, and before leaving Independence.

"From the numbers you have," Woody said, "how far are we from Santa Fe?"

"Two hundred and seventy-five miles," said Pitkin. "We are a hundred and forty miles from the crossing of the Arkansas. We are in the extreme northwest corner of Indian Territory. Shouldn't we be out of reach of the Comanches?"

"Not necessarily," Woody said. "I wouldn't consider us out of their reach until we've crossed the Canadian River."

Pitkin sighed. "At least another seventy-five miles."

Upper Cimarron Spring. July 23, 1869.

It became their first camp after leaving the Cimarron. The spring flowed into a ravine, which in turn, emptied into the river four miles distant. There was fresh water, flowing beneath towering cliffs, spires, and crags, through wild currant and plum thickets, its banks a profusion of grapevines. The trail passed over the ridge more than a quarter of a mile from the spring, and the remains of old campfires attested to its popularity as a campsite.

"After the desert," Naomi said, "I'm thankful for any water, but before we leave here, let's fill all our water barrels with this fresh water from the spring."

Slowly but surely, they began passing landmarks on the trail that had been included in the map Pitkin had.

"That must be Rabbit Ears Peaks up ahead and to our

right," said Pitkin. "According to the map, there's a spring at Round Mound."

Round Mound, a round-topped cone, rose more than a thousand feet above the plain, and was by far the most prominent monument on the trail. It was visible for two days before they reached it.

"I want to climb to the top of it," Nell said.*

"I think not," said Pitkin.

Half a dozen miles west of Round Mound, the outfit reached Rock Creek, and for the first time, they began having trouble with the wagons. The dry air of the high plains began playing havoc with the woodwork of the wagons. Tires rattled loose, spokes backed out of the hubs, while wheels began to wobble. The chuck wagon was the first to show signs of collapse, and ironically, Wiley and Whit Stubbs had a solution to the problem.

"We got water here at Rock Creek," Wiley said. "We'd best lay over here for a day or two, until the wagon wheels is watered and swole."

"Yeah," said Whit. "We was havin' to do it all the time, back in Missouri. Old wagon we had was so near used up, we spent most of our time fiddlin' with it."

"Startin' with the chuck wagon," Woody said, "show us how to cure those rickety wheels."

"Be glad to," said Wiley. "Y'all been mighty kind to Whit an' me. We'll do both your wagons 'fore we do ours."

Wiley and Whit proceeded to jack up the chuck wagon, and with four pillars of rock supporting it, removed all four wheels. These they rolled down to the creek and submerged in the water.

"We'll leave 'em there all night," Whit explained. "By in the mornin', that wood will be swole so tight, them tires

---

* The view from the top of Round Mound was truly spectacular, the climb worth the effort. To the south lay a varied country, rolling to level, with mounds and hills. Far to the north were vast plains, with occasional peaks and ridges. Beyond these was a silver band—the snowpeaks of the Rocky Mountains.

an' fittings won't work loose fer six months.''

Quickly they removed the wheels from Pitkin's wagon, and finally, the wheels from their own two wagons. All were put underwater in Rock Creek.

"There is much to be learned on the frontier," said Pitkin. "It appears that every man has at least one skill that may be foreign to the rest of us."

"That's gospel," Nip Kelly said. "There's considerable more to ranching than just the knowin' which end of a cow is which. You'd do well, addin' Wiley and Whit to your payroll. You're headin' for snow country, where you can't depend on grass. A wise rancher grows his own hay, and that—like removin' and soakin' wagon wheels—just ain't cowboy work."

"Mr. Kelly," Pitkin said, "that is a most astute observation. I shall consider it."

"Don't just consider it, Father," said Nell, who had heard the conversation. "Do it."

"Perhaps I shall," Pitkin replied, with a hint of a smile. "We seem to have developed a tolerance for others, of late, and it is most becoming."

"If you are referring to my once shoddy treatment of the Stubbs family," said Nell, "you are quite right. I have found them to be . . . more than I expected."

Nip Kelly laughed. "Nothin' like spendin' some time with Bonita, naked in an Indian camp, to temper one's judgment."

"Precisely what I was thinking," Pitkin replied.

They were speaking of Nell as though she wasn't listening to every word, and for just a moment the old Nell surfaced, prepared to become furious. But then the truth of it got through to her, and she turned away without a word.

Wiley and Whit were up and about before first light. Before Gonzales had breakfast ready, the wagon wheels had been removed from the creek and each was mounted on the wagon from which it had been removed. The dried-out wood had swollen to normal size, and Pitkin appraised their

work with appreciation. Wiley and Whit still were a little
in awe of the Englishman, and got hurriedly to their fee
when he approached.

"I am impressed with your ingenuity and willingness,"
Pitkin said. "Unless the two of you have other plans, upon
reaching Santa Fe, I'd like for you to become part of my
outfit. You may consider it until then, if you wish, before
making your decision."

"I reckon we can make that decision now, sir," said Wiley. "We been wonderin' what in tarnation we was goin'
to do in New Mexico, once we sell these wagonloads of
whiskey, ain't we, Whit?"

"We have," Whit agreed. "Paw needed us to help him
with the wagons, and we didn't know what we was goin'
to do, beyond that."

"Starting today, consider yourselves part of the outfit,"
Pitkin said.

"We're obliged," said Wiley, "but it wouldn't be fair,
until we rid ourselves of these wagons. We can't take no
wages until then."

"You can, and you will," Pitkin said. "Despite the wagons, you will be expected to do what must be done, such
as the manner in which you reclaimed those wagon wheels,
as well as defend against Indians or outlaws. Agreed?"

"Agreed," they answered in a single voice.

Nell had spoken to Woody about Wiley and Whit the
night before, and Woody had an idea what Pitkin was pro-
posing. He was sure of it, when Pitkin concluded his conversation, and his appreciation for the Englishman rose
another notch.

"Head 'em up, move 'em out," Woody shouted.

The trail, during the course of the day, passed through
rough sandstones and emerged near Point of Rocks. It was
a rock spur striking to the south, with a good spring below.
The rocks of the range were like jagged teeth, rugged, and
all pointing southwest. Finally, beyond Point of Rocks, the
outfit reined up. If Pitkin's map meant anything, they were

more than six hundred miles from Independence, and less than two hundred from Santa Fe.

The Canadian River. July 31, 1869.

"This is the first damn river since leavin' Independence that's had a genuine *ford* with a bottom of solid rock and a decent approach from either bank," said Woody.

"Not only that," Vic observed, "but it's no wider than a creek."

It was true enough, and the wagons were crossed immediately, without difficulty. The horse remuda and the herd followed.

"Now," said Woody, "I'd say we're well out of reach of the Kiowa and Comanche, but we can't be any less vigilant. There may be outlaws."

But the outfit had entered a region known for torrential rains, violent hailstorms, and dangerous lightning. Such a storm began building in the far west, and a massive bank of dirty gray clouds swallowed the sun two hours early.

"If I'm any judge," Woody said, "whatever's on the way will hit us sometime tonight. I reckon we'd better prepare our shelters and stay where we are, until it blows itself out."

Deuce Rowden and his five companions had chosen their camp well. West of the Santa Fe Trail, along the Canadian River, they had been waiting for two days. Each man had taken a turn on daytime lookout, watching for the Pitkin outfit. While they had approached the Canadian crossing, Watt Grimes had watched from a distance. Now he made his way to his horse and rode back to warn the others.

"They was riggin' shelters between the wagons," Grimes reported. "That means they'll be there through the storm."

"All the better for us," said Rowden. "We'll strike in the mornin', while the storm's at its worst."

* * *

Gonzales had supper ready early, allowing everybody to eat ahead of the storm, and Woody spoke to them.

"Every rider in the saddle until the thunder and lightning has passed. We'll do our best to keep them from running, but don't do anything foolish. I'd rather take the time to round up the herd, than take the time to bury one of you."

"Wiley an' me will help," Whit said, "if you got horses for us."

"You're welcome to mounts from the remuda, and there's saddles in Pit's wagon," said Woody. "We're obliged to you."

"It's our job as much as yours," Wiley said proudly. "Mr. Pitkin's hired us."

There were smiles among the riders, while Nell Pitkin had a special one for Bonita.

Thunder rumbled, distant lightning walked grandly across the horizon, but there was nothing of a terrifying nature to spook the herd. The rain came in gray sheets, whipped by high wind, and it became difficult to keep a single fire going, for hot coffee. As long as there was a possibility the herd might run, Woody had kept every man in the saddle, but as the thunder and lightning diminished, he allowed them to seek shelter. The herd, helping itself to the available graze, was strung out along the river, and even through driving rain, could be watched from camp. The rain was cold, and as the wind died down, there were more fires as the riders sought to dry out. By midnight, the rain was steady, with a promise of lasting the night and beyond.

"Lucky we crossed the Canadian while she was just a branch," Vic said. "By mornin', it'll be bank-full."

But while they could hear the rushing of the river, the rain slacked and finally ceased an hour before dawn. Nobody was more surprised than Deuce Rowden.

"We can still pick some of 'em off with Winchesters," York Eagan insisted.

"No," said Rowden. "We been paid to kill 'em all, an' where they're holed up, there's no way we can git close enough. We got to git ahead of 'em and lay an ambush."

The sun rose with a vengeance, but there was an abundance of mud, while water had collected in every arroyo and low area.

"I think we'll remain here for a day," Woody said.

While the only heavily loaded wagons were the two belonging to Wiley and Whit, they now were part of Pitkin's outfit. Like it or not, they could progress no faster than the two wagons would allow.

"I believe," said Pitkin, "that we are within a hundred and fifty miles of Santa Fe."

"I've changed my mind about that map," Gavin said. "I reckon I believe it now."

Woody laughed. "If it's goin' to be right about something, now's the time."

"Head 'em up, move 'em out!" Woody shouted.

The outfit again took the trail the day after the storm. Once the herd was moving and the riders had them under control, Woody again rode ahead. According to Pitkin's map, there were springs, creeks, and rivers enough to provide adequate water the rest of the way to Santa Fe, but something kept Woody riding ahead.

"I reckon I've been on too many drives through Indian country," he told Nell. "I just can't get it through my head that the minute I let up, everything won't go to hell in a hand-basket."

She laughed, but he did not. He continued riding out ahead of the herd, looking for something, never knowing exactly what, but unsatisfied. Three days beyond the Canadian, Gavin spoke to him.

"I've never seen you so unsettled. Do you know somethin' the rest of us don't?"

"No," Woody said "I reckon I can't get over the Indian threat. It ain't costin' us anything, me ridin' ahead. Let's just say I have a feeling—a bad feeling—that's been on my back since before we crossed the Canadian. I don't know what it is, but I don't feel right unless I'm scoutin' ahead

of the herd. I reckon this will be my last drive, and maybe
that's gettin' to me.''

''Three days,'' Watt Grimes grumbled, ''an' we're no closer
to ambushin' that Pitkin bunch than we was at the Canadian.
If they git much closer to Santa Fe, we might as well let
'em go. You forgettin' Hankins told us he wanted 'em
gunned down a long ways out, so's Indians would git the
blame?''

''Pitkin's got six riders, himself, two teamsters, an' a
cook,'' said Deuce Rowden. ''The rest are females. Tomorrow, we're goin' to light a fire under that bunch, make
'em throw caution to the wind, an' come after us. We'll
choose the time an' place.''

''How do you aim to do that?'' Haynes Wooten asked.

''You'll know tomorrow morning,'' said Rowden. ''Now
we're goin' to find us a place to wait for 'em, and I promise
you, they'll be there.''

''Head 'em up, move 'em out!'' Woody shouted.

Once the herd was moving without difficulty, Woody
rode ahead. There hadn't been a problem with water since
leaving the Canadian River, but still he scouted the trail.
Three hundred yards ahead, overlooking the trail, was a series of stone abutments. He rode wide of them purely from
habit, for in Indian country the terrain was perfect for an
ambush. He rode for what he believed was fifteen miles,
and wheeling his horse, rode back to meet the oncoming
herd. Approaching the stone abutments, he reined up, studying them. Then in the stillness came the roar of a Winchester. The slug struck Woody in the back, puffing dust
from his shirt. He pitched over the withers of the horse and
sprawled face-down. When he didn't move, the horse
snorted and trotted on, escaping the smell of blood.

''A Winchester,'' Gavin said.

The other riders had heard the shot, and they weren't
surprised when Gavin raised his hat in a signal to mill the

herd. Rusty, Naomi, and Nell were riding drag. Reining up his teams, Pitkin shouted at Rusty.

"What has happened?"

"We don't know," Rusty shouted back. "There was a shot. Something's happened up ahead."

He said no more, galloping to join his comrades. Wiley and Whit leaped from their wagon boxes, demanding the horses Jania and Laketa rode. Riding hard, the outfit came together. Half a dozen miles ahead, Woody Miles lay unmoving, blood soaking the back of his dusty denim shirt . . .

19

Nell Pitkin's mind swept back to that night so recently when she had tried to joke with Woody about his obsession, his constantly scouting ahead. But Woody hadn't laughed, and she could now see him lying dead somewhere on the trail. Kicking her horse into a fast gallop, she pounded after the riders ahead of her. She had to get to Woody . . .

"They'll have heard the shot," Deuce Rowden said. "Let 'em get within range and then cut 'em down. Make every shot count."

"Pitkin may not be ridin' with 'em," said Grady Beard. "What do you aim to do about him?"

Rowden laughed. "We can git him anytime. What chance has one Englishman got agin all of us?"

Wiley and Whit caught up to the rest of the riders, and the seven of them thundered along together. Long before they reached Woody, they could see his horse standing with dropped reins. When they could see Woody lying on the ground, Gavin began shouting to his riders.

"Ambush," Gavin shouted. "Rusty, you and Vic ride wide of that bluff, keepin' to the east. Rest of you come with me."

Gavin galloped his horse up a rocky slope that would

lead them up and behind the high rock abutment ahead. But Nell Pitkin was of a single mind, knowing only that Woody was hurt. On she galloped.

"Nell, no!" Rusty shouted.

But Nell paid no attention, and Rusty had but one chance to save her. Urging his horse into a fast gallop, he raced after her. But she was within range of the hidden bushwhackers, and rifle slugs began kicking up spurts of dust all around her. Lead slammed into her horse, and the dying animal screamed. It went down, pitching Nell over its head, and she stumbled to her feet. Somehow, slugs whining all about him, Rusty reached Nell. Leaning out of the saddle, he swept the girl across the withers of his horse and galloped away. While Vic had no visible target, he was blazing away at the stone abutment whence had come the rain of lead. It subsided as Rusty rode out of range. The left sleeve of his shirt was bloody. Reining up, he slid Nell off the horse, and she looked in horror at his bloody arm.

"Woody," she cried. "I only wanted . . ."

"I know what you wanted," said Rusty, "but you were playing right into their hands. Woody's been bushwhacked, and the varmints aimed to use him as bait to suck in the rest of us. We got to flush them out, before we can see to Woody."

His words were punctuated by a sudden burst of fire somewhere beyond the stone abutment. Suddenly, a man with a Winchester scrambled into view, and Vic shot him off the bluff. Speechless, Nell clung to Rusty. As suddenly as it had begun, the firing ceased, and the next sound they heard was a shout from Gavin.

"Four of us are hit. Get Woody on his horse and back to the wagons, if you can. Any of you wounded?"

"Me," Rusty shouted, "but I'll live. We're goin' after Woody."

But Nell was already there, seeking a pulse. She looked at Rusty and Vic, and tears streaked her face.

"He's dead," she cried. "Woody's dead."

"Maybe not," said Vic, leaping from his saddle. He

lifted Woody, feeling for the large artery in the neck. There he found a faint pulse.

"He's alive," Vic said, "but not by much. Rusty's hurt. You'll have to help me get Woody onto his horse. You mount the horse and help me raise him bellydown over the withers."

Nell did her best, fear for Woody adding to her strength.

"Now," Vic said, "hold him in place and get him back to the outfit as quick as you can. Rusty, you ride with her. I'll go help the others in whatever way I can."

Gavin and Ash had bloody shirts, while blood still pumped from a hole above Gavin's right knee. Ash led his horse, while Gavin leaned on his, gripping the saddle horn. Blood ran down Wiley's left arm and dripped from his fingers. Whit was bellydown across his saddle, and Wiley led both horses.

"My God," Vic said, "is Whit . . . ?"

"He ain't quite," said Wiley wearily, "but I'm scared . . ."

"Where's Nip?" Vic asked.

"He's the only one of us that wasn't hit," said Ash. "One of the varmints run for his horse and got away. Nip went after him."

Vic helped his comrades to mount their horses, and with Vic leading Whit's horse, they rode back toward the herd and the wagons.

"My God," Gladstone Pitkin said, as they rode in. "Will someone tell me what's going on?"

"Woody was ambushed," said Vic. "They used him as bait to lure the rest of us."

"But . . . why?" Pitkin persisted.

"We don't know," said Gavin. "Somehow, Woody seemed to know . . . to suspect . . ."

He turned away, to the blanket upon which Woody lay. Gonzales had Woody's shirt off, and Gavin breathed a little easier. The wound was high up, near where the arrow had been removed.

Vic eased Whit off the horse and onto the blanket beside

Woody. Bonita, Jania, and Laketa were there, removing Whit's shirt.

"I'll take care of Whit and Wiley," Bonita said. "Jania, you see to Ash's wound, and Laketa, you take care of Rusty."

Already, Nell was doing her best to help Gonzales tend Woody's wound, while Naomi was removing Gavin's shirt. Everybody was occupied except Gladstone Pitkin, and it was then that he missed Nip Kelly.

"Where is Mr. Kelly?" Pitkin asked nobody in particular.

"One of the bushwhackers escaped," said Gavin, "and Nip went after him."

Nip spared his horse as much as he could, and the bush-whacker ahead of him seemed to be doing the same. The day was young, the sky clear, and they both knew that before sundown one of them would die. Watt Grimes had seen the Texans coming, and while his comrades had died, Grimes had run for his horse. His only hope—if he had one—was to ambush his pursuer. It would be a difficult—if not impossible—feat, for Nip Kelly was expecting no less. Before topping a rise, he dismounted, proceeding afoot. Only when he could see a distant dust plume did he mount his horse and continue. The bushwhacker must get far enough ahead to double back, and Kelly hadn't allowed him to do so. It was Kelly's intention to crowd the outlaw until his horse played out, forcing him to take his stand where destiny decreed. The showdown came much sooner than Kelly had expected. Wary, seeing no telltale dust, Kelly proceeded on foot until he could see a grazing horse. Lame, the animal limped toward him, nickering. Kelly threw him-self flat, and three slugs from a Winchester ripped the air just inches above his head. He rolled away, taking refuge behind the trunk of a huge pine. More lead tore off pine bark, and it showered down on him. He had been so busy dodging lead, he hadn't been able to learn where his ad-versary was holed up. Using a yard-long dead stick, keeping his eyes straight ahead, he lifted his hat high enough to draw fire. It did, and he saw a puff of smoke rise from behind a pair of boulders. There was a crevice in between, apparently just right for a Winchester barrel.

"You got me by the short hairs, hombre," Kelly said to himself, "but only as long as I'm stuck right here in front of you."

Slowly, he began inching his way backward, using the enormous trunk of the pine for cover. He was about to do the very thing the bushwhacker would fear the most. Once out of the line of fire, he would be free to circle around and come up behind his antagonist. It would then be the bushwhacker at a disadvantage, for he wouldn't know where Kelly was, and to move would risk a deadly case of lead poisoning.

Kelly moved fast, for it was only a matter of time until the gunman grew desperate enough to risk changing position. There was a new volley of shots, as the bushwhacker sought to draw answering fire, to be sure his target hadn't shifted. But Nip Kelly was deep enough into concealing brush that he got to his feet and began flanking the gunman. Once behind the man's position, Kelly called out a challenge.

"I'm behind you, mister. Leave the weapon where it is, and get up."

"Don't shoot," cried a frightened voice. "I'm gettin' up."

He got up with a Colt in his hand, but his shot went wide, and he hadn't a chance for another. Nip Kelly's Winchester roared, and the gunman was flung backward into the pair of stones that had concealed him. Kelly was there in an instant, kneeling beside the man.

"Why the ambush?" Kelly demanded. "Why was your bunch after us?"

The dying man said nothing, his eyes clouded with pain.

"Tell me," said Kelly. "You have nothing more to lose."

The man's laugh was bitter. "The . . . joke's on . . . Hankins. Tobe Hankins . . . Santa Fe . . . tell him . . . tell him . . . Watt Grimes said . . . go to . . . hell . . ."

His eyes were open, but the soul had departed. Nip Kelly stood there, his Winchester under his arm, and his mind drifted back over the years. Tobe Hankins. Was it the *same* Tobe Hankins Nip had known so long ago, in Missouri? Whoever the man was, what could he possibly have against Gladstone Pitkin and his riders?

"It'll bear some lookin' into," Kelly said aloud.

Taking the outlaw's Winchester, he returned to his horse. From his saddlebag he took a small notebook and a stub of pencil. He then wrote a message on a clean page in the notebook:

> If you don't see me again, look for Tobe Hankins, Santa Fe. Bushwhackers. Nip.

Kelly then did a strange thing. With all his strength, he took the Winchester that had belonged to Watt Grimes and drove its muzzle deep in the ground. Pulling back the gun's hammer, he eased it down on one corner of the piece of paper. Mounting his horse, without looking back, he rode away. Along the Santa Fe Trail . . . seeking Tobe Hankins . . .

Whit's and Woody's wounds were by far the most serious. While the lead had gone on through and hadn't hit anything vital, they had lost enormous amounts of blood. Nell Pitkin had worked beside Gonzales, treating Woody's terrible wound, While Naomi had taken charge of Gavin. Bonita and Vic had first doctored Whit, and then Wiley. Jania and Laketa had taken care of Ash and Rusty. Gladstone Pitkin had been kept busy with the heating of water for the cleansing of wounds. Finally all the wounded had been tended to. Woody and Whit had been given whiskey, and were snoring noisily. The other wounds, at some time during the coming night, might require whiskey to fight infection. Until then, they were painful, but not life-threatening. Fortunately, when the outfit had milled the herd and gone to Woody's aid, they were near a spring with adequate runoff.

"The graze ain't too plentiful," Vic observed, "but it'll have to do for maybe another two days."

Nobody mentioned Nip Kelly. There was virtually no sleep for those who had not been wounded, for every man with a wound required regular doses of whiskey to combat the threat of infection. Woody and Whit required almost constant attention to keep bandages in place so that the bleeding didn't start again. By dawn, Rusty, Ash, and Wiley had begun to sweat, and the worst was over. It was near the end of the second day when Woody and Whit began to sweat, evidence they had won their fight with infection. After supper, Nell went looking for Rusty Pryor.

"Rusty, I . . . I've been wanting to talk to you, but Woody's been so sick . . ."

"I understand," Rusty said.

"I want to ask a favor of you," said Nell. "An awfully big favor, and I'm not sure I've the right to ask."

"Give it a try," Rusty said.

"Please don't ever tell Woody . . . what I did . . . that I could have gotten you killed."

"I don't aim to speak of it to anybody," said Rusty. "It was a fool thing to do, and in no way could you have helped Woody, but I understand your feelings. If it had been Vic or me, instead of Woody, I expect Bonita or Laketa would have come to us, just like you tried to get to Woody. I can't fault you for that."

"Thank you," Nell said. "Naomi and I owe all of you so much. I never thanked you properly for rescuing me from the Comanches."

"It was my pleasure, ma'am," said Rusty. "I never seen *anybody* visit so much grief on a pair of Comanches as you and Bonita did."

Nell laughed. "I couldn't have done it without Bonita, and neither of us would have had a chance, without you, Gavin, and Vic."

Rusty turned away, embarrassed by the unaccustomed

praise. The second day after they had been wounded,
Woody and Whit were conscious but weak. Gavin spent half
an hour with Woody, telling him what had taken place after
he had been ambushed.

"I'd have been dead a couple of times," said Gavin, "if
it hadn't been for Wiley and Whit. They waded in and did
their share."

"I'm not surprised," Woody said. "They don't have
much of their paw in them. Where is Nip Kelly?"

"One of the bushwhackers escaped," said Gavin, "and
Nip went after him. I'm thinking some of us ought to go
looking for him, if he hasn't returned by tomorrow."

"Some of us should have gone today," Woody said.
"Nip's no slouch with those twin Colts, and I reckon he
can shade any one of us with a Winchester. It ain't takin'
him this long to track down one bushwhacker."

"Not a man of us left unwounded, except Nip and Vic,"
Gavin said, "but you're dead right. I ain't in prime condition, but I can ride. I'll go at first light."

"I reckon it's just as well this will be my last ride as trail
boss," said Woody. "Every time there's a need for me, I'm
flat on my back with arrows or lead. You're wounded too.
Why don't we talk to Vic?"

"Talk to Vic if you want," Gavin said, "and he's welcome to ride with me, but I'll be goin' at first light. I believe
in a man ridin' for the brand, but Nip's pretty far out on a
limb, right now."

Woody said no more, nor did he approach Vic. It wasn't
the first time he and Gavin had disagreed, and he was sure
it wouldn't be the last. The more he thought of Gavin's
stubborn stand, the more certain he became that the man
was right. While he—Woody Miles—had been out of his
head with fever, Nip Kelly had likely gotten himself neck-
deep in trouble. Perhaps even more than the resourceful
Missourian could handle. In so many words, Gavin hadn't
said he didn't want Vic trailing Nip, and like a revelation,
Woody believed he knew the reason. Vic Brodie was more
headstrong than was Nip Kelly, and even with his back to

the wall, wasn't inclined to seek help. Troubled, Woody silently cursed the bushwhackers and the wound that sapped his strength. Wounded or not, he was still trail boss, and Pitkin would be looking to him for some decision regarding Nip Kelly. Knowing Gavin McCord, Woody was certain he wouldn't speak to Pitkin of his decision to follow Kelly, but within minutes of Gavin's departure, Pitkin arrived with questions.

"I am concerned about Mr. Kelly," Pitkin said.

"So am I," said Woody. "Gavin's goin' after him at first light."

"Gavin has an unhealed wound," Pitkin replied. "So does everybody, except for Vic and myself. Perhaps it is time for me to assume some of the responsibility for this outfit."

The Englishman was dead serious, and Woody almost laughed.

"None of us have ever doubted your sense of responsibility for this outfit," Woody said, "but we don't know that Kelly hasn't walked into somethin' that won't ensnare all of us, and every gun we can muster. I promise you, when we ride as an outfit, you'll be in the thick of the fight. Until we know what's happened to Nip, this calls for the eyes and the ears of a frontiersman. Wounded or not, there isn't a man alive more qualified than Gavin McCord."

"I am unprepared to contest that," said Pitkin. "Gavin has proven himself."

He turned away, and Woody was left alone with his thoughts, until Naomi came looking for him.

"Woody, Gavin's wound isn't healed. Why is he riding in search of Nip Kelly?"

"His choice," Woody said. "Why don't you ask him?"

"I have. He refuses to discuss it."

"Naomi," said Woody wearily, "a man generally bears enough of a load, without havin' a woman question his judgment at every turn. If you want Gavin, ease up on the reins. Give him his head, and I *don't* mean on a platter."

For a moment he thought she was about to lose her temper, but she didn't. Without another word she turned away.

Santa Fe, New Mexico. August 4, 1869.

Nip Kelly had ridden almost a hundred and fifty miles. He immediately found a livery, leaving instructions for his horse to be rubbed down, grained, and watered. Of necessity, he stopped at a cafe and ordered a meal, and before leaving, he asked about Tobe Hankins.

"Fanciest saloon in town," the cook told him. "You can't miss it."

Kelly had ridden all night, and it was still too early for the saloons to be open. There was no mistaking the place, when he found it. In gaudy red and gold letters two feet high, the name—"Tobe's Saloon"—was emblazoned across the false front. It seemed plenty large enough for living quarters, and Nip pounded on the locked double doors.

"Vamoose," growled a surly voice from inside. "We open at eleven. That's three more hours."

"This ain't saloon business," said Nip. "I'm here to see Tobe Hankins."

"What's yer business with Tobe?"

"None of yours," Nip said shortly. "It's between Hankins and me. Tell him Nip Kelly's here."

"He don't generally git up till ten," said the same voice, a little less surly now.

"He will this morning," Nip replied. "Tell him I've brought him a message from one of his *amigos*. A gent name of Watt Grimes. His dyin' words, in fact."

That got almost immediate results. When the door eventually swung open, it revealed the bearded man behind the surly voice. A Colt revolver had been shoved under his belt, and under his arm was a sawed-off shotgun. When Kelly stepped inside, the door was shut and locked.

"That's Tobe's office, down the hall," his host said. "You can go in an' wait."

Cautiously, Nip opened the heavy door and stepped inside. The interior was dim, the only light being the rays of the morning sun through a single window. At the far end of the room was a desk, and behind the desk, a door. Nip took a chair against the wall, from which he could watch the door through which he had entered, as well as the door behind the desk. As he had expected, Hankins entered through the door behind the desk. Nip got up and stood before the desk. Hankins said nothing, and it was Nip who spoke.

"It's been a long time, Tobe."

"Not near long enough," said Hankins.

"I wish I could say it's good to see you again," Nip said, "but I'm just not that big a liar. How well do you know a gent name of Watt Grimes?"

"He comes in the saloon occasionally," Hankins said. "What are you leadin' up to?"

"An ambush," said Nip. "Six skunk-striped varmints waylaid the outfit I'm ridin' with. I trailed the only one who got out alive, leavin' him for the buzzards and coyotes. Before he cashed in, he said the ambush was your idea. He also said, tell you to go to hell. Now I'm here to settle with you, Hankins."

Hankins laughed. "You'll never leave this room alive. Do you think I invited you in to talk of old times?"

"I got more confidence in a rattler than I have in you, Hankins," Nip replied. "Do you think I came here alone, without the rest of the outfit knowin' where I was headed?"

Again Hankins laughed. "Won't make no difference. There's no statute of limitations on murder, Nip. I can kill you legally. Remember, you left Missouri on the dodge. I still have one of the wanted posters."

"You bastard," Kelly said, "it was you that provoked that gunfight. You drew first."

"Yeah," Hankins gloated, "but you fired first, and it was your slug that struck poor Celeste Tilden. Funny thin' was, she was afraid you'd get in trouble for shootin' me, but it only got you in deeper. It was you that rode away.''

"You told me she wàs dead," said Nip, "and I knew I couldn't count on you to speak up for me."

"You was always puttin' me down," Hankins replied. "Celeste always preferred you, and even after you rode off, that didn't change. She hated me, and I had to fight for the favors that would have been yours."

"What in tarnation are you saying?"

Again Hankins laughed, savoring the torture he could see in Nip Kelly's eyes. When he spoke again, it was with an evil hiss.

"You was a damn fool, Kelly. You've always been a fool. Celeste Tilden wasn't dead. Your slug only creased her. It took some doin' on my part, but I convinced her you didn't want her, that you was fiddle-footed. I had her for five years, Kelly, but you spoiled it for me. She cussed me, slapped my face, and went to St. Louis. I heard she died there, spendin' her last years in a whorehouse. For ten years, you rode the outlaw trail, Kelly, for a no-account whore who *should* have been dead."

"You lie, damn you," Kelly snarled.

But the misery in the man's eyes told the truth, and the acceptance of it was enough to contain Nip Kelly's anger. For a long moment, his hands trembled over the butts of his twin Colts. Gradually he became deadly calm, hooking his thumbs in his pistol belt. Much to the surprise of Hankins, Kelly spoke.

"So there was no deception on Celeste's part, Hankins. Just your lies. I can feel better about her in a whorehouse, or even dead, than in your filthy hands. Now, let's get back to my purpose for bein' here. You hired that bunch of scum to bushwhack Pitkin's outfit, and I have the truth of it from a dyin' man. Before I kill you, I want some answers."

"This time," Hankins said, "I don't mind givin' you some straight ones. There's a railroad comin', Kelly, and I aim to own the land they'll need for the right-of-way. Just who do you reckon owns that land now?"

"Gladstone Pitkin," said Nip.

"Yes," Hankins admitted. "Now I aim to make you an offer you can't refuse. I figure we might have been friends, if we hadn't let a no-account woman come between us, but all that's in the past. With you or without you, I aim to take that land from Pitkin. I aim to walk tall in this territory, and this is your chance to side me. Will you?"

"Never," Kelly gritted. "I won't betray a man who's treated me white, who accepted me for what I am, without questionin' my past."

"Not even to save your own hide?"

"Not even then," said Kelly.

The shotgun bellowed, its heavy load blasting a hole in the desk, but Nip Kelly wasn't there. He had hit the floor, pulling a Colt, rolling away. He came to his knees, his Colt spitting lead, but Hankins was bellydown on the floor, behind the ruined desk. While the bearded man hadn't reloaded the shotgun, he had drawn the Colt. He fired twice, and both slugs slammed into Nip Kelly's back. He lay facedown, his life leaking out on the office floor.

"Good work, Jake," Hankins said. "Wrap him in a blanket and get him out of sight. After dark, I want you to take him as far along the Santa Fe Trail as you can—at least fifty miles—and drop him."

"Hell," said Jake, "why go to all that trouble? Why not just plant him somewhere?"

"Because, by God, they'll come lookin' for him," Hankins said, "and I want to be sure they find him."

Hankins left the saloon and climbed the back stairs to the second floor of the Pecos Hotel. He silently cursed Deuce Rowden and his bunch for the bunglers they were, lamenting the loss of the three thousand he had wasted on them. He wouldn't make that mistake again. When he knocked on a door, he was admitted by a Mexican whose twin pistols rode low on his lean hips, thonged down with rawhide. Hankins came right to the point.

"Sanchez, I need some men. Man killers."

"*Si,*" said Sanchez. "For where, Señor, and how many?"

"Fifteen," Hankins said. "Here. In Santa Fe."

"The law, Señor?"

"For the next few days," said Hankins, "the law will be mindin' its own business."

Gavin saddled his horse. In his saddlebags was enough jerked beef for three days, and additional shells for Colt and Winchester. Naomi spent a few final minutes with him. After her talk with Woody, she had said nothing more to Gavin regarding his decision. The girl had begun to appreciate Woody's wisdom, for Gavin seemed relieved. Obviously, he had expected an unpleasant confrontation with her. She knew he must speak to Woody and to Pitkin before he rode out, and and she yielded to them.

"I won't be back until I find Nip, or get some word of him," Gavin said.

Pitkin nodded, and Woody spoke.

"Tomorrow, we'll be movin' on. We'll look for you somewhere between here and Santa Fe."

Gavin tipped his hat and rode away, knowing they were concerned about him, knowing they were reluctant to speak, lest it be taken as a lack of confidence. Before he lost sight of the camp, he reined up and looked back. Naomi raised her hand. Gavin swallowed hard and rode on . . .

20

*G*avin had ridden not more than a dozen miles when he reached the macabre sign that Kelly had left. The abandoned Winchester said that Nip had caught up with the lone bushwhacker who had run for it. The written message, however, left him puzzled. Apparently, Kelly had learned something from the bushwhacker, but why had he ridden on alone? True, most of the outfit had been wounded, but if Tobe Hankins—for whatever reason—had hired one bunch of killers, he certainly was capable of hiring others. However resourceful Kelly might be, taking on a gang of killers single-handed wasn't his responsibility, yet he appeared to be ready to do just that.

"Damn it, Nip," Gavin said aloud, "why didn't you ride back and tell us whatever you had learned?"

While Gavin had word as to Kelly's whereabouts, he was reluctant to simply return to camp with the information. They still would be faced with the need to join Nip in whatever difficulty he had encountered, yet every man—with the exception of Vic and Pitkin—had been wounded. Gavin rode on, believing he was not more than a day's ride from Santa Fe. When he eventually found Nip Kelly's body, it was late afternoon. Try as he might, he was unable to find Kelly's horse. Riding a mile farther toward Santa Fe, he figured it out. He found tracks of a lone horse *from* Santa Fe, and tracks of the same horse, returning. Nip had died in Santa Fe, yet someone had taken the time and trouble to ride out and leave his body where it was sure to be found. Why?

"Damn it," Gavin said, through gritted teeth.

Sadly, he wrapped Nip's body in a blanket, tied it securely, and draped it over the withers of his horse. With the animal carrying double, he dared not hurry it. He eventually reached camp just minutes before the second watch began. Rusty, Vic, and Ash watched him approach in the starlight, needing no explanation. The slow plodding of the horse soon awakened the camp, for they all feared something had happened to Nip Kelly, and not one had been asleep. Gonzales had lighted the lantern. Silently, Vic helped Gavin remove the blanket-wrapped body and ease it to the ground. Beyond the dim light from the lantern, there was the sound of weeping. Nell, Naomi, Bonita, Jania, and Laketa were paying tribute to Nip Kelly in the only way they knew how. Gavin rolled Kelly over, exposing the pair of bullet holes in his back. It was all they needed to know of the manner in which Nip had died. Without a word, Gavin removed the written message from his shirt pocket, passing it to Woody. Gonzales held the lantern close, and Woody read the brief message aloud. With a minimum of words, Gavin explained where he had found the message, and finally, where he had found Nip's body.

"For some reason, he rode to Santa Fe alone," Woody said. "Do any of you have any ideas as to why he did that, instead of ridin' back and tellin' us what he had learned?"

"I have nothing more than a suspicion," said Gavin, "but I believe Nip knew, or at least thought he knew this Tobe Hankins. He may be somebody from Nip's past."

"Maybe," Woody said, "but why did Nip have to go after him alone?"

"He never talked much about himself," said Naomi, "but he once told Nell and me that he was from Missouri, that he once knew a girl there, but that she was dead."

"We are speculating," Pitkin said. "Tomorrow, we shall bury Mr. Kelly and resume our journey to Santa Fe. Gavin, have you any idea how much farther we must travel?''

"I rode a good sixty miles before finding Nip," said Gavin. "I'd say we're a hundred miles out. Another week, at most."

"When we have reached the place where you found Mr. Kelly's body," Pitkin said, "we shall leave the herd and the wagons there, and ride to Santa Fe. I shall ask all of you to load your weapons and follow me. We shall see that Nip Kelly has not died in vain, gentlemen, if we must demolish the town, leaving not one brick atop another."

Sadly, they left Nip Kelly in a lonely grave along the Santa Fe Trail. It would grass over and become one of many, lost to the ravages of time . . .

Upper fork of the Pecos River. August 11, 1869.

"Just a mile or two beyond here is where I found Nip," Gavin said. "For the sake of good water and graze, we'd better leave the wagons and the herd here."

"Father," said Nell, "why must we remain here with the wagons and the herd, while all of you ride to Santa Fe? Naomi and I can shoot, and I know Bonita, Jania, and Laketa can."

"Precisely why all of you will remain here," Pitkin replied. "Gonzales will be here, and I suspect we may need all of you to tend the wounded."

In Santa Fe, Jake pounded on Tobe Hankins' door. Finally, Hankins opened it.

"Devlin just brought word," Jake said. "They're on the upper fork of the Pecos, and it looks like they aim to stay a while."

Tobe Hankins nodded. It was time to alert Sanchez and his band of killers . . .

Santa Fe, New Mexico. August 12, 1869.

Gladstone Pitkin, Woody, Gavin, Vic, Rusty, Ash, Wiley, and Whit rode along the narrow streets of Santa Fe. For the occasion, in addition to their Winchesters, Wiley and Whit had been supplied with Colt revolvers.

"We don't know where this Tobe Hankins is," Woody said, "but he'll be waitin' for us. That's why they left Nip where we could find him."

"Look over yonder on that other street," Rusty said. "Tobe's Saloon."

"Maybe that's what we're lookin' for," said Woody, "but let's be sure."

Woody trotted his horse across the street to a livery. With the butt of his Colt, he pounded on the door. A gray-haired old timer opened the door just far enough to poke his head out.

"Pardner," Woody said, "we're lookin' for Tobe Hankins. Would that saloon be his?"

"Yeah," said the liveryman. He saw the mounted, armed men and quickly closed the door. Woody rode back and joined his companions.

"That's his place," Woody said.

"I hope you don't aim to ask the varmint to surrender," said Gavin. "If we can't hang him, let's at least gut-shoot him."

"He hires men to do his killing," Pitkin said. "I don't expect him to be alone."

"Neither do I," said Woody. "We can't surround the saloon, because we don't know how many are waitin' to greet us, or where they are. There are too many false-fronted buildin's close by. There could be a man with a rifle on the roof of every one."

"If it becomes a matter of driving Hankins from the saloon," Pitkin said, "I may have the solution in my saddlebags. I took the precaution of bringing dynamite, caps, and fuses."

"Pit," said Woody, "welcome to the frontier. You'll do. All of you spread out among the buildings surrounding the saloon. I aim to call on Hankins to come out. If nothing else, that should draw some fire, and we'll see where the killers are holed up."

There was a vacant building across the street from the saloon, and Woody managed to reach a door that hung on one hinge. He ducked inside. Taking aim with his Winchester, he shot out the glass in the upper portion of one of the saloon's double doors.

"Hankins," he shouted, "this is the Pitkin outfit. We found our *amigo*, Nip Kelly, dead, and he left evidence pointing directly at you. Are you comin' out of there on your hind legs, or do we have to level the place and drag you out?"

"I'm Hankins," a voice bawled, "and I have men all over town. Don't start something you can't finish."

From two different directions, shots rang out. Lead slammed into the sagging door, ripping it from its single hinge. There were answering shots, as the Pitkin outfit bought in. It appeared the defenders had not holed up in the saloon, but had attempted to circle it, with the intention of ambushing anyone approaching the building. Suddenly there was the rattle of gunfire, and Pitkin literally threw himself through the open door. There was a bloody gash across his chin and his hat was missing.

"I brought some dynamite," he panted.

"You might also have gotten yourself killed," said Woody.

"It is capped, with an eight-second fuse," Pitkin said, producing four sticks.

"I reckon we'll have to use it," said Woody. "If Hankins has men scattered all over town, he'll never come out."

"Warn him," Pitkin said.

"Hankins, we have dynamite, and we're gonna blow that place to hell and gone, if you don't come out," Woody shouted.

It brought another volley of shots, some of them coming from the roof of the saloon. Pitkin had lighted a match, and Woody touched a fuse to the flame. With a sputter, the fuse caught. Woody held it a second longer, and then flung it high above the saloon roof. There was a screech from somebody on the roof, followed almost immediately by a puff

of smoke and an explosion. The entire front of the saloon
collapsed, but still nobody left the building.

"Damn it," Woody growled, "where *are* they?"

Beneath the saloon, Hankins and six gunmen crept along
a tunnel Hankins had created for just such a purpose. Gavin
and the rest of the outfit had been returning fire from the
roofs of several buildings, but suddenly all firing ceased.

"They're gettin' ready for somethin'," said Gavin.
"Keep your guns handy."

Suddenly there was shooting from a dozen different quarters. Vic took a slug through the thigh, while lead tore a
furrow across Rusty's back from shoulder to shoulder. The
gunmen had worked their way to the outer perimeter of the
town, and were seeking to trap Pitkin's outfit in a cross-fire.
But they had overlooked the resourcefulness of Pitkin's outfit, as well as Pitkin himself. Three riflemen had Pitkin and
Woody trapped, firing from behind a huge pile of stacked
firewood. Pitkin lit out in a run, lead spurting dust around
him, finally taking refuge under a porch. From there, he
lighted a dynamite fuse, throwing the explosive directly into
the woodpile. The explosion silenced the three rifles.
Emerging from the hidden tunnel, Hankins and his companions crept toward an alley that would take them within
range of most of the Pitkin riders. But Wiley and Whit had
each taken a few capped and fused sticks of Pitkin's dynamite. While they had no targets at which to shoot, their
eyes had been busy, and they saw Hankins and almost half
his gunmen coming down the alley, across the street. Each
lighted a fuse off the same match and flung the powerful
explosive into the alley. Following the horrendous explosion, there were screams of anguish and then silence. Tat-
tered bodies lay in the alley, but Hankins had rolled under
a house, escaping the fury of the blast. Crawling to the other
side of the house, he crept out alone, a Colt in his hand. To
his dismay, he found himself facing Gladstone Pitkin, holding a Winchester under his arm.

"I reckon you're Pitkin," said Hankins, cocking the Colt.

"I am," Pitkin said.

Pitkin dropped to one knee and the slug went wide, but Pitkin's shot didn't miss. The Winchester roared once, and the heavy slug ripped through Hankins. He lay unmoving, in a pool of blood. Several of the gunmen Hankins had hired began shouting in Spanish, and suddenly all firing ceased.

"They're runnin' for it," Rusty shouted. "After the varmints!"

"No," said Pitkin, who had walked to the middle of the street. "Hankins is dead, I think, and while we may never know his motivation, it is enough to be rid of him. Are any of our riders wounded?"

"Vic and Rusty," Woody said. "Everybody's accounted for, except for Wiley and Whit."

But Wiley and Whit had been busy. After throwing the dynamite, they had seen one of Hankins' men hiding under a house. He had been gut-shot, and his time was short, but Wiley and Whit had dragged him out.

"We reckoned you might want to talk to him," Wiley said.

"You reckoned right," said Pitkin.

"I ain't sayin' nothin'," the wounded man snarled.

"Hankins is dead," said Woody. "You have nothing to gain."

"What can you tell us about Nip Kelly, and about Hankins?" Pitkin asked.

"I'm Jake," the wounded man grunted. "I come here with Hankins, from Missouri. It was there that we knowed Kelly. I . . . never liked him. Was me . . . that shot . . . him."

"Why?" Pitkin insisted. "What did Hankins have against me?"

Jake groaned, and by the silence, they thought he was dead. But he opened his eyes and spoke just once more.

"Your land . . . railroad . . ."

"There it is," said Gavin. "There was talk about the railroad when we first reached Independence. The right-of-way must be comin' across your land."

"I trust it won't interfere with the raising of cattle," Pit-

kin said. ''I didn't come all the way from England to contribute to the building of a railroad.''

The citizens of Santa Fe watched in wonder as the eight
men rode out of the village. While many Americans had
come down the Santa Fe Trail, few of them had been the
equals of these men.